To the ones that deserve a second chance and to those that don't.
For those that wanted to become a treasure hunter as a kid.

BURIED IN SINS

JAMIE FRITZ

WARNING

Before you start reading, I want to give a warning that this is intended for mature audience/readers. As I do in my day job, I want to give transparency. Here are the trigger warnings:

Abusive relationship/ Domestic Violence (past, flashbacks)
Death of a loved one (off page, past)
Anxiety
Gun violence
Grief and loss
Attempted murder
Trauma

Also,
While this series is within the realm of treasure hunting, some aspects have historical accuracies and some fictional. While the madames are fictional people, majority of the French history is correct, between the culture and historical timeline. I am in no means a historian like Gwendolyn, but I have done my research and in some aspects hope that my search engine does not tip off watchful eyes.

I meant for my search engine to be innocent.

THE TREASURED OUTCASTS

JAMIE FRITZ

1:49   4:10

The Crew

Gwendolyn Griffin- The Mastermind/Leader: Historian
Quinton Griffin- The Coordinator/2nd: Psychologist
Dominic Stephens- Weapons Master: Ex-Military
Winston Diggs- Driver: Mechanic
Xara Kennedy- Linguist: Wild Card, Hacker
Elijah Langley- Architect: Muscle
Zacharias Langley- Medic: Ex-Army
Yankee Thomason- The Con Man: Socialite
Jacob Hartley- Hacker, Security: Tech genius
Massey- The Benefactor

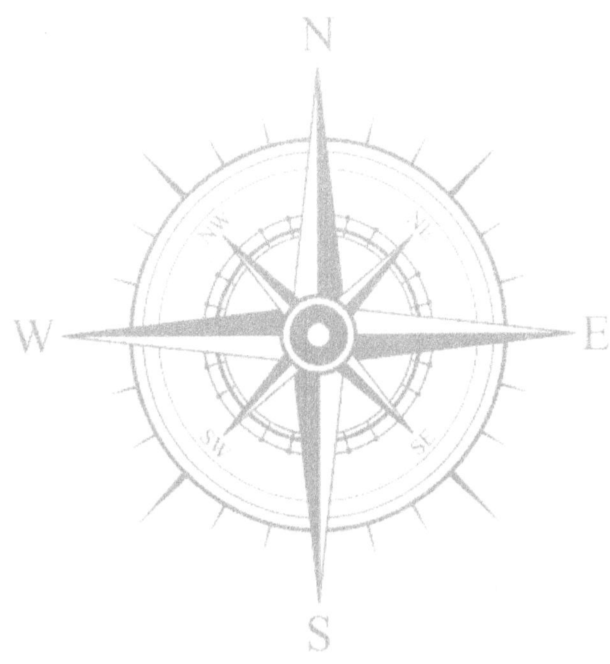

Chapter 1

Gwendolyn

Our family has lived by a motto, "Even lost things will always be found."

When they say that your chosen family is more important than blood, the ten-year old little girl and her older brother who was raised by her uncle wouldn't believe you.

Quinton and I were raised by the last living relative we had that didn't turn their back on us. Uncle Maximus, the eccentric collector of the family and the black sheep. Everyone in our families had written him as the "special" family member. I think they were looking for the word extravagant or extraordinary. Uncle Maximus didn't hesitate when we needed someone to care for us.

Honestly, it was the best decision that was made for us.

Consumed by all things historical and lost, we thought he was mad until he had brought us along on his quests, searching for the last missing treasures of the world. He believed that we could learn more, immerse ourselves in the world around us.

Literally the world was our playground. It was as if the world was endless and waiting for Quinton and me to unravel the mysteries.

At thirteen, I was free-climbing mountains, picking locks (courtesy of Maximus), climbing into crevices, and learning how to handle guns and various weaponry including my beloved Desert Eagle. I was eighteen, don't worry.

At sixteen, I had more knowledge and intellect on every historical fact and mystery of the Earth including secrets of the Egyptians, hidden treasures of the Incas and the Mayans, mysteries of countries' royalty, and even the lost cities that were once a powerful force. I was consumed by finding everything I could. By eighteen, I had gone through more passports than the average jet setter.

The world was my playground and the mysteries they gave me were my candy.

You could say Quinton and I had a well-rounded education, even world class education. We loved every minute of it and still do.

In the end, we were preservers of history and collectors of lost things. We were an adventurous trio whose soul mission was to collect history. We were thick as thieves, sometimes he was more the brains, my number two during these adventures and myself the leader.

My darkest time came when my guardian, my mentor, my only family other than Quinton left the earth. I thought my adventures were done; I thought that life died out when he did. I remember crumbling to pieces, I remember my voice was gone for weeks.

He passed away in my sophomore year of college as I studied ancient history and archaeology. The news of his passing shattered me, knowing it was just Quinton and me to continue what Maximus had started. That darkness left a hole in my heart.

I didn't know if I would survive. The pain made me almost leave my education to deal with my internal crisis. I didn't know if I wanted to adventure anymore, to seek out and recover history. It didn't feel right without Maximus, without his dramatic takes of history to unfold the mystifying tales of the world around us, without his infinite wisdom and rants, and without his encouragement to keep going.

The drive to continue any adventures was gone.

The flooding of memories for Maximus reenacting the tales of long ago as if they were bedtime stories sometimes were too much. He let our imaginations soar into the heavens as if the constellations were to tell the story, flashing images across the night sky.

Weeks after his death, we had been going through the childhood home, or the manor as most people would know it as that was left for us, with plenty of room and more than we could ask for. Maximus did very well at his job and had room doubled over. We had gone through his office that was connected to the massive, antique library. I don't think Quinton, or I had the heart to toss anything away.

His office was littered with maps, some rolled out, some rolled up, journals and books on every topic. From ancient Babylonian times to the samurai and even historical records of royal bloodlines across the waters.

The one thing about Maximus is that he never had a true plan of action. He had an ongoing list of fascinations and curiosities. He never knew "where the wind would blow" and whether it would be in his favor. He kept a little notebook with his list, and I knew that it kept growing, especially after our last quest, together.

"What if we just straighten up the desk?" Quinton had suggested, perhaps wanting to keep the memory alive. I didn't blame him, I would have done the same thing. Or would have just waited another week or so.

Quinton was sweet like that, considering others and keeping traditions alive. That and the psychologist in him tried to handle my grief.

When I was studying ancient history, he studied psychology and went on to get his graduate degree. He had a knack for understanding body language and the tones of people, what people were really thinking, what they were hiding.

He was a modern day lie detector, I always joked with him that he better hide from the FBI, knowing that they would find talent in that. Give him two minutes with someone and he would tell you in detail everything from what stresses them out to what secret they were hiding.

As we rummaged through Maximus' office, I got the feeling he was enthralled with endless ideas, always thinking about the next adventure. I had watched Maximus' mind spin in thought and curiosity, analyzing every clue and historical fact we found, and his office reflected that tornado of interest. Going through his stuff was tough. I went through so many boxes, through his memories, his hopes and dreams. I sat in his seat, the big cushioned one he loved so much, rifling through his desk drawers.

I sat in his seat, the big cushioned one, going through his desk drawers. There was one that was stuck. I didn't remember that drawer being stuck. I grew frustrated trying to get it to open for me, spiraling into the same madness Maximus would if he got stuck on a puzzle.

With one final tug, I yanked the draw open. The noise itself from the drawer was enough to think something was wrong or the very least, broken.

At first, I wondered if I had ruined the desk drawer, fearing that there was damage to it, then I wondered how I could cover this up without judgment. Quinton had heard the frustration and noise from the pulling of the drawer.

"Please tell me that you didn't damage anything?" He looked at me sternly for more answers. I tend to get forceful, especially when anger arises.

"No, I didn't break anything."

"This time," he finished for me, he groaned. "What were you looking for?"

I sighed, "The drawer got stuck and I wanted to see what was inside," I said, rummaging through like there was treasure.

Most of it was paper, documents that didn't make sense to me at that moment. But hidden underneath the papers laid a small brown leather-bound notebook, something that I recognize from my childhood. The worn-out leather was rough under my fingertips, memories started to become vivid once again. Images of lost treasure and Maximus's list of his impending adventures and conquests.

Excitedly, I thumbed through the list, which dated back longer than Quinton and I had been alive. His most notorious adventures were crossed off, his exploits spanning the globe.

Part of me wanted to create a standing map with pushpins of the locations, with different colors for where he was and where we were all three together, just to see the jumbled zigzag his need for adventure took him on. A soft smile spread across my face.

"Is that what I think it is?"

I nodded "Yeah, buddy. Maximus's journal and list." The book felt heavier in my hands. A piece of Maximus in my hands.

"I thought we lost that, or it ended up being buried with him in the casket." I shook my head. Although we both wouldn't have been surprised if it was in his casket.

Quinton circled the desk and leaned on it, folding his arms across his rolled-up button up shirt. "You know, we could continue the legacy."

I was taken back. Out of the both of us, he was more of the cautious thinker, observant type. But he said that in quick thinking. Did he really think that we could do this? Especially on our own?

"That might be the grief talking." I started to tuck the notebook back in the drawer. Almost forgetting about the world that awaited us. I tossed the idea away, it wouldn't be the same.

Quinton stopped my hand, grabbing the notebook, "I'm serious. Why not?" he asked me.

The sense of adventure was calling us as we would go on his quests, crossing off the quests without just felt wrong. It felt like it wasn't my place anymore, that I didn't have the right or expertise. The sinking of feeling that he wouldn't continue as we continued on.

"What do you expect me to do? I still have to consider school and maybe even finishing, getting my degrees." I wasn't kidding. I had more to consider this time, when we were younger it was easier.

"You and I both know that he was preparing for you to take over one day. Like the rightful heir to the land. We could make a team." He started to say, staring back at me with those Griffin blue eyes. "Also, he would throw something in anger hearing that you aren't considering finishing school." Quinton tilted my chin up to meet his eyes when I turned away from him.

I held back so many tears at that moment. The hesitation of the maybe.

I scoffed, "Okay genius, are you expecting a "team" or "legacy" to fall out of the sky? Plus, I'm not ready to lead a team." I jerked away from his hands.

"It's going to take time, but when do you ever back down from a challenge? Need I remind you that you were the one that challenged the village chief to a pepper eating challenge to gain passage in their valley. Because someone couldn't wait for uncle's pilot contact to come and get us to get us across the area." he pointed out. He wasn't wrong, my stubbornness and eagerness sometimes rewarded. I faced challenges great and small and overcame them, even in my most dramatic flair.

"We're the last ones. We're the outcasts." I said in a small voice. "We have no more family, the very least anyone that would care for us. We are all that we have left." We've lost so much in our younger years.

"So, we will find a new family and find those outcasts," he said, jumping up from his spot to across the room. I guess that is what big brothers are for, to pick you up when you doubt yourself or get lost.

So, over the years, that's what we did. We searched the country through interactions and moments in our life that it was like the fates had spoken.

One of the first ones was Xara, my Harvard freshman year roommate. She was the child of an American diplomat. A daughter with certain expectations to uphold and Xara, through her own way of life, rebelled and wanted to choose things for her own, not a life that was planned for her. Her parents wanted her to get into government and politics, she had her mind made up.

By the time we finished our junior year, Xara had created her own underground information network utilizing her language skills, the woman could speak seven languages fluently, to help advocacy groups and take a bite out of corrupt governments. She was a no-brainer, by the time we graduated, she already had a room in our home. She's a powerful house and with one look that could kill, no one underestimated her.

While Xara and I were finishing school, Quinton ran into the cousins. Elijah and Zacharias.

Both impressively built for muscle, but both different as polar opposites. Elijah was a man of sunshine and good times, but can be very observant as Quinton himself. Elijah had a fondness for architecture, not afraid to get hands dirty. You could give him a time in history, the background of an individual or family, and country, and he could spin a story about the structure of their home and pinpoint the weaknesses.

Zacharias was our resident ever grumpy troll of an ex-army medic, it was fun to push his buttons and get under his skin. He was quick to judge, assessing every situation we were in, which helped him as the medic in the group. He's definitely has patched one or few of us during our quests. But the man can be an opinionated annoying man.

Quinton and I wanted to build an unstoppable crew. While Zacharias and Elijah were some the muscles, their skill set were mainly need elsewhere. We needed more muscle and special skills. Quinton could hold his own, but he didn't have the training that I did. The cousins were useful, and somewhat easy on the eyes. Well, not Zacharias. He was just fun to roast.

The team didn't stop there. Fate has a funny way of intertwining lost souls.

One day I had returned home, my birthplace before my parents' accident, reminiscing about a time long ago and a moment where I needed to clear my head. It's what happens when thoughts cloud your judgment, and you need a moment to breathe.

All of a sudden, my jeep had crapped out on me as I was heading out of town and I couldn't get to a car rental place. A small town in South Carolina nestled outside of Clemson.

Small meant small businesses. I had it towed to a local garage and as I couldn't be patient anymore because I didn't know what was going on and I had so much research that I needed to do over the next few weeks, I plummeted through the open garage. After which I got yelled at by a giant man with skin as dark as night and muscles that could toss me across the room with a feather.

My spitfire ass got into a screaming match. But there was something oddly familiar about him. His eyes, brown with little flecks of golden honey looking down at me. His height was almost towering over me. When I noticed his name tag reading "Winston" but I didn't know him as that.

"Win," I said looking up and down at him.

"Winnie," he said, dropping his tool and squeezed the life out of me.

Back then when we were kids, childhood sweethearts some would have said, we were the infamous Win and Winnie, best friends. The local sheriffs had known us by name, little kids who got into the most troublesome days after school.

But once my parents had passed away in their accident, I lost all communication with him. After reuniting with him, I convinced him to change his path and join the team. We needed someone who knew vehicles and machinery, and how to acquire them. Winston was the man for it, on top of being a bit of the muscle.

And I would be lying if I said part of me wasn't attracted to him in the beginning. Nothing came out of it in the beginning but there was always a spark of warmth when he flashed his beautiful smile or even when he caressed my cheek from time to time.

There were six of us, and at twenty-three then I was still working as a traveling museum curator taking my expertise across the country, when my other travels weren't taking up my time. Being entrusted with the safety of artifacts and historical attributes. It wasn't a bad side gig, it allowed me to feel like the smartest person in the room.

That was when I met Yankee. I didn't know his actual name at the time, but he had run a con during one of the events that I put together for an organization. After I let him have his fun, I found him out and from that moment, he become a friend.

His charismatic attitude and insight into the wealthiest people and how these events go was what we needed. He was a con man, a thief, and a fellow historian. After he told me that he wanted more to do with his life and see more than just the country, how he was never fully accepted by his family, I knew I was an outcast when I saw one. It didn't take a whole lot to convince him to join the crew. Soon, he made his way into our home.

Well, more like popped up when the time came.

I guess while I was on business and meeting Yankee, which was when my brother got himself into trouble with the dark web and plunged himself into a rabbit hole. Quinton is not completely technologically advanced like the rest of us. You would think that the man had been born in a completely different time period.

Luckily, he was able to catch up with a college friend, Hartley. The technical genius had built a cyber security business and was booming. Hard to believe a once scrawny student hidden away in his dorm turned into a beautiful lean business man, that sometimes sent shivers down your spine with one look. He was a flirt, in the most "I don't think you can hide from me, I'll find anything" kind of way which came in handy a few times before when the charm was needed.

But on the side, Hartley had been a hacktivist, taking down organizations for the good of local communities. When Quinton told me about him, I knew that Xara and Hartley would get along swimmingly, and if we weren't careful, might be a dangerous pair. Hartley was made for the crew, and possibly an essential part as well. It took more convincing for him, but I have a way with words, and perhaps a pretty face and charming personality had something to do with it.

After a few months, we were more than a team, we were a family. A family of outcasts, people that you would never think twice about. A family where we looked out for each other and continued to be there even when we hit a low point.

I thought that Quinton and I would never have a family anymore after Maximus, but I like to think that he had something to do with the family we found. Like he said, "Even lost things will always be found".

After a year, we grew to trust and learn each other's stories, on top of charting around the world. Little by little we threw down the walls of our lives and accepted each other.

But something was missing, a tiny little part.

Every group has that one person that sort of just showed up into the mix. Closing out our crew was Dominic, the oldest of our group.

Unfortunately, Dominic lost his wife and child while he was on tour in the Army, and had dedicated the rest of his life to his work whether in the military or in his private security. The oddest thing was, is that Dominic knew Uncle Maximus from his various adventures.

According to a letter that Uncle Maximus wrote, Dominic was welcomed to be a part of the family adventures when he was through with his service in the military. Dominic never found anyone after his wife passed away, and limited family around the area. Quinton and I welcomed him with open arms, as long as he would tell us stories about uncle before we came to live with him.

After Dominic, we were complete. Only time would tell when we would start adventure and the world was our playground. I could only imagine where we would go from there.

The days were coming when adventurous lifestyle would turn into obsession and selfishness. The obsession with legends and adding my uncle's list was consuming me, eating me alive internally. Ideas would flow through my mind, it felt like it was an endless cycle, going down the rabbit hole with no way out.

Unfortunately, the end of our little band of outcasts came faster than I thought it would. And later I would be taking complete blame and turning away from the life.

My thirst for completing the quest got us in the biggest trap and near-death experience. Our mission was to find the Guild of King Liam, but what happens when you lose track of what people meant to you and over power it with the feeling of getting what you want?

I was greedy, a quality that I knew would get me into trouble. But I didn't realize that I would be losing more than I anticipated, I didn't just lose the feeling of victory, but I lost my crew. When we got back to the manor, it was an all-out bashing session full of rage and fury.

My mind chose to block it out, but it was Quinton who had said we needed a break and what I thought would be a couple of months has now been two years. More like I feel they have left me, because most people in my life tend to leave me. I knew that I was to blame, but in the end they were the ones to make the choice to leave.

Then never to return.

Do you know what it's like to have enough space in the world, and still feel hopeless and lonely?

I did. I have gone stir crazy, spending the majority of my time in the library researching and getting ideas of what to do next, but I needed something more. Like an unwanted itch.

It had been two years, I needed my family back, I needed them more than ever. For the one adventure that I have been dreaming about and tasting since I was a little girl.

But in order to make it happen, I needed the crew back and I knew who to go to first. I just needed to make an appointment.

CHAPTER 2

QUINTON

T ime is a tricky thing.

One moment it's a day that passes by, then it turns into a week, then a month. Finally, it becomes a year later and then another.

I thought that it would be a good idea for the team to break for a period. Tensions had been raised high, I could sense that there was going to be further damage if something didn't happen. In all my years of training, a break is needed as a way to heal or work through a problem.

Our crew had a problem that would turn traitorous.

We almost lost Hartley as a result of Gwendolyn's pride and thirst to complete quests, trying to prove her worth to our uncle.

Or the very least, the memory of him.

I tried not to play the therapist in her case, but she worried me. She worried us. You could see the amount of control and undeniable greed. I thought Maximus had troubles with his conquests, but she took it to another level, some would call it selfishness, I would call it her "escape", an escape from the reality of her life.

We were young when we lost our parents, we had Maximus to play the part of guardian. She grew attached, even though they already had a strong relationship. Granted, Maximus had his love for me as his nephew. We had our own bond over subjects like the mind and philosophers.

When he had passed, it was something in her that broke, I saw her eyes and her spirit, the way that they fleeted away. I saw the way she carried herself, defeated, lost.

I didn't think Gwendolyn would recover. I thought we would have lost her for good, she would have been a shell of a person, truly empty inside.

The break was the best solution I could think of at the moment. Emotions and tensions were high. When we returned from our last adventure, we needed the break. At least that is what I kept telling myself over those two years.

She needed to ground herself again. Her obsession got the best of her, and I worried that if we continued, the crew, the team would be a thing of the past.

It was my hope that six months tops, we would regroup, she would come to her senses and perhaps mature a bit.

Just a break.

But what was supposed to be six months turned into two years. We could chalk it up to the fact that we didn't know when to come or who needed to make the first move.

I would have understood that there were many fingers pointing in the opposite direction. As well as some that would be turning back. Time could heal.

Gwen had some hard feelings, I imagined she might have felt betrayed, angry, and even a bit of grieving when we all parted ways. I don't blame her for feeling resentment towards me, specifically, I had actually expected it. The memory flooded me of how it started, when I gave her the reality we were living in.

"You can't be serious, Quinton. This crew is family. It's the only family we have, and you're asking everyone to leave." She *rests her hands on the desk in front of her, hitting them down almost forcefully.*

"Gwendolyn, we almost lost some of that family," I pointed out.

"But we didn't. They're here, alive. We just need to regroup and research more. We know what went wrong. We can fix it." She rushed the words, almost like she's trying to convince herself. Or trying to convince me that I was making the mistake.

I hung my head, knowing I probably won't be able to convince her. "And what if they weren't? What if they weren't alive?"

"But they are," she said again. Almost pleading for me to stop.

"You're missing the point, dear sister. It is sheer luck that they're still alive. You've become obsessed." I spelled it all out for her. At least someone had to be blunt. "Are you willing to lose the crew all together because of your obsession and greed? Or do you want to save our family?"

"You're putting the sole blame on me?" she hissed.

"I'm merely saying, since the obsession of completing the quests, you've rushed us and instead of saying anything earlier, we didn't dare get in your warpath." What else was I going to say to her that hinted at the severity of the situation?

Rash decisions, impulsivity, she was almost manic.

I gave her the choices, but she didn't take it well. I can see the tears welling in her eyes. She thought crying was a sign of weakness, that if she allowed herself to break down her walls or show signs of humanity, she'd lose everything.

I don't think she's willing to go through that again. We've all seen what betrayal does to us, and she's no different.

After a painstaking silence, she answers me. "Fine. Everyone leave then. I don't fucking care. If they want to walk out, that's their choice." She waited a moment before her infamous last words on the subject left her mouth, "Everyone leaves us at some point." She collapses into one of the resting chairs, avoiding all eye contact.

Those words haunted me, echoing every day since we left. Two had flown by, I had faith in my sister.

Fortunately for her, I didn't wander off too far for her, but far away for her to have space.

I remained close within the same state as the manor and kept my distance. I tried to reach out to her, at least to check in on her. But she has not responded, the others were different. I felt we have all come to an agreement that it was different without each other, but the promise of tomorrow was better right now than living on the edge.

We missed our adventures, but there were too many close calls.

Myself, I was waiting for the day that Gwendolyn woke up and became the sister I know and the smart woman that has been dominant for a while.

As for me, it was another day in private practice nestled in a small town in Rhode Island. I could have put my experience and education to use in a practical setting or gone into academia, but something called me into private practice. All I had was a little loft and a downtown that thrived on small businesses.

Every morning seemed the same here with my morning routine, getting up and getting ready for the day, picking up my coffee order before heading into the office, with four or five clients on my schedule, and even having the local newspaper in my hand to relish the wonders of the news. The little bell rang at the front door of the office, signaling that it was the start of the work day.

"Good morning, Dr. Griffin," Ms. Nancy, our practice's receptionist, softly said.

"Good morning. Any messages this morning or new appointments?" I said, approaching the desk, barely looking up from my paper. Rarely was there anything new.

"Yes, sir. You have a morning consultation that was added to your schedule last night with Professor Wendy Panning. She is waiting for you in your office," she says, handing me the message of the consultation.

It was interesting that I could have a consultation first thing in the morning. It left me wondering.

"Thank you, Nancy," I walked away through the double doors into my corner office.

Even at thirty-three, I have been proven to have more experiences than my fellow colleagues resulting in a bigger space for practice. Call it a world class education.

I didn't recall Professor Wendy within the field. I thought it was a curious mind that wanted to know about my work or my connections.

I opened the door, "Good morning, Professor Wendy," I say, noticing the stranger at my desk, with their feet propped up on my desk, leaning back in my chair, with a psychology journal in their hands, covering their face. Dressed down to their boots, ripped jeans, and a green rustic leather jacket.

A lot of gumption and audacity, some would say unprofessional. But this person was no stranger to my life, if anything what I thought was a ghost.

"Oh, please. We can drop the formalities. You can call me Gwen." She dropped the journal, showing that rounded face and peachy cheekbones. Her blue eyes glaring at me, the same Griffin blue eyes as me. Her sun kissed brown hair, cascading past her chest in loose waves. "Or sister if you prefer, big brother." finally dropping her feet off my desk.

To say I wasn't stunned or in disbelief would be an understatement of the century. Knowing my sister, she wasn't there because she had seen the error of her ways, but perhaps she needed something. I glared at her, she had a sly facial expression, the cocky smirk, the carefree eyes.

She was here for something.

Her gears were moving in the most curious ways.

"Gwendolyn. Must you add the dramatic flair. They made a wonderful invention of the telephone." I put the paper down on the mini coffee table near the couch where my clients chose to relinquish all their thoughts and motives and wonders of life. I sat down, folding my hands in my lap.

"Where's the fun in that? Plus, I like catching you off guard, which adds to my fun." She wiggled her eyebrows.

She had a passion for theatrics and the unexpected. She once plotted against a former ex-boyfriend who double crossed all of us in an early mission putting her back into a dark and hurt place; so she plotted a ruse to make him chase a faux hunt that resulted in him vanishing from the world, no trace from him and everyone else had a hand in his downfall. Sometimes I thought she may have killed the man, leaving him in a grave where no one would have found him.

She was hurt and for once, I saw actual fear from her. Like it had captured her soul and wasn't letting loose. The devilish grin on her face after seeing that he cowered in fear, knowing that he learned to next cross her or come at our crew was enough for her.

"It's been two years, sister. To what do I owe this unexpected visit?" I said, leaning back into the furniture. Watching her facial movements, waiting for her tells of lying or hiding the truth which in her case are completely different.

"Six months, two years, time is a cruel mistress." She sucked on her teeth, looking back at me. "I'm sorry that I didn't call or email like everyone else did for me... Oh wait, no one did." She muttered, swishing around the desk of forms and assessments.

I stood up, walking towards the desk to gather the papers to prevent any more threats of breach of confidentiality.

She snickered, knowing how to get under my skin. She jumped up from the seat scanning the room to peek at the artwork placed on my walls.

"Might I remind you that it was a two-way street. And six months was the original plan, but perhaps we found a greater purpose from the split."

"Cut the bullshit, found a greater purpose. I'm not one of your clients that needs reassurance that the things in my life are not my fault but I can battle them and become a better person." She glanced over her shoulder, batting her eyelashes.

The sass from her lips brought back memories of how she used it for her charm, especially amongst her quests and certain people.

"I am merely suggesting that while I understand your anger and emotional state currently, your goal was to refocus on yourself." I sit in my chair, watching her. "But obviously you are still harboring some hurt feelings."

"Quinton, you of all people should understand that I can't be left alone, in my emotions. In order to "refocus" on myself, I needed others around me. You don't think that I regret my behavior on the last adventure. Do you not think I realize what the consequences could have been?" Her voice raised in anger that was still brewing inside. "And the one person that I thought could help, my own blood, left me to carry out this plan."

"This is good. Keep going." After the words left me, I suddenly realized that I overstepped professionally and personally.

Gwendolyn saw red, "I'm not one of your goddamn clients. Don't shrink me. I needed you then like I need you and the rest of them now."

There it was, the moment of truth. She couldn't hide it. Her eyes growing wider, her facial features had softened, she was caught. She didn't just need me but she needed the crew, and perhaps for a reason we all know would be true amongst Gwendolyn Griffin.

"You found another historical treasure, no, an adventure fit for yourself. Tell me if I'm getting warmer," I eased back in my chair, waiting for her to finally admit that she is not here for a family reunion but that she wants something and for her own selfish reasons wants the team back for her. Some things do not change with her. She doesn't say anything, but she doesn't need to, I could see her mind spinning.

"Something big enough that you need a whole crew... something that you have been chasing... for years." Something was clicking, all the pieces coming together. "No. You didn't find anything, and yet you did." The strings of thought built the bigger picture.

"I did," her nose scrunched up as she grins. "What if I said both? I want my family back and I found my, I mean our next adventure," she leaned against the wall, folding her arms across her chest.

"Gwendolyn, do you think that's wise?"

"It's been two years, it's time for people to come home."

"And what happens if they have made a new home for themselves? Or don't want to come back?" I asked.

She hung her head at my words. I can feel the worrisome thoughts scurrying through her mind; this was the last thing she wanted to think about. She didn't want to face the idea that the others are happier without us. I would be lying if I didn't miss the crew, the rest of the outcasts, but I'm not delusional.

When we formed the team, I thought of them as the team, but she said that we were all outcasts, we were a family. We were ones with pasts that haunted us, where we only trusted certain people. All of us had a dark secret or a past.

The few years we had as a team were marvelous and memorable, and the adventures unbelievable. But those two years were easy and less worrisome. Those last two years were safe and if that meant I knew my sister was home and not putting herself on a suicide mission to prove points or even to stroll back into dangerous habits, this was better.

"Please, brother. I am asking for a second chance. I am asking for my family to come back. You have to be honest, we all did not work through our last moments. You proposed an idea and the next morning, everyone was gone." She straightened up her back, appearing proud, but something in her words and her expression tells me she was genuine.

She wanted us back. Maybe she was right and if we came back, something in her would come back to reality and we could continue to be the crew we wanted to be.

"I proposed the idea, but I didn't set out to hurt you or force anyone to do anything. They left because of their reasons. Yes, six months turned into two years. But sister, did you learn anything during them?"

Her silence was an answer that echoed the loudest. But her breath hitched before she truly answered.

"I learned that I cannot survive without my family. I want a chance to get it all back. And I have a plan to do so. But most importantly I need you. My older, intelligent, brother."

"I don't think that is what you learned. Do you not see some fault in this?"

She hung her head, again. "Maybe."

To be fair, I've mulled over our history and where my sister went off bounds. She meant well. We were the ones that lived with our uncle after our parents had their accident. We didn't have a horrible childhood as many thought so, Maximus loved us as his own children, and took a chance.

Sure, we were not normal children who went to public schools, but we were taught the importance of family, the sense of the unknown, to continue to feed into the curiosity of our minds, and that even lost things can be found.

I let out a sigh, knowing that my sister has her hooks into me now. The air hung heavy as a plan started to brew. "So, are you going to tell me the grand scheme of ours to get our family back?"

The quickness of her smile sparked that glint in her eye that tells me our adventure has yet to start. She pranced to the couch, where I finally noticed her messenger bag, the one she used to carry everywhere we went, loaded with the history and lore we needed. I used to call it her mystery bag, as she would pull random things out of it from compasses to books to first aid kits to even random knives. She pulled out random papers and files. I pulled out my readers, looking at the papers and piles noticing that they have names. "Wait, did you seriously..."

"Did you really expect me not to come prepared? Of course, I have some leeway on everyone's whereabouts. Jeez, brother, your memory is getting hazy in your old age," she shuffled through prepping to show me the way.

I snorted, "I am older than you by four years, not forty years."

"To get this right, to bring everyone back, I figure we divide and conquer," she started to suggest but I quickly shook my head at the plan.

"No, if you want to prove to me that you want this second chance, we go in together. You want people to trust you again, then we appear as a united front." I saw the wheels turning in her head as she took it into consideration. She wanted to say no, but I knew she wouldn't.

In the end she knew I was right. She sighed in response, ruffling her hair, pushing it all on one side.

"Fine. We go together," she scrunched her nose.

I chuckled, barely holding on to my laughter, "How did those words taste?"

"Fucking bitter," she coughed out. I chuckled at her response, there's my little spitfire sister. Maybe there was hope for her after all.

"Okay, I guess I need to start packing. Tell me who is first on the list," I started to pack up my desk about to put in my two weeks, something a bit unethical, but when family calls, sometimes you answer.

"First one is someone I know wouldn't hold too much of a grudge against me," She gathered her items ready to go, putting the plan into action. It was obvious who she was speaking about.

The one other person from the group that knew more about our family and the legacy of the family. It was time to visit the Windy city.

CHAPTER 3

DOMINIC

Every Wednesday was the same.

If there was one thing I learned in the military it was routine and regulations. Being back in my hometown had allowed me to come back to a routine. The last few years I wondered if I was getting too old to travel across the world. Still, I enjoyed the spontaneous adventures and wonders.

But one thing I missed was visiting my wife and child.

Once I got back, I made myself visit the grave site and talk. At least, that is what my therapist suggested I do, keeping the memory alive and the grieving process on my own time. It's taken a long time for me to admit that I needed therapy for myself.

If you'd asked me after once I discharged from the military if I had anticipated my life being the way it was, I'd told you to fuck off and then some. Never did I imagine getting tangled up in a treasure hunting team, fulfilling a legacy of a man that I met in my early years as he trotted across the globe.

Nor did I think that I would be asked to watch over his family as I got to know the man before he took his seat in the heavens above.

"My good man," Maximus had said walking into my office of my private security business. I was barely a year into the business.

"Maximus Griffin, what do I owe this pleasure? Not on some death ridden mission of yours? No sand in your shoes?" I went

to shake his hand, his grip had weakened since the last time I had seen him. He gave me the faintest smile.

Every time I had seen Maximus, he would appear with grand gestures and ostentatious, bizarre behavior. But the man had a good heart and over the years has been a supportive friend. The gray hair always throws me off, he always appears to be youthful. His wrinkles and aged skin were showing more at that moment. That time was not being kind to him.

"You didn't come for a chat, did you?" I asked him, showing him a seat. He shook his head.

"I need one last favor, old friend," He plopped on the couch, adjusting his famous suit.

"Old friend? I believe I am younger by many years." I started to pour an old scotch from the counter, offering him a glass, but he declined. I poured one for myself. "What's going on Griffin?" I finally asked.

"I'm going on a hunt and the children" meaning his niece and nephew that I haven't met yet, "are off in their academics. I have a feeling that this might be the hardest one. But I have to do this for myself."

"A solo mission like the good ole days right. I'm a bit lost." I softly laughed. His expressions grew graver.

"If something would happen to me, I need you to just look after them. Not completely in their lives or replacing anyone. But watch out for them, especially my little firefly Gwendolyn. She might be the hardest one. They don't have anyone else after me, other than themselves. Dominic."

He's asking me to be there for them or keep them safe. But why? "You didn't tell them, did you?"

He shook his head. "They think I am going to vacation at home in England."

"Maximus, I know you operate on your own terms, but these two are your family. Why don't they know what is going on or *even the risk?" No one should feel like they were not returning home.*

"Guilt my friend. I have taken them away from being around peers and people in their generation. And they are both thriving. That is their adventure," he gave the slightest smile. He wore his heart. "They would be here if I asked them, but I can't. I can't ask them to drop everything and risk their life." he said solemnly.

"But yet it's okay to risk your life," I turned it around.

He was silent after that reply. One last favor for the man I called friend. "This is one quest that I need to do. Alone. Even lost things can be found."

I couldn't do it. It wasn't fair. In the end, I don't think he wanted me to tell them. At least not the truth. But in the end someone needed to look out for the Griffins.

"I will do it. Not for you, but for them. I know what it's like to lose the only family you have."

I sipped on the scotch, easing in my seat.

A couple months, I was fulfilling that favor for him.

My routine had been predictable the last few months. But some normalcy, I would be lying if I said if I wasn't bored in some areas. That life felt too safe, too cautious. The only positive side since the split was that I was closer to my wife and child. It had been over twenty years, and yet some days it feels like it was yesterday.

When Gwendolyn and Quinton approached me to join the team, I took it as a sign from Maximus to continue that promise and be there for them. Little did I know that not being on a routine or regular schedule allowed some freedom and ease.

I remember seeing the spark in Gwen's eyes, the same one Maximus used to have. Her ocean blue eyes sparkled in the sunlight, but could turn dark when tough times arose. I could have said no, I didn't have obligations to Maximus or the Griffin's name.

I could have gone back on my promise to a dead man. But that wasn't who I was.

Gwen had called me an outcast, when I looked at her confused, she laughed and told me that it's not a negative thing. She clarified that being an outcast is not a curse or a derogatory term, but a term to be feared, a sense of freedom, a way to be a safe haven when no one else has anyone else.

When outcasts find their family, they are sure to overpower those who underestimate them.

Impactful words from a strong, clever woman.

I agreed, leaving behind the business as something for another day and began to travel the world. The team they put together seemed odd at first, but nothing I couldn't handle. I had been around young bucks who wanted to make it big in the military and had no sense of direction. Over the years, they were starting to feel like family and I couldn't help feeling like being a part of it. It turned from less of an obligation, which they will never know, to a new sense of purpose.

Soon, that spark in Gwen's eyes caught up to her. Slowly, I started to see the obsession and began to worry about it. Maximus had a sterner head on his shoulder, but it was everything to her more than anyone on the team.

It was one quest she couldn't complete and it messed with her head.

A feeling I know all too well. I wish that I could have stopped it sooner but she was relentless and brushed it off. Her anger, her need to prove something to someone, it cost her more than she realized and possibly our numbers could have dwindled.

We all had "should ofs, could ofs, would ofs".

I'm not saying that she was fully to blame. Whether we all agreed or not, we had a hand in the outcome. There was something perhaps we all could have done. But it wasn't my responsibility to be a parent.

For once, I wasn't the leader of this pack, which fell into the hands of Gwendolyn. Then it slipped out of her as we all left.

Since then I have kept my distance, at the request of Quinton. He knew his sister better than all of us, but in the back of my mind I wondered if the length of time was necessary.

Six months had passed and then nothing. Time kept going and the silence grew louder.

It was absolute silence, I wondered if they all decided to continue their separate ways. It was a decision that most have made, one thing never settled well with me. We didn't have an appropriate farewell. It's one thing about my family, that I never was able to say goodbye, but another thing to leave behind the people that had impacted my life more than I could describe.

It was a cloudy day, and I sat on the blanket next to the headstone in the cemetery. One that had been collecting leaves and nature around it.

"Hey there lady. You'd thought I'd be late. Never. Unlike you on our wedding day, I'm always on time. You remember when the wedding car wouldn't start and then we ended up being late to the reception. Oh, your mother was so pissed. I thought she was going to blow a gasket." I started up a conversation.

The imaginative conversation.

It seems ridiculous to speak to someone who is not there, but something about being able to unload what is going on as if they were here. I imagined that she was watching carefully, tucking her hands under her chin, listening to every word that I say. Her strands of curly brown hair coiled in twists flowing in the wind, in a tangled mess.

I let out a deep sigh, my mind was in twists. Like when you're stuck in a corn maze, just wanting to burst through the walls, but can't. I knew that she would tell me to stop hanging around and start living my life. It's easier said than done when your mind would rather plan out the adventures you should have been taking with her and your child.

"We could have been traveling. Oh, you would have loved Greece. Especially the food and the people. I think you would have found the place to be magical." I leaned against the stone, resting my head on it.

"Greece did have a wonder about it, didn't it Dominic?" a voice came from behind me. A deep chuckle makes me turn.

Turning to find a sharply dressed man, deep olive skin, and unmistakable curly brown hair pulled into a bun. His dress shirt had two buttons undone. A sight that could have been mistaken for a ghost. But the infamous blue eyes that ran deep in the family told me it was no ghost.

"Dr. Griffin," A grin spread across my face. I grasped his hand pulling him into a long awaited embrace.

"Dominic Stephens. Looking good for a man of your age. Even adding salt and pepper to the look." He pulled back, flashing the typical Griffin smile.

"You'll be climbing up on that ladder soon."

"Not too soon," he laughed.

I folded my arms across my chest. Not that I wasn't excited to see this man, but no heads up, no contact. Typically that was a page out of Gwen herself, not her brother. Something was throwing me off.

"What are you doing here Quinton?" I stared at him intensely. He looked at me, he was definitely hiding something.

"We are getting the family back together," he shoves his hands in his front pockets. He said we, not himself.

The magical term we. He wasn't alone. Of course, she wouldn't be too far from this.

I raised an eyebrow, "We?"

He nodded his head. The slight smirk gave it away.

"Where is she?" A small smile spreads across my face. It was damn time.

CHAPTER 4

GWENDOLYN

I hid behind the tree, afraid that Dominic wouldn't accept the invite if he knew I was here. My gut told me to trust that he'd come back with no problem, but my mind said otherwise, replaying the last moments.

I never got an understanding of his expression when they left. But the slight hint of happiness of asking where I was, I felt a little warmth igniting inside my stomach. The closest thing I had to my uncle, the last connection other than my brother was feet away.

"Where is she?" Dominic asked, a twinge of happiness in his voice.

"Never far away, old man," I said, coming from behind the tree leaning up against it. Dominic towered over my 5'7 frame, his arms engulfing me in a tight embrace.

He may be the oldest of the group but never would I have associated him like a father figure or a replacement for Maximus. He was a caring man who honestly was the glue in many of the heated arguments or fights we had. Most of the time, the giant man would grab us by the shirts, lifting us off the ground to separate any fights. There was something about him that made him feel like the protector, that and his experience with the military.

"Always one for the flair," He pulled back, taking in every inch. "Looking good for a woman who turned into a lone wolf."

"Lone wolf who wants her pack," I said as I brushed past him, making my way to my brother still casting a shadow. "Don't think this is an appropriate place to have this conversation. Coffee?" I suggested, turning my back towards them, knowing that they would follow me.

"How did you find me?" Dominic shouted behind me.

I glanced back in his direction. "Buy me a coffee and I'll give you all the secrets," I winked at him. I was rewarded with his big smile.

Soon we found ourselves inside a local dinner in the heart of the city, a young lady pouring two cups of coffee, and handing over the tea bags for Quinton.

I'll get my caffeine from a better source. He would say. The hustle of the place gave an ambience, like a well-loved oil machine. Enough noise to keep some privacy.

I splashed a thing of creamer and a pinch of sugar into my coffee and mixed it together. The clinking of the cup started to irritate Quinton, knowing that it is the one thing he can't stand. I peeked over to him, seeing that I was given the "if you don't stop" look. No matter how hard he tries, Quinton wished he would win in a fight.

Putting him in charge would be a challenge for me. Though he didn't know it yet, I couldn't have him as a flight risk. I know I screwed up in the past, I caused emotions to fly.

I started off slow knowing that Dominic possibly hadn't given up on me.

"Are we going to talk or are you two going to keep playing this sibling annoyance gimmick?" Dominic said gravely.

Quinton looked at me, giving me the okay to explain myself. I needed my family back to get back to our lives, I didn't want to risk anymore, but still can't shake the feeling of abandonment. I looked across the table, Dominic waited for my answer.

"Dominic, I need to get my family back," I looked back down at my coffee, not wanting to see his expression. The only one of the group that I don't like to disappoint or get sparing judgment from. I didn't know whether it was because of his age or because he was another extension of Uncle Maximus. I didn't want to disappoint him anymore than I possibly have been already.

"I'm here to ask you to come home."

His facial expression when I looked back at him wasn't what I expected. I expected a heated face, ready to blow the roof off the dinner. I was expecting more of an outraged look, thinking that I must be crazy to think that it was a possibility. Even a simple laugh off would be appropriate in this case.

"Come home? If you haven't noticed kiddo, I am home. Have been for two years now," he sipped his coffee. The sting of the way he said *home* and *two years* hurt like hell.

I shook my head. "Not that *home*. Home back with us," I admitted. "I... *we* need our family back and to go back to the way things were." I must have hit a small nerve because his facial expression changed, and I felt Quinton grip my thigh to back off.

"Go back to the way things were? Do you remember the reason behind why we left? Why we needed a break in the first place? I know you're young, but I know you are not naive," he spat out, almost like a small dagger aiming for my heart.

I wasn't expecting bitterness from him.

I straightened up, not showing a light of weakness that was slipping out. The wince of disappointment. It brought back small memories of when I felt like I disappointed Maximus. "I think we can all agree that after six months, none of us felt like going back, we can't place blame all on Gwen." I turned to Quinton, staring at him, feeling I got slapped in the face just for a moment.

"Two years, but it started with her," Dominic added in. "But you can't speak for everyone, I don't think it was that no one wanted to come back. We didn't know if you were okay or if everyone was ready to come back."

"I don't think she knew that it was up to her. I didn't communicate well with her. And I am ashamed of that.," my brother chimed in.

"She's right here you know. You could just speak directly to me," I waved my hands in front of me. "Look, I admit that I *may* have gone extremely overboard and put the lives of others on the line. I didn't see the line that I crossed. But after six months, no one came back. I thought everyone would just come back on their own. This is what happens when you assume." I started composing myself to not trail into emotion. "Things were rushed. Half of you all were ready to leave as soon as we got back," I started to play around with the cup's handle. "But I think it's time to come home."

"The Gwendolyn I know doesn't automatically spit out the words that someone wants to hear. So I'll say this, and I don't need the words to be misconstrued," Dominic started as I looked back at Quinton who was dunking this tea bag in his cup. I know he was listening to every word.

"Proceed," I said to Dominic.

"You were turning into Maximus, and not in the most honorable way." Dominic reaches across the table to grab my hands. "Maximus had a thirst for adventure, and you went a little crazy, like you were trying to prove something. So, my question for you is, who are you trying to be? Are you trying to prove something or someone? Why do you want us back?" He paused for a moment. "Gwendolyn Griffin, are you sincerely sorry for what happened? Or did your brother coach you into saying those empty words?"

I jolted back from his words. Had I learned a lot from the time I was given? Not completely. Was I fueled by personal gain? Honestly, who isn't nowadays? But this was the reaction I was looking for, the one that told me I was part of the problem, if not the beginning of it.

But I wasn't going to admit that, that easily at least.

Quinton sat there smugly, nodding his head in agreement with Dominic, waiting for me to answer. I wasn't ready to admit defeat, but I know that is what they are expecting me to say. Admit that I was in the wrong.

I couldn't admit to something that I didn't truly believe or wasn't ready to admit even to myself most days. Dominic was asking the tough questions, I shook off the thoughts of being worse than Maximus. I wanted to say that I learned my lesson, but the truth is, I don't think I truly have. Maybe Dominic had a point. But what if; what if I was worse than Maximus. I couldn't say anything, but it did hit a nerve. I avoided eye contact with him for a reason.

The truth can fucking hurt.

"Why do you want the family back? What's so important that you need all of us?" he starts off.

I couldn't hide my expression, I sucked in my lips.

"Wait," Dominic must be connecting the dots now. "You found a new obsession," he said bluntly. I avoided his eyes even more. "And it's something that you have been wanting." The small smirk on his face told me he finds this a bit amusing. He knew me very well, seeing the light in my eyes. A moment ago he was telling me that I was worse than Maximus but here we were.

"The Seven Deadly Madames," I said forcefully, trying not to let anger or fear bubble up from the top. Quinton looked back at me, waiting for something else to come out. "I found new evidence."

He didn't believe me, at least not at first. "You're lying," Dominic spits out. "That has been a dead end for years, even Maximus couldn't find anything."

And yet, I'm worse than Maximus. I was one step closer than Maximus.

A small sense of pride raked through me.

"I did. I found something or rather something was sent to me with a favor I will pay, and..."

"Up until you realize that it was bigger than you, right?" Dominic folded his arms against his chest. "Even if you were to get everyone back, what makes you think that something of an apology will be enough? Or will it be easy or if everyone will want to get back in the game?"

That was when my bright idea started to shed some light, "Because I won't be the lead on this mission," I said.

"Then who? As far as I know Massey hasn't been our benefactor in a couple years and we're all too individualistic to not have someone lead the lot of us."

"Leave Massey to me." I responded back. "But it will be Quinton. Quinton will lead." I took a sip of my coffee again, while Quinton choked on his tea. His coughs grew louder in the diner as a few heads had turned to look.

I hadn't told him yet that I had an idea to make him lead as a form of trust. Perhaps that was my only saving grace. Maybe I should have said something earlier before Dom.

"You'd let your brother take the lead on the *one* mission, the one quest that you've been obsessing over? You must be desperate enough," Dominic chuckles deeply.

Yes, I was desperate enough, but I wanted my life back to normalcy. After twenty nine years of it, I deserved it. I have had enough loss in my life, but I'd be set.

Between heartbreak, grief, and death, I was set for a lifetime. Quinton would have a clearer head than myself, and the team would trust him right now, before they would put me in the back seat, and perhaps even on the road to forgiveness, whatever they needed to get back to us.

"Gwendolyn, I don't think that is going to be a good idea," Quinton muttered out. I think I caught him off guard. "It's a brilliant idea," I said back. "The problem was that I was leading everything and I was the reason why people got hurt. Am I now coming to terms with it, yes."

The noise of the diner swelled, almost overpowering our conversation. I bumped Quinton out of the booth so I could get up. I scooted out and pulled out my wallet from my messenger bag and tossed a couple twenties on the table and started to walk out, knowing that they would follow me.

I left the diner, waiting by the street, highly debating whether to grab a cigarette from my hidden pocket or not. I didn't typically smoke, but when I did it was in times of high stress. I reached into the bag, my hands on the carton. Then I heard the bell from the door of the diner ring, I quickly yanked my hand out of the bag.

Go ahead and keep running.

"Gwen, do you think this is a good idea?" Dominic touched my shoulder. I turned to see him. "I want everyone. Even quiet, head games Hartley, no matter how many times he tries to play his mind games or make me fluster."

Okay, I missed the head to head games with that man. He and Winston were the only ones that could ruffle my feathers.

"It was his way of having fun with you, sister," Quinton chimed as he was putting on his sunglasses, looking around the streets.

"Trust me, I know it was for his enjoyment," I couldn't blame him. His twisted mind and demeanor were alluring to some not just me. But not fully my cup of tea.

We all knew who your heart belongs to, even if you did screw it up.

"We all deserve to go back to the way things were. Are you telling me you would rather sit back at home, take a case or two from the agency, and have an actual routine?" I walked further down the sidewalk heading towards the parked cars. "Are you going to lie and say that you haven't been itching to get back to going on missions or quests? The adrenaline in you isn't begging to be released?"

I knew that Dominic had been missing the adventures and the sense of calling.

"Are we going to talk about this more and your plan? Or are you just going to leave me here on the streets?" Dominic yelled out as I left them in the dust.

I turned back and gave him a smile. "Invite us back to your loft and then we can talk."

"That's very demanding of you," Dominic smirked back. He shook his head before saying, "Wait, how did you know I had a loft?" He sounded a bit surprised.

"I'm just a woman who knows what she wants and can keep a secret or two," I unlocked the car and got in the passenger side. Quinton soon followed suit and we headed back to Dominic's loft.

I knew that Dominic was well taken care of due to the splitting of the profits and his savings. He was not like the others, needlessly spending and putting it towards "toys" or "investments" or even guilty pleasures.

He was smart, so knowing him, he got a loft in the heart of Chicago, within distances of the cemetery, and to keep normalcy, he opened back up the private investigation business, taking on random clients. The smartest one of the bunch, when it came to practicality.

Walking into his loft, I fully expected it to feel like home, antiques or classic furniture, possibly industrial interior design than anything else. But for someone who has lived here for two years, it feels barren and unlived in. It was still an empty shell of an area, limited to sentimentals. I think someone may have been lying to me.

I thought this would give me leeway to make my point, Dominic was ready to come home months ago it would appear. I walked through the loft, the clicking of my heeled boots echoed even more. I promised Quinton I would take the answer "no" if it was genuine. I still had to learn and accept that the majority of this was on my shoulders and my responsibility. But something told me that Dominic would give in. I saw him take a seat at his island table, waiting for me to speak.

"Gwendolyn, I think the time for dramatics is over, stop playing around and talk with Dominic," Quinton sneers at me, his patience wearing thin.

I plopped on Dominic's brown leather couch, expecting a softer landing. "You were my first stop, then at Quinton's request is to gather everyone else and plead my case. And then like before I will relay that Quinton will be team lead, I will just use my skills accordingly being the historian of the team. Now that he knows the plan and I am not holding back my plans. Quinton would have been the better pick, he has more of a level head than us." I said, spreading my arms across the couch.

"Regroup and move on." Quinton added. Dominic huffed, offering little retaliation.

"So, how did you all find me?" Dominic asked.

"Program left by Xara and Hartley," I said bluntly, shutting down the side conversation. I think we all have that deflection technique because something in our lives led us to be this hurt.

Partially me.

"We're not all perfect, we all have faults. I failed as a brother and I'm coming to terms with that," Quinton said. Only thing is, I never believed he failed as a brother. I couldn't blame him for being human and having emotions.

"And you started with me," Dominic said, walking around his kitchen.

"Because to say you have a sweet spot for little ole me. Plus you know Maximus would have wanted you to come back," I leaned forward, resting on my knees. "Please Dom, if you say no, I know there's no hope for the rest of them." Although he was the easiest to convince, it didn't mean I could bank on the fact that he would say yes. I didn't know how much damage was done.

I saw Quinton glancing over in the direction of Dominic. I could see Dominic taking everything into consideration. The wheels in his head turned. I silently pleaded with him to say yes, to help bring us all back together. Silently asking him for a second chance.

Then I started to doubt myself in all this. Dominic looked back at Quinton.

"You have been very quiet in all this my man, what do you think?" Dominic asked Quinton, staring at him, those inquisitive eyes. Quinton leaned against the wall allowing room for me to talk, since all this was my idea.

He pushed off the wall and said, "I think we all deserve the chance to try again. She may need this as much as we need this. We were happy. We were a family. And we still are that chosen family that we created, we truly are never parted. I think we should try again." His words were ringing true, we won't know until we know. "But with the agreement that after this last conquest that if we all want to go separate ways, then that is the end."

That was the agreement, a harder pill to swallow.

With a deep sigh, Dominic pushes off from the table, hanging his head low, but releases a grizzly laugh. "One last try, but I'm not making any promises. What do you need me to do in the meantime?"

I couldn't help myself but be giddy and jump up from the couch and entrap him into a tight hug. The sign of a possibility that this would work is all I need. "Thank you, thank you."

That was the bode of confidence that I needed. Dominic was coming back and made my heart jump out of my chest. Not everyone would have the same reaction or influence as Dominic.

I released him and grabbed my bag, "Try to get back to the manor by next week, I have a feeling that Quinton and I will have a tougher time getting others. Make yourself at home, get anything else in order." I kissed him on the cheek and signaled Quinton to move.

And with our goodbyes at the door and Dominic back in the game, I felt like walking on cloud nine, a sense of pride that would be what I needed.

"Where are you heading to next? Who's next on your list? Damn, it almost sounds like a hit list now that I say it out loud," Dominic asked before we headed out the door. I knew who was next, because this person had known me longer than anyone else except my brother. And I couldn't deny him anymore.

"Time for a childhood reunion, my way," I answered him, and before I knew it we were heading back to South Carolina, determined on getting my engine checked on at a local garage.

CHAPTER 5

WINSTON

There's nothing I hated more than someone who has no business changing their own oil, because they thought that YouTube would save them money. And if you don't know how to actually do it, then you ruin your car if you screw up.

Some people honestly are just that stupid and will do anything they want.

"Mo, come put this up on the racks. Let's take a look if there is any more damage to this truck," I yelled at one of my mechanics in the back who was flipping through a manual to check the gauges on one of the other cars in the back.

"You got it boss," he responded and started to push the truck up on the racks.

He was a hard worker but sometimes he wasn't the brightest crayon in the crayon box. Lucky for him, the next moment, he was out of the way before a dusty sage green jeep charged into the open garage. The rev of the engines echoed loudly in the open garage, charging into here with a death wish.

Either someone had a target on their back or someone wanted to royally piss me off.

They had halted to a stop when I grabbed the nearest large wrench, ready to wring some necks. No one came into my shop to start a fight. The dust started to settle and the rage in me was simmering.

I wasn't an overly aggressive man, but nobody came into my business and messed with my garage or workers at the very least.

I started to storm towards it, "Are you kidding me, man, you better get out of the damn car so I beat your fucking ass," I stepped further towards the jeep to find a familiar woman with a cat-like smile.

The smile that could sink a thousand ships. A smile that affected me months ago, something you couldn't let go nor forget. Gwendolyn.

A simple wave of her hand, her playfulness that sent shivers down my spine.

She was the Helen of Troy, bringing men down to their knees.

Stupid, not again. Not again!

After two years, this was how things were going to go down. I dropped the wrench with a loud thud onto the ground echoing in the garage. Mo looked at me with a slight fright in his eyes, not knowing how to react or what to do. He looked like a cartoon character that had smoke coming through his ears from thinking. He was still holding the remote to the racks.

I gave him a death stare, hoping that he would scatter off, but he already looked confused, lost even.

Gwendolyn got out of the car, leaning against it, like she was ready to command to get what she wanted. The one person that knew how to get under my skin and press all the right buttons, but the only person that could melt my heart.

People always talked about the one that got away, well she was still very present and stood in front of me. It wasn't my decision to let her go, that was hers and as a result, left a part of me that was bitter and angry.

We were childhood best friends, always either starting trouble in the neighborhood or being each other's alibis. At a young age, the sheriff shouldn't have known our names, but we didn't care at that age.

Truth be told, I loved the damn minx, no matter how much was going on in our life. She was the one person I possibly could not say no to, but something told me that this would be the first time.

"Winston." The purr of my name rolled from her mouth. I fell under her spell one other time, and honestly, never thought I would recover from it. It took only one word, one name to spiral me back into a delirious state.

I shook it off.

"Ms. Griffin," I said, refusing to give her back the power. I refused to give in to her, she had made her decisions. Just like I made mine.

I transported back to the memories of being back home because of her and her stubbornness, her actions, and her rejection.

A broken record with the sting of rejection hurt more than leaving her, that's what it felt like. Even as children, she made most of the decisions, she created trouble, I just went along with it because I saw what was in her heart.

All I wanted was to be in her life and make her mine. I could see having her in arms and only mine for ages to come, but I guess I was a fool to think that was what she wanted no matter all the intimate touches she would give.

"Come on, Win, really? The formalities. Are you still upset with me?" She took a step forward in my direction.

I heard the passenger car door open and shut, producing her brother, clean and dapper looking. He's just as bad as her, just with fancier words that made you examine your own life.

The nerve of this woman.

Still upset? Upset didn't cover the emotions I had, I was still furious and bitter. I used to laugh and smile around others and part of me was buried when we split. Therefore yes, I was still upset with her.

The gleam in her eyes told me something was in motion and I didn't know what was coming but I had a feeling that she had something up her sleeve. She had some sort of plan. A feeling that she was pulling the puppet strings and she dragged her brother in her mess again.

"You can go back the way you came," I growled out, picking up the wrench and pushing her back far back in my mind, "I'm sure hell is missing one of their mistresses".

I turned and walked away from her. I snapped to Mo's attention. He was still standing in the corner with mouth opened wide, I grew concerned that he would swallow flies pretty soon.

I wiped my hands on one of the rages in the toolbox. The light steps of Gwen did not help me. Her light rose scent from her perfume filled my senses, flooding back memories of her falling asleep in my lap in the library, the small caresses and sneaky little kisses on the cheek. Everything felt so innocent with her, afraid to push the damn boundary.

Memories of her in her element, getting lost in the cities we were in but perfectly able to navigate and find our true destinations. It was all in the past.

"Winston, it's been a long time," she cooed, leaning next to me, facing the opposite direction.

"And whose fault is that? Certainly not mine." I snapped back.

She started to speak, I pointed at her, "Think before you say. One lesson I thought you would get by now." My words came out harsh with a bite.

She shrunk down, darting her eyes to her brother, as if to ask for help.

"Time to come home, my friend," her brother interjects. He knew how to command a room, it must be a family trait, running through their veins.

"Last I checked, this is my home." I threw my arms out, showing up the space that I came back to after the split. I honestly tried to fight it but Gwen, the ever stubborn woman she is, made it possible for me to leave. "You think just by showing up here, batting your eyelashes at me will make me say yes?"

She was thrown back for a moment, I knew that if I said truly what I wanted to say, I might have ended up with blood on my floor.

Anger started to boil up, and resulted in steam rovering over my head. I walked away from her, acted like she was not here, acted like she didn't cause all of this.

I started to get back to work on the vehicles lined up in my shop. I have kept the business afloat, even when I was away across the oceans, spending every last moment questioning what was going to happen next. I didn't have much family left, of course like last when she walked in my garage, I didn't realize that I would receive a family I didn't ask for.

Between the cousins and even Xara, we were all a tight knit group. Even Yankee with his mysterious quirks. The money flowing in from our travels allowed me to keep the shop going and allow my mechanics to keep working while my distant cousin took over the managerial duties. "Mo, grab brake pads for this Ford, lord knows this one will go through them in a couple months or so."

I glanced behind to find Quinton talking with Gwen, holding the back of her arm to stop her. I sensed the fire in her eyes, her impulse to fight.

Bring it on Winnie, we'll see who comes out on top.

Someone cleared their throat, noticing that it was Mo with the pads in his arms. "Do I want to know, boss?" he grunted out.

"Ghost from the past," I mumbled under my breath.

"Looks alive to me." That she was, part of me that wasn't furious with her would be ecstatic about that.

Instead of the minx, Quinton walked in her place, still respecting my space. The light brown mustache that he has kept over the years added to his age. No more could you see the young faced, baby faced professional, but the mature gentleman.

I'll give it to him, he had class and etiquette, a lesson from their uncle. The heavier steps of his dress shoes clicked against the garage floor. "Winston, give her five minutes. If not her, then please do me the favor," Quinton pleaded with me.

"One good reason. Give me one good reason." I said to him, the words tasted bitter.

"Because you look at her with the same affection and infatuation that you always have had. It's just being covered up with anger. I'm not blind. You have been pining after her for years." the slight confidence in his smile.

"Don't try to use your mind tricks." I shook my head getting back under the car to check out the rest of the car.

"I'm saying this as her brother. You have been trying to be that one person that she would count on, then she broke your heart. Therefore, you are still angry with her. Honestly, I don't blame you. How many times did we all try to reign her back in? How many missions did we go on and have too many close calls to where we, her family, even said okay what's next," His words started to ring true and empathetic.

"And what after two years, she decided that she wants me back, wants you back? I find that hard to believe."

Time to come home.

It's not just me that she wanted back, we wanted everyone to come back. "I'm not the only one."

Quinton shook his head, "No, my friend you are not, she is on a mission to get everyone back. To get all our family back home." He shoved his hands in his pockets, kicking around the floor. "Five minutes all I'm asking. Give her a chance. She'll be on her best behavior." I had to laugh.

"You and I both know that won't happen." I responded back. He shrugged in response.

I released a loud sigh, wiped my hands on my uniform, attempting to clear the oil off my hands. I walked over to her, towering over her, her big brown eyes glistening in the overhead lights, her brushing her hair to one side, tilting her face up at me.

"Five minutes, my office. Now." I growled out walking away from her and headed into my office, expecting her to submit to follow.

In any country or world, she was the image of sheer dominance in a man's world. "You could say please," She called back, words getting under my skin.

This couldn't have been happening to me, after six months had passed I thought we were all done.

She didn't reach out, no one else kept in contact, our crew felt officially over. I think at one point I doubted myself, a brief moment of weakness that left as quick as it did when it came.

I opened the door to the back office, paced a few steps before I saw her standing in the doorway, watching me, waiting for me to say something. She chastised herself to the seat in front of the desk, crossing her toned legs over each other. I folded my arms and leaned against the desk. This was not my show to take charge.

A few seconds went by and something, I began to wonder if she had spaced out. I cleared my throat, "I said you had five minutes. I think it's more than enough time to say what you need to say and then leave." I grumbled to her.

I had enough games from her over the last decade of my life. She took a deep breath and boosted herself up from the chair, taking a step between my legs.

I have seen this move before, when she truly wanted to melt and bend to her will, she'd bat those thick eyelashes, step between my legs nestling close, drag her fingers lightly on my upper arms. And if she really wanted to get her way, she'd cup her hands behind my head and lightly scratch there. I would turn into a putty in her arms. Her wicked grin would spread across her face and you knew she won that round. She was working her move, attempting to win me over.

"Winston," she said breathlessly. Her fingers were about to trace the muscles of my upper arm. I stopped her, pinning her arms by her side.

"Not this time. Either talk or walk." I stared into her eyes, leveling with her. Her eyes searched for a way in. She relaxed in my hands, a slight break in her walls.

"I tried." She took a step back, "I guess words will have to do."

"What did you think would happen? You show up here like the first time and wiggle yourself back into my life. Need I remind you that, you came here for one thing. And it wasn't *me*," I had to let those words fly. I sensed it the moment she came barreling through my garage.

"What if I actually did? What if I came here because I needed you back in my life?" She took a step back and looked back at me. She started to wander around the room. She was staying close, but giving distance as well.

"Then I would say that you were lying or hiding something," I said. She stopped in her tracks. *Gotcha.* "I'm right, aren't I?" I couldn't help the crooked smirk on my face. I know her too well.

"Yes and no," She admitted. "Winston, it has been too long. I want the crew back under one roof."

"And do you recall why we all left?" I spat out. We both know who was at fault. I tried to reason with her before we all left, but sometimes words are better not spoken. Some words lead to heartbreak and honestly, I don't think they could ever be taken back.

"So that's it, I slip up and everyone agrees to separate for six months. Sounds more like running away." Gwendolyn said angrily, putting my clothes back into my closet after I had packed them up. She didn't want me to go.

"Winnie, it is just a break, we'll come back. We have to focus back on ourselves, then when we are ready, we'll be a crew again."

"I know I screwed up, but leaving in a time where we have to recenter ourselves, we need each other." She truly didn't see what happened. She didn't see the overachieving, the over-stressed, the greed in her eyes when we were in that tomb. I worried more and wondered if she would recover.

"No, you need us to stay because we have been your family for a long time now. But I'm not truly leaving you. I'm going back home." I started to say, nervous about saying the next part, "You could come with me."

Looking back at her with a sweater in my hand. Silently pleading that she would say yes. I walked back to the dresser across the room.

"This is my home, and you belong here. All of you do. Instead of staying and talking like adults, everyone is leaving," the next part was a whisper I almost missed, "almost like cowards." I slammed the dresser drawer loudly. There was dead silence.

"Coward? You calling me a coward?" I spat at her, she jerked back surprised, as if I didn't hear her.

"What else am I supposed to call people who run away from their problems?" She yelled back, pushing off the bed.

"Human, we are human. Especially when the people we love push us to the breaking point." I tried to reason with her, but I have a feeling with everyone's emotions running high, including hers, I was not prepared for this fight to end peacefully.

"That is not love, that is someone who is afraid of facing the problems head on, that's not someone I love."

"You're saying that you don't love your brother, the cousins, Hartley? Not even me?" Emotions were running high, "Because the moment we need a break after the amount of danger we put ourselves in, you don't love that you didn't get your way. Poor Gwendolyn, so used to people doing what she wants and how she wants it. You may have that gracious, kind heart that I have known for years, but that green greed monster has surfaced." The bitter truth arrived and I'm surprised she has lasted this long.

Her stunned silence is enough noise to fill the room. She gently got up from the bed and walked to the open door of the room, leading out in one of the wings. She stopped dead in the center of the door, not looking back, I couldn't see her face and if there were tears or anger twisted there.

"And poor Winston will never get what he truly wants because he is too afraid to go after it himself." Her words burned inside. Echoing loudly, being too afraid to get it himself. She walked out. She could have come home with me and spared the hateful words, but she chose her own. She chose to be selfless and walk out on me. Here I thought that she would say yes to me.

"Mine. I caused this. Is that what you wanted to hear? I screwed up and I shut everyone out because I felt that you chose to leave me over everything else." Her voice was low.

"I gave you a choice. You proceeded to shoot it down." I growled a bit back.

"I didn't know what to do. You know I don't handle anger well."

"Understatement of the year. But also a poor excuse," I said.

"What did you expect me to say? That I regret my behavior, that I am not the same person anymore? I lost something and someone. I don't know if I fully learned a lesson, I don't know if I can be the person that everyone is expecting me to be," she said, plopping back on the couch.

"You have yet to answer an important question. Why now? After two years." I leaned forward, inches away from her face. A slight temptation in me was holding me back.

"The Madames," her wicked smile came back.

"Fuck no." I jolted back.

She had been after that lore for years, well before I had entered her life again. She was mystified with the legend of the madames, yet there was not enough research of history to truly pinpoint the accuracy of the legend. She had combed through countless books through the huge library back at the manor and never saw the end of the shelves, visiting academic libraries to check their catalogs. She would get a bit of a lead and then fall into a dead end. It was heartbreaking to see her on the verge of defeat.

But the Gwen we knew, bounced right back. Someone would call it an obsession.

"It's real this time." She piped up, with excitement in her voice.

"You have been saying that for years, but look where it got you. You truly think me or anyone else in the crew would come back to help you fulfill some kind of obsession?" I whipped back around my desk, placing my hands on my desk.

"I got one of us back." She raised her eyebrows.

"Who?"

"Dom."

I laughed, "Of course, the one person that was closer to your uncle than anyone else. And who is willing to do anything for your family."

"Our family." She corrected me. "What if I said that I truly want my family back and I wouldn't be in charge of our movements?" she finally said.

That got my attention. There was no way Gwendolyn Griffin would give up control even to her own flesh and blood. The only one was Maximus when he was alive. She's giving up the one thing that partly defined who she was, a leader. Giving up control wasn't something that came naturally to her, but that was just the team aspect.

"I'd call your bluff," tilting my head, waiting for her to up the ante.

"Quinton will lead until the crew feels that I could handle it. I will do the research, play my part aside from leading the group." She laid out her plan.

"And what if we all decide after that we are better off? You let us go?" I hung the question in the air.

"We'll cross that bridge, if we come to it." she fired back. There was a softness in her eyes, "Please Winston, out of everyone, you were my hardest one to talk with, we both know why. I can't do anything without you. You and I both know this." her eyes almost watered up but she fought back the tears, standing firm in her ground.

For a moment I had to think.

Two years of washing my hands of her, two years of leaving behind the adventurous side I had locked up even before.

Two years without the friends I had come to know over the years. One thing I couldn't walk back to was being as close as I was to her. I had thought that she would choose me, her words rang in my ears almost everyday.

"And poor Winston will never get what he truly wants because he is too afraid to go after it himself".

Those words broke my heart, and I wouldn't let that happen to me again, even if it means moving on from the woman I cared about for years. It would be hard when she is a walking temptation and I'd do anything for her.

I swallowed my pride, and decided that if she wanted me for me, she would have to work for it. If she wanted a second chance at me, us, or the team, she'd have a lot to prove.

"When do we leave?" I said, not looking at her, knowing that she would have a cunning smile, feeling like she had me wrapped around her little finger.

I would give her one more chance, perhaps there was a chance. But why did it feel like I made a deal with the devil?

CHAPTER 6

Honestly, I didn't think that Winston would say yes, but those blue eyes actually worked on him, or at least for the most part in the meantime. He was on the track to wrapping up his ties at home. Gwen and I had five more family crew members to wrangle and the next one on the mental list was in Florida, hugging the coast.

This one, according to Gwen, was harder to track down as she was like a ghost and changed location every week. Our wild one, our wild card, Xara Kennedy. It w expected, something admirable about that, something about it was alluring.

Xara was the daughter of an American diplomat family. She was supposed to be raised, married in a dignitary home, with the image of the future diplomat or politician on her shoulders. But we all know what happens when people have different ideals or morals than family, they tend to revolt and pursue a different lifestyle.

In the end, Xara had created her own underground information network utilizing her language skills to help advocacy groups and take a bite out of corrupt governments. The woman could speak at least seven languages, a gift that definitely became useful. Within our group she was our linguist, and wild card. The woman was a genius.

Out of anyone in the crew, she was smooth talking, very cunning even more than my sister, and could overpower anyone, well maybe not everyone. Gwendolyn had found out that she had arrived back in Florida from a trip in Bali. Most likely she had used her charm and connections for a free trip.

Before we went our separate ways, I thought that she would speak her mind and have choice words. But she was quieter than others. I had attempted to reach out to her multiple times, but my own mind said to move on. I didn't want to let her go, I didn't want to keep chasing her when there was no direct possibility.

I missed a lot about her, but I wouldn't admit that in the crew's presence. Everyone thought that she was the one that could control me or sway me with anything, if only they actually knew that the little demon was *mine*. And I was hers, though words were never spoken true. I gripped the steering too tight, my hands at the point of being pale.

"You're thinking hard over there, brother. You nervous or something about Xara?" Gwendolyn woke me up from the daydream.

We headed into the state, I honestly did not know what to expect. I would imagine that she would be like the Godfather, sitting back as the world burned at her feet or seducing her latest affliction. Xara lived a very different lifestyle than myself or my sister. I was intrigued with her mind and we both saw each other in a different light and shared that passion. That was how she was in the light, in the daytime. Within the shadows and between us, there was just us, if only we took the chance outside.

"Well, after two years, one would wonder if havoc has chased her or she's chased havoc." I said nervously.

There was a small snicker that came from Gwen's lips. A bit more cynical than I would have liked. I looked over at her, she was hiding her big smile. "She still makes you nervous. Oh, my god you're blushing. It's the embarrassment that sets it all to fact." Always teasing, always joking to sometimes set the attention elsewhere.

"Yes, a grown woman that executes dominance in the world we live in today."

Maybe not so much behind closed doors.

"No, you're afraid she'll say no and pull out her knife. And then you would ask for more." Gwen said. "I swear I kept thinking I was the kinky sibling, but brother dearest may have beat me."

You have no idea, dear sister.

"The only other woman who has put me in my place," I muttered under my breath. To be fair, I'm the only person who could ease Xara. As my sister would put it, I was putty in Xara's hands and she was putty in mine. There was something that spoke to me, the power struggle or switch between us.

"I'm sorry, what was that?" Gwen leaned over the armrest, "No? Nothing? Thought so."

Gwendolyn knows how to get under my skin and stay there. Like the pest she is. I could feel the anger boiling to the surface.

Save the rage for something else, not the time or place.

We didn't have a lot of time especially with Gwendolyn's rushed deadline, she wanted everyone home at the manor next week, towards the beginning of November. Unrealistic in my opinion. But I didn't dare say that in fear she would not get her way and would result in her withdrawing from the world once again. Gwendolyn was blinded to the point she didn't look upon others. Xara being one of them.

Xara had seen her through the beginning of tough times and when Gwendolyn came back to school, Xara gave her that tough love that I couldn't. Xara knocked my sister down a few pegs when Gwendolyn decided to go on a self-destructive path.

I should have been concerned that Gwendolyn had found everyone, using the systems that Xara and Hartley had used and created. It should have signaled me that she was more ready to confront the quest rather than admit her mistakes.

"Whatcha gonna say to her once we get there?" I questioned my sister.

In her typical fashion, she responded with her smug grin. "I know exactly what to say to her. You just sit there and look pretty," She tapped me on the shoulders, condescendingly.

After countless traffic stops and parking in a packed parking garage, Gwendolyn walked to the elevators in confidence, the kind that runs in the family. "I imagine you've run a number of scenarios in your head, and have planned accordingly." I said in hopes that she thought about this before we walked into the chaos that she would think of the consequences.

But a part of me was anxious to see Xara after all this time.

The elevator takes us to the main lobby of this building to another set of elevators, Gwendolyn punched in the floor number and I peered at it seeing that it was the top floor, the penthouse. Xara must have done well since our time apart. Last I knew she had taken a step back from her underground organization of hacktivists when she joined the crew.

The elevator dings that we are the floor. The clicking of the boots on the ground echoed in the hallway as we made our way to her door. My heart raced faster, a bead of sweat rolled down my neck. My sister gave a few hard knocks at the door, waiting those few seconds before an answer was a hard moment. She pushed me to the side away from the view of the door. The light opening of the door, a shadow at the door gave us the slight hope that we needed.

Xara peeked through the door opening, "Damn, you're not the delivery guy. Stay there, I'll call the garbage man." She tried to close the door, but my sister's boot stopped in her tracks.

A brief silence fell upon us. "Vips, let's talk."

The old nickname that Gwendolyn had given Xara when they were in school. Vips for Viper meaning that Xara was a deadly person, ready to strike fear and at any time. People underestimated her in quick fashion.

"You want to talk now?" Xara spat out, followed by a short snort.

"I know. I know." my sister responded.

"You know what, Gwen?" Xara opened the door, revealing sweatpants and a loose black shirt that hung off her shoulders exposing her smooth, fair skin.

Sit there and look pretty.

I couldn't stand to the side any longer, Gwendolyn was losing this battle and quicker than she anticipated.

"She knows that she hurt people and screwed up." The words came out faster than my mind could process, pushing off the wall and coming into the light. "Hello, Xara."

Xara stared at me, not responding. We locked eyes, time was standing still, and I could see the small fight in her eyes to stop. The curve of her smile was concerning, thinking that this is a ploy. "Wow, she must have done a number on her own brother, if he quickly turned back into the trusty sidekick."

For once, I couldn't read her, I feared she was talking about me hidden in her words.

"Hear her out." I mumbled. Pleading with her. Maybe if she let us in, we might have a chance. Staring into her dark brown eyes. She was absolutely beautiful, even in the mid-morning. The doubt in her eyes was familiar back when we left. I saw a hint of shock.

"It must be a cold day in hell if you spoke up." a slight laughter escapes her. Very rarely do I take a lead against my sister. I guess if Gwendolyn was going to put me in charge, I might as well start now. "I'm giving you ten minutes and that's it." She walked away leaving the door open with an invitation.

I grabbed my sister's arm before heading in, "Let me do the talking."

The small grin on her face and a hint of a chuckle told me that she underestimates me. She looks back at me, "She's going to eat you alive."

Good.

Truth be told, I wanted that fight with her.

We walked through Xara's apartment gawking at the wide open area separating the living area and the kitchen. The ceilings opened widely and spaced out even more. I wondered where she was hiding her equipment and even more how long she was staying in this place.

Xara had rummaged through her kitchen and found an old winding kitchen timer. Part of her ploy and game. Twisting it to start the timer for ten minutes. She slammed it down on the table with enough strength to break the table. Xara plopped into the oversized size chair that could fit two or more on it. She stretched out her legs, crossing them, throwing her hands behind her neck. I blanked for a few seconds. Gwendolyn and I looked at each other hoping the other one would speak.

"Did not think it would take some geniuses to figure out that the timer means you have a time limit." Xara said.

I whipped around the couch, quickly sitting down, leaning my knees, hands folded together. How was I going to convince this woman, a symbol of strength and power. Don't let her toned statue fool you, she could take down a heavy weight champion without breaking a sweat.

You know firsthand.

But Xara is a smart woman, she can easily pick up on the tone of words and the slight inflection of syllables to tell that you are lying, compared to my examination of body language and tales.

My sister was on the bar stool, watching anxiously, her legs shaking with anticipation. I was surprised that she had not intervened at that time.

"You look good Xara. Staying out of trouble." I said to break the tension. My words still had not been formulated adequately.

"That's your opening Quinton? Come on, you can do better than that. I know you can," Her cheekiness came out. She would see right through my words. She shot over a wink in my direction.

"We think it's time to come home. Back to the crew." I rushed to the point, why drag it out?

Xara sat up, she was shocked to say the least.

"*We?*" She said, pulling her body closer to the edge of the chair, tension in her voice, pointed to Gwendolyn, "No, I think you mean her. *She* thinks it's time to come back to her crew. I should have known that she dragged you along. Back down to wonderland," She shook her head.

I inched closer to her, we played this push and pull game and some come out a winner.

Let me back in you damn strong-headed woman.

No matter what feelings I had developed or still had over the years with Xara, she was family. We all make mistakes. Maybe I should have done better to keep track of her and still be there for her in the end. I glanced back at Gwendolyn, watching the pain in her eyes twinge, the past being uncovered again.

"Xara, I'm sorry. We all weren't supposed to go this long. *I* thought that I was doing what was best for everyone." I said softly, peering into her eyes.

She just snickered, "Look where that got us."

"Separated and broken." I said, inching closer and closer. For a moment I wanted to forget Gwendolyn was in the room, and that I was apologizing to someone I care about. Perhaps deeper than I let on.

"You can't break me. You. Couldn't. Break. Me." she sneered out. It was a challenge. Her history was coming out, rearing it's ugly head.

"Gwendolyn, could you please step outside for two minutes." I commanded, my eyes narrowing towards Xara. Xara did not break contact.

"I'm sorry what?" Gwendolyn said flatly.

"Two minutes. Now." I rarely raise my voice, let alone to my sister. My sister complied and went outside and shut the door behind her. Once the door closed, I started to remind Xara that there was a person she could not fool.

"We both know we could break each other in one minute flat." I said sternly. She stilled.

"Perhaps broken is the wrong word but Xara. You and I both know that you can't be broken," I started to get up and move towards her.

"You think that you can come back here after two years and try to take control?" She teased.

"No, little demon, I haven't earned that yet. But soon I will." I started to caress her arms, trailing a finger along the way, walking behind her. Bending down towards her ears. "You can't tell me that you have not missed it. You haven't missed the crew, the adventures, the thrill, and even the closeness of all of us." I continued. "And I mean us."

She looked over her shoulder and looked at me, "You were fun. I would try to lie and say otherwise but someone can sense my lies."

"And they can taste very sinfully sweet." I said walking back to my spot. "Just hear her out."

"Why?" She questioned me.

"Closure? Reeking havoc?"

Coming back to me?

"How do you know I haven't already had my peace? Found some nice woman or another man?" She tried to lie.

I chuckled, "Because we've both ruined each other for another person." I said. "Hear her out."

The ticking of the kitchen timer kept echoing in my ears, waiting for an answer from Xara. I thought that I got under her skin a bit. I waited for her to respond. We both push and take, and one day I had wished that we would be more than fun. I brought Gwen back into the mix.

"You can't be happy with the life you have now." I resumed the previous conversation.

"I have all I need and more." She stood up straight with her arms out wide. She had spun around "This is mine, something in my name." She walked away for a moment. "You are doing a shitty job of convincing me. You have five minutes, pretty boy," she said.

Oh, a sweet lie.

Time was ticking away and I knew that she was going to be the toughest one to bring back into the fold, let alone convince her to come back to our crew, our family. Something told me I needed a different approach to her. Seduction, our old games were not completely winning her over. Perhaps bluntness.

"Gwendolyn wants us all back for one chance to prove that she has changed and that in her words 'truly belong with each other'. I wouldn't be here if I didn't think that she had the chance of being right. I know it's hard to forgive her. Hell, I don't think I have forgiven her myself," Gwendolyn started to protest, but quickly backed down when my attention darted in her direction.

I turned back, "But I am being a bigger person and going to push past this because at the end of the day, Xara, we *are* family. We had each other and she lost sight of that. She needs you back. Just as much as..." I had stopped myself before I let more of the truth render out of me.

I was sure that the more that I spewed out that I would regret, or push her away.

But she looked at knowing exactly what I was going to say. One thing about Xara, too, is that she is calculated. She knew the truth before the next could come out of my mouth.

Xara leaned over the chair, looking back and forth between my sister and me. She scuffed. "I think that is the first time that you spoke more than your sister. Someone must have put on their big boy pants." When she finished, I made a mental note that she would pay for that comment, and I couldn't wait.

I was surprised that my sister was frozen, like a gargoyle in the highest church. Watching everything take place but not interjecting herself into the conversation. But it wouldn't be too long.

"Viper, I need you. You, your brain, and the witty charm you have on others," Gwendolyn said softly, resulting in Xara glaring at her.

"You just want us back because there is something that is unattainable for you and you need the crew and their skill set. So, what is it that you require everyone back?" Xara walked over towards the kitchen then leaned against the couch, staring at my sister waiting for her response.

"Damn, am I really that predictable," Gwendolyn asked.

"Yes," both Xara and I responded.

Inside I felt that she ignored me on purpose. This push and pull relationship we have had was enough for someone to lose their mind and I was a glutton for punishment. Myself, being one of those people.

Gwendolyn sat there, not responding, the time was ticking away and my sister was one who was stubborn. "One last adventure and then if we all feel that it was not worth it, then we officially go our separate ways. I will respect that, I won't stop anyone, anymore."

Where did that answer come from? Gwen's face twists in a nervous, reserved look. She wasn't pretending.

"What kind of flowery, bullshit answer is that? What happened to you Gwen? The Gwen I know wouldn't just let people walk away again. Seems like you're just saying something to appease someone." And quite honestly, I'm a bit bored of this act. You have two more minutes and then you can find the door." She started to walk away. "So why now? What sparked the idea of wanting a reunion?"

"The Madames," I let out, almost like a growl. Part of me was already getting annoyed with Xara's behavior and lack of empathy.

"You're shitting me. This fairytale again?" she laughed, practically fighting to breathe, Gwendolyn started to get defensive. Xara had an inch on Gwendolyn's height, but when the two appear to square up, they always appear at eye level.

"A fairytale you once wanted to chase, too," Gwendolyn said defensively.

I rushed over between the two of them, Xara's body pinned up closer to mine, enough to feel the warmth of her skin. Tiny memories came rushing back.

"Xara. Please. We are a family and families fight, they don't get along, and occasionally someone ruins it for all until we learn to trust each other again." I shared.

There are no lies in my words. Xara peered up at me, there was a slight softness from her and for a second I saw the familiar person that once made my heart beat a little faster.

And once devoured.

Gwendolyn stepped around me, grabbing Xara's hands into her own. "I screwed up." My sister's words were careful, but I am starting to see that there is hope for her, the more people expose her to her truth.

"And it took this many years and the loss of you and everyone else to realize that I hate to be lonely. And that I wanted and needed you back. You are my best friend and have been through everything that has happened when I lost someone." Her words were sincere and almost believable. I knew my sister, and there was a grander reasoning for her wanting everyone back than what she said.

"I'm still not hearing those other two words." Xara countered.

Two words and Xara was there. But then, the timer dinged and that brief moment of success faded into failure.

Gwendolyn looked back at me, Xara let go of her hands. "Time's up."

She started to walk away, but I blocked her. Baring my hands on her shoulders to turn her around to focus back on Gwendolyn. Gwendolyn's soft footsteps closed in on us. Gwendolyn's eyes watered lightly, enough to allow a tear to roll down her cheek. She looked up at Xara.

"I'm sorry, Xara." She yanked her closer into a tighter hug and I could see the struggle from "Those were three words." Xara gave in, softly returned the embrace. They stayed like that for another minute.

Sometimes embracing our battles is better than forcing out words. I leaned against the couch until they broke a part. Xara straightening herself out, composing herself.

"Motherfucker," She let out. "This does not mean I forgive you and I sure as hell will have some stipulations before I go anywhere with you."

"You can put them in writing and give them to the leader of this." Gwendolyn smiled from ear to ear. Hinting that she was not going to be in charge.

"Who's the team lead, if you are not." Xara started to clank in the kitchen, possibly looking for alcohol, which I don't blame her. But I had a feeling that this would be a shocker, as it was for me. I stuffed my hands in my pants pockets, crossing my legs, leaning against the couch. I couldn't wait to see the look on her face.

"Me. If you have demands, you can have them in writing to me. Unless you have a problem with that." Xara slowly turned around, cocking her head in astonishment.

"Truly a cold day in hell if Gwen let go of the reins for *you*." She walked over to me, closing the distance between us. Her chest was bumping closer to me. I could smell the sweet scent of orange off her skin. To say I wasn't drawn would be a damn lie. "You think you could handle it, being in charge for once." She trailed a finger along my chest, she winked, fiddling with a button or two. She knew I could.

"You can't break me," I uttered her words she spat at me earlier.

"Oh, but I can try. And we both know I could." She tapped on my cheek and turned to walk away.

"Five days Xara. Your room at home will be ready for you." Gwendolyn shouted at her.

"I'll be there with my list. You know the way out." She continued to shout from the room. The satisfaction on my sister's face says it all.

We walked out of the penthouse, and my curiosity got the best of me. It felt too easy for Xara to cave in. Sure, there was some fight, but not enough for her to say no.

But knowing my sister, she had a plan and as soon as we rounded everyone up, it would be my turn to take charge.

"Where to next?" I asked as we got into the rental car.

"We have a flight in four hours to Colorado." she replied but with a slight playful grin, "I think I might need to see a doctor."

CHAPTER 7

ZACHARIAS

I couldn't wait to end my shift. Running the graveyard shift at the local Emergency Room sometimes felt like the worst decision since we have been back in our home two years. But that was what we have succumbed to for us, Elijah, Hartley, and me.

If you asked us, this is not what we wanted for our life, but we weren't given much choice. It seems like eons ago, with the days dragging on.

"I don't like this, man. It feels like we are just running away again." *Elijah had noted, as we were packing up the trucks to head back home.*

We almost lost Hartley on the last quest, the guild. Normally he would stay behind, looking after the monitors, tracking movement, analyzing data as it came to us, and even hacking into systems when needed. But we needed the extra hands.

"We aren't running away. You heard Quinton, we need to take some time. Too much could have been lost." I said knowingly, and I wasn't willing to stick around and see what happened if we stayed.

Usually it is Elijah that is the voice of reasoning, the one that observes everything and can share a smile or laughter with you, but I felt that he might have gotten comfortable here and this had been our normal for the past few years.

Maybe it was the thrill of the chase or this passion to use his knowledge base on these quests.

"Look I get it man, but six months is a lot of time in between. What if..." He started, but he and I didn't want him to finish that statement. We had promised we would leave behind the "what if's" and just let life take us for a ride.

What ifs lead to a downward spiral of thoughts that both of us cannot afford to go down.

"Eli, look we'll be back in six months once the dust has cleared and boss lady cleans up her act, then maybe we all have the chance to live a few extra years."

"Seems kinda sudden. It's a bit drastic."

"Would you rather a world war happen in the midst of all this?" I questioned him.

He shook his head in response. I had told Quinton that we would take Hartley with us until he was feeling better to make his own plans. He had been in and out of consciousness, vitals were okay, though not enough to stay and find out. I would have felt better knowing that he would be okay, even if it meant keeping an eye on him.

We had been back in Colorado since then and honestly, it was rough. Hartley had made a recovery, but his left side gave him some trouble, which still concerned me. Combined with physical therapy, his recovery had been fine. I think we all went through a period of depression and uncertainty, especially when a so-called team never reunited.

No one was reuniting those six months after, we didn't know if to reach out or not. We never got to fully say our goodbyes, but when no one came back, we had to accept it and do what we had to do.

And accepted we did.

After a few more months of hope and no reward, we moved on. We had to make a choice, even though it seemed her and her brother made it for us. I had to do what was best with the family I had left. I didn't press or bring it up anymore. To protect us from any more hurt or possible injury, we stayed and didn't look back.

Hartley opened his business back up and had his space over our garage. Elijah did some contracting jobs on the side and consultation. I went back into the medical field, I needed a place where I was pulled in different directions, where my attention wasn't worried about my own blood and my friends dying on me. I had seen a few in my time during the Army. As for me, I got lucky and went into the Emergency Room department of the regional hospital.

We fell into normalcy after the split. The three of us became a pack, looking out for each other. Trying to get back into a "normal" life, possible relationships, being a part of the community here locally, we have been trying our best.

But we didn't speak about the others, nor what else happened. We missed it from time to time, dinner table talk turned into memory lane. Hard to even say that we missed a certain blue eyed demon that caused my head to hurt from her spontaneous nature and obsessive thought pattern. The way she would get under my skin.

She knew what she wanted and more, though greed and pride was an ugly sin for her.

The indulgence of adventure, the reward of something historical in your hands, that was what I thought everyone was missing. I don't think Elijah and I ever imagined doing something like this. We didn't have much but we at least had each other and we looked out for each other.

The graveyard shift wasn't too bad, I got some interesting cases and momentous stories to tell my colleagues and others. Within a couple of hours, I knew I was going to enjoy my bed and my blackout curtains, drifting into a deep sleep. The shifts turned me into the night owl, where back in the day I was more a morning person, or at least did the morning watch when we staked out places before raiding them.

The word raiding made me flinch, an automatic response.

I'd get smacked in the head by a certain devil woman if I said that word "raiding". The automatic response of myself flinching had been normal, unfortunately. I knew that we weren't raiding, but bringing back a piece of history where it would belong, and if we made a little profit, then we wouldn't turn down the reward.

"Hey, Dr. Langley, new patient, room 12," one of my charge nurses said to me, handing me one of the working tablets. I looked at the name, *Peter Panning*.

I was sure this man was teased and bullied growing up with a name like that. I wasn't one to say anything. Even the name made me want to steal the kid's lunch money.

I knocked at the door before entering, taking a look into the chart of my patient. He had come in with possible appendicitis symptoms. Typically, I didn't get cases like that here. Most common are overly celebrated teenagers or college students, hikers with dehydration, or the occasional bar fight that continued on in my ER.

I opened the door, setting the tablet down and grabbing hand sanitizer beforehand. "Alright Mr. Panning. What can I do for you this morning?" I asked, then I looked to find the infamous blue eyes.

It wasn't possible. All I could think was *no way in fucking hell.*

"Zacharias," Quinton Griffin grumbled out.

He was lying in the hospital bed, his legs crossed over each other, his hands folded in his lap. He looked comfortable as if he was ready to have a therapy session with me.

"Son of a bitch. What are you doing here?" I slammed the door shut before something came trailing that I didn't want to resurrect.

The nerve.

Coming back here after all this time with no word, and that was how he wanted to come back?

"Before you say anything you cannot take back, perhaps you should have a seat." Quinton started to get up, swinging his legs off the bed.

I would have given anything to knock his uptight, proper ass out of that hospital. Send him back to wherever he came from.

"Oh! *Now,* you want to speak. After two years, you want to speak to me?" my voice boomed. Anger bubbles up.

There was no calm exterior that would be normal for me. But I could feel my blood pressure rising. my head pounding in anger. I was at the point of whether I wanted to keep my job or release some pent of tension and anger.

"Mistakes were made, and I acknowledge that-" He started to say and I cut him off, "Don't start that shrink shit on me." Anger seared in my body.

"Zacharias," he started again, straightening up. I once called this man friend, practically family.

"Stop! You and your sister are not just going to waltz back in here, acting like everything is okay." I charged towards him. "You have a lot of fucking nerve showing up and in my hospital." I paused.

Wait sister?

She was missing from this situation, but if he was there she wouldn't be too far away, "Where is she? I know she's got to be here."

I started searching the room, as if she could hide the small exam room cabinets.

"Would you let me finish, before you defend your ego and do something that is going to bring anymore unnecessary antics." He stood up, with us facing each other within distances.

Defend my ego? Quinton has a way of talking down to you without talking down to you like a child about to throw a tantrum. He should have used that skill on his own sister back in the early days.

The last words that this man said to me was, "We'll be back. This will all pass over."

Little did we know that those words wouldn't ring true. As much as Quinton thinks that he is capable of handling situations, it was his sister that he couldn't handle. Gwen was our friend, a confidant, but we saw where that led us. She risked everyone's lives and didn't bat an eye. And at that time, she would have done it again.

The hairs on my neck stood up as I heard the creaking of the door. The air changed, and I didn't know how I was going to react.

The she-devil walking on mere mortal land, with an ice cream cone in her hand. The signature smirk, her flowing long brown hair. She had roped her brother into her scheme.

"Zach," her melodic voice rang out. The way she said my name was her own annoying, pestering self that sometimes made my skin crawl.

"Gwen." Saying it like a curse.

Maybe if I say it three times, she'll disappear back into her cave.

"Looking well, got some more meat on the bones." She chuckled. I had to look down at myself again not believing her teasing statement. I straightened back up, looking at her dead in the eyes.

She thought she could bat the eyelashes, flash a smile, and everything would be okay. Time had taught me a lesson in how to stand on my own two feet, be more of a leader and put others first.

She started to circle the room, looking into the cabinets, with her ice cream still in hand. She opened the cabinet doors, pulling out the instruments and playing around with them. The playful, devil-like, cunning behavior that made Gwen, Gwen.

"That's what happens when you ghost everyone," I turned to face her, walking towards the door trying to usher out. "I don't have time for this. Obviously this was a classic ploy to get my attention, but kindly get out of my hospital and fly back to wherever you came from. Gwen that means you must return to the hell you belong to," I quickly opened the door and gestured to them to leave.

"You're so cute thinking I'm the devil, have you looked in the mirror there Zachy?" she said, playing with the otoscope, the light shining in my face and placing back where she found it.

"I'd say you should look in the mirror, but that requires you to have a reflection," I snarled back at her.

"Takes a devil to know one," she teased back. She turned back to her brother. "You didn't tell him, did you?" she snickered, like a goddamn child.

Gwen plopped in the chair near the bed, still enjoying her ice cream, after she had gone through all the tools, too bad there weren't any syringes. My mind started to wonder if I could knock her ass out with a sedative.

Quinton shook his head, "Attempted to but you walked in as usual, right on cue for chaos to erupt."

"Why are you even here? And why did you fly all the way from Rhode Island?" I rolled my eyes, closing the door from behind me.

"Actually, we flew from Florida," She said, crossing her legs, not making eye contact.

"Good for you? Go back there," I said, confused about the significance. About to give up on it, gesturing to them to leave.

"Xara says hi," she said proudly.

I turned white as a ghost. Gwen was cooking something up, scheming, and she successfully found Xara. And Xara foolishly agreeing to it, so I took it. It made me wonder what exactly was her plan and how did I fit back into it? How did *we* fit back into this scheme?

I shook the thought away. I wasn't going to risk the lives of others for someone else.

"You all can leave." I didn't want to give them a chance.

"Zacharias, we are getting the family back together." Quinton said moving towards his sister, snatching the ice cream out her hands as if a child was in trouble, tossing it in the trash.

She pouted, "Rude, I was going to shove that in his face like old times." crossing her arms.

Truly like an annoying sibling. I couldn't forget the endless pranks she pulled on me and others back in the day.

"Funny, family implies that you all give a shit about us" I said, spewing out anger, accidentally speaking on behalf of the guys. Elijah was going to freak out that she was here.

Quinton continued, "We all made mistakes and hasty decisions that impacted how everything ended up."

"Did those mistakes include someone acting like a spoiled brat when she didn't get her way because everyone left her," I folded my arms.

All the times that I reflect back on that day, I can remember her shutting everyone out, acting like it was our fault and no blame was to be brought upon her. In her eyes, we betrayed her, and gave into mutiny.

In our reality, she didn't put anyone else first. She'll act like it from time to time, but in the end it was a mask of her own personality. Some would call it being young or even spoiled.

"Ah, name calling. I've been called worse," She rolled her eyes. Cocky woman.

"And what, you just show up, with your family's theatrics for what? Your own fun and games?" I asked, the anger slowly showing its teeth.

"Because we need you and the guys. We can't do anything without all of us." Gwen stepped into the conversation.

I still wasn't hearing anything remotely close to how we could benefit or even an apology.

The light went on inside my head, *she* needed something. Everything came back to her. Her wants and her thrill for the unknown and the lost items. We weren't stupid, we knew all that wild, excited look in her eyes. That wild look in her eyes that told us that we lost her in the passion and the quest. I started to laugh, I got what she was going to do.

"It's not us you want. It's the skills. You want everyone to be roped into another item of history that you want to cross off. You think you can convince us to come back, push past all the hurt and the uncertainty we have had?" I folded my arms across my chest.

I made my move, I wasn't going to allow her to wiggle her way back into our lives. She wanted something, she could put in the work for it. "You want something? Tell me Gwen, what made you desperate to seek back this "family"? Something you truly want." I grinned at her, that took her back a moment.

She regained her composure. "You're not fun to annoy anymore. Too much anger." She sighed, "You grew a backbone while we were gone, didn't you?" her coy smile, flashing across the room. She stood up and brushed herself off, "Tell me Zachy, which is your favorite deadly sin?"

I was stunned.

"You didn't," I challenged her. There was no way that this woman had produced enough evidence to make a legend a fact.

"Oh, but I did. And it's time to come home." She smirked, what Winston saw in her, I'll never know.

"That's a myth. Your own fairytale." I answered her. "There is no way that you found a lead into that. Even your uncle noted that it was a legend, there was no direct connection."

His notes on the subject made it impossible for her to let go. She didn't want to believe that there was no connection, she was relentless. A mad dog with a bone.

"Oh, but I did. I found the one thing that will be worth the chase," She said, Quinton stood up, taking the moment away from his sister. His own annoyance and impatience was showing.

"What she meant to say is, she is looking to get the family back together and treat this as a second chance to prove that she is in control and knows that she can't lose herself in these anymore," He clasped a hand on her shoulder, forcing a demanding look in her direction. She shut down for a moment, there was something in her eyes that softened. Like she had been caught up and needed to step back.

"You expect me to believe that you've changed, that you are scheming your way of saying pretty words?" I pressed her.

Her expressions changed when she looked at her brother and then looked back at me, almost sincere, "Sometimes we forget what we had until we don't have it anymore." She said softly, and for a moment, I saw the girl I met in the beginning. The mischievous, loving, caring woman that just wanted to find lost things.

My mind started to spin and for a brief moment wondered if I wanted to come back. I worried if we did, if it would be like last time, on the verge of losing someone close to us. "How do we know that it won't be like the last time? We almost lost Hartley, and I'm sure the man has some lingering effects." I spat out, it wasn't overly exaggerated.

"Because I won't be in charge," She said, letting it resonate, keeping her quiet.

You're kidding, Gwendolyn Griffin was an alpha female, she doesn't let anyone walk all over her. "It can't be that easy. You expect me to believe that Gwendolyn Griffin isn't going to be in charge. No way," I laughed hysterically.

Gwen was nothing but control and confidence. It would be a cold day in hell to know that she would easily give up on her control over the quests and leadership. But as my laughter died down, the brother sister duo didn't budge.

Either this was a cry of desperation or reality.

"She has relinquished her role as leader for the time being." Quinton said.

"Then tell me, what bright genius thought they could take her place and lead a unique and chaotic group?" I asked, waiting for the punchline.

Gwen looked at her brother and her brother looked at her.

"I am." Quinton stepped up like it was a medal of honor. I was probably more worried about Quinton being a leader than Gwen taking back her role.

"I'm sorry what, you want Shrink here to be the next leader of this. Wow. desperation is not a look for you Gwen." I continued to debate on whether to entertain this or not, much less let the guys know what is going on.

"Look enough with the dramatics, aren't we a little old for that." Gwen spits out.

I gasped, "Me being dramatic, damn that mirror must have been broken. Here stand in front of this mirror, if it breaks you owe me a new one." I started to pull her towards one of the mirrors in the room, and she punched my shoulder. Fucking hell. She hadn't lost her spunk nor her punches.

She sarcastically whined, "I'm so hurt, Zach."

I had to take a pause and think. I knew where my mind was leading, but I was one voice.

"Okay, let me put this as blunt as possible." I stepped toward her, Quinton shoving an arm between us. "You put the team in danger when we were in those caves. You knew how unsteady that foundation was and the known fact of the tremors. Yet, you were power hungry and obsessed with finding the guild, you had this drive of getting what you want, no matter the cost."

"And I realized that price later than I should have." She raised her voice. All laughter and sly factors escaped her. Her voice was full of intention.

I had looked at her, thinking that there was a sliver of hope. Hope that she had learned her lesson or at least had gotten helped her realize what she had lost. I had to question her, if not for myself than for at least Hartley or Elijah. I could move on and be content but it was those two that I knew if anything could possibly forgive and move on or return to the adventure that ahead of us

"How come you just realized this now?" I asked, feeling all emotions drain from me.

"Because it took me losing everyone, every family member again, for me to finally understand that I screwed up. Did it come when I needed something again? Yes. Because the people I had were the ones that helped me through every step when I couldn't and if it takes me, groveling and apologizing and proving that what I did was wrong, then yes I will do it Zacharias," her chest rose and fell, her words full of passion.

Her words were like a weight that had been lifted. But I wasn't easily persuaded, I had my doubts. You can call it a mistrust in her, I called it safety. This might be enough to let my thoughts entertain the second chance.

"You should have saved that speech for the guys." I said, starting to walk out the door.

"Does this mean you'll do it?" Quinton had asked.

"I get off in thirty minutes, we'll meet in the parking lot. It won't be me that you'll have to convince." I said coldly. Gwen had muttered something under her breath. I chose to ignore it.

I had hoped that this part would not come back with agonizing regret. I wasn't going to lose them again.

Chapter 8

Gwendolyn

Zacharias had grown with more back bone than I imagined, which could have been a blessing or a curse, depending on how you look at it. My error in judgment resulted in this, more consequences to my actions.

Sure, I had been stubborn from the beginning and there I was thinking I could wiggle myself back into their arms or back into their lives. Getting everyone to trust me again was going to be harder than I thought. I hated to admit it but maybe Quinton was right, maybe I have more work ahead of me.

I had been thinking about my mistake, because the mistake cost me everything. I was going to have to beg and plead with them to be back even if it meant that in the end I had to let them go completely.

I slowly realized that I did screw up and I was blinded by my own anger and bitterness that I didn't see the error of my actions. We were sitting in the parking lot waiting for Zach to get done with his shift. I knew that he wanted me to speak with Hartley and Elijah before anything else. Every possible rejection or denial scenario ran through my head.

Shivers spread through my body, like every memory of that day came rushing back to me. Every echo of words, every emotion of movement, the memory of my mind choosing the quest over them and nearly losing Hartley.

He wasn't even supposed to be there.

That thought echoed louder than anything. It was true he wasn't, but guilt weighed heavier on me, though I wasn't going to let people see it.

I felt a gentle push from my brother, his hand grazing my shoulder, I looked over at him. "Did you get lost in your conscious mind?" his therapist's voice resonated through his words.

I offered him a small smile, knowing that he saw me get lost in the thoughts.

"You've come this far, Gwendolyn. And yet you look like your demons are coming back to fight you," He said.

"More like the demons are winning," I couldn't help but respond.

"You knew that this was not going to be easy, and that everyone would be emotional over the past couple of years," He reiterated. He had said the same thing when we were flying to see the boys.

I looked down at my hands, there was a tiny part of me that was worried that I was expecting too much, that I was over my head with things. Quinton reached over and lifted my chin.

"You can't expect them all to say yes when you bat your eyelashes. This is your time to reflect on how you want them to still look at you. Whether you want them to see a cunning woman with a hidden agenda or the Gwendolyn that remembers why we started this, the sense of family and adventures," Once again he was correct. I couldn't expect people to fall at my whim anymore.

I came to realize that everyone had the same thought, that I was blinded by my own selfish reasons.

My eyes flashed up as I saw Zacharias leave the hospital entrance. He signaled to follow him. Quinton started up the rental car, following Zacharias down the winding, long highway roads, exiting off to the large increments of land and homes. I was starting to get fearful that the guys had secluded themselves, but I knew I shouldn't be judging.

I should have done better with looking after them. I should have done better, but that is something I won't openly admit. I wondered if the boys did well or if they thought about us. I missed the antics and the pranks around the manor. I missed the quiet reserve of Zacharias, the laughter of Elijah, and even the subtle eyebrow raises from Hartley. I started to bite my lip, the nerves were about to tremble through my body.

Dominic, I could handle the oversized protector that he was. Winston, I knew, still had a soft spot for me. Xara, I had to shut up and just turn on the charm. But the boys, you can call it the fear of rejection or the feeling of disappointment. I knew that I deserved whatever was coming to me.

"I know you're worried," Quinton said, barely even looking at me.

"Out of everything that we have ever done, these three terrify me the most." The truth hurts. Words felt like bullets to the chest.

"A few days ago, the woman that came into my office propping her feet up, would never have admitted that. I'm not saying I'm worried. But you look like your thoughts are unraveling," my brother kindly said but I knew that it was his psychological mind that was speaking to me.

Something was unraveling, bringing back this family, these people that I called mine, feels like bringing back the dead. I knew I couldn't bring back the dead, and here I was. Resurrecting something or some people thinking that this would be a good idea. I couldn't bring back my parents. I couldn't have one more day with Uncle Maxx. My self-doubt that I had buried a long time ago within the sands of my old life was starting to come back.

I shook my head. I couldn't let this slip out, I couldn't let myself be dragged down this rabbit hole. I'm afraid that if I let myself slip back, I will truly be gone. I was afraid of this for two years and every time I pushed past it. Finding new projects to attach my name to, distract my mind, never allowing myself to think fall down the hole of what ifs.

Our rental had hit a bump, and brought me back to the moment. Preparing myself to plead my case to the guys.

"You back from looking into your dark soul?" Quinton joked with me. I flashed him a coy smile, waiting for us to arrive at the guys' place. I could tell that the men found this better for them, as the sun peeked through the mountain views. The way the light grazed the secluded areas, finding the small cracks to shine through. It was beautiful all around us.

A hidden paradise from the cruel, brutal world.

We came to an opening to their entrance. Another wave of dust coated the rental. Zacharias was still within sight. "I wonder if Hartley did any security for this place?" Quinton questioned.

He had a good question. Hartley was known to do our security, being our eyes in the sky while we welcomed ourselves to places that were not suited for us. In the end nothing was damaged, as if we were never there. No footprint or evidence to prove that we were there. I wouldn't have been surprised if somewhere along the road Hartley had put extra measures of protection.

As we continued our path to the house, Quinton and I's mouths had dropped. We were expecting a typical family home with a ton of land behind them. But we were greeted by a modernized mountain home. Glass walls allow the sun to shine through, probably giving off that warmth that you would want to feel on your face. I could only imagine the openness inside, enough room than they needed.

The intrusive thoughts of wanting to explore their little kingdom.

"Damn, they did well for themselves." That was all I could say, allowing the initial shock of it all. They had moved on with their lives, almost forgetting that before the crew they had lives of their own.

"What did you expect? That they wouldn't adjust well?" Quinton retorted back.

"No, but I didn't imagine they would get all of this. Bet this was all Elijah." I snorted.

Elijah was the mastermind of our lay of the land. He had a curious mind for buildings and architecture that we trusted him for knowing about the structure and the unique features of these historical buildings. Before he had joined in, he was a prime architect and a sought out project manager for construction companies. His skills had amazing use with the team.

And you didn't listen to him.

The thought snaked into my mind. The sting of errors.

We pulled into the curve of the driveaway, Zacharias had pulled his truck into the garage, which Winston would shit his pants if he saw that, a huge home garage, probably loaded with motorcycles and other expensive cars.

"You ready little sister?" my brother asked me.

Truthfully, I don't know how much longer I could take more stabs at my mistakes, but this was a bigger team. "Let's get this shit show started," I slammed the door behind me.

Winter hasn't come yet for Colorado, but I could imagine they could be brutal and the amount of snow that cascaded through here. Zacharias had walked over to the car and tapped on the window. His bronzed skin radiated. I knew that the final decision wasn't his, but if he had his way, the answer would be no.

The true answer would be from Elijah and Hartley.

"I can't promise anything more than what I think is going to happen," Zacharias called from over his shoulder as he led us through the front door and up the stairs. Quinton was trailing behind me, his presence close by. "Why this place?" I blurted out, curiosity hit hard. I could see the smugness of Zach's smirk.

"Truth?" he inquired.

"No Zach, I wanted you to lie to me and make it pretty," I said sarcastically.

"There's the snark we know all too well." Zacharias chuckled softly. Was there a brick that fell down? Was there light at the end of the tunnel?

"Elijah designed it. He had this place built a few years back and then I guess you could say we had a reason to use it," he said, taking us to the main floor with the living room and kitchen area. The glass walls or windows gave into a mountain view that is worth every penny of land. But the pain of his comment stung. At that moment, I didn't know how to retort.

"He outdid himself, the man is a genius when it comes to designs." Quinton filled the empty air.

"I like to think so." A booming voice came from the landing bridge from above us. I whipped around to watch him as he made his way towards us.

Elijah, like his cousin, had golden bronzed skin that looked like the sun had been blessing them. His jet black hair was short, cascading over the side of his face. His muscles still toned and could strike fear in anyone who would be there. The curl of his lips into his smile frightened me.

Although the man was an Adonis in flesh and blood, he would make some other woman happier.

But something was missing from his expressions.

Surprise, shock, anger? Hell, even confusion.

"Looking good shortie," He continued to say as he made his way down to the living room.

Okay, color me surprised. But something was missing. The subtle use of my old nickname stunned me. He made his way across the living room and spread his arms open, grabbing me into a tight hug. I was lifted off the floor.

"Not what I was expecting," I muttered against his chest. I was pressed tighter, but honestly that wasn't the shockest thing. The words out of his mouth was what could have been on my gravestone.

"Does this mean I need to dust off the passport?" His smile spread like a cat from wonderland. I pushed against him, knocking him back a few steps.

"Drop the act, Elijah." Zacharius snarked.

"What act?" He looked back at his cousin who was debating on whether to add whiskey or creamer to his coffee.

"Your cousin already spoke his mind. Just say what you need to say and don't hold back," I raised my voice. My skin started to itch at the thought of walking out and giving up, I have had enough of my own mistakes thrown in my face. These three terrified me with the uncertainty.

One was bright, full of sunshine, and brilliant. His soul could light up the darkest room.

One was protected, sarcastic, and dare I sat daring. Though grumpy, he was admirable.

The other was an enigma, one that tap danced between awe and frightening, one that acted like he was a dark shadow whose smile was enchanting.

"You got carried away, I can't fault you for being you." He relayed putting his hands on my shoulders, "You mistake me for my cousin. I can forgive and not hold grudges." He said, squeezing my shoulders.

He was right, he didn't hold grudges, he was more free spirited than his cousin. "Question is, are you ready to move on and be ready for the next thing?" His grin was contagious in the most positive way. Oh, I have missed this. I missed his smile and his attitude. I remember that he didn't want to leave the manor practically begging his cousin to stay, I could remember the conversation I overheard as I had stalked through the hallway.

I hurt everyone and he was one of the worst ones I felt. His innocent, loving nature was always refreshing to have.

"I'm ready. I'm ready to get back to the way things were." I caressed his cheek. "But you, my friend, are one in few that are ready to come back. I doubt that Hartley would feel the same."

Zacharias was an obstacle but Hartley I doubt he was willing to come back. I was the one that had Hartley come with us in that cave, I was the one that caused him to almost lose his life.

"Apparently, it's not my decision," I glared at Zacharias, who was giving me the middle finger as he was scrolling on his phone.

Elijah walked over to his cousin and gave him a shove. "Like you haven't made some decisions in your lifetime that have come with consequences."

"Not me, I'm an angel," Zacharias chides.

"So was Lucifer and look where he ended up," I snarked back at him. I shook my head, there had to be a catch, Elijah gave in so quickly. "So, all three are in agreement then?" I plopped on the couch.

"I don't think that is going to be the case," my brother noted. "You only spoke to two out of this trio. There are certain eyes in the sky that require convincing."

"Since when are you against me?" I spit out.

"Not against you, I'm merely pointing out that before you give in to victory in your mind, there's a third party person that should have his voice be heard." He crossed his arms, leaning against the wall. Now he wants to be vocal in this.

The cousins chuckled, they knew that I used to have a hard time getting through Hartley and the man made me nervous.

"You aren't a leader just yet, brother." I reminded him. We hadn't truly started yet and I still have some control. Do I have control issues, yes, but will it be worth giving up some control for the better of us, that answer I hadn't found yet.

Hanging my head in defeat, I simply asked, "Where is he?"

"Down the hall and up the stairs on the left." Zacharias had responded, not looking at me, but that dirty smirk on his face was enough for me. He was silently still hoping that everyone would say no, and he could go back to the way he wanted things.

The other question in my mind, had he changed?

Chapter 9

Hartley

I already knew she was coming.

The little vixen attempted to use the program I "left" for her. Did she really think that my system wouldn't let me know when it was in use? She was relentless. Rounding us up like lost sheep, thinking that we needed her back in our life to reclaim what life we had two years ago.

Then again, I was filled in on what happened after we returned from the mission, why I was in our home in Colorado rather than in the manor. I wasn't given much of a choice given my state at the time.

It was only a matter of time before she would come and round us up again in hopes we would find the lost history and mysteries in that notebook of hers. Her hunger for lost history was unfathomable.

One thing she wouldn't admit is that she has the hardest time speaking with me. She'd sometimes avoid eye contact and the tiniest bit of blush sat on her cheeks. But I watched this woman take on so much and never blink an eye. The one time she lost control, well the results were not varied.

She might find you attractive and intimidating, Elijah and Zach jokes.

I'm not a hard person to get along with, but I'm not afraid to be blunt and honest. Some would call it a hard exterior, somewhat cold. Mostly, people underestimate me, thinking that I would not have the brains for large operations.

I didn't know how I felt.

Did it feel weird for the past two years to get out of the tech room and into the streets of the world we live in? Yes, and the pure enjoyment of being around others like me that don't fit in but belonged together at the same time.

I couldn't help but snicker when I heard her voice on the main camera in the living room. A small smirk was curling on my lips. Zacharias I know was hiding a laugh, wanting to see her fumble over her words. It was cute that she stumbled over her words, or sometimes fell for our conversations that would make her flustered. But she got stronger, she knew the game and how to play. We all have a dark and twisty side.

I'd never make a move, I left that to Winston, trying to push their buttons to see what would happen. Well, that's partly true. I had my other reasons, but just like she gets under Zach's skin, she made it easy to mess with her.

But over the years it was fun teasing her, making her blush even when she was trying to hide it. For once, I think she gave in, because I was one of the two people that could get under her skin and challenge her, she liked the game and the banter. I just wished a certain mechanic would have taken the bull by the horns, no time like the present.

Her small, soft footsteps almost went unnoticed until the soft knocking of my door. Show time. The knocks are faint, but enough to know that she was there. I got up to answer the door, fully expecting that she would be slouched over, avoiding all eye contact with me.

I knew that this wasn't what she had expected to do, acknowledging her mistake, being called out, being judged all over again. She probably had hoped that the guys would come to me first and "speak on her behalf" but Zacharias had a different idea, making her work for what she wanted.

I opened the door, her arms crossed, head hung low. She was truly avoiding eye contact. I couldn't help but laugh and smile at her.

"Well, if it isn't the world famous Gwendolyn Griffin, gracing me with her presence," I said, opening the door wider allowing her to come in. She brushed past me, saying nothing to me. But she stopped in the middle of the room.

My space was huge compared to what she had for me back in the manor. This space was like a studio apartment without the kitchen in it. In that space, I had my tech spread out, surrounding me with the world I know. I knew that I wanted to keep my world close to me, and keep a close eye on the things I cared about.

Sure, I didn't let go of the world that I left behind two years ago, and I would be lying to myself if I had said I didn't miss it. In that moment, the opportunity to reignite that missing flame was here.

"Gwendolyn, if you would like something, speak," I said, I suppressed my chuckle.

She jolted up, as if she was startled. She turned to face me, "You got... bigger," She said, turning her head quickly. I think she was lost in thought.

"Two years, and that is all you want to say to me." I couldn't deny that within the last two years gave me the chance to grow in strength, but keep a reminder of who I was.

"Glad to see that you're not dead." She said, nervously.

"I mean I would be a sexy-ass ghost. But I guess you didn't come to tell me that?" I walked around her to go sit at my desk where my monitors and system were hard at work.

She sucked in her lips, not expecting the playful comment that came from me. "Okay Hartley, are we going to pretend that I don't know what you already knew I was coming, even before I was in the house." she folded her arms back.

There was that feistiness, that bark that is not worse than her bite.

"Well, when you use a program that I designed, did you really think I wouldn't get a notice?" I stretched out my arms, putting them behind my head. "Oh, how was the little reunion with you and Winston? Break his heart again?" I had to laugh.

Winston was madly in love with this woman, and she was too infuriating to tell him the same. It was cute, their little push and pull game. I couldn't lie, it was fun on my end to see them squirm when someone pestered them about it.

"You're worse than Quinton. Am I that predictable? You and him seem to know everything," she scoffed.

"You can't forget Yankee was the cherry on top, he had the best snapbacks." I added.

She went silent again.

"Shall I skip to the part where I know why you are here and I tell it to you?" This was why Quinton had brought me into the mix. My curiosity led to my addiction, finding the truth and knowing what was going on around me. I may have been the eyes in the sky, but seeing everything came with a price, a price that sent you down rabbit holes.

When she activated the "white rabbit" program, my alarms went off and I followed down the path.

I leaned forward on my knees, looking straight into her bright blue eyes. Her hair fell in her face. "You found something that fed back into your obsession. You got the one piece of evidence that would tie everything you have been searching for. You thought after two years and you're newly minted evidence that you get the team back together, a team that in your midst would have to convince and grovel even to get back together. But your obsession came with a price." I got up, walked towards her, starting to walk around her. Like a vulture circling their prey. Her breathing was beginning to hitch.

I knew the appeal that Winston saw in her, her intelligence, her dominant side that begged to not always be in charge, her breathtaking blue eyes that with one flutter of her eyelashes she put a spell on anyone that crossed her path. The way she bit her cheek or stuck her tongue out in hard concentration.

But Winston can claim her, if she doesn't run away again.

"But what price did Ms. Gwendolyn Griffin have to pay for that? Admitting that she was wrong? Trading something for the evidence? No, something more that is not easy for her." I knew what it was, but I had two years to catch up with the woman, to crawl inside her little twisted mind.

We're taught never to play with our food, but I never listened to that lesson.

"It was a price that I'd be willing to pay over and over again if that meant that I got everyone back. And some to fully forgive me." She let out with some spite like the words were sour in her mouth. She was trying to win this battle.

"Ah, the price of what? Control." I said. She stilled. I was right. Again. I typically was.

I stood behind her. "Control over the team. Over the "family" that you say you built." I leaned closer. "But deep down it's not about the obsession that is your weakness. Oh no, it's about the family that you found and created."

Okay, call me dark and twisty, but when you stand behind a screen you analyze everything in front of you.

"A family that you were a part of," she added.

"You want me back?" I released a chuckle, waiting to see how she would interpret the question.

"For someone all knowing, that was a dumb question," she diverted the question.

"Admit it," I crept closer. She turned around and shoved at my chest. I laughed deeply. Oh, it was a game between us, who can break first.

"Asshole. You know it's not fair when you act..." She started.

"Sensual, psychotic?" I replied.

"A twisted son of a bitch," She gave me a punch to my shoulder, which she had to extend out due to the height difference.

"Admit it, Gwen. You missed our little games. Ruffling those feathers. I kind of expected more of a fight from you," I started walking away from her. Heading into my closet, I grabbed one of my big duffels.

She didn't say anything about the last part of my statement, but I didn't push it.

"When do we leave?" I asked. I had my mind made up.

"I'm confused." She said, her puzzled look told me that I threw her off and she wasn't expecting my answer so quickly and with haste.

"Oh, for someone who wants everyone home, you act surprised." I told her.

She walked over to the bed and leaned forward, looking to see if this was real or another mind game. "You're not going to ask for an apology or make me grovel. Beg on my knees." She stopped herself because she knew what was coming. She hung her head because she knew what was coming.

Oh, this was too easy. "Little Gwen, save that part for Winston." I winked at her.

She made a silent squeak that made me want to laugh. I didn't harbor a lot of feelings. Some things are worth being able to move on.

"Oh god. I have missed your twisted humor Hartley. But look. I'm sorry for what I put you through. You know the old saying, you don't realize what you miss until it's gone." She started to sit on the bed, she was starting to sound sincere. "I took a bigger chance and put your life and others involved."

"You let your obsession dictate your actions." I simply put.

Her eyebrows furrowed, I could see the instant fight that she was about to rip me a new one. She was probably trying to be a smart ass and make a comeback. I put a finger to her lip to attempt to stop her from speaking.

"Before you start saying something as a smart ass, you can deny all you want. But I will always be right when it comes to you." I teased her.

She muttered something, but I didn't catch it. I grinned at her. She knew that I knew her well enough to know her next moves or even her thoughts.

Again, call me dark and twisted.

"Fucking vulture," she muttered under her breath. "Why are you being forgiving towards me compared to Xara or Winston? I did something wrong, put your life in danger, most of everyone's lives were in danger." I started to turn back to my closet, grabbing the essentials. "I let out my anger when Quinton said to take a break and I fought against it. Practically digging my grave deeper."

"And you mean to tell me that no one else has made mistakes. Remember Prague with Zacharias or New Zealand with Xara?" I was trying to make a point, while not answering her question like she wanted. "Gwen, we make mistakes, we say things that we truly regret saying. We're blind to our actions until we are left to reflect and guilt starts to eat us up." I turned back to her leaning on the closet door frame. "I'm not saying that what happened wasn't the result of your actions in that aspect, we all had something to prevent what happened."

She sighed as I continued, "But I think we need to move on, and stop harboring feelings about what happened and who did it."

She gently nodded her head. Who am I to judge someone's dark obsessions? We all have them, it takes a certain amount of control and creativity to mask what we don't want others to see.

"You make it sound like it was easy to forgive me."

"Why would I want to hold on to hurt, or even anger?" I said, knowing it wasn't worth having any regrets pent up.

"So, you really would come back?" She asked, stuttering her words, wanting a simple answer instead of pressing every button to make her work for the answer.

I grabbed one of my sweaters and jeans, walking back to the duffel. "Yes. I'll come back. Even if it might be the last time."

She goes silent for a moment. Her eyes were avoiding me, no way to search for what was going on in her head. If I could bet money, she was trapped in a thought, a memory rushing to her from the last time, possibly the hurt and the pain.

Give me something Gwen. Let me know that my friend is okay, was all I thought.

She took a breath, her chest filling with air, releasing whatever was trapped in her head.

"I can't lose anymore people in my life, Jacob." she whispered.

She shocked me, hardly anyone used my first name, even her. But she was serious. She couldn't lose anyone else. Between her parents then her Uncle Maxx, she would truly be broken if one more person left her.

I walked around the bed and gathered her in my arms. She tensed up, but slowly succumbed to accepting the embrace. She needed to know that at least one or more people wouldn't let that happen. At least not again.

"You aren't going to lose me, kid. It's just about time you got yourself back on track." Squeezing her tight. I wasn't surprised that for once, she didn't have to put on a brave face or a mask to hide herself. It wasn't something she was used to.

It wasn't long before she shook her head and struggled to get out of the embrace. "Jesus Christ, Hart. You big oof, you don't have to suffocate me." She pushed on my arms to get out. All I did was laugh, the slight essence of herself was coming back.

Although, something was off about her. As if each movement or thought was fragile, or holding back.

CHAPTER 10

GWENDOLYN

Hartley knew exactly how to press certain buttons and watch someone crawl out of their skin. It was twisted, but that's part of what makes him unique and an outcast. He used that advantage in any way he could, even to just have a little fun.

There was some relief that he didn't hold any grudges or placed any guilt on me.

He followed me back to the main room, and the pompous look on Zacharias face told me that I surpassed his expectations.

Surprise dumbass, not everyone holds strife and resentment like you.

"Either you didn't succeed and Hartley came to give us a piece of his mind or you bewitched him and we're screwed," Zacharias was going to be the tough cookie to completely win over again.

"Well at least something wants to screw you," I snapped back.

I didn't blame him, but something that Hartley and Elijah said stuck with me and wished that Zacharias would take to heart.

At what point do we learn to let go and move on, why harbor all this guilt and mistakes?

Because you were the one that broke the chain and caused this reaction.

My mind got lost in guilt and self-punishment.

"Maybe someone had a voice of reasoning," I snarked back at Zacharias. "Hartley wanted to give it one more shot before we completely say that we are done." I could feel the warmth of his body behind me. Like a grave shadow radiating warmth behind me.

"So, what's the plan?" Elijah popped in. He must have migrated from the kitchen while I was in with Hartley. Him and Quinton were on the couch deep in a conversation. "Are we getting the band back together?"

"It would seem that the majority says yes. At least one more time." I said almost defeatedly. Wanting to hold back the slight possibility that they could leave after everything.

"It's going to be the decision of everyone of what they want to do after this quest. Whether we stay and continue stepping into history or make our own as we go our separate ways," Quinton chimed in.

"Time for the big family reunion." Elijah grinned, like a boy at Christmas. "Now we can finally let the creepy uncle out of the basement."

"Technically it's the suite over the garage." Hartley jokes.

A burst of laughter filled the room and for a moment it was like old times where the guys would joke with one another, cracking insults trying to outdo one another. The times where Elijah would be in the kitchen attempting to feed an army or two, knowing that no one was going to eat it. But it would turn into a food fight that would result in someone cleaning the kitchen and it wasn't going to be me.

Something snapped me back to reality.

"Gwen, where did you go?" Hartley whispered in my ear. Scaring the shit out of me. Like a dark spirit presenting themselves.

"Sorry, stuck on a memory." I pushed away from him. "Okay, tie up the loose ends here and first of November, it's time to come home."

"Then you will let go of control." Zacharias eyed me, hoping that I wasn't forgetful about the task at hand.

I flipped the bird over my shoulder. I didn't hear what he said after but one could assume that I was being called choiced names.

"Yes, my brother will be in charge and I will remain the historian. Any other smart ass remarks." I answered back.

"I'm curious as to what Winston had to say when you approached him." Another sarcastic tone from Zacharias.

Internally I was ready to wind up and deck him. This was why people mistake Zacharias and me for being siblings rather than Quinton and me.

"Don't think he had much of a choice when approached." my brother chimed.

"Story time, spill. How did it happen?" Elijah bounced on the couch. Mayhem waiting to happen. "Wait, let me guess. It was in true Lady Griffin style." He said with a weak regency mimicked the charmed look on his face. "I can just picture it now, you burst through the front door and demanded that Winston come back to you and say yes to you." He continued with his accent, fanning himself like a lady of court.

And they call me dramatic.

"More like drove her Jeep into his garage and almost ran him over, the poor bastard." Quinton joked with him.

"Well that's one way to guarantee he comes back, just knock his ass out. Attempted murder. Remind me who broke whose heart first?" Chimed in Zach, again.

I rolled my eyes, "Well obviously it wasn't you, that would mean you have some game and have a heart," I strode into the kitchen grabbing a cup to get some coffee.

"Oh and you had a good track record before Winston." Zacharias pointed out.

Shivers ran down my body. I had long forgotten the shadow of my egotistical ex-boyfriend. I dared not think about him. The slime of a man. He crept his way into my life and nearly pulled it apart and showed me the true colors of his soul. Wanting me to fit perfectly to his image and reminding me that I wasn't going to be good enough for him, finding every way to break me down, piece by piece. He had betrayed everything we built and became competition with his black market deals with historical artifacts that we had found. He had friends in all corners of the world. And his way of using words to harm me, belittle me, make me weak.

In the end, the crew and I bested him and since then he has not come near me. But then again, Winston would have been at bat ready to defend me.

"Damn Zach, you keep putting her into her flashbacks, we'll never leave." Elijah jerked me from my memories.

"You've been doing that more and more. Are you sure you are ready for this to happen?" Hartley asked me.

I nodded my head but no words were coming out. "They are just memories, nothing more."

The way my mind replaces every memory that resulted in fear and brokenness caused me to pause for a second and think if this was the best thing. My brother started to grow even more worried about me. I attempted words, but I think this was the strongest flashback I had. They had been coming back more and more and I'm sure the clinical and analytical mind of my brother would tell you exactly why this was happening.

"I'm ready for everything to go back to the way things were." I said half-heartedly. "But do whatever needs to be done for you either that's tying up loose ends or putting other business ventures on hold."

"The plan is normal or our standard procedure. Research, plan, execute." Quinton stood up adjusting himself.

"And expect to have two or three backup plans." Elijah stated. He wasn't wrong either. I was beginning to think that we were very predictable. They were the necessary evil.

We had parted ways from the men, praying that they would stick true to their word. We only had a few days before November would come to us.

There were a couple of things that were still missing.

At that point, we had everyone except one person.

Yankee.

He was a mystery even as time went on. There was something very strange about him but that is why he had become a good friend and one to stir the pot. If I knew Yankee, I wouldn't have to find him, he would show up. The crew thought I had a flair for the dramatics, Yankee was a class act himself.

I remember when I first met him, it was the opening of a museum focusing on contemporary art. Although I am the historian, I was called in to do a favor for a friend and helped organize the event. As the night was flowing, I had heard whispers of an artist that was being shown that night, and I knew that it wasn't true.

I kept my ear out and low and behold, Yankee had been posing as the artist. I had memorized each piece and the perspective artists I studied for days. We had a show of questions and answers, waiting for the other one to give in. Unfortunately, he had kept up the act. After the showing that night, I exited the building and headed to the parking lot and found Yankee hanging on my car.

"I'll admit I have never had someone challenge me and go full force into a battle." He said, his hands stuck in his pocket, legs crossed, leaning on my car.

The cat-like grin spread across my face. "I was right. It's okay to admit it." I teased him.

"Maybe. How did you know?" He asked.

"I organized the event and met with the artists. You are not one of them, and yet posed as one of them. I was waiting to see if you had the guts to keep it up."

"You underestimate me, my friend." He commented.

"Why did you even come if you have no connection with the art or the artists?" I asked, I should have been mad but he was a special character and I respected someone that charms their way in and can hold their own.

"If I told you that I wanted champagne, would you blame me?" He chuckled. I laughed with him. I should have seen him as a con

man, a trickster. But I tipped my hat to him. I thought Uncle Maximus would get a laugh out of him.

From there on, Yankee had become a friend and a must at social events. He would pop in without even a word from me, claiming that he was there for champagne. He was and still is a mystery but an important part of the crew.

We got back to the manor, knowing that the rest of the crew was soon going to be coming in the next day or so. I knew that Dominic, Hartley, and Elijah would keep their word and give it one more shot. But Zacharias, Winston, and Xara were the ones that I would have to continue to prove to them that I was genuine. I was going to earn back my way.

Rhode Island, although small, surrounded us with later childhood memories. Times when my brother and I would explore a new corner of the manor, feeling like it kept getting bigger and bigger.

But Quinton was holding back on something he had been questioning. Although I knew the answer to the question, I was waiting for him to say something. As we entered the main garage area, rather empty but not for long. The clicking of my heeled boots echoed, filling what room there was.

"Home sweet home." I said.

"The team isn't full," Quinton noted.

I walked away from him, "No, we got everyone".

Quinton cleared his throat, "I think you miscounted, sister." His voice, long forgone the brush of southern he had, now sounded like he was a proper gentleman. I mean that was credited to Uncle Maximus.

"Oh, I didn't miscount," I walked through the staff kitchen towards the foyer, catching up on packages and mail from the time we were gone.

"Gwendolyn, we don't have time for games. You forgot someone. A person that I know that you would have mentioned before we came home." Quinton followed me as I flipped through the packages and mail. I wasn't too worried.

I headed into one of the living areas. I didn't bother to turn around knowing his face was scrunched up or confused.

Sometimes it's still the best to be a little sister. I plopped on the couch and propped my feet up, opening the packages, and envelopes from the previous museum curators or my contacts offering their help into the mistresses.

Quinton stalked over to the couch, poked my head, tapping to see if my mind was still there. "I don't think your mind is comprehending the concept of we do not have all the team. You said you found everyone." He turned to join me in sitting.

"And I did," saying to him, paying him no attention.

"Enough of the charades. It was cute in the beginning but now it has become an annoyance. You're missing the last person in this team," he grew frustrated, along with strain.

I grinned so wide, my cheeks. For once I had the element of surprise with me. And in that moment, he was about to take back those words.

"Yeah, I don't think she was playing charades, my friend. Also, you should really look into that lock on the back door, someone might actually come in and rob you," A booming smooth voice echoes through the living room.

My brother whipped his head toward the sound as a sweater wearing, freshly shaved man walked with a bowl of popcorn gracefully coming into the main room.

Yankee held no surprise. I wasn't worried. Yankee had the ins with everyone and it was only a matter of time before he figured out the band was getting back together. He was a sucker for gossip and knowing the dirty secrets of others and used them to his advantage and sometimes benefitted the mission. He had been a confidant.

"Son of a bitch." Quinton murmured. Brushing a hand through his hair.

"Oh my god the world is ending, Quinton cursed!" It was a rare occasion and it was perfectly timed. I beamed a little proud of my brother.

Yankee bursted into laughter and my brother was still stunned that he was wrong. "How? She never mentioned finding you or anything." My brother wanted to know. I grinned a bit knowing the secret of Yankee.

"Technically, she didn't. Heard it through the grapevine," He shrugged. "When is the rest of the crew supposed to be arriving?"

"Within a few days. Your room is ready if you want to settle in." I pointed out to him, turning my attention back to the mail and the readings from fellow historians. "If you'll excuse me, I'm going to retire into the library," I stood and moved past both of them.

Leaving my brother to do whatever he needed to do and Yankee to get into whatever chaos he wanted. Maybe venture back into town and find a man to conquer.

I made my way to the library, part of my sanctuary and where the majority of my work was. I took over Maximus's office and maintained and expanded the library throughout the years. But I wasn't going to be alone, for a shadow was following me, but maybe that was the paranoia in me.

I had high hopes that Maxx's might spread some inspiration.

CHAPTER 11

YANKEE

The manor had become more of a permanent home than I was ever blessed with. When you grow up in the foster care system and have limited blood relatives, it was nice to have a family to call my own.

But any amount of separation can change a person and sometimes not in the most positive light. We all tried to make the most of the event and hoped to thrive.

Gwendolyn didn't have to find me; she knew that I would catch on and know it was time to come back. I was ready to come back. I had become bored over the two years, hijacking social events, throwing in a couple cons, and even started a rumor that I was a mob boss. But who says it's a rumor?

Everything lost its luster. I had heard from a professor at Harvard about some research into French monarchy and courts. I knew she was back on the trail.

Also, I may have peeked into his emails and saw she needed the information from him by a certain time. It didn't take a genius to figure out the connection.

I'm not saying that when the crew split and the limited contact that I was angry. But I wasn't going to keep being angry or furious with her. Friends don't do that. The best thing was to give her the space to piece herself back together and allow us to give her the room that she needed.

Once she figured out her crap, and sent the signal, the crew would be back. But part of me wasn't going to let my friend out of my sight until I knew from her what her game or ploy was.

I had followed her to the massive library that only a bibliophile would dream about. She hadn't changed. She was the same beautiful, dark haired, muscular, intelligent, cunning woman I met. But there was still pain in her eyes. Something if you weren't attentive, you'd miss. She still appeared to be the person every one deems her to be.

But something was still off.

She turned into the library and went straight to a shelf that had the ladder placed in front of it, she started to comb through the texts. I thought that she knew that I had followed her. I sat down on one of the leather couches in the middle of the room.

The library was nothing short of what you were to expect from a family of treasure hunters. The bookshelves spread across the room and were divided into two floors. If anything, the library was a quarter of the manor. A ladder was placed on both floors and off to the side of the library was the office that Gwen would spend most of her time. She would say it was to be close to Maximus as if he was there, coaching her along the way.

It had been a few moments that she had been combing through the bookshelves, almost lost in a trance. I cleared my throat, waited to see her react. She jumped a bit, her body jolting in fear. "Jesus Christ."

"Wow. I didn't want to believe it," I joked.

"Believe what?"

"You'd be the one to come find us. The woman I know isn't much of a groveler. What happened sweetheart?"

"I have no idea what you're talking about." She huffed out.

Normally, this woman would be noticing everything, the smallest details, like she could see someone's move or the plan move two steps ahead of her. And here she was, jumping at the fact that I cleared my throat.

"You, my friend, may have turned into someone I know you're not. Your edge, your self-confidence, begging to be someone again." The hard truth.

I saw the mask.

"You would too if your mistakes were repeatedly thrown in your face. I started out as if I knew exactly what I needed to do, but I was wrong. It's like getting smacked in the face over and over again, peeling back every layer you have." She started to say, she trailed off, as if to chase a thought. "Maybe you have been gone too long." She adjusted herself.

"Well, I was never too far from you. Come on, it's me, you can talk to me. When have I ever judged you... not including when I judge your taste in men you date." I regretted that last part.

I knew her taste in men, I would know all about it, have that memory fester in my mind. Resting on the couch across from her, my body slumped even further.

I folded my hands to my chest, twiddling my thumbs, waiting for her to take the moment and let it all out without it leaving this room.

I may be a con man sometimes, but I do listen and some things are kept under lock and key in my mind.

Her shoulders slumped over and taking a deep breath. She turned back to me and her eyes almost welling up. Her pure look of defeat almost broke me.

"Gwen, come on. What's really going on inside that head of yours?" I questioned her, thinking that being alone for so long, she bottled up some things.

"I thought this was going to be easy," She finally said. A brick of her built up wall in her mind breaking off.

"Talk to me."

She made her way towards the middle of the room. Her hands grazed the top of the other couch across from me, leaning into it. "I saw the pain of everyone, Zach, Xara, Winston. Was I really that inconsiderate? Fuck, I had gone on for so long. And honestly

Yankee, how did you all not stop? I became a monster in their eyes."

"Time and hurt can make you see what you didn't." I simply told her the truth. "You didn't put anything else on you. In your mind, everyone betrayed you. Perhaps, maybe we did." I sat up, leaning on my knees. "Sweet cheeks, perhaps we were rash and instead of helping you see, we followed Quinton's lead and thought of our own selves."

The wheels of thought turned in her head. It was the thought that we didn't think of staying and rectifying the situation.

"The question is, why are you holding yourself back from understanding or accepting all of it? And then moving on?" I had asked.

"Pride? Pressure of being something I haven't had to be?" She questioned herself. I mean, yes, but something was more.

"Possibly," I offered.

I patted the couch next to me. She slowly sank into the couch. I wrapped my arms around her, bringing her close. I could smell the vanilla and whiskey scent on her. No wonder Winston was widely affected by her, if she were someone else, I'd bottle that up and bring it with me everywhere.

"*Mon amie,* there is more going on in that mind. Tell me more." She was still holding back.

"I can't lose anyone, not anymore," She sounded defeated. I needed to help her get back to the spitfire woman she was, not this shell of a woman. Call it kindred spirits but I thought that she and I were along the same history. Family leaving us, making us feel like we are abandoned and then when you finally found someone close to you, they leave you.

Everyone leaves at some point.

"What are you most scared about?" That question hung in the air like it was an unthinkable question. She chewed on her lower lip, her body eased more into me. A weight that was continuing to let go.

"I'm scared of a lot of things Yank, one, I will disappoint everyone, again. You know what Dom told me, that I was worse than Maximus. Almost losing Hartley, acting like a brat, throwing a temper tantrum," She sunk down into my lap, burying herself in her guilt. But not the guilt that she thought she was supposed to have.

I started to comb my fingers through her waves. "I don't think you are worse than your uncle but crazed for a moment or two or five, yes." Comparison is an ugly bitch, no matter how confident you are with your life.

"Dom is right, though. What kind of person doesn't feel guilty when someone almost dies, someone that is a friend, that's family?" She said louder, throwing her hands in disbelief.

"One with trauma of people leaving, *mon amie*," a simple observation.

"Maybe I turned heartless," she said.

"You want advice, or are you wanting to rant," I asked. I was growing weary of the self-pity party.

I had hoped that while we were gone she wouldn't spiral, but I guess some people you couldn't help but wonder what happened when push comes to shove.

"Advice," she said in a small voice.

"Oh, my friend, you're not heartless. You care immensely. Sometimes when we love others too much, that is when we push them away." I caressed her cheek. "Tell me what else you are scared of." I thought I knew one of the big thoughts because it was the same one that broke her heart before.

"I'm scared that everyone will leave again. And I'll be the one mentally and emotionally lost." her voice was as soft as a whisper.

There it was.

The amount of loss with her was unfathomable. "That's why you wanted one last hurrah. One last time, hoping that we all would stay. But baby girl, we can only focus on what is in front of us. I think what screws us up is when we think too much of the future instead of the now."

She let out a deep sigh, sinking even further down onto the couch, into me. The vulnerability was a step in the right direction whether she thought it was a sign of weakness or not.

"I thought you were going to say seeing Winston again scared you the most. By the way, how did that go? And did Xara throw anything at you?" I wanted to distract her, not wanting her to continue on the down spiral of her toxic thoughts.

The soft chuckle she let out, I couldn't see her face but I imagined there was a small grin on her face.

"Winston is another crack in my foundation," she said.

I saw the way they looked at each other, and the moments that they had together. She wouldn't admit to the connection but I knew she wanted him, especially after her last relationship years ago, she stuck by Winston's side.

"Things will get better. I mean you see him and everyone when?" I checked my watch.

"In the next couple of days. He's never going to forgive me though, I already know. He wanted to say no when we saw him."

"But he said yes because a certain brunette siren charmed her way and reminded him of what he wanted. The boy is obviously infatuated and y'all will live happily ever after." I drew out a southern charmed accent.

She smacked my leg. "I fucking hurt him," she said.

"Well. you tore the man's heart out, told him you didn't want to go with him, and I think there was a mention of being a coward," I wasn't going to deny that I was eavesdropping on their conversation that night. But practically the whole manor could hear it.

"I can't take back the words even when I don't mean." She responded.

"I know but it will take time. If you want him, let him come to you on his own time, I mean if you have to get down on your knees, he wouldn't say no." I teased her, knowing a little release of sexual frustration will do them some good.

She propped back up and leaned against the backboard, "You ready to do this?"

"Bring it on, baby."

Chapter 12

Griffin Manor was a beacon for all our treasure-hunting hungry souls. Years ago, it didn't feel like home, but after losing most of my family, the manor turned into a home.

It was clear that Gwen accomplished more than I gave her credit for, she convinced everyone or partially everyone to come back. The cousins had arrived, with Hartley in tow. Xara had arrived in the driveaway right behind me. Dominic was earlier than the rest of us, which was not surprising.

Dominic was the first one she came to find.

The cousins greeted me with an embrace and Hartley a simple nod. Hartley was a puzzle, and couldn't say I didn't miss the times that he made Gwen fluster. Memories flood of all the times we had in the manor. Between the jokes and the pranks, and the moments where we didn't have to think about what's next, we could just be us.

"Winston, my man. Couldn't resist her, could you?" Elijah joked, spreading his infectious laugh.

"No, it was the afterthought, once she plowed over him with her truck." Zacharias yelled from behind.

"It was more like I wanted to say no, but..."

"The damn minx." The cousins finished my sentence.

There was a time when I would do anything for her. I'd move the world, protect her from anyone that wanted to cause her harm. I'd call her mine if she would let me. At that moment, I didn't know what she would allow me to do, other than my job.

I saw Xara come towards the huddle, her hair short now razored on the side, but the top swept across her face. Dressed in dark jeans, a halter top, and a dark green blazer, seeing the edge in her steps, as if time gave her the motivation to do what she wanted, no one holding her back. A woman in charge or at least dressing the part. I was surprised that she was able to crawl out of it or at least Gwen was able to pull her from it.

"Boys. Time did you all well. I guess all that anger turned into gym sessions." She cooed. "Are we ready for this shit show?" Her sunglasses disguising any expression in her eyes.

"How did they get you to come back?" I asked.

"It took some convincing." She bluntly said.

"She talked you into it?" Elijah asked with a smirk on his face. She shook her head, "No, her brother."

I was shocked. Was this serious enough that Quinton stepped up? It was hard to believe. Someone was starting to relinquish her control.

"Anyone heard from Yankee?" Elijah asked. He was ever the observant one.

"Fifty bucks says he's invaded the wine cellar when he arrived today." I said.

"Fifty bucks says that he never showed up and is in the tropical" Zacharias piped up, extending out his hand.

"I'll take that bet," I grabbed his hand. Why not make a lite bet during this time that not everyone wanted to be here.

"Count me in, but I bet he was already here when they got back." Xara extended her hand. Zach and I looked at each other and grabbed her hand to shake on the bet.

There was a tingling sensation, a small shiver that ran down my back. A sense of familiarity. The crew had their fun and games and times where childish fun and antics were everyday.

"Shall we? I bet everyone is ready to get back to this manor." I grumbled.

"You're starting to sound like Zach, here," Elijah started, head-locking his cousin. Zach started to struggle getting out of it.

"Seriously, why are you chipper about this than we are? This whole situation also affected you. Or did you just forget that?"

Elijah started walking in front of all of us, but then stopped at the manor door, facing us, "I'm going to tell you the same thing that I told Gwen when she came to see us," He started directing it to everyone, not just me. "Why am I going to hold on to grudges? What good will it do? We can either move on and try to fix the part of ourselves that was hurt or we let it continue to fester and make us even more bitter than we already are."

It bothered me that he was siding more with Gwen. He was the opposite of his cousin, even in this opinion.

"Big man is right though. But I suggest we continue this inside with the rest of the crew." Hartley chimed in.

With my head hung a little low, we marched inside with our bags in tow. The grand foyer hadn't changed, it was still historical and welcoming, opening the manor to everything that was there. But it wasn't Gwen or her brother that greeted us, it was Massey. Everyone stopped dead in their tracks, more stunning than quiet.

"How?" Xara asked.

"Plot twist" Elijah laughed.

"Hell has certainly arrived." I said.

Gregori Massey.

A man that is distinguished and that has ostentatious taste. Friend of the family.

A man that is a ghost with the money that allows him to do whatever he pleases. He was our benefactor, the one that financed the extra bit we needed for our quests.

Massey preferred to stay unknown and unattached but according to Quinton, he was a longtime collector and friend of the family, but still very unattached.

Massey reminded me of the older man from the old dinosaur movies, dressed in white linen with a gold and black cane. But add a Cuban cigar.

After all the shit that went down two years ago, all of us were surprised that he would even show up.

"Well, well. If it isn't the Outcast Crew once again." His cheery disposition told us all we needed to know, but his English accent rang out.

The fact that he didn't have all the information or just the story that was spun to make a certain person or two look like the victims.

"Wouldn't go as far as once again there, old man." Xara teased, but bounced up to the old geezer and planted a small kiss on his cheek.

"Ah, but you're all here. Come, come. We are all meeting in the large study." He wraps his arm around Xara's shoulders, leading us to where we all needed to meet. The boys and I just dropped the bags in the foyer, not knowing how long we were going to be there.

"Say Massey. How they get you to come back?" Zacharias poked around.

Massey just chuckled. "What makes you think it took convincing my boy?"

This man might have been more demented and twisted than Gwendolyn.

Gwendolyn.

Win and Winnie.

Her name still affected me. Images of what could have been and what should have been.

Elijah slapped me on the back to bring me back to the surface.

The large study room was on the east wing of the manor. Mostly we had used it for bringing together a plan or working on the problem areas once we traveled into a new area. Sometimes it would be weeks on weeks, even months for certain ones.

Sometimes we would find Gwen passed out on the couch never making it to her bed.

Our bed.

The thought crossed my mind when there were times she would ask me to stay to help chase away the night terrors. Her small frame almost melted into my body.

Most of the time it would be Gwen mainly in the room or Yankee when he would ramble on and on about certain historical periods or even Xara when deciphering codes or languages.

But we were all there for a reason whether it was for a second chance or a last hurrah. Better start getting to work.

We bursted through the doors as Massey yelled out, "I found some scoundrels entering the manor, they wouldn't happen to belong to you all."

"The family is all here." Gwendolyn turned around, dressed in her usual jeans and regular tank that carved out her body. Quinton peered through his reading glasses, closing a book. They had the corkboard in the beginning stages.

"Family is an interesting word to describe this," Xara sneered out.

"Aren't you are missing the one person that could be hiding in the basement for all we know." Hartley jokingly said.

"Huh, I don't see myself in a basement. Too musty. Now a wine cellar..." Yankee said, sneaking up behind us like a damn ghost.

"Let me guess, that's where they found you?" Zacharias asked, proving an answer for the bet.

Yankee sipped on his coffee cup and grinned as he headed to one of the seats. "Oh no love, I was already here when they got back. Gave Quinton quite the scare," Not the answer we were looking for, both Zacharias and I slapped a fifty in Xara's hand. She would have had to have known or else she would not have bet.

"Welcome home, everyone. You know the drill, so let's begin." Gwen ushered us all in.

The large study allowed for optimal seating between a brown leather coach to a hardwood table seating four to even the random L-shaped desk in the corner. Large bookshelves also coated the walls. Some would call it a smaller version of the gigantic library on the other side of the house.

"Before we all sit, I think we'd like to see this *evidence* that led you on this wild hunt again after seven years, perhaps even more," I grunted out. She had rounded us up stating that there was evidence that would prove her suspensions and lead to another discovery.

She looked at her brother for approval. The transfer of power must have started before we showed up. "Tell them, sister, Winston is right. The time for secrets ends," Quinton folded his glasses and stuffed them into his coat pocket. His mannerisms always got me, like proper gentleman etiquette.

She started to pull out a book, a leather bound loosely woven book. She held it as though it was her last breath, her last plea.

"I have the diary of the last five years of Narcisse Renaud, the youngest daughter of Lord Renaud. Sister Pride of the seven deadly Madames."

CHAPTER 13

GWENDOLYN

As soon as I started to show the old journal, holding it close to me, there was an uproar of disbelief. I held in my hand practically the map that would lead us to the secret room. But not everyone believed me. Chaos erupted, madness tangled around us.

"There's no way that the journal of one of the sisters just showed up. You know the amount of people that would kill to have that little book in your hands." Zacharias, being the first one to yell out of disbelief. "We're not going to be in the crossfire."

"How do you even know that it is what you say this is?" Winston yelled out. The sting of his voice shocked me.

"Fuck this shit, there's no way that is real!" exclaimed Xara.

I didn't blame them, I didn't believe it myself, until I felt the material of the journal in my hands. The most delicate thing.

But I interjected, "Once everyone sits down, then we can get started." I climbed into the seat in front me and everyone took their own time and sat down, each one of them muttered under their breath. The time to get to work was now and I was ready.

"Let's start from the beginning. Shall we?" I pointed to the corkboard. I have told this story many times, but each time felt like the first.

A few nods of heads and a couple eye rolls responses and began the tale that had fascinated me since the time Maximus had told it to me. Little eleven-year-old me, gazing into his eyes watching every storytelling movement, capturing my attention.

"Throughout history, women have been overlooked, used as possession, used as a pawn in a man's world, used for contracts. They were to be seen, never heard, and be submissive to the man in their lives. Noble birth meant that you were born into wealth, power, political status, and privilege. Unlike their opposite gender, women tried to keep to the societal rules and behaviors. Until there were seven French sisters that would prove to the world that women are more powerful than you think. Whispers of these sisters roamed through the country of France. The Renaud sisters.

"Each sister is said to have kept historical journals, portraits, and treasures that represent them and each from their own conquest. Their influence sparked revolutions, trade agreements, power, and politics. The whispers of their influence struck through Europe. Whispers swirled that each sister resembled a deadly sin which influenced the historical events in their time. Each sister grew powerful the more they claimed their own legacies.

"Ameline, the sister of Sloth, the oldest and the first. Then came Martine, the sister of Wrath. Then Nanette, the sister of Gluttony. Then the twins, Esmerie, the sister of Envy, and Désirée, the sister of Lust. After came the sister of Greed, Frastine, and last but least, Narcisse, the sister of Pride.

"It was rumored that a secret place holds the key to important historical mysteries, tucked away in the bowels of their home. Mysteries that would link different events to each other as the works of these sisters. Secrets of trading routes and influential writings and discussions. It is said that whoever was to find the secret trove, the room filled with rumors that stand the test of time, must find the keys to unlock those mysteries. Each sister held a key that unlocked these secrets." I finished. I wanted to bow like I gave the most notorious monologue of my lifetime.

There were a few moments of silence. Then Yankee spoke up first. "So, you mean to tell me that you just happened to come across the one journal that is the answer to everything."

Troublemaker. "Yes and no." I said. Quinton cleared his throat.

"I think you are going to need to expand on that. Lay out all the cards." He tried to command the room, but there was a slight timid tone.

If he was going to step up and fill my shoes, while I prove to the crew that they are in the place they need to be, he was going to have to do something.

"Dr. Landis over at Yale reached out to me and said that he had an interesting piece of French history from the eighteenth century. Landis indicated that he had acquired it from an auction that had a rare book. He had worked with the Harvard department with authenticity. And fortunately, Yale was in possession of the said rare find." I simply put it. I left out that I owed him a favor or two and included a month worth of guest lecturing for all his seminars for the transfer of the possession.

"What price did you have to pay? Or should I ask what account this came out of?" Massey asked, knowing that I still had the inheritance that was left for me.

"That price is on me," I answered him.

Or a favor in return.

"Explain how the diary is the answer. Mind you this is one of seven sisters and the youngest sister." Elijah chimed in. Logical question. "Also, she married one that was beneath her than the rest of the husbands which means architecturally, her home had little significance."

Elijah had a point. The status of wealth was not just by the clothes one wore, but the size and structure of their home.

"Narcisse was the most arrogant and overbearing one, the *prideful* one. She believed that she held more power and leadership. She would be concerned with what everyone else would think of her, that she or her status, that she would have information that would put her in a position of power. And where do most people with power keep their secrets?" Quinton furthered on, proving my point.

"What kind of nobility would keep entries written, could it have gotten into someone's else's hands?" Zacharias boldly stated. We all have certain weaknesses and history was not his strength.

"Narcisse was the youngest, most likely judged for being the baby of the family, wanting to prove to her family that she was worth something," I added to Quinton's point.

"Let me guess, her words will lead to each individual key? To form a what, another key?" Zacharias questioned. Taking any chance he had to find a flaw.

"If you listened, I said *each* sister has a key. I've already started to dive into the journal, finding out what we know versus what we don't know. If you would let me explain..." I raised an eyebrow at them.

"Keep going, Gwen, the elevator will go up sooner or later." Hartley said, giving Zach a shove for me.

"Each sister had a key that was their own. Now, somewhere along the entries, I have seen it mentioned that the lock to the room is round or circular, maybe even an oval. Martine designed it so that all the keys have to be present in order for everything to unlock. This prevented any of the sisters from going in just alone," I explained.

"Or each sister guarded their own key from someone else taking it from them." Quinton shared his suggestion.

"What we need to do is research more leeways to each of the sisters' lives and find an inkling on where each of the pieces are. I think I have figured out Narcisse or at least the location." I started to ramble. My obsession was getting the best of me.

"So, with each key, we have no way of knowing what the keys are actually their keys? Even back then, it was easy to make a fake." Xara asked, with a slight laughter in her voice.

I nodded my head because that was the mystery. All we have to go on are the details and entries of the diary and dive into the tales of the other sisters. These are the sisters that history has no clue what their identity was. All legends have a spark of truth, hence why the library was a myth to most, but a historical point I wanted to show.

"Well, I think you're completely crazy." Zach chimed in again.

I rolled my eyes, slightly regretting bringing him back. If bringing his judgmental, grumpy ass back meant him questioning our every move, then I would have just gotten Hartley and Elijah and called it a day.

"My friend, we have gotten further with way less than we have now. That's what we loved about this, the mystery, the puzzle," Yankee chipped in.

I laid out all the cards. Waiting for an answer was agony. I showed everyone my plans, my research of everything I had.

"Massey, you've been awfully quiet. Care to chime in and say a few words? Like saying no to this wild goose chase." Zach, beginning to be the thorn on my side, grunted out.

Massey plastered a large grin on his face, "She's the chip of the old block. A chase is what you all needed. To band again and find the.. Gwen, what is it that you say or Maxx used to say?" I knew what he was talking about.

"Lost things will always be found, Massey."

He smiled, pointing at her in agreement, "Right, my girl. Go on this goose chase and of course, if you ever need anything." He started to say with a wink. Tapping his cane before meandering out of the study.

Deniability.

"I think we all need to clear the air and move past this. Some of you, if not all of you, harbor ill and hurt feelings against my sister. You have every right to that. We all understand that Gwen can be quite obsessed, and once in a while selfish." Quinton started but I cleared my throat.

"Excuse me? I'm right here." He set his hand on my shoulder, telling me to quiet down and let him work the room.

"You have every right to feel what you all went through. But we all knew that six months was the goal and between miscommunication and us waiting for any word to come back. We're back. We're going to bury the hatchet once and for all. If there is something that you feel you need to help move on, say it now or just let it go." Quinton took the lead.

They each looked around each other, waiting to see if someone would speak up first. I had imagined it would be Zacharias due to the amount of doubt that he had in what was in evidence. But it was Yankee that broke the silence.

"I know to say that everything was Gwen's fault would be wrong. I know I could have done better with communication and being aloof. I'm ready to move on and learn from what happened, to never have it happen again." A soft smile landed on his face.

"I think Hartley and I were ready to move on and let it go. I can't fault Gwen for having an obsession. We all have our obsessions that blind us. Yeah, she could have been better, but so could we." Hartley nodded as Elijah spoke.

"She apologized to us individually or at least attempted to, I think it would be best while everyone is here, to actually apologize as a group. One last time to somewhat bury the hatchet," Xara suggested.

At this point, I was tired of the finger pointing, forgiveness was going to take time, and over time I thought it would be easier for everyone to move on. I wasn't ready because I was still coming to terms after some reality check. The question in my mind raced, do I give them a half-hearted apology or do I give them the truth?

"A group apology? That doesn't seem like a bad idea." Quinton grinned, agreeing with Xara, like I had a chance between them, admitting a bit traitorous on his side of things.

I bit the inside of my cheek, a nervous tick, I unfortunately have picked up. All eyes were on me, attentively waiting for me to say something. One pair of eyes, especially, burned closer to my heart. Our last words echoing in my head, making my heart race.

"I'm going back home." he started to say, there was an edge to his voice like he feared the next part, "You could come with me." he looked back at me with a sweater in his hand. I couldn't say yes, everyone else was leaving me, and the one person I wanted more than anything was ready to leave this all behind, everything we had built.

He walked back to the dresser across the room.

"This is my home, and you belong here." I meant to say he belonged here with me. "All of you do. Instead of staying and talking like adults, everyone is leaving," the next part was a whisper "almost like cowards."

He slammed the dresser drawer loudly. The words came faster than expected and I sucked in my breathing, wanting to take those words back. But everyone is running and leaving out of fear.

"Coward? You're calling me a coward?" He spat at me, I jerked back surprised, from his words, the loudness in his voice.

"What else am I supposed to call people who run away from their problems?" I yelled back, pushing off the bed. My anger was blinding me and I was holding back tears. I saw both our hearts breaking and I couldn't stop it, I couldn't take it back. What was said was said.

"Human, we are human. Especially when the people we love push us to the breaking point." He shook his head.

"That is not love, that is someone who is afraid of facing the problems head on, that's not someone I love." I threw it back in his face.

"You're saying that you don't love your brother, the cousins, Hartley? Not even me? Because the moment we need a break after the amount of danger we put ourselves in, you don't love that you didn't get your way. Poor Gwendolyn, so used to people doing what she wants and how she wants it. You may have that gracious, kind heart that I have known for years, but that green greed monster has surfaced." My silence was enough noise to fill the room. I gently got up from the bed and walked to the open *door of the room, leading out in one of the wings. I stopped dead in the center of the door, not looking back, he couldn't see my face and if there were tears or anger twisted there.*

"And poor Winston will never get what he truly wants because he is too afraid to go after it himself." I walked away. The echoing of the door slam.

A gentle shake woke me from my distant memory. "Gwendolyn," Quinton's voice pulled me out of my trance.

A heaviness weighed in my chest. The long heartache that wanted to be fixed hurt and weighed even more.

"If there is one thing I have in common with these Madames is the obsession, wanting something more. My obsession back in the caves and the guild risked everything we had. I screwed up. It took two years to realize and I'm still realizing that today. I'm sorry. I'm willing to prove my forgiveness. I just want a second chance." My shoulders slumped, knowing each will take their time.

"Please," my voice shook.

They waited for a while, waiting for approval or someone to make the first move. Xara stood up from her chair. She walked over to me, I stood to meet her, waiting for a reaction, and unexpectedly she grabbed me into a tight hug. Her true answer and possibly her forgiveness.

This was the beginning.

CHAPTER 14

XARA

That was growth. Gwendolyn Griffin rarely apologizes, let alone to a whole group of people that may have held a grudge. She was trying, which is more we could give her credit for, but it wasn't an easy fix. Rather a step in the right direction.

After the apology, instead of getting back into the swing of plotting out the next moves, we all disbursed to our rooms. Taking the time for the information to process.

They weren't kidding when they said they had kept everything the same, as if we never left. Old photos were still decorating my wall. I only packed a big duffel, waiting to make my mind up whether I was staying for longer or not. These photos were making a small impact on giving into the whole thing.

I came across a picture of Gwen and I in our junior dorm and it was homecoming weekend, and my date had bailed on me, knowing my ex-girlfriend would, Gwen had made a call to her brother and a few hours later, he was suited up for our homecoming gathering. I touched the picture reliving the memories and I could help but smile.

A creak at the door told me I wasn't alone.

"Ghosts of memories of the past visiting you?" That smooth voice boomed through the room.

We've tipped toed around the idea of us, but I think the chase was more enduring than the continuous of that thought. He was fun to play with and he definitely returned the favor. If I was honest with him, I hadn't wanted to be anyone, male or female or non-binary since we left.

"Yeah, Doc. They have a funny way of pulling you in and convincing you to say yes to anything," I turned briefly to look at him. The mustache combination was certainly a look and still didn't know how I felt about it. I bet if I convinced him, he would shave it, just for me.

I wonder what that mustache feels like somewhere else.

I shook the thought away. I wasn't sure after this quest if I was staying or going, therefore I was not going to get attached. "You and sister certainly had a way to get us all back here."

I looked back at the pictures and heard his footsteps come closer and behind me. His body touching my back, his warmth cascading around my body.

"There were other ways to convince you, little demon." He said, leaning down my ear. "Want to know what they were."

Little demon.

It had been ages since he called me that. He had his predictable signs, how his body responds to me, I knew how to shut him up or have a little power over him. Taking back control. Where others might think he was submissive, that certainly was not the case in the shadows. At least between us.

But sometimes it was the other way around and that is how we liked it. Knowing what the other person needs.

"Dr. Griffin, are you trying to start something we both know I will finish?" I teased him.

He slowly grazed his hands along my side, then taking one arm around my waist, pulling me closer to him, and his other hand trailing a finger along my collarbone. I would be lying if I said that it didn't send shivers down my spine.

"You want to rethink your question?" He growled in my ear, giving me the opportunity to rethink my response. His hand that once was caressing my collarbone was then gently wrapped around my throat. I could feel how hard he was, he had been waiting.

"Dr. Griffin, have you been thinking about me?" I asked, changing my question.

Had he been thinking about me? Has he been seeing other people since we left? We fought the attraction the best we could, but one drunken night and sober thoughts exposed, the truth came out.

The cold exterior that I put on for others, he could see right through, I'd make him nervous, but the look into my mind and soul, he could break me out of it. It was nice to have that, a break from the appearance I gave others.

He let go, his hand around my throat, his arm around my waist. But he didn't let go for long, he spun me around, forcing me to look up into those blue eyes, the intoxicating Griffin blue eyes.

The one person that accepted my chaos and my lifestyle, who didn't want to change me. There was a starvation, a primal look in his eyes, as if he was waiting to take his possession, his claim back. He backed me up against the photos, pinning my body against the walls. The wall vibrated a bit.

He tilted my chin up, not forcefully but with power, a hunger in his eyes.

"I thought about you every damn day and regretted not hearing your voice everyday, or the feeling your skin prickle under my touch." He held my gaze, watching every facial movement, waiting to spot a lie, "I regret that I let you go!"

I looked behind and realized he had closed my door.

Then in a flash, his lips were on mine, the passion flamed higher and brighter and suddenly I was at his whim and I didn't want to turn back. His lips trying to claim mine and I let him. Both of us are hungry for each other, trying to make time stand still and make up for the times lost. He smelt of fresh woods, and sea air.

I had missed this.

I slipped a moan into his mouth, the ecstasy racing through my veins. He lifted me, wrapping my legs around his waist. I was starting to become breathless. This was a long-awaited kiss. But he pulled back and I let out a whimper, I didn't want him to stop.

"I'm giving you a choice. I can and will remind you that you belong to me up against this wall or I will prove it to you in the shower or in the bed." His voice hinted with some gravel.

Too many choices, I wanted all three. I wanted to be greedy and I wanted to make the decision. It had been too long since there was anything. Every fiber of my being ached for him, even when he appeared at my doorstep.

And if this was his apology, then I'd gladly accept it. Fortunately, my silence gave him his answer for the both of us.

Us.

A weird concept that time allowed me to ask myself if I wished to explore that with him.

I bit my lip, looking at him.

"Someone is trying to be greedy, not making ,a choice," he chuckled.

I softly nodded my head. He pulled me off my blazer, started kneading my breasts, they were peebling through.

My skin, my body begged for more. I let out a small moan, but I started to reach out for him, towards his belt. He swatted at my hands.

"We have two years to make up for and I don't intend on rushing," he said, placing his forehead on mine.

He stripped me of my halter top, lazily throwing it on the ground. I tried to fumble with his clothes but he grabbed my chin and jolted my head to the side, giving him access to my neck. He trailed kisses along my neck, heading further down my body. He stopped though. He stopped and stared at my chest piece.

Something had changed from the last time. I needed a simple reminder that I felt good once with someone I trusted, even cared about.

Over the past two years, I added more ink onto my skin. But one hidden feature, within an intricate design featuring skull and crossbones, was a pitchfork. A simple feature.

"Oh little demon. You missed me," he chuckled, before taking my nipple in his mouth. Tasting, teasing me. The sensation shooting straight through. The sensation sending me into a lustful haze, blinding everything around me.

My hand grasped his head, "Maybe a little bit," I was rewarded with a small nip from him.

"I think it was more than a little. I wager that if I reach in your pants, slip my fingers through that little fabric, I'm going to find you soaked. And ready for me to feast."

My eyes widened at the thought of him between my legs, his tongue sucking on me, eating me like a starved man in a desert. "Please," I whimper.

It had been too long, and I wanted this. I wanted him.

"As she commands." In a flash my jeans were gone. But no underwear. His devilish grin appeared as I looked down. "You were ready for me, weren't you." He inserted a finger, and jerked back. The teasing motion

He captured my lips, lust surging through. Both of us are a heaping mess. He started pumping in and out, adding another finger. Wetness flowing down my thighs, I wanted to come, practically begging him for a release.

With a devilish smirk, Quinton took his fingers out and slipped down onto his knees, hiking one of my legs over his shoulder before he dived into my pussy. The first feeling of his mouth on me had me jolt out of my skin. The slightest touch of his breath made me weak in my knees. Then the more ravenous sound came out of him when his groans as his mouth zeros in my aching pussy.

He took his time, plotting out every movement with a swipe of his tongue, tasting every ounce of my desire. His licks were enough to keep me on edge at his mercy, sending moans straight from my mouth, to the point of begging him to let me come. My hips met his licks, his nips, his sucking of my clit.

Quinton paced himself, slowly teasing and torturing me into my impending orgasm. The waves of pleasure were rolling and the moment he curled his fingers inside me, hitting that one spot that would shoot you off like a firework.

"Fuck," I let go, as the orgasm ripples through me, Quinton hasn't let go and at that point my legs were ready to give out. I started pushing his head away, but he whipped off his belt and in a blink wound the belt around my wrists and held them. "I can't. Please." I barely say.

I was at his mercy, completely. He was the greedy one, taking my pleasure for himself and giving more than I felt I deserved.

He looked at me with darkened eyes, "I want one more. Can you do that for me?" He pulled back. I slowly nod, and the sinister chuckle. "That's my girl."

They say what you lacked in your childhood was what turns you on.

Praise, any praise from him made me melt. He worked himself pumping in and out and sucking on my clit. It wasn't long before the crashing of my second orgasm roamed over me, leaving me in a pile of heat and ecstasy.

Quinton finally released me, standing up and my release coating his mouth. He grabbed my neck and pulled me closer to where I am tasting my own release.

He started to fumble with his sweater and all I wanted to do was take him in my hands.

"What do you want Xara? I need your words," He started to shake off the sweater, pulling it over his head and then slowly undoing his pants. I could see the outline of dick, pushing against the seam. My chest was still trying to find my breath. "Name it." He growled out.

"I need you inside me," I whispered, practically begging.

"Doing what? I can't do anything without your words," He said, gently, his voice full of sex, lust. He kept teasing me in every blissful, sinful nature. The sweat dripping from the both of us glistened in the light.

I gulped. It had been a while, but he wanted words, he wanted to give me choices, he wanted to hear what I needed. "I need your cock in my pussy, please."

"As you wish." He yanks me up and strolls over to the bed, it was freshly made, the clean scent surrounding me.

He gently places me on the bed, laying me out, bare and naked. No slow, no love-making, just us in lust and passion.

The anticipation might kill me in the end, if not a third or fourth orgasm from this man. My eyes watch him as his pants start to lower and he is finally sprung free. Right then, my hunger grew uncontrollably. I knew I wasn't making a mistake.

He stroked himself a few times, taking his time to tease, making me wait. He crawled on the bed, slowly like a tiger stalking its prey.

"Two years, Xara, two years I have been craving, wanting you again." He said.

"I'm here, Quin," I told him, but his words sent me over the edge.

"And I'm never letting you go again," He said as he thrusted in one solid stroke into my pussy. I yelped, in one swift movement, I felt full.

He slowly tantalizingly fucked me, his hands in my short hair. I missed my longer hair at that moment, but it was still enough to grab onto with power.

"I swear on this somewhat green Earth, if you do not fuck me like you mean it, I am going to kill you." I growled out, needing more from me. He knew how to drive me crazy, all the buttons to push. He peppered a few kisses along my jaw.

"Then let's remedy this, I have plans for you," With grace, I went from being fucked on the bottom to impaled on the top. I placed my hands on his chest to steady myself. It was like being full of different parts of yourself.

"Ride me," He commanded, and I swear if there was a term for being even more turned on and wanton I'd invent one.

I heeded his command and felt the power back on me. I moved my hips into a pace that I needed and I was going to take from him. This was mine and I was going to claim it. Something came over me. I had never been this possessive, but with Quinton it had become easier.

I rode him to make sure we both chased a release.

A flood of memories, of stolen moments rushed through my head. A piece of comfort, something that was missing for a long time. I wanted to be his, but feared that I would never be enough. That's why I never chased it. I worried he would have his fill of me and move on.

I think Quinton saw a bit of worry in my eyes because he grabbed my face and pulled me into a deep kiss and whispered, "I want you here and now, and for all times." I continued to ride his dick and both of us on the cusp of an orgasm.

It wasn't until he took his thumb and rubbed my clit that for the third time I came. I came hard, I started to see stars bursting my closed eyes as he followed behind me.

He gathered me in his arms with him still in him. These were the moments I missed the most, the closeness, the feel of his heartbeat against mine, and the feel of safety, like the world is staying still and freezing this moment. He kissed my head.

He returned to the soft, caring man that I adored for many years.

He whispered, "I'm sorry I left you," My heart beat faster.

"Take us to the shower. We have a bit to talk about you and I." I kissed him back. With enough strength and him still in me, we headed towards my private bathroom, and took the hottest shower.

Quinton and I went a round or two more before we finally dressed and started to talk. He leaned against my desk and myself sat on the bed. Once the bed was actually made. Exhaustion hits, you don't realize the lack of stamina you lose when you take a break.

"I have my list of demands, as requested." I said, waving a small list in the air.

"I was quite surprised when it was you that embraced my sister. What changed your mind?" He questioned me.

I couldn't answer it myself at first, but Gwen saw me through all the moments of my life that I wish subsided. She saw and supported me through my fall out with my parents. My parents wanted me into politics and I went rogue and paved my own way. The only person left in my corner at the time was her.

"She needs us."

"That's not it. Try again without lying."

"But you like when they are sweet lies." I winked at him, but he just cocked his head at me. "Fine. I hugged her because I know it's not easy to admit when she screwed up, let alone in front of everyone. I'm still trying to forgive her," I began wanting to finish my statement, but stopped myself. There was a little bit of myself not ready to completely tell him.

"I think everyone still is." He said, brushing his foot against the ground.

"Have you?"

He shook his head. "But everyone tends to forget that I was the one that asked for the separation, the split to give us clarity."

"I think everyone has suppressed that fact for a reason. It was the tantrum that came from her that resulted in everyone actually leaving, but with the understanding that everyone might be coming back within six months. But with all the haste, we waited for word instead of taking action, it was her silence. But in turn, we led our lives." I knew I started angrily rambling when Quinton started to flinch at my words.

"You said to bring my demands and I brought them." I unfolded my paper, leaning back on my bed. Quinton started to inch closer. I popped my foot out to stop him. "No, you don't, I am taking back the power right now, you stand there like a good boy and listen." He smirked at me, but I stared at him letting him know I was serious.

"Proceed."

To be honest, I knew I should have thought of more, but it was harder than expected. Something I didn't want to admit.

"One, I receive a bigger stipend for any additional equipment or persuasion for those we encounter." I wasn't going to pass the opportunity, with some areas of the world, we had to get creative with the people we interacted with.

"Approved. Next."

Damn, I thought it was going to be more challenging than anticipated. "Um, second. The group has the second say so, before your sister." I had to admit this to myself, it was a little bit harsher, but necessary.

"Up for discussion. I am not going to neglect my sister's opinion."

"You misheard me. I said that the group's opinion is taken seriously over your sister's. At least for the time being. This was her obsession, she wants this, which means that she will not stop for anything."

There was a slight nod, very slight. But I knew he heard me.

"Any more demands? I expected a longer list." He snarked at me.

I had one more, *Don't let me run away from you again.* I read the words again in my head, but crumpled up the paper, destroying the evidence.

My mind stopped me. He just crept back into my life and has given me multiple orgasms, which clouded my judgment. "No, I think we are all good." I said to him, hiding the truth, the one piece that I wasn't ready to let loose.

He just gave me a look like, we'll see. One day Quin, maybe one day. I'll find the courage to say what I really wanted. For now, I was wrapped in the arms of this man for a while.

CHAPTER 15

GWENDOLYN

You ever get lost in thought and time ticks away in a flash? Well, that's what it felt like as my brain racked with the translation of text, analyzing all the words and sentences, making sense of the rambling nonsense.

It took a couple of weeks before everyone finally settled into their routine and moved in. There was life that sprung back in the manor and my heart felt full. I knew that people still needed to get issues resolved and I had to continue to prove my word, but it was a step and I was content with that. Each person dived into research.

Elijah and Zacharias were looking into eighteenth century French architecture and topography of the land, giving us the visuals that we needed. The main image we needed was where the family was from and their birth home. From there it was a matter of the timeline of each sister's marriage and further upbringing. Hartley worked within the dark web, continuing to notate any rumors or whispers of the sisters or connections, searching into every text we could get our hands on.

Winston and Dominic had maintained the garage and basement with fine tuning and cleaning the weapons and vehicles. They kept busy with plotting what we needed and what we could use in case of emergencies.

My brother on the other hand was always the odd ball. His background and skill set was more on human behavior past and present, he would wait for one of us to bring information and continue to analyze it and place it within the puzzles. He sat back and let us do what we did best. I didn't overstep, I took his training wheels off.

Xara, Yankee, and I took the diary looking into the historical features and breaking down the translations. Xara was already a step ahead of me, with her computer programming that allowed for accurate translation, I took the longer route and journal and notated my special way of the translation.

I knew what I was looking for, something that no computer could tell me.

I was immensely thankful for being fluent in French and Greek. Yankee was researching and utilizing the library for further research on the French culture and historical timeline.

Each one of us took our part back, except for me. I was back to being a main historian, separating fact from fiction. To be honest, it felt like I was splitting a part myself, one I was so used to being.

The one thing that kept this mystery going was how detailed she was and diligent she was in writing. The journal was thick, but every page was a new pathway, new answers, but also leading into questions that I had no idea how to answer.

By the time everyone was getting settled, I had been halfway through the journal, I felt like I was holding up progress. My own notes and annotations, most nights I didn't return to my bedroom but stayed in the library, surrounded by possibilities and insights.

It was starting to get colder and colder in the November month, and the fire in the library was illuminating the room. The crackling of the wood, fire blazing was the only sound and sight that had welcomed me most nights, especially that night. The night greeted me like an old friend. Everyone had turned in for the night, but my mind kept seeking out the answers that would feed my curiosity.

I had come across a poem that Narcisse had written, seven verses. I imagined seven verses were for the seven madames, her sisters.

Something wasn't clicking or making sense, Narcisse seemed to ramble on and on. I couldn't get an accurate translation for certain words. It felt like a scramble psychotic delusion.

I roughly translated it. But something wasn't right about it. There were certain words that had not been translated before, but when I got it, I would check with Xara and Yankee to hear their opinions.

I had been working on the rough translations when I heard the creak of the door. Everyone I knew was asleep, passed out from their days' work. But one person and I had hoped it was the one person I wanted back, someone that knew where to find me.

Winston.

He broke my concentration. A dark majestic angel looming over the room. I could stare at him all day and never be bored. I could study all the muscles and ridges of his body and still want to explore it. I had my chance, but I kept making him chase it. Then I ruined it.

My rimmed glasses at the bridge of my nose, I had terrible night vision, but I knew what heavenly sight was before me. I had sat at one of the tables in the room, all my notes sprawled out. Papers covering the table, books opened and ready to read. A mess within a chaos.

"I figured you would be in here." His voice was low enough to rumble the earth and send shivers down my body.

"I'm a creature of habit, Win. Did you expect anything less?" I tried not to gawk at him, continued to look at the poem, I had half of it translated. Older or traditional French could have multiple translations.

He scuffed at me, probably at his nickname. I didn't have time for the attitude nor the distraction. *He was never a distraction. Give me a distraction.*

"Oh, I'm sorry, does the name Win make you hate me even more?" I sneered at him. It was late and I was not in the mood to fight, I was tired, burning my own candle to the brim.

He took a step closer into the library, apparently not backing away from this conversation, let alone me. I had given him space to have him adjusted back to this life, but I wasn't going to interfere with him and his process. Quinton had advised me that if I wanted him back in my life that I needed to let him do it on his terms and timing.

But I didn't promise that I would be nice about it. I could still add some spark to it.

"I never said I hated you." he said softly, grabbing my attention.

"You sure act like it. Especially when I came to the garage. By the way, I would have never run you over, but you were certainly cute with that wrench in your hand." I said, throwing my glasses off my face and onto the table. I leaned back in my chair and folded my arms.

"Do you want me to lie and pretend that I'm not angry with you or at least still hurt?" He didn't raise his voice, there was a small softness to it.

"No." I responded back to him. "I'm not expecting a warm forgiving heart either. I certainly don... You know what never mind." I threw the idea of saying I don't deserve him out the window, because I didn't deserve a lot of things.

"Funny, you acted like there was more to say. Something more about maybe, us?"

"Maybe there was." We fell silent. "Look, I'm sorry. How many more times do I have to fucking apologize? To you? To everyone? I didn't know what I lost until everyone was gone and it took something this big to realize it even more." I was starting to raise my voice, but softly said, "I just want my friend back, Winston." There was a lump of pure emotions in my throat that I swallowed down.

"You just want me back as a friend there sweetheart?" He asked very smoothly. I quickly shook my head before I realized what I had done.

The truth and emotion hit hard as the words came out.

A few weeks ago I had schemed and planned my way, still thinking that I truly didn't do anything wrong. I had turned into a version of myself that was ugly and cold. And I didn't want Winston as a friend. We had grown closer and sometimes I pushed away.

"Those are nice words Gwen. Pretty even. But it doesn't fix everything," He said, stepping closer to the table.

"Wow, some genius you are, you don't think I don't know that," I started to get up, but suddenly with enough force he moved the chair away from the table and trapped me by his arms as he latched on to the chair.

He was close enough for me to smell the clean scent from his soap and see the fresh stubble from a couple of days old shave.

"And it would take a genius to know that words can't be taken back." He started to level himself to my eyes.

"As I remember there were two people in that conversation." I threw back at him.

"You walked away." The final punch of the hardest memory in my mind.

I walked away. I hid all the emotions that threatened to be exposed, I didn't want to appear weaker than I already was.

"And poor Winston will never get what he truly wants because he is too afraid to after it himself."

"That door slam has haunted me. Every. Day." I didn't look at him, avoiding him. Because at that moment, I didn't feel like I had the right to call him mine. The hardest punch to the heart.

He tilted my chin to look at him, releasing my chin, he tucked a piece of my hair that had fallen from my bun behind my ear.

"There wasn't a day that I didn't think about you. I have one question for you." He started.

His touch was warming my skin, the brief touch sparked so many memories during our travels and when back in the manor. Our playfulness, our embrace, the way he could just melt all my problems away and me return the favor and promise.

My childhood best friend turned into my almost partner, but I couldn't cross the line, not again. Before the split, we were getting closer and moments happened even more. With all the tension, I danced with the line. And then my mind said no, the heart said yes. My mouth echoed the words and my body walked away from him.

I wanted him and only him. I was just too fucking stubborn to let it happen.

"Yes, Win?" I said softly.

"Are you ready to stop walking away from me?" His voice turned sensual. My eyes grew wide. I couldn't say yes and apologize any quicker. I couldn't speak. "I didn't hear an answer."

"Yes."

"Yes what?" He growled.

Jesus, if this is what happens when we separated for two years, I would hate to see the dominance of this man after a lifetime.

I searched his eyes for an answer. There were two ways I figured he would want me to answer. Submission or admission. The power in his stance, the commanding presence. He had changed, he wasn't the same man that I left behind. The edge of heartache took a turn and I didn't know if I was turned on or scared for a moment.

"Yes.. Winston?" I questioned the possible response. He chuckled, shaking his head. That was the wrong answer.

"Try again." He leaned closer, pushing our foreheads together. Once he was putty in my hands, but how the tables had turned. He was taking control of it at that moment. For once, it was a breath of fresh air. It was something new that stirred in pleasure.

My heart raced, my mind telling me to speed up this process, plotting the next moves.

I looked at his face.

"I'm tired of walking away from you, Winston." The phrase took enough breath out of me.

I fully expected him to take me right then and there, throw me on the table, pushing everything off of it. Splay me across the table, like a meal ready to be devoured.

But he just kissed my forehead and backed up. He had a cocky grin on his face, like he knew I didn't want a damn kiss on the forehead.

"That's it?" I asked.

He shrugged. "That depends on you." He started to walk away but stopped mid way when I started to speak.

"I just told you I was tired of walking away. Do you see me running? Do you see me slamming any more doors?" I stood up, taking steps closer to him.

I wasn't done with him. I stepped up to him, and grabbed him by his shirt, yanking him to me. I slammed my mouth on him, at first it was hard and almost painful, but once his shock wore off, we eased into it. He felt more like home, like he was supposed to be where he was supposed to be. With me.

My hands released his shirt and my palms just rested on his chest, he took over our kiss, cupping my face, holding me in place. Sinking into it further and further. But he broke it first, resting his forehead on mine.

My mind hid the words I wanted to say, *Winston, finally. I'm sorry.* I started to choke back the tears. Then my mind started to wonder.

"Why were you looking for me?" I asked.

"Curiosity." He answered. Backing up, letting me go. A twitch of sadness started to spread. I was so close and he was backing up, "I wondered if you had gotten back into your obsessive habits or not."

Lies, that wasn't it.

"Look who's lying now," I pointed out.

"I'll answer your question if you answer another one of mine first," He said, taunting, teasing me.

"Fine. I'll play your game." I walked away from him, pretending I was looking for something else. He wasn't going to win this game so easily. He made me work for it this far, his turn now. Revenge wasn't his normalcy, but two years could do a lot for someone.

"Out of everyone on the team, other than your brother, why didn't you come to me first?" He asked. I knew the answer, but I'm cunning.

"You weren't the closest. It was Dom," It wasn't a complete lie, but not the truth.

"Try again," He said, grumbling almost.

"You weren't on the list alphabetically." That lie was a stretch.

"I'm going to give you one more chance." He growled out.

Shivers, goosebumps. Oh this man, what this man was doing to me now and how I wished he acted on it. He followed after me, coming closer and closer to the bookshelf.

I turned back, back straight against a bookshelf. The shelves poking me in the back. I stared into his eyes. Sinking my bottom lip between my lips.

"I feared you would turn me down before I could get anyone else. For the moment, I just wanted you to say yes. You could have ruined my plan and confidence." I fiddled with my necklaces. "Obviously, I didn't have to worry."

I don't know if that was the answer he was hoping for but it was the answer that he got. For a man that hated me or had his heart broken and just let me kiss him passionately, he was awfully close.

Before, I was the one that flirted with the line of our relationship and friendship, testing to see what he would do.

Two years. That was all it took for this man to command his presence and be seen. To get a taste of the past, and take charge in the present.

For the first time in a long time, I saw him. And it was me that craved him. For more of his touch on skin. For his words spoken sweetly to me but reminded me who had his heart. Question was, was I worthy of his heart or was I still having to mend it because I broke it?

"I think there is a second part to it," He said. The heat from his body was tantalizing, I just wanted to reach out and touch him, grab hold of him and wash the feeling of regret off my mind. I doubted that he would let me, in that moment, it felt like a game or a trick.

"Maybe there is."

"When you're ready, you'll tell me what you truly feel," He inched closer, "But you want something now, Winnie?"

Oh my childhood nickname, maybe there was hope. His legs wedged in between mine, trapping me more in the bookshelf. His hands are bracing the bookshelf behind me.

God, I wanted to say yes so fast. I wanted to give in and say I'm his, but he won't let that happen, not yet. I nodded my head. I could feel my arousal soaking my underwear. I wanted him to sear a powerful, awakening kiss.

"I think we both want something." I said. He could deny all he wanted but eventually his primal urge to take what he wanted would give in.

"One more than the other." He said, backing away.

I let out a whimper, silently begging that he wasn't walking away after I said I was done. I grabbed his arm, maybe with not enough strength, but this was the first time it was just him and me, I wasn't ready to end that yet.

"Winston," It was all I could say. My words weren't going to fix everything, it wasn't going to mend his heart.

"I'm still here, Gwen. Maybe not a hundred percent," He turned away, heading towards the door. "I would never walk away, I never wanted to." His shoulders slumped. He was holding back, he didn't want to give in first, because look what happened the last time he tried. He almost left. And words stopped him.

"Stay with me." I gasped back. Those were the same words he asked me. To stay with him, to go with him back home. Now I knew what those words meant. It was a plea. It was a command but with a possibility. "Please." I asked again. Holding back all the tears.

"You want me to stay? Where?" There was a hint of anger, not sadness in his voice.

"What do I do, brother, once I have my chance?" I asked Quinton. I was clueless.

"For once Gwendolyn, tell him what you want and how you are going to prove that you change and have changed from the last time."

"That's it? How that is so simple," I rolled my eyes.

"You want more from him? Prove that you've earned forgiveness. For you, that means being honest and allowing time. Now, if you'll excuse me, I have my own bonds to mend."

"Winston, I want you here, in this room, sitting in silence with me, making sure I don't pass out on the table. I want you in this house, because you made it more of a home. I feel safe with you. I want you in my bed, helping me be rid of nightmares and prove to me that it's you and me. I want you in my heart and I want back in yours." The rush of emotions, I had my legs shaking. He turned to face me, I sounded like a lunatic.

It sounded too much, but my brother suggested honesty.

He stood there, my hand still grasping his arm. He fell quiet. I worried that I frightened him or rushed the timing.

"I'm going to be honest, I don't think I am ready for everything." It was a start.

"But you're ready for something?" I said softly. "But I will give you whatever time you need. I don't want to walk away any more."

"Okay." He said.

"Okay?" I repeat back. I was shocked that he agreed.

"Okay, Gwen." He said hopefully.

A pang of hopefulness fills my heart. "Okay. so, can you at least stay with me tonight." I just wanted him near, even if things were going to be taken slow. He nodded his head.

I returned to the table and he settled on the couch picking up a book that laid on the table. I'd glance at him at any chance I could get.

By the end of the night, I wasn't at the table anymore, I had rested my head on his lap and passed out, the book feeling heavy in my hands. But Winston held me for the rest of the night until the next morning I woke up and the sun through the windows peeking through, shining and illuminating his smooth, chocolate skin, like he was sculpted by gods. I would be like Michelangelo, chipping away to find the rest of his godlike figure.

My fingers caressed his cheek, his soft skin. I slowly inched up from his lap, being careful not to fully wake him. I got up just enough to softly kiss him on his cheek as he started to stir. A small smile escaped me. I started to get up, trying to respect his space knowing that if I go any further I might push him away even more.

But someone grasps my hand and looking back seeing his dark brown eyes showing specks of ember in them. One look and could melt away.

He yanked me back towards him, my legs cradling his hips. His hands started to explore through my hair, coming back to caress my cheeks. He held the sides of my face in his hands, staring into my soul.

"I've missed you, Winnie," stealing my lips with his plush lips. I sunk into it, being where he is, afraid that after this he might back slide from me. It was a start.

CHAPTER 16

A month, which was how long it was before we made a plan, but it wasn't complete. Gwendolyn found a turning point, the one that made it seem like all the puzzle pieces were coming together.

Each section of the poem was broken down by each sister. At first, the stanzas would appear to be gibberish, random rantings of the one sister that made it seem like it was all about her and who she was.

For each sister we had to understand where the location of their keys needed to unlock the library, and even locate where the library was hidden. Our two historians were stumped, and I didn't know what to do.

I was stumped as well, I had no indication of what would need to happen next. I felt out of place. I knew how to run groups of different populations or conditions, but running a group of intelligent, independent, and stubborn opinionated individuals, I was better being second in command, following what plans were already in place.

I didn't want to ruin this for my sister, she needed closure, this last adventure to possibly be better than the one before. She relied on me, and I knew the fear of disappointment all too well.

One night, I was alone in Maximus's study, my sister resting on the couch in the main library. The desk lamp illuminated everything I needed to figure out the rest.

"Narcisse rambles too much, sometimes it is pure nonsense." Gwendolyn had said.

I am my own person, no one else's image but mine.

A Reflection of myself tells me everything.

Never go against those who are full of pride.

Needless to say this was Narcisse, calling herself pride and her own person.

Money holds the crown and country

Taking more than what is needed.

She keeps everything Safe and sound.

Greed. Frastine was married into a nobleman in the treasury, it was obvious Narcisse would mention money.

Venus, herself, gifted her beauty.

Distracted are those whose eyes wander over.

The one she truly loves holds her Heart.

Desiree was the only one that was duchess, which was rare unless you married a true nobleman. But whispers of a torrid affair threatened her position. Gwendolyn believes that she loved two men.

Her eyes desire the lives of others,

The taste of succession above those she looks down.

Green are the heavens coated in stone.

I was starting to believe that the statements of nonsense were true. Unless we had the translation wrong, this was the fact. Esmerie had become a widow at a younger age than her sisters and unfortunately became the overseer of the family estate and finances, becoming a spinster in those times.

Indulgence, excessive, all hers.

Punishment even more, behind Ironclads.

Beg forgiveness and ask for more.

Gluttony. The moment of indulgences. Being a glutton of punishment, something within that line puzzled us.

Love has taken a soul and fed revenge

She sits waiting for gates to open,

To seek fury and Hell to tomb Earth.

Revenge, fury, a woman's scorn. Wrath, Martine. The wife of a general. From what we knew, one of the true passionate, faithful pairings out of her sisters. Her husband was killed in the line of duty, some say it was betrayal from his second in command. I could only imagine her world crashing down on her at the news of her husband.

No dedication to Almighty power and heavens,
Little effort, no movement, no Bells to ring.
She can expect the unexpected, no one else.

Then we were back to the nonsense. The amount of time we spent looking at this board coming up with theories.

As the weather grows colder, Massey kept asking if we were any closer and to be honest, after a month for us and two years for my sister, we were nowhere closer than anticipated.

I had called for everyone one night, as we gathered together, around the board with copious amounts of Chinese take out. My sister was standing by the board, looking at everything, notes of the family, each stanza, lay out of the former family's estate. Her mind spinning in different paths, sometimes seeing things before anyone else, a bit like Maximus. Xara and Yankee were right behind her at the table, Winston watching her every movement, and I couldn't help but admire the way Xara's eyes bounced around from one side of the board to the other.

"Can I ask a dumb question?" Zacharias had piped up with a mouth full of food.

She had turned, "For you, it's just a regular question." Not the time to throw a dig at the man, sister.

"See, you still have your bite." He snarked. "But seriously, I don't think we addressed this. I understand that the beginning of the lines were capitalized, but Gwen, you capitalized other words," Silence fell, because for the first time, he was on to something.

"That's just how it was," Gwendolyn waved off the statement, looking back at the chicken scratch of notes.

"Can we just look at it again, why did you capitalize these words?" I asked. Eyes shot back and forth between the group.

I looked at the stanzas and the son of a bitch may have been on to something.

"Yeah, when I translated the text there were words that were capitalized, therefore I capitalize the translated word. I didn't make a mistake," She started to get defensive.

"That's not what I was getting at there, Sherlock. What I was trying to say is, what if there is a significance of the words that are capitalized?" He continued. I could see the wheels turning, as if the furnace had sparked a fire.

"Rock for brains actually may be on to something. Wait, okay. I see what you're trying to say" my sister admitted, "Keep talking." She sat back in a chair.

Zach had wiped his hands on his jeans, then clapped them together to stand up and bring attention to himself. I could only imagine what was going through his head.

He walked up to the board, presenting himself to show off his point. "Gwen, you said yourself that Narcisse was detailed, she had the in and outs of the family. Look at the poem. The stanza we all know that it's her; it's pride. But look at the word that is capitalized, reflection." He pointed to the word. "What has a reflection? Recall what she says, I am my own person." He was waiting on her or anyone to come up with the rest of it. I had never seen my sister curious and stunned at the same time.

"Looks like I'm going to have to finish this thought," Zach sighed. "Pride is about herself, saying that it is a reflection of myself. Come on Harvard! Connect the dots." He continued to wait.

But I think my sister had overexerted herself and she was overthinking. But I was starting to see what he was saying.

"A mirror. Seeing herself in a mirror, more like her personal mirror is all she needs, to view herself the way she does. The mirror in her married home," I finished his thought.

"Probably behind a mirror if I were to guess," Zacharias stated.

My sister was still rendered speechless. Zacharias was on to something. "Holy shit. You grumpy ass bastard figured it out!" She yelled. She squealed.

"So wait, the poem wasn't nonsense, it hid clues as to the location of the sisters' keys?" Dominic spoke up, "But why? We thought the sisters wanted to keep things hidden?"

He had a point. All things of records, accounts, historical ledgers had vanished, without a trace. History didn't want them to be found. Or someone didn't want the name to ring out. As if they were erased from history.

"Narcisse wanted someone to find their secrets. That's why she wrote everything down. Think about it, someone so prideful doesn't want to be forgotten. She did something that her sisters wouldn't figure out. She kept all the dirty secrets of where the sisters hid their keys." Gwendolyn explained.

"She kept an account of everything or at least the majority of it, and the secret to pass down where to uncover their sins or their history. Little devilish woman." Dominic sat back in his seat.

"That she is, that's why she was careful when she planted those clues. I guess the legend is true. Only those who are worthy of uncovering their sins, she didn't want her own sisters to have what she wanted for herself," Xara pointed out. "Sneaky bitches. God, they are fascinating."

They weren't the other ones who were fascinating.

"Okay, so obviously we have Narcisse who hid her key behind the mirror. What about the rest of them?" Winston asked. We were all on to something. Everyone read through the stanza again.

"What do we know of Frastine?" I asked, taking notes of each sister again. Frastine was the sister known for greed. I was beginning to think their parents were seers if they named each other daughters with a connection to known sin personality.

"According to the books, or at least the journal, she was the wife of the city treasury office. She married up, considered to be a part of the nobleman society," Yankee peered into his notes.

"She talks about money, greed, and power but then Narcisse talks about the country and crown controlling it, taking more than needed. Narcisse is making it seem like there was saving grace," Xara continued.

"But the word here is safe. I don't think she is talking about safety as in safe." Zacharias pointed out.

"No, not safety. What if she is talking about a safe like a safe, like a pin and tumbler?" Hartley chimed in. There were some historical conflicts. But that could have been me. "This is going to sound off the wall, but is the safe box or lock safe even back that far?" I asked.

"Actually, yes. The first pin and tumbler safe, the beginning of what our modern day safe looks like now, was first introduced in the 16th century. Before that there were different types of safe or even puzzle boxes." Hartley pointed out. I was not surprised that the man with the security experience would know that.

"Okay, so a safe? Where?" Elijah questioned.

Good question where?

"Money... Where would someone who is the wife of the treasury nobleman place the safe and the key together? The old royal treasury department. Well more like the main repository of the crown jewels back in the day. But now most are in the Louvre due to the Revolution. There are some surviving artifacts, we would have to do some digging and possible breaking and entering." Yankee added in.

Gwendolyn started to write on the sticky notes and posted it on the wall next to the names. We kept going through the list. "Greed and Pride are done. Let's look at Desiree, the sister of lust. The word is Heart. Heart being who she truly loved." I said.

"Well, we know she was not faithful to her husband with accusations of cheating, the question is who is the person that held her heart." Hartley said. Someone had been listening to the history lessons that Gwendolyn gave.

"Xara any idea from the readings? Yankee?" I asked. I was getting more comfortable taking charge, and the momentum was going.

Xara and Yankee looked at each other, before one of them spoke. "That is to be determined, she is still a mystery but we'll dive into it," Yankee announced, writing in a notebook to further research.

"What do we know about Esmerie?" I continued on, getting up from my seat to walk around. Sometimes movement can help with the thought process.

"She's the envy sister right?" Dominic asked.

"Correct, one of the twins," Gwendolyn continued.

"From what we know, she was the youngest widow during the time they gathered," Dominic leaned back in his chair.

"She lost her husband due to an unknown illness. Instead of marrying again, she took over her family's finances and estate. Uncommon, but not far-fetched," Xara noted.

"Was it her influence from her deceased husband that gave her an edge?" Winston asked.

A woman exerting power, much less the middle child. There was a slight rebellious aspect to consider. "Her purpose for the rest of her life was controlling the family. She became manipulative, domineering because her envious nature made her controlling and seek out to prove that she still had power by taking over the family estate and power." I noted.

"But she doesn't have a capitalized letter in her stanza that Narcisse wrote." Elijah continued to point out. He was right. We all looked back at the board, under her stanza there was no capitalization.

"Could it possibly be that Narcisse held a grudge? Not support-ing her sister's status in the household?" Zacharias asked. Good observation.

"Maybe that is the clue, or the answer. The fact that she was in charge of her family... What if her key is still at the estate? Or in a family crypt?" I suggested.

"That's not a bad thought though." Gwendolyn credited me.

"So, we have keys that are hidden in a mirror, a safe, with a mysterious lover, and now a tomb. I take it that these women wanted certain things to be buried." Dominic recapped, making sure everyone was on the same page.

"Certainly seems like they don't want anything unearthed," I muttered.

"What's next?" Elijah asked.

"Gluttony, or Madame Nanette," answered Gwendolyn. I was beginning to see that spark in her blue eyes come back. She had become down and depressed, worried that this would have been a waste or disappointment. She felt like the spark was dimming and I hated to see that happen again for her.

"What's the story about her?" Hartley asked.

"The wife of a prison governor in the Bastille." Gwendolyn noted.

"I'm sorry the sister of gluttony was married to a warden? That does not make sense." Dominic said. I didn't blame him, but at first I was confused and now the pieces were coming together.

Yankee stepped up towards the board with a wide grin on his face, he had connected the dots.

"Gluttony wants more and more. Narcisse says Ironclads. Iron-clads, prisons. Ever heard of the phrase 'glutton for punishment'. Nanette may have had a desire for punishment, maybe she fancied it herself." He turned and winked at everyone.

A few of us laughed, Zacharias not so much.

"So, we have to break into Bastille and look where?" Zacharias was starting to get antsy.

"Well, it is just a start, we'll have to get into her mind and think where would hide the key." I said with hope. No one else said anything but I don't think anyone was convinced that it was in Bastille prison.

Two more sisters to get through. This was the most headway we had since everyone arrived and I didn't think we would get this far. My sister was determined and the crew slipped into a routine and old habits. I started to see relationships form again and some were taking it slow into their own relationship. I think this was the right move.

"Wrath," Xara said with a hint of fight in her.

"Martine Renaud, a temptress and warrior in her own fashion. What does the stanza say again?" Hartley said, looking back in his notebook.

"The word was Tomb and Hell." I read off again.

"Yeah, but look at what it says before that." Winston pointed.

"Sits waiting for gates to open." Elijah read off.

This time Zacharias spoke up. "She's waiting for someone who died. Wrath is full of vengeance. She wants to wait for the gates to open and Hell to be unleashed. Who died?"

"Her husband. A captain in the king's army."

"Another tomb to visit again?" Zach said sarcastically.

"Maybe a tomb, maybe a catacomb. Did we not learn anything in South America?" Elijah laughed, bringing the memory of Zach falling through a tomb in a catacomb ran through my mind. "That was one time," Zach growled.

"And it was still funny, cousin," Elijah bursted into laughter.

"Okay. Six down one to go." I commanded the room, a couple heads whipped in my direction.

"Ameline. The oldest sister." Hartley echoed.

"Was Almighty intentional, or was that just regarding the term of God?" Dominic asked.

"The sisters were not religious, or the least devoted. I would think that Almighty was intentional in the sense of a clue." Gwendolyn was studying the board again.

"Let me guess, she was married to a minister." Zacharias turned back and sat at the table.

"Not exactly, but a highly devoted nobleman. But she had some influence in the church. That's why I am thinking it is the church where her family would attend. Or one that her married life took her." Gwendolyn suggested.

The room fell silent, partially in disbelief, partially in amazement. This was what Gwendolyn wanted, the crew to come back together and solve the one puzzle that had gotten to her. We had solved or partially the clues to the sisters and we were on the path set for us.

"Wow." Dominic exclaimed, letting out a deep breath.

"Seems like we have some travel plans to get through. Let's shoot for a timeline of a week, wheels up." I said, letting everyone take a sister and look into the background and sites of where we were going.

CHAPTER 17

HARTLEY

We were actually going to do it.

We had come so far into this. We knew one thing for sure, we were going back to Paris.

Paris was the central location where the women had grown up and married into. There were certain locations like the Bastille and Treasury of Saint-Denis that were in Paris. There were a couple other locations that we needed to find first like the lost lover and the mirror. Narcisse did not remain in her hometown, but we weren't certain of the last location.

Elijah and I worked on the schematics of the city compared to eighteenth century Paris and modern day Paris. Elijah was more in his zone than before, cracking down on what history had given us. Architecture and the structure of the grounds was where he thrived, solving what time used to be.

We had come into the tech center in the manor where Xara and I set up shop. Fortunately, during the time that we were back, there wasn't any unusual activity regarding the sisters or mention of the secret library. We weren't the only ones that may have been searching for it.

"I still can't believe we are here. Thought I'd never see this place again," Elijah plastered a smile on his face.

"I think a lot of us did." I said.

I had my doubts but the determination of Gwendolyn and the support she was getting back gave me a little ease. The little sparks of hers were coming back and the team was in a good place at least for now. If Quinton could keep Gwendolyn in check and controlled, we would be in for a successful mission. We were waiting on Massey to release the funds needed for this quest.

"Bastille is going to be a challenge," Elijah noted, looking at the screening with the blueprints of Bastille or at least the eighteenth century Bastille before the French Revolution. The medieval fortress turned into a state prison. And then the French Revolution happened.

"What do you mean?" I pondered his reasoning.

"Honestly, I don't think the location is Bastille. Bastille isn't standing, Gwen knew that, if anything it's in shambles or and anything left risked looters or thieves." Elijah sounded disappointed.

"But parts of it still remain, right?" I asked.

"Let's ask an expert," I suggested.

I dialed Yankee, wanting to run this by him first before taking it to Gwen. The little spitfire would spiral if we went down a rabbit hole and it was too early for that. A few moments later, Yankee came into the center and plopped on top of an empty desk.

"I have been summoned? What can I do for you handsome gentlemen?" He flirted a bit. That was his style. Suave, gentleman-like, and an ex-con man with a heart.

"The one location is not Bastille." Elijah blurted out.

"Well, I would assume that Bastille, the actual place, is not intact. Neither is Bange de Tolon." Yankee said matter of factly.

I shook my head, "Wait, if you knew it wasn't then why didn't you speak up?"

He laughed, smiling from ear to ear, "Because my dear friend, we haven't found any other reason to believe it was somewhere else." He leaned on the desk, looking between Elijah and me.

"Then it can't be Bastille. No safe would have been recovered after the French Revolution. At least not without notice," Elijah continued.

He didn't want the impossible, neither of us wanted a wild goose chase. We had been on this quest for more than a month and already the signs of burnout were being raised to the surface.

"Don't be coy here, Yank. We need to get this down. We already have two locations we are unsure about, we don't need a third." I said, commanding that there be an end to this.

We didn't know when we were leaving for Paris but it seemed like we were running out of time.

"Ah damn, no time for play?" He pouted his lips, then rolled his eyes once he saw that we weren't amused. "Fine. You boys are no fun right now. Bring up the information on Nanette's husband?"

I turned back to the computer and pulled up the file of information we had on Nanette. I had skimmed through the file and looked for the information on her husband. Yankee jumped off the desk and smoothly walked up behind me, hands in his pockets.

"He was a governor at first at Bastille. As we know, but that couldn't have been his only posting?" I said. Yankee glanced at me with a cunning look, eyes daring to prove me wrong.

"Not that we have found. Unless your supercomputer can prove me wrong." Yankee challenged me. They all had looked into the history before but never utilized my system.

"Shall I time you man?" Elijah was getting on with this bet.

I started to cross reference Nanette's husband with any private records and anything within the eighteenth century prison records. I was confident that my system would find something, it always finds the loose strings.

It was a matter of putting the right references and knowing the timeline. After a few minutes, longer than I would have wanted, there were records of her husband's transfer papers. It didn't mean much for her unless she unexpectedly went to her husband's transferred post. Which, if we were thinking of Nanette, a glutton in true fashion, she would not pass up the opportunity.

"Well looky what it shows, a transfer from Bastille to Château d'If," Yankee announced, feeling a sense of pride.

"The same place that the dude from the Count of Monte Cristo was imprisoned," I asked.

"I thought that was a sandwich?" Elijah said innocently.

"Oh, you beautiful man." Yankee pouts, "The Count of Monte Cristo is a fiction book first and foremost. Don't worry we'll add that to your summer reading list." Yankee patted Elijah on the head.

The images showed a structure, standing still in the middle of the water, noting that it was still a tourist historical attraction.

"It's still standing." I pointed out.

"Give him a cookie ladies and gentlemen, he's a smart boy," Yankee batted his eyelashes, as he teased me for pointing out the obvious.

"Easy." I growled out.

"Looks like we'll need a boat added to the expenses." Yankee smirked. Sometimes we should be concerned when Yankee smirks, meaning he had a thought and was waiting for it to play out.

"Shall we go to Quinton and relay the news?" Yankee asked.

"Smart thing to do since he is taking the lead on this." I said.

"I don't think it was a smart choice to leave him in charge. He has been in the background majority of the time. More of a sounding board." Elijah confessed.

He was ready to go when we were back in Colorado, but something shifted in him.

"He may not be the strongest leader, but you don't see any one of us taking the helm," I comforted him. Quinton deserved the chance to get himself on the board to take charge. "Plus no one wants to truly have a handle on Gwen."

"I think you are forgetting about Winston." Yankee smirked.

"That's a different kind of handle there my friend," Elijah laughed.

We had a notch in our plan, one location we thought was where we were going to end up rerouting the plan.

We gathered around the meeting room with the new information and with Massey in the room, well over the phone.

"We'll be based out of Paris, I take it we have secured housing and security?" Quinton walked around us heading towards the board.

"I have a contact in Paris that is able to house you lot for a while." Massey calmly said. "How long are you anticipating being there?"

"No less than a month." Quinton said.

"Oh, Christmas in Paris. That should be a *fun* holiday." Yankee claps his hands.

"We are doing business Yankee, that means no hookups." Dominic, ever having the father figure perspective. Yankee raised his hands in defense.

"Why are you automatically assuming I'm going to be the problem? What about Xara, the woman can pick up anyone and leave them in a heartbreak," Yankee exclaimed, I laughed because he didn't know what I knew.

Quinton already laid claim to Xara, and I don't think Xara is going to push back no matter what she may have said.

"That's going to be a problem," Quinton said lowly, looking at Xara who just winked at everyone.

"I'll be the perfect girl scout, cross my fingers," Xara said smugly.

"We have the majority of the known locations, we'll just have to be diligent and proactive. Also, we have to work hard on the other locations. Hartley, are you still looking into any leads about Desiree's lover?" Gwendolyn stepped up but she quickly looked at everyone and Quinton and sat back down, remembering that she was not the one in charge or being the mastermind.

"Yeah. The system is checking any source between the entries to text to every inch of the continent." The system was checking everything but sometimes it's not easy to find something so hidden. That's why we were all in it for the chase.

"So, we have five locations in Paris. Come on class," Quinton wanted to add a dash of humor, but some found the annoyance. Usually it was Gwen who would rapidly fire the case and we all moved on. We all looked around waiting for someone to break the ice.

"We all know the prison will be last because it is on an island." Elijah prided himself in that, even though a few moments ago we had found out.

"Then there's the Treasury or the Louvre," Winston noted.

"The family home is on the outskirts of Paris," Zacharias said.

"Martine's husband's tomb," Dominics pointed out.

"And the church of Ameline's husband," I said. Which was yet to be known, but churches were something better than nothing.

The three historians, Yankee, Xara, and Gwen beamed with delight. We had five locations, four in Paris and one island. "Do we know what we are looking for?" Zacharias said.

"Pardon." Quinton pondered.

"What I'm asking is, do we know what we are looking for? As in does Narcisse's journal indicate what these keys look like? I mean we might as well be going on a wild goose chase." Zacharias had a point. We have the locations, we have the means and the goal, but the access to the treasure would be wise.

Gwen slammed down the journal opening up to a page with a drawing. It looked like a skeleton key, but there was a gem attached to it.

"We hunt down the locations, grab the keys" Gwen said, crossing her arms like she was ready to defend herself in a manner.

"And with all seven keys, we unlock the history." Yankee clapped his hands together.

"Why do I have the feeling that this is the most dramatic quest we have had?" Dominic entered the conversation.

"Because these sisters were dramatic, yet influential women in that time period. Women didn't have influence on their society. It was parties, marriage of convenience or arrangement, and traditional roles of being lady of the house. So, yes these women had a bit of flair to them." Gwendolyn spoke to Dom and Zach.

"One final mission and as agreed if you still want to leave and go back to your lives," there's hesitation in her voice, "then I won't stop you. But we have come this far, I don't want to turn back now when we are so close." She worked hard to get us here and we are close. We can taste it, well most of us.

"One last hurrah." I said grimly, giving everyone a chance to react. The next morning we all knew one thing. Dominic will have to either be knocked out or be drugged up.

CHAPTER 18

DOMINIC

Out of all my years of duty and private sector it was airplanes that I hated the most. I hated flying. I refused to fly but when I joined the crew I had to get over the fear or at least find something that wouldn't set off my anxiety or air sickness.

We all headed to the local airstrip where Massey had arranged for our transportation. We had packed up with the intention of being in Paris in a matter of hours. I felt a rough pat on the back from Elijah when we got to the strip and unloaded the van.

"Just like old times." He laughed.

Yeah, old times indeed never felt like old times.

Maybe our last.

The thought spiraled in my mind, I didn't think we all would walk away, for some it might be easier. There were still a few that were staggering behind feeling that this would be the last time.

"You got your patches?" Zach came up, grabbing his bag and supplies.

I tapped my breast pocket on my coat. These had been a lifesaver for long trips like this. Something about flying makes me pass out, didn't bode well back in the Army.

"Ready to get the show on the road and be done?" He asked me.

"Zacharias, let me ask you something?" I peered at him through my sunglasses, he cocked an eyebrow. "Why are you so adamant that this is going to be the last time? You, Xara, and Winston are all very hesitant to say why you didn't want to come back. So, be honest brother," I swung my duffel over my shoulder.

I gave him a few moments to collect an answer. He, out of all of them, was giving the most lip and push back, other than figuring out a crucial element, it seemed like he just stood back, watching everything, putting his own input when it wasn't warranted.

For someone that was in the medical field, promising to care for others and do what's best, I don't think his best intentions were lined up. I grew concerned with him even with the month that we had been at the manor.

He looked down like he couldn't give me an answer but he sighed.

"It wasn't your family's lives at stake." He put.

Elijah looked at me then at his cousin, probably searching for a way to apologize for his own cousin's words. I started to walk away, because after all the years that I had seen him and had come to me for advice, he'd start thinking more about this team as a family, rather than a ride along.

I yelled back at him, "You may be right, but thought you considered us all family at one point." I headed towards the plane, knowing that take off would be soon.

Stepping onto the plane felt right, although I wasn't looking forward to the chance of being sick.

Gwen was sitting on a larger couch section, but she had sprawled out and let her size take up half the couch.

I grabbed her stretched legs and put them over my lap to sit next to her. I felt bad I hadn't checked in with her, remembering the promise I had given her uncle many years ago.

"Little one, how are you holding up? First quest that you aren't in charge of," I patted her legs, she gave me a soft smile, her blue eyes sparkling.

"I'm okay." She started to say. I gave her legs a gentle squeeze as she continued, "I mean, I don't entirely like it. I feel like I'm not seeing the entire board in front of me. I don't feel like I see the whole board," She felt like she wasn't doing enough.

"I find that hard to believe. You have worked so hard and without that journal, we would still be separated and this library would still be lost," I tried to comfort her. "But what I want to know is, have you made amends with him over there?" I nodded my head in Winston's direction, he had pulled out his tablet and headphones, spacing out from the rest of us.

"A few weeks ago, but the man was stubborn. I tested the line, every bump, every chance I had, but he has been stagnant." She said in a low voice, I didn't know whether she was ashamed of herself or the situation. "I told him I wasn't running anymore. I laid out what I wanted. Who knows if it will be enough. Attempted to be patient."

"And what is it that you want?"

She glanced away, mumbling something, until I nudged her. "I'm sorry I can't quite hear you over this mane of your hair." I said.

"I wanted him to be more. I wanted what he wanted back then."

"And you want it now." She couldn't fool me. She had been wanting to be closer to Winston, but youngsters don't always know what they want, especially when it comes to love.

"Obviously." There was so much in her head that I wish I could have helped work out for her.

"Give him what he needs. He'll come around." I said to her, patting her legs one more time. "He was hurt, he was ready to chase you anywhere, but you didn't want to chase him. Time is what he needs."

"When did you become a wise old man?" She started to get cheeky.

"I may be old, but I can still whoop your ass."

"Bring it on, gray hairs." She said playfully.

I remember when I met my wife and the happy life we had built, that was all I wanted for them. At a young age she lost her world, I knew what that felt like and it was not something I would wish for unto anyone. But she had love right there. Maybe I just need to give a little more push, in the right direction.

The engines were starting to roar and I had slapped a sickness patch on my neck, ready to go. Gwen didn't move from her spot and she had been comfortable where she was. She had buckled up, as did everyone else.

Everyone was loaded up and ready to take off, until Hartley yelled, that surprised us all. The boom in his voice was enough to startle even the birds on the runway.

"Son of a bitch." He had yelled, which is not very often.

"What happened Hart?" Quinton taking off his glasses.

The impending silence was deafening. All eyes were on Hartley, the look in his own eyes was grave.

"Apparently we are not the only ones looking for this library." He started to get cryptic.

It wasn't the first time this would happen. We had been on quests before other interested groups had come along. They'd come along and challenge us to a foot race to take what we wanted. In the end, even if we lost it, we'd get it back in the end.

"I mean, that was part of your job, to look out for interested parties, why you making sound like it's the end of it all?" Winston snapped for a moment.

"I was doing the same thing as you were." Xara popped in, yet sounded offended. "I haven't found anything."

The anticipation kept all our eyes on Hartley.

"Get to the point, Hart," Quinton said.

"Might need to tell the pilot to stall for a moment, this is going to blow a few gaskets." Hartley was trying to be strategic.

Quinton exited the cabin to go see the pilot in the cockpit and came back, bidding a few extra minutes, the engines had grown quieter. Hartley started to control the monitor that was in the front of the cabin and staring us in the face was someone we thought had vanished years ago after someone had put him in his place. The same wavy blonde hair, tailored dress shirt and slacks. The snake of a smile with a curl on his lips. A camera image on the busy streets in France.

Augustus St. Germain.

A low-life bachelor. A socialite from a wealthy and well known family in Europe.

A thief

A con man.

And Gwendolyn's ex.

Her body had gotten cold and clammy against me. The life of her warmth escaped her, her walls coming back to defend what hope she had left in this world.

It was one thing that she, I know, regretted her entire life, allowing him to manipulate her and mess with her mind. She was still afraid of him in her eyes, her own kryptonite that threatened to bring back the darkness that once flooded her mind.

Winston jolted at the pictures, probably ready to bury someone once and for all. His body tenses, as his breathing became harsher.

"How?" It was Zacharias that spoke up. A question we all wanted to know the answer to.

"He's resurfaced after all these years. It's been, what, five years?" Elijah interjected.

Six years actually.

She had reached her own breaking point, where we could talk with her and get her out of the situation that flooded her life like a toxin. The flashes of a worn out woman, a woman who could barely stand on her own comes across my mind, haunting the time for a moment I thought I failed her uncle.

"He's going after the Madames as well. Not surprising. But why now?" Xara said.

Gwendolyn had stayed quiet and when she remained quiet, you could hear all the thoughts in her head.

Winston didn't move, but I could sense anger in him boiling to the top.

"Please tell me this motherfucker is not going to get in our way, again," Winston seethed with steam.

"We don't know that for sure," Quinton tries to calm everyone down and in my opinion, is not doing well.

"The snake comes out when he gets a sniff of what is going on. He had to have a tip, or something. This is no coincidence. No way that this man, the lowlife of a man, just comes back after all these years," Zacharias goes into a tailspin.

"If he is after the Madame's library, we have to be ten steps ahead of him. We are smarter than he is, and seeing him should be more motivation for you all to want this more." I said, commanding a bit more than what Quinton had to offer.

"He fried our systems last time we tried to out smart him, he knows what he is doing. He may be a pretty face, but the fucker knows his shit." Xara reasoned again. "He's lucky I didn't put a hit out on him on the dark web."

"Let's just get to Paris before we fall behind. We don't need the past to affect our goal. If you'll excuse me," Quinton brushed past everyone back to the cockpit.

"That's all you got?" Hartley spoke up.

The noise and commotion stood still, Quinton gathered himself to look at his friend, "What else do you want me to do?"

"Fight back? Give us some sort of encouragement that we are a team, I don't know," Yankee chimed in.

Quinton hung his head in defeat, already giving up easily. How much more fight could one person have?

Everyone pretty much spoke except Yankee and Gwendolyn, well until Yankee broke from his silence. Yankee was already pulling out his flask from his inside jacket pocket. Gwendolyn remained silent.

"Hey. Look, you have your family back, he is not going to touch you." I coaxed her. Silently wishing that Winston would move his ass over and take over.

We remember the last time he had his hands on her. The crew was ready to take action. It was a horrid scene, seeing her in a ball, almost like a shell of a person. She wouldn't say anything about what happened but it doesn't take much to see that whatever happened, it did some damage. He was a snake, cunning, and charming in the most disgusting way.

"Come on Gwen. Focus." her legs still resting over my lap, like a statue unable to move. Her face was pale, cold even to the touch. "Come on kid, I know this is a shake up, but you can't let him overpower you again. You are a Griffin and I know if Max was here, he'd say what to you?" I peered into her eyes, waiting for a response.

She finally turned as the jet engines turned on, "Face it and Conquer it."

Maxx used to say that to me whenever I told him that he was nuts about doing what he did and going where he was going. He passed on the wisdom to her.

"Atta girl."

"Thanks Dom." She offered a soft smile.

Before we knew it we were up in the air, being transported to the other side of the water. Everyone had settled into their positions, off on their own little mindset. Gwendolyn went back to flipping through her notes and the journal, Xara and Hartley went back to accessing their systems and mainframes.

Winston was still to himself, hadn't moved since we were on the tarmac. This was not the same group that started it all years ago, and frankly they all needed a kick in the ass. Honestly, I was not afraid to do it. No better time than now, before we land people to go off in their own direction.

I moved Gwen's legs off of me. I didn't care if my air sickness was going to get to me, but I would be damned if I continued on seeing what I have been seeing. Gwen was startled, the books falling out of her grasp. I stood up, clearing my throat.

"Alright. I'm going to say something and y'all better listen before things get ugly. For the past month or so I have seen your ghosts." Everyone raising an eyebrow, questioning me, possibly concerned for me. "You all can act like nothing's bothering you or you are working for forgiveness. Honestly, we might as well turn the damn plane around," I wasn't going to be gentle. I stayed silent for a longer time, just watching.

"I'm sure that everyone is going to say that everything is fine or you all will work on it. Drop the act and start acting like yourselves. You all act like you don't care, that this doesn't excite you. I am seeing less of a team or a family than before." I pointed at Gwen. "She just saw an ex that tormented her and nearly broke her, and not one person said anything about her well-being. What the fuck is the matter with you all? Did you all become selfish over the years?" The anger that was pent up for a while is fuming.

I couldn't believe that this was once a unified group.

Quinton tried to stand up, but I shook my head. "No bud, your sister put you in charge and instead your ass has been acting a sidekick, just acting like he was the leader. Do better." He sat back down.

Zacharias tried to say something but I glared in his direction. "Zacharias, I know damn well you aren't about to tell me it isn't about you either. You act like you don't want to be here. You are your own person, you didn't want to be here, fine, leave. You have been helpful and that is not going unnoticed. But brother, stop acting childish."

Winston just stared at me and I was ready to speak my mind. "I'm not going to tear you all down, that's not who I am, but I sat back quietly letting you take control of what *you* needed and I was sick of it. If we don't get our act together, someone is going to get hurt like last time." My stomach was getting nauseous, I had to sit down. Everyone was lost in thought.

"I haven't been a fair nor right leader." Quinton admitted. "Truthfully. I don't think I was the right person for it."

"I have been an asshole." Zacharias commented. A few snickers spread across the plane. He wasn't wrong.

"We're going around saying what's wrong with us?" Xara asked. She sighed, "Fine, I've been too much in my own mind to know what I want and it affects me." Then daggers in her eyes, "Anyone repeat that, they'll wake as FBI's most wanted." She would have no guilt on her face.

"I just wanted to be back around our crew again. I missed the action and way things were." Hartley flashed a devious grin, made a few chuckles at that.

"I wasn't ready to go last time. But I'm not overstepping people's boundaries." Elijah remarked.

Winston crossed his arms, pursed his lips. "I let my hurt dictate what is in front of me and forgot to be a friend to everyone." He looked back at Gwen.

"I was the one who ruined it for everyone and put my own desires before everyone." Gwen admitted. "And screwed up something good when I had it." That was only for Winston.

"Yankee anything you want to say?" I turned to him, normally he was never quiet.

He cleared his throat and made a big gesture, opening his mouth. "I just wanted to cause mayhem with you all like we did in Rio."

Flashbacks of Elijah in Carnival and them trying to find Xara, Quinton, and Yankee after a wild night.

"Families fight, they go through a period of hate, but deep down they do love each other. Enough of the pity parties, it's time to get to work." I sat back down.

I was too old for this shit, these childish games that I didn't want to be a part of.

Quinton leaned forward, over the table in front of him. "I'm going to make a suggestion." He paused, "I'm removing myself as leader."

"That wasn't the deal buddy." "Can't do that brother." Xara and Gwen yelled together.

He raised up a hand to interrupt. "No, but obviously there is one person that is better than me," He looked at me, "Dominic."

Well, I didn't see that coming.

That wasn't the plan. I left leadership a long time ago and allowed others to do that. "Obviously you were more ready to kick our asses and straighten us out. I have failed to pull the team together in that direction, so Dominic I believe it should be you, the rest of the mission."

"That wasn't my plan." I said defensively.

Gwen put a hand on my shoulder. "But it's the plan we need. I haven't won everyone over to take over nor do I need to."

"You'd leave the old man in charge?"

"We would be leaving the right person in charge." She reassured me.

"I mean Dom, it's not like you're herding a bunch of cats or anything." Yankee commented.

"No, more like a bunch of teenagers with raging hormones." I muttered.

I thought for a moment, if everyone is putting their trust in me, that has to mean something. I nod my head, accepting the position. For once, the crew seemed happier even if it's just for a moment.

"Stop acting like children and start being the people we need you to be," I said as we jetted to Paris.

CHAPTER 19

GWENDOLYN

Maybe I should have put Dominic in charge in the beginning. My brother has many wonderful and useful qualities and maybe I jumped the bullet and thought I could make him a leader. But there was a better, obvious choice. I stayed quiet the rest of the trip. I was trapped within my own mind and thoughts.

I saw that figure on the feed, and my nerves were shot. I left everything in the past and it got me again. I could feel the weight of it all, putting pressure on me. Everything I survived and suppressed coming back like it was a new experience.

August was no ordinary man. He came from power and high society, he had hidden protections that made him invincible. He wasn't who my mind made him out to be. His words were too smooth to allow me to see clearly. His tone muted everyone around me. And the regret I feel was I tried to convince myself like I did to others that he wouldn't hurt me. He had manipulated me, I was his puppet. I had fallen for a monster, someone that was covered in ugliness.

There was a point where I called him out on what others were seeing and when he answered if backfired on me. Broke me mentally and physically.

"You were easily fooled. A pretty face with foolish hopes."

"You thought I loved you, oh princess, you were just another body. One I'll keep using for my own pleasure."

"You wanted my attention, even brought me along to the crew. You made me richer and gave me access to a world of possibilities."

"You think you can get rid of me that easily? I'll come back one day, princess. Just you wait."

Those were just previous words that ran through my head. I learned to silence them. I can blame all day for my actions, I was the one that put myself in that situation and dragged everyone into it. I just didn't know that a couple years later, I would do the same thing again, severely hurting someone else.

Winston moved closer to me on the plane, but he couldn't look at me. I didn't need him to treat me like I was precious or fragile, I just needed him to provide a small bit of comfort and pull me out of my haze.

We landed near Paris, being waited by Massey's contacts to be transported into the city. One of the gracious contacts of his gave us access to a flat, occupying an east and west wing. Thankfully it wasn't at the very top or the stairs would have screwed us.

Everyone buddied up with rooms to make it easier on space. There was a sense of calm, but I think there are still going to be some things that have to be worked out. Including a tall, muscular, dark skinned man that has not made movement. But that was going to change.

"Round up everyone, we have some planning to get through this week." Dominic called out, getting everyone to the main room. They had set up shop with the boards and the notes we had back in the manor.

The first key to find, ended up being trickier than expected. We knew that the key was originally in the Treasury of Saint-Denis, but during the French Revolution, items were lost and some survived. Through Yankee's knowledge and understanding, surviving pieces had been presented to the Louvre and have been archived in their facility.

That was going to be fun. At least, I had hoped that for once I'd feel the rush again, even if it's for a moment.

It was going to take a con artist and a couple of hackers to be geniuses once more.

Thanks to Elijah and Hartley, we had the schematics for the Louvre, understanding the points of impact and where the cameras and or security might be. We all would be in place throughout the levels of the museum and ready at will to be distractions, as long as nobody ends up being locked up at this time.

"Do we need to go over this plan? I feel like anytime we go over a plan, it ends up being thrown in the trash because one of us is not prepared or it's not working out the way we need it to," Zacharias whined.

I glared at him to shut up, we were finally in a good place and we were ready for this.

I started to move, ready to lunge at him, "Quinton or Winston, calm her ass down, she's ready to pounce and I don't think in an enjoyable way." Zach cracked up, my nerves were already shot, I went to move, and two hands were placed on my shoulders, I turned around to see Winston pushing me back down.

"Easy Winnie, save it for later," He whispered in my ear. There was a slight hope in those words.

Dominic just ignored him, and Zacharias pouted in his seat like a petulant, grumpy ass child.

"Alright, now, Yankee, thanks to his thieving ways, was able to swipe access down to the archives. While he's down there, he will be requesting to visit the section on Saint-Denis, since it was a previous exhibition. He will be on comms, while Xara and Hartley will be on duty for cameras and sensors. Everyone else will scatter, because once Yankee is back, we only have a few minutes before the archive workers will figure out that something is missing." Dominic scanned the levels and pointed out everyone being on each level.

It was a solid plan, one that many would see in movies, and sometimes it doesn't go as planned. But each of us were talented and skillful enough.

"Hartley and I will erase any data that comes through with Yankee's identity, though I wouldn't mind seeing what his real name is." Xara grinned.

"And y'all will never know," Yankee mused.

"I will remain on the second level or -1 level, gravitating towards the stairs for a quicker round up. As soon as Yankee leaves the second basement, everyone will need to migrate out leaving the levels." Dominic instructed.

"Gwen and I will be on the zero level, mainly near the stairs toward the Greek and Roman antiquities." Winston gripping my shoulders. He was putting us as a pair into it, this was going to be interesting.

"I will be on the level up, ready to go, for any distractions." Elijah grinned. "I know the place can be a maze, but stick towards the main stairwell, when exiting. We all know the meeting point after?"

We nodded, just a couple of blocks was a small cafe that we had scoped out earlier in the day.

"We have the identification for Yankee to use, but the Louvre has been updating security measures and we don't know what Augustus is up to, since the CTV, there has been no additional sighting of him, but we should be aware of our surroundings," Hartley warned. There hasn't been any more sighting of him, but the snake knows when to pop up and strike when the timing is right.

"I promise to be the most well-behaved man ever," Yankee gave a flirtatious smirk.

"When hell burns and God steps down. Just don't land yourself in jail," Zacharias joked, which was surprising.

"Please, I look good in handcuffs," Yankee winked.

"Any questions?" Dominic asked before we all dispersed and rested for the evening. We all looked around waiting for anyone else to speak up or even comment. After a few moments, we all left, some left the building to venture out into the city, I stayed behind, I typically do.

Quinton jokes that I see everything, every hidden clue or puzzle, I stayed behind focusing on if there was anything else I was missing, answering any roaming questions. The building was quiet, you could hear every footstep or creak of the floorboard, to say I was surprised who ended up in my room, loaming over me, was no surprise at all.

"You know you can come in, no need to lurk in the shadows," I said, calling from the bed I had landed on after everyone supposedly left.

I had cracked open my computer and the journal and my journal as well.

Winston's heavy footsteps creaked on the floor, his body leaned up against the door frame, I looked up through my glasses. Something was on his mind. He didn't say anything but sulked into the room, twiddling with the fixtures in the room. It wasn't a highly decorated room, but a comfortable set up for the building and aesthetic.

"Win, please. If you want to talk, then talk," I told him.

Ever since the library, he has pulled away again and I feel I have given him space and tested when appropriate at times. But everything was up to him, it was the respectful thing to do. I know in the end, he wasn't trying to punish me, when you grow up in the lives we have, many deaths and people leaving us, it's never easy. That is why we hang on to everything we have, and protect it.

He sat in a chair across from me, his arms stretching behind him, rubbing his neck.

Take the hint, Winston.

"I'm sorry Gwen," his voice solemnly said.

Sorry? Why was he apologizing to me?

"Was there something to apologize for?" I raised an eyebrow.

He couldn't look me in the eyes. "Winston, why are you sorry?" I asked again, wanting to reach out to have him in my hands.

"I wasn't there for you on the plane." He confessed. He looked ashamed, guilty that he wasn't there.

"I wasn't expecting you to do anything. It was much of a shock to me as well as everyone else. Even Yankee froze, I was half expecting that he would have been halfway through his flask," I reassured him.

But Yankee and I understood the reason behind it. That would be another story for another day.

He shook his head, not agreeing with me. "I should have said something or at least came to you or something, I don't know. I don't know why this is hard." He put his head in his hands, there was a moment of confusion, of vulnerability.

"Winston, things don't have to be perfect. I gave you space for a reason. You chased me through the years, my turn to do it." I hung my legs over the bed, striding my way to him.

He was still hanging his head, and at the moment, I needed him like he was for me in the library, showing what strength was when your childhood crush broke your heart and came back in the beginning for selfish reasons.

I reached for him, cupping my hands over his hands, forcing him to look up at me.

"How long are we going to punish ourselves for being imperfect and wanting each other in our lives? How many times is fate going to give us a second chance, or a third chance? I'm sorry that I confused you and allowed you to feel like you didn't know what to do." My thumb rubbing his face, his dark hungry brown eyes looking into mine.

Come on Winston. Please.

"You don't have anything to apologize for. I think we have done enough of that. Are you ready to stop?" That's all I could think about.

I stopped sulking around, feeling down for not doing something. I had one more attempt up my sleeve.

"If you want to apologize for not being there for me, then do something else for me," I said, holding his gaze at me, "Please, erase him out of my mind, erase the thought of his touch from my skin. Let there be you, and only you."

I pleaded with him, and before I knew it, he kicked the chair back and lifted me like I was a feather, allowing me to wrap my legs around him.

"No more running," He snarled. The deep bass melted me. I shook my head in response, "No more running."

"Only me." he said, kissing me fiercely, possessively, ravishing me, like an animal that has been starving for decades. I moaned in his mouth. Years of pent up tension and frustration, years of yearning for the chance.

The guilt and horrible feeling of screwing up, melted away. It was like our bodies were one, like we were complete. His passion fused within the kiss and I just wanted more and more from him, anything he would give me. This would be the last and only man I would sink down to my knees for and never regret it.

I nipped at his lower lip, and let out a chuckle. "I told you that was for later." The slight twinge of animalistic nature in him unleashed, almost like a caged animal finally being released.

"You little minx," He mumbled against my lips. He walked us to my bed, both of us landing like a rock. I had the slight fear that we would go through the floor. Winston was no lean man, he was massive in the most endearing, drool worthy.

And he was mine. Finally.

He didn't move, almost like he was taking in the moment and letting things happen. I reached for his face, caressing his face, he turned his head kissing my palm.

"Erase all the bad memories, it's you and me. Win and Winnie." I sighed.

His hands went into my hair, gripping as to anchor himself, but pulling my chin up towards him. His knees were in between my legs, kicking them apart. "I am the only one that can kiss you like this." He worked his way from the top of my head, kissing every inch. Tracing the outline of my face, trailing down my neck to my chest.

I ached for more, like a boiler ready to let out steam. As his mouth started to explore my upper body, his hand that was once were in my hair was traveling lower, unbuttoning my jeans, slowly taking the zipper down. My hips guided his hand to know what I needed, what I wanted.

"These are in the way." He snickered.

"Sounds like you need to do something about it." I teased him.

His touch ignited a fire within me and I was burning up. Like a fireball hitting my chest, expanding across my skin. All the anticipation led to this.

"Are you fond of the shirt or the bra?" He asked.

I shook my head, and like a flash he ripped open the shirt, a couple buttons landing on the floor. He rushed to take it completely off sliding off the bra straps and one handed snapped opened my bra.

I was bare, or at least half way there. He sat back on his knees, straightening up like a beast assessing his prey before he devoured it whole. He stared at me, and his gaze made me shiver, enough to make my nipples hard.

If this man didn't put his hands back on me, I was going to take charge.

He strips off his shirt, and slowly leans forward just hovering over me. I reached for his pants trying to unbutton and speed this up before I combust. He swatted at my hand, grabbing my wrists and pinning them above me. "Don't make me find some zip ties or Dominic's cuffs."

"You wouldn't," I dared him.

Yes please.

"I would." he studied me, finding my amusement in the idea of restraints. "You'd like that a little too much. Don't worry, there will be time." His grip tightened on my wrists, my body arched to meet his, "Let me take my time, I have been waiting for this for a long time, Gwendolyn Griffin, and I will take my damn time enjoying every moment, just to finish and start over and do it over and over again. Do. You. Understand." His voice was gravelly, demanding, hot.

I nodded my head in agreement.

"Yes."

"Yes what?" He tested me, waiting to see if I was finally released from the barrier I held up for a long time. The dam that he busted out of me, one that wanted nothing but to be his.

"Yes sir," I said, trembling.

"That's my beautiful woman," He sinisterly grinned.

His hand still pinned my wrists above my head, his other hand yanking my jeans down. I wondered how long it would take him to notice, it's just my jeans.

As the fabric was ripped from my lower half, he let out a small fake gasp, "You weren't wearing anything this whole time?"

I shook my head, "Did you really think I waste good underwear when I'm just relaxing in the room?"

He shook his head, "Let's not tell pretty lies. You were waiting for me."

I gave a gentle shrug.

"Mm, it's just easy access." He said before his thumb started to rub the sensitive clit, I was past the point of aching, now I was just wanton, in a lustful state.

I whimpered, he knew that this pace was killing me internally. "I'm going to let go of your wrists, you're going to be good and let me have this." I nodded my head.

Yes, take what you need.

Winston spreads my legs apart giving him more access as he sunk down, his thumb still roaming over my clit. My hips start to buck against him. He started to nip inside my thighs, then replacing it with tantalizing kisses. I started moaning louder and then quickly silenced myself, hoping that no one would come back early and hear me.

"You won't be keeping silent for long, babygirl," And with that his mouth closed over my pussy, beginning to ravish me. His tongue flicking over every sensitive nerve, sending what feels like fireworks through me. He began sucking on my clit and pumping a finger in and out of me, sending me in oblivion, I was beginning to feel everything let go.

Every stress, every bad memory being erased. The only person I want touching me, making me feel this way with me. He continues the pattern, inserting another finger, I become more and more of a sloppy mess, but it doesn't bother him. I'm right there on the edge, I was close, I was clenching around his fingers, and he... stopped.

My breathing became heavier and I wanted to scream, I was close.

But before I could knock some sense into him, he already had his pants and briefs off. I whimpered, wanting him back to me. I sat up and reached him, I wanted to play as well. But he shook his head with his beautiful smile and guided me back. "There will be plenty of time for that. I think I know what we need," he said.

"I was close!" I whined, a bit of being a brat.

"I don't want you coming around my fingers, Gwen. When you come, it will be around cock, the one you have be desperately wanting. You want it stretching you wide, taking every bit of that orgasm. Only to have you milk me dry. That's what you want isn't it?" He teased me with the cock rubbing outside of my pussy ready to thrust inside me.

"Yes, Winston. You wanted me, have me, take me." Every tease he sends me, I start to whimper. "I'm on birth control and clean. Please." I begged him, both of us worked up to this moment.

"There has not been anyone else since you came back to me the first time. I'm clean."

"Fine, you're clean, I'm clean, and no babies! Now can you just fuck me!" I growled.

A simple *smack* on my clit made me jumped off the bed, "Such a dirty fucking mouth."

We got that out of the way, we both knew what we wanted. Nothing between us. Just us two.

Winston plunged himself inside me, taking every inch of him. He pulled me in a bruising kiss, as my legs wrapped around him as he drove into me. My hands on his back, my nails digging into his skin. He growled at the sensation.

Each thrust was everything I needed, everything we needed. His hips guiding into movement. He picked up the speed faster and faster until he was hitting me deep inside. Nothing between us but the pure desire to be one.

The growing pleasure wanted to explode at the pace that he set.

"Winston, please let me come."

"Asking permission, are we?" He chuckled then slowed down his pace. "You want to come, little minx," He took his cock out, and got off the bed. "On all fours, ass towards the edge of bed and up," He instructed me.

I crawled towards the edge of the bed and on my hands and knees, quickly not to lose the momentum we had. He stepped closer to me, running a hand down my spine. He dug his fingers into my cheeks.

"One day, I'll paint these red, and every time you sit down, you'll remember one thing." he said.

"Remember what?"

"That you are mine. And I am yours." He said huskily. Then he dove back into me with a deep thrust. It hit every spot that would make the stars sing.

Fuck, I have been stupid for not taking a chance sooner.

He picked up speed, I could feel myself dripping, from sweat, sex, and ecstasy. His one hand that was on my spine and then threaded into my hair, taking a grip of it. The pain added a new sensation that I was slightly getting addicted to.

"Fuck, please." was all I could say.

A mixture of my moans and his grunts, we were both close. "Rub your pussy. Come for me."

He didn't have to tell me twice. The tightness of tension building ready to release. Between rubbing my clit in circles and him thrusting into me, a few moments later I was riding the wave of pleasure, allowing the Paris night sky to not be the only one having stars tonight.

I think I must have screamed his name as I came around him because in a few more strokes, he was chasing his high. He collapsed over me. Giving soft kisses over my shoulders.

We stayed like that for a few moments, catching our breath, waiting to see if our bodies would catch up after the rush.

He finally left my body and left me to crawl back onto the bed all the way. I could feel him dripping down my leg. Normally, it is not my style. But for Winston, knowing that it's his, marking me as his and only his, slowly was going to be my favorite thing.

He came back to the room and brought a warm washcloth. Through sleepy eyes, I watched reach for my legs, opening me back up. He started to wipe himself off of me.

We were both in need of a shower, but I rather lay there with the man that had my heart for a bit longer, even if I had told him that I started to fall for him and that I was stupid for not taking the chance earlier.

But that would be another time for that. He softly kisses the inside of thighs and reaches for his briefs and his shirt. He had pulled his briefs back on and given me his shirt, more like he dressed me.

Winston laid between my legs and rested his head on my stomach, wrapping his arms around me. I saw a small smile of content on his face. We were in our safe spot. Moments of bliss. I wanted to freeze the moment.

Finally, Win and Winnie were back together and Winnie would never mess it up again, so at least I prayed that I didn't.

CHAPTER 20

YANKEE

It was the day that we would be one step closer to unraveling the truth. The Louvre is the most exclusive and well-known icon in the world. To say that it would be easy to just grab and go is an understatement.

We all gathered in the main room gearing up for the first part of this quest, some of us had an eventful evening the night before. I looked over at Gwendolyn and Winston, there was a better aura around them, something warm and loving. They just appeared lighter than the day before.

The softest hint of a smile as Winston assisted Gwendolyn with her items. That, and we all saw them pass out in her bed, we didn't say anything, also they didn't close the door, we let them have their moment, even though some of them wondered where Xara would end up. *I knew.*

Xara came up behind me giving me the badge and identification I would need to access the archives. "Seriously, no bullshit. In and out. That's all we need. We have to get to the other keys before anything else." She warned me.

"I promise, *Dr. McCormick*, will be on his best behavior." I said, crossing my heart.

Dr. Alec McCormick, a professor and historian from Oxford, or at least that is the identity that they gave me. I needed a likely backstory and enough of a mindset and knowledge of that world to fool anyone. It's the person of the disguise you have to worry about trusting more than the man under it.

"I'm willing to put money on it if you do something stupid and raise awareness down there." Hartley betted.

"I'm betting against that. You underestimate me, my dear boy," I threw out the British accent as part of the guise.

Hartley shook his head and grabbed the keys from the table in front of me. "Come on Xara, we need to get there before everyone else," Xara and Hart left the flat, to move on to their next step.

The plan was for the tech geniuses leave before us to gain access to the mainframe without detection, allowing them to remain "our eyes" with all the cameras and security that circles the place.

Everyone else would stagger in, taking their positions ready to start a distraction if something were to go wrong, which it wouldn't. Everyone would have their comms and their phones. Gwendolyn especially because although she was the notorious by name historian of the group, she would be recognizable, and since we have a ghost that has emerged, it was the safer route. No one was truly expecting me.

We were all on more of a high alert because of Augustus.

His name created goosebumps on my skin, like a negative energy leaving your body.

I didn't know if that was fear, bad memories, or even guilt.

His picture woke up something in me, and Gwen saw, and she felt it. She knew I still carried around guilt because of him.

If it wasn't for me, he wouldn't have entered her life. For if it wasn't for me and introducing him to her that night at the gala, she wouldn't have gone through all that she did.

The crew didn't know the whole story of how they met, well more like the half truth of where they met. Just not how they met and by whom.

Each one of them left a few minutes after each other, I didn't activate the comms until I arrived. I grabbed the rest of the gear and made my way out the door. It doesn't take long for me to arrive at the Louvre. According to the schematics, my entrance was separate from the common one.

I twisted my earpiece in and soon I could hear everyone and chatter.

"Yank has arrived. Everyone in place?" Dominic's voice boomed in my ear.

"Gwen and I are in place." Winston echoes along.

"Same." Elijah announced.

"Yep. Ready. Can I ask something though?" Zacharias said.

"Technically you did." Dominic laughed.

"I don't think some of us look like they belong in an art museum." Zacharias said, I'm still failing to see the question.

"Zach, ever the brawns never the brains sometimes friend. You have to remember that this was no museum but a historic castle. That's why at the bottom you can walk the original moat." I said, giving him a brief history lesson.

"I feel like I stick out like a sore thumb." He said.

"No one told you to wear plaid," Xara booms through, arguing with him like a sister would.

"Quinton, any help here? Help him blend in," Gwen suggested.

"Zacharias, the more you worry about if you fit in here, the more you are going to have eyes on you. Just enjoy the level you are on and take in the sights," Quinton had the brilliant mind of settling nerves or second thoughts.

"Focus, keep the comms clear, in case we have to go to plan B. Yankee, do you have the glasses?" Dominic reminded me. Hartley and Xara were able to pull together a pair of glasses that allowed everyone to see what I'm seeing. This would come in handy than rummaging through the archives here, looking for a mysterious key that we don't know what it looks like.

"Hart, are they working?" I asked to make sure that they function properly.

After a few clicks and noises, Hartley came back on. "Picture is decent. Not the best, I'll try to work on the resolution. Gwen, can you check on your phone?" He asked.

"Picture is fine on my end, I think there is a small lag. Like the picture freezes for a moment and then goes back to normal," Gwen analyzed the screen she was seeing.

"We'll fix it on our end. But we are clear. No snakes, no vultures on camera." Hartley said. I wasn't surprised that they had hacked into the system, taking control over the feed and if necessary making it seem like we were ghosts.

I approached the welcome desk in the building, looking for navigation on where I needed to go. The hustle and bustle of the museum echoed like a cave. Murmurs of individuals roaming through. Groups of students filled the entrances ways. For everyone it was a typical day, for us it was another day in the office.

"*Bonjour,*" Greeted the receptionist.

"Hello," I said in a British accent.

"Ah, English. How can I help you?" The thick French accent came out, barely understanding her.

"Yes, I have an appointment with Professor Laurent. I believe he is expecting me," I leaned forward, flashing a smile.

"*Oui.* Dr. McCormick. *Un minut, s'il vous plait.*" She said, dialing her phone to call downstairs I imagined.

"Doing well, Yankee." Dominic cooed in my ear.

"We're not out of the woods yet. Play the part. Get in, look through, get out." Gwen said.

I imagine the crew roaming through the hallways. Zacharias questioned the art pieces that cover the walls. Elijah admired the structure around him, taking in every bit of design and architecture ingenuity. Quinton looking around people watching, analyzing the body language of others.

But the two I was curious about were Gwen and Winston. After their night last night, I had hoped it wasn't a fluke. I needed the distraction from my nerves.

A con man that gets nervous, who would have guessed it.

"Heads up, receptionist is returning." Xara echoed in my ear, I turned my attention back to the front desk.

I flashed a toothy smile her way. "Professor Laurent will be with you momentarily. Is this your first time?" Her thick accent was starting to get hard to understand. I started to underestimate myself. I was hoping that Xara was listening in.

"She's asking you if this is your first time at the museum, you dunce." Xara sneered over the comms. Thank you goddess.

"*Oui.* My first time in Paris. Especially around this time of year." I said, trying to hide the nerves.

Had it been that long that I started to doubt myself and skills? The receptionist nodded and looked back at the main desk. My heart started to race, like the thumping was overpowering my ears.

"Yank, I hear the nerves. Settle down. Remember when we first met?" Gwen softly said. I followed her voice through memory lane. "Don't respond. But you know you almost had me there. You were so convincing that I second guessed myself. You are brilliant and mischievous. Use that. Get out of your head."

I got out of my head to see that someone was coming my way and from the sweater vest and slacks combination and the balding head this was the man I was to meet with. Not my type, but he seemed kind of cute, innocent, and precious.

"Ah, Dr. McCormick. Nice to finally meet you." He extended his hand to shake.

"Yes, thank you for meeting with me on this matter." I returned the handshake as we made our way through the winding stairs and hallways. We traveled downstairs to the lower levels and down another hallway or two. I wiggled my comm which was the signal to check in with the feed.

"I can hear you buddy." Zacharias said. "The sooner we get what we came for the better."

"Camera feed is holding steady." Hartley confirmed. I adjusted the frames.

"Doing well. Keep it up." Gwen cooed.

"Speaking of keeping it up, Winston, you good over there big fella." Xara laughed.

I had to keep my composure, suppressing the snicker that was in my throat. But internally I was dying of laughter.

"There's a difference between watching out for trouble with the camera and being a stalker." Winston growled out.

"Well, if you didn't make it obvious, no one would see." Gwen giggled out.

"Well, if someone wouldn't rub her ass on me, I wouldn't have a boner." He growled out.

"I didn't need to know." Quinton groaned.

"Neither did I," Dominic said.

"Come on Dom, you can't tell me that wasn't funny. Xara can you see where their hands are?" Elijah popped in.

"Jesus, and I was worried I was going to get kicked out of the museum. I think I'm in the clear." Zacharias bellowed.

"Focus, or I'm pulling everyone out of the museum. We said we needed in and out." Dominic brought back the focus.

We finally got to the archives which were hidden behind two secured doors. Glass panels giving a glimpse of the minimized collections of artifacts. The once glorified colored artifacts now muted in tone, but if one would listen history was still speaking.

The majority of the archives had been transferred to another facility and when we were doing research we wished that we didn't have to go there. Thankfully there was a previous exhibition of the Treasury on display and we had some time.

"My understanding is that there is a piece of the former Treasury that you need to examine in person to look for details on a person you are researching." Laurent had reiterated the cover story.

Technically he was not completely wrong on why I, or we, were there.

"That is correct. I was hoping that I'd take a look at the former exhibit and see if there were any connections that linked." I had to sound somewhat academic.

He hummed, "Well, I'm not sure how much you think you are going to find. If your person of interest was dated before the 18th century, I'm afraid that your person of interest may not have as much as you hope. The French Revolution was a rough time for French History. Most items of the treasury were looted or never recovered." Laurent explained to me.

I already knew that. It's here, we all knew it.

"I understand, Professor. I am not hoping for a miracle, just hopefully a glimpse," I reassured him.

"Atta boy Yankee." Gwen cheered in my ear.

"Very well. If you will follow me." He continued on, accessing the doors to unlock and let me into the treasure trove of the found. He typed into a keypad for access, I made it seem like I wasn't looking, but I did. He scanned his badge and waited for me to follow him through.

"Lucky for you, the exhibit has not been fully transported to the new archive location. Please follow all the protocols and if you must step out for any reason, please come find me. I have set aside a place for you to work. If you require anything else, do not hesitate. I trust a man of your background in academia will not cause trouble." Laurent looked at me from the side, as if he had a hint of mistrust.

I cleared my throat, "My friend, you have my word, which is my honor. I am very appreciative of your generosity. I think this is the start of a humbling friendship." I flashed him a smile, and he nodded, walking away as soon we arrived at the area of set up.

Something in me panicked as everything in my ear was too quiet. Not a snicker or an inappropriate comment was made.

All I knew was that I was looking for a key. It could be a skeleton key, or something resembling a key. I tapped my ear with my comm, signaling the crew that we were in business. I didn't hear anything, it made me worried. Thankfully, I was supplied with a notebook and pen. I flipped to an empty page and aimed the glasses down at the paper.

Were the comms down?

I worried that after we had passed the threshold of the door into the archives, silence was greeted. I imagined the panic everyone was experiencing. I hoped the glasses were working. I wasn't a true historian, no degree or formal training, but I knew enough and could learn enough to pass through and go along for the ride. I was exemplary at researching.

I could do this. I could make it on my own. Silence greeted me again. All the voices were gone, no one was with me, I was alone but I had to keep moving. For all I knew the feed on the glasses were limited range.

I would have to go in blind. My palms under my gloves were getting sweaty. I would have to be put to the test to see if I could do this.

I silently prayed that somewhere there was someone looking down and wishing that I would be able to find his unknown key.

I walked through the archives. Shelves after shelves of historical treasure and artifacts laid there, waiting to retell the stories of long ago. Some of these treasures were exquisite. I knew that Gwen must be throwing a fit wishing that she could get her close up with these artifacts.

We thought that maybe there would be a safe or something like a box that would hide the key but between the Brooch of Saint Louis to even the Ring of Saint Louis. I was starting to lose hope. Some items were relatively small. There were a couple vases that are from a series of vases called *vases de Sugar.*

I doubted that Frastine would hide a key in plain sight, let alone her sisters. But sisters couldn't have known about the French Revolution beginning in their later life. Or did they, and they had inklings of whispers that became like shouts. But where would you hide your key?

I doubt that the key would be in these vases or ewers. Someone would have found something by now even in today's modern world. I had to turn over "every rock". I wasn't going to leave there knowing I could have done more.

I tapped my ear again, hoping the frequency would pick up again. But there was no luck. Something tells me the walls are blocking the signal and Hartley and Xara are like raging bulls that see red right now.

I glanced over to see if Laurent was nearby, afraid that the antique vases would make a sound. I ran back to the table and grabbed a mini flashlight from my bag. Running back to the shelf, I had limited time. I'm the last one to know what is plan B, in fear that I would screw it up somehow some way.

Okay it happened one time, but we all recovered and all limbs were attached.

I looked into Sugar's Eagle, and it was a heavy piece. I am not the strongest but I can hold my own but this piece was heavy. The heavy vase has a gold work chiseled up the neck and facial features, and rock crystals covering the body. There was no time to admire the work, but in my earlier days, this would fetch a fair price. Apparently these vases were in a cabinet during the time in the Treasury and it survived the revolution.

I pried open the neck portion and wiggled it out, flashing the light inside to see if there was anything. The hollow sound told me that nothing was in there. I placed the top portion back and placed the vase back onto the shelf and moved towards the next one.

The Sardonyx ewer, definitely from the Greeks, if I had to guess and from searching it was from the Byzantine Empire. The details of the work and the floral design and colors. It was quite the treasure. I had to stay focused, my window of opportunity was diminishing. I was getting distracted and being pulled back into my earlier days.

I nudged the top of the ewer, shining the light into it and I couldn't see anything. I was beginning to be disappointed. Usually by now, we would be halfway through a quest and knew the end result. The Madames were beginning to be the quests of quests. But that was the most intoxicating part, where history keeps you on your toes.

One last vase that could likely hide something. As soon as I moved it, there was the slightest *ting* sound. I don't know how these workers missed it. But I saw a shadow within the glass vase. The gold work and crystals were astonishing but I had to figure out a way to get into the vase. That was concerning. If I moved around a lot, Laurent would notice and we would have a big issue at hand, with the Louvre taking the key.

I turned the vase upside down gently, giving it a gentle shake and a swirl, trying to inch the key out. The key was wrapped up in some brown cloth. Perhaps that it's why no one truly noticed. It was at the bottom and could have been mistaken for the bottom of the vase in coloring. I thought the keys would be decent size, perhaps noticeable.

The cloth was coming slowly through the top portion of the vase. "Come on, come on," I whispered coaxing.

There was a squeak from a chair.

Fuck.

"Everything alright, doctor?" Laurent asked from down the room.

I rushed through, trying everything to make the key get out quicker. But Laurent's footsteps were coming quicker and quicker. I could see the cloth coming into view and almost in my hands. Out of the corner of my eye I could see the silhouette of Laurent inching closer.

Finally, the cloth was in my hand. My heart was racing and my hands were shaking. I hurried and put the vase back and stuffed the cloth into my pocket. Just in time for Laurent to present himself through the archive shelves.

"Everything alright Dr. McCormick?" He asked. His dark eyes peered at me with concern.

"Quite. I was trying to use my phone to check notes and emails from my associates and unfortunately cannot get a good signal. Mind if I step out? I think I was on to something but not quite sure." I adjusted myself trying to calm down my heart from exploding out of my chest.

"Oh yes, the doors should let you through. I will be here if you need to come back." He offered. I think I made it through and didn't raise any flags. The fabric and key in my pocket are waiting to be revealed.

I quickly walked over to my messenger bag and rushed out, waiting for the doors to release me. My comms had been silent and as soon as I passed through the threshold, I held my phone up to my ear to pass as if I were on the phone.

I tapped my comms hoping that it would wake them up or stir the uneasiness and commotion.

"Earth to humans. Can you copy?" I smirked.

I flinched when the sound barrier broke through my comm. Then all the shouting came through.

"Oh my god."

"Jesus Christ."

"He's okay."

"Cancel plan B."

"Awe, you all missed me." I gushed. Weaving through the hallway and the stairs. I tried not to bump into anyone.

"What the fuck happened?" Zacharias snuck through the lines.

"The hell should I know, I heard you all one moment and once I entered the archives, my comm went dead."

"They must have some kind of jammer or security system." Xara stated.

"Shouldn't you have seen that?" I asked. It was a fair question.

"Yes and no. Right now is not the time to argue. Did you find something?" Hartley stopped the bickering before we all lost it.

"I did, it's in my pocket, I think we all need to move and head out. Now. I don't know if the Professor suspected as much. But he was very curious." I recommended.

"You heard the man return home. You know the drill. Be careful the museum is getting busier by the minute." Dominic had said.

"Do you have your exit buddies?" Elijah joked.

"I'm heading out now," Zacharias said, "Elijah I'll meet you on your level."

"I lost Gwen?" Winston said, practically blaring through the comms.

"Wait how?" Quinton yelled.

I hurried out the doors before I could go back and help search for her. This was more at stake here, but I worried for my friend. She was already on the edge from August's reappearance and so was I.

"She was right behind me, and then." Winston stuttered out.

"Xara, Hartley, where is she? Winston, I'm headed your way. Zach and Elijah find Yankee and head to the meeting location." Dominic barked out orders.

My friend, where did you go?

CHAPTER 21

GWENDOLYN

I saw him. I knew my own eyes didn't deceive me.

Not August.

I saw Maxx. My ghost of an uncle, alive and watching me.

I knew he has been gone for years. But I wasn't hallucinating. He brushed past me in the exhibition hallway. I felt him.

As we were leaving, I was behind Winston, Yankee had recovered what we hoped was a key. and we were one step closer to finding the library.

Then I felt someone brush past me and he was there. The same curl of a smile, the wicked grin that felt like the cause of mischief. I had to see if my mind was playing games with me. But in my heart, I knew it was him.

I left Winston in a hurry, moving past people in the hallway, focusing my attention on him. He was there, I wasn't seeing things. I had fully convinced myself that he was there.

I took out my comm and put it in my pocket, I didn't need any other distractions. Anxiety crawled in my chest. The weight of the "what ifs" were heavy once again. The shadow

There were many people and he was at the end of the hallway, so I turned a corner around another hallway to cut him off.

Winston was not going to be happy that I left his side, but I would suffer any consequences at a later date or time. I needed to know.

Maximus left for his own quest and returned home to us in the grave we weren't ready to bury him in. Something never sat right with me about his last quest. Something in me didn't want to believe his death wasn't real.

The crowd of people were getting to the point of frustration. I wanted to scream, I lost him. In the crowd of people. I pushed past them all, turning every corner, looking for him. I wanted to shout his name to see if someone would turn around.

Without warning, I smacked into someone built like a great stone statue. I looked up and found Dominic, clutching my forearms.

Just holding me. His eyes were full of concern and anger. He wasn't too happy about my stunt.

He bent down and looked at me. "Why did you run?"

"I saw him, Dom. I saw Maxx," I blurted, preventing my emotions from toppling over.

He drew back, "He's gone Gwen. Sweetheart, Maximus has been gone for years now."

"I know what I saw. It was him," I said trying to convince myself I was hallucinating.

He shook his head, trying to convince me that it wasn't true.

"We'll talk about this later. Right now, we need to leave. Now." He nudged me in the opposite direction.

We started to walk and I glanced behind me hoping that there was some evidence of what I saw. I wasn't seeing ghosts. It was him, it had to be him.

Winding through the crowds and the hallways we come to the exits, loading onto the escalators and through the doors. I felt his looming body language, like he was disappointed in my actions. I swear sometimes he can act like a father figure, the way he looks at you like I should have known better.

He was quiet the whole walk down the blocks to our meet up location. Everyone had made it safely, no one was missing except almost me. I saw Winston's eyes full of fury.

I'll suffer the consequences later.

"Found her," Dominic walked me to the table we had in the back.

It was a discreet restaurant that gave us privacy and away from heavy foot traffic, and especially from street cameras that are around the city. It was enough to allow us to convene and then leave when necessary. Plus, they have good wine.

"Miss the exit?" Elijah asked. The ever sweet soul, like a concerned brother.

"Not the place or time right now," I sheepishly said, knowing that we needed to meet, make sure we acquired what we needed and then head back to our flat. Winston glared at me, I know he's mad, but the way he looked at me, he was ready to give me consequences. I could feel the heat rushing through my body. Everything that day was the wrong time and place for things.

Yankee reached into his pocket and placed the item on the table. We all just stared at it, as if it was going to move or do something magical.

"In a cloth?" Xara asked. She cocked an eyebrow.

"In a Sugar vase. The key was wrapped in this at the bottom. I don't know how the historians missed this or didn't see this. But it was there." Yankee explained.

We all just sat there, silent, waiting for something magical to happen.

"Well, are we going to unwrap it or just stare at it like we are two and want to poke it with a stick?" Zacharias brought up a good point.

They were looking to me to tell me to do it. For once I shied away, I wasn't the leader, I was to sit back and prove that this was more than just about me.

"Dominic, you're on point," I said, allowing him to take the first step.

Maybe it was the sense of disappointment that I feared. What if this wasn't the key, what if it was another clue? What if it was a dead end or even worse, what if we were not the first ones that found it?

Dominic nodded his head, everyone leaned forward on the table and waited with anticipation. His fingers undid the knot on the top, allowing the strings to fall against the table again.

The air hung thin, the anxiety was killing some of us.

Winston had grabbed my hand under the table and squeezed it. He was trying to be there for me, in his own fashion. I glanced over at the table noticing that Quinton was awfully close to Xara.

The strings were swept away from the cloth, my legs started to bounce, beginning Dom to hurry up and reveal what we all were hoping. The cloth started to unravel, the package did seem small, even the smallest package can lead to something extraordinary.

Finally, we were welcomed to the sight of a discovery. That was the true adrenaline rush. Knowing that you are soon to embark on a journey that you least expected to go on. In the palm of his hand laid the first piece of the Madame puzzle.

He placed it in the middle of the table, all of us gawking at it.

A skeleton key with a small emerald on it, the light green gem shined in this restaurant.

Green for Greed.

Green for monetary power.

"Fucking hell," Quinton exclaimed.

"I'd be damn," Elijah sounded surprised.

"They are real," Winston said.

The sounds of disappearing doubt gave me a spring in step and a cocky grin on my face.

"Does this look like the tale of a legend? A myth?" I sat back letting the anxiety leave my body and a sense of pride came to us.

I knew it. Uncle Maxx you were right.

"All thanks to that little journal." Dominic said. "You were right, Gwendolyn."

I liked the feeling of being right after so many times being told that these women did not exist. Or even that history was fully explained when it wasn't.

We were getting close and all we had to do was keep going. This little key was about to change the course in our lives and we didn't even know it yet.

"Come on, let's get out of here. Remember to stagger." Dominic commanded again.

He wrapped it back up in the brown leather wrapping and handed it to Hartley, possibly putting it in a secured case.

Everyone staggered out, except Winston and me.

I got up and he pulled back. Something or someone told me we weren't going to be going back to the flat right away.

"Sit,"he commanded. A slight invitation in this voice.

Shit.

I sat back down, sinking back down in the chair. He forced the chair to face him, with strength to grab it and turn it in his direction. He leaned against the table to the side and didn't say a word. He waited before he spoke, thinking of the right words to say to me.

His eyebrows furrowed, his eyes staring into my soul, trying to read my mind, my movements. I crossed my legs and sat there, my arms folded across my chest. Both of us were stubborn enough to wait for the other one to say something.

If I was back at the flat, I'd tease him, possibly bat my eyes at him, distract him, make him rethink his train of thought. After last night, I wouldn't be surprised if it worked. Both of us wrapped around each other's fingers. That's what happens when you give in.

"You wanna explain why we turned to exit and you bolted in the other direction?" He asked.

He didn't yell, he didn't throw an attitude at me, but his voice was sharp in command. I didn't know how to explain to him that I ran because I thought I saw someone that was supposed to be dead, buried in a grave in the states. It would just paint me to look like a fool, like I was seeking attention.

I understand Uncle Maximus has been gone for some time but it's been the hardest few years without him. Without his encouraging words and his light British accent, life had an emptiness to it. I know if anybody could understand that it would be Winston. I could only imagine that this man was thinking I ran away from him again, part of me didn't blame him if that was his train of thought.

"Are we just going to sit here and pretend that you didn't bolt?" He asked.

No one was pretending, at least I wasn't.

I looked up at him meekly, and stood my ground. I had to answer him. "Winston it's not like I ran away from you again I think last night made that pretty obvious." Quick flashes of the night before ran through my head.

"Then what did you see Gwendolyn?" He rarely uses my full first name and for a moment I was scared and slightly turned on. He seemed more pissed off than worried.

"I thought I saw him, Win," I rushed the words. He looked at me like I was saying I saw August, "I thought I saw Uncle Maxx. There, you happy? I bolted because I thought I saw my dead uncle walking through the hallways and I needed to see. I needed to know that the slightest bit of emptiness that I am still feeling could be filled, could be whole again." I scuffed.

It was a loaded answer, more than expected.

He blinked, just staring at me confused, as if he was wondering what my next move would be or if I was lying. and honestly I didn't want him to think either.

"Well, aren't you going to say that I was crazy. And if you are, I think Dominic beat you to the punch on that." I threw an attitude at him and part of me knew that was a very bad idea.

He scrunched up his eyebrows, I think I struck another chord with him, "Never said you were crazy. But we are in a new city, a new quest, and the timing of all this, what else am I to think." He threw those words at me in such frustration.

We were both getting heated at the moment and if one of us didn't settle down who knows what the ending would have come out to be. I took a breath before the next words that came out of my mouth.

"I would hope that you would think that I wasn't running away again." I said calmly. Begging for a little hope there.

"Gwen, with August popping up and not knowing his movements, I was more worried that you bolted in revenge. Or worse, that something happened to you. Could you imagine if something actually happened to you and nobody could get to you?" He was serious, I could tell. "What if I couldn't get to you?" He finished out.

It wasn't that I was running away from him but that something could eventually happen to me. I guess you could say that was his biggest fear now, never returning because of my own impulses. It was no longer me running away from him again, but that I would never come back if something happened to me much like Maxx.

"I have a feeling that no matter where I am, you would come and find me. Or I would fight my way to come back." I grabbed him by the shirt pulling him close to me with our faces and close proximity. "Now you have two choices, Win. One, you could either sit there and keep gawking at me like a child who's in trouble or two, you can kiss me and we can go back to the flat and I can make it up to you and prove that I am not going nowhere." I offered him a proposition that something told me he couldn't refuse.

I wouldn't have minded the second option.

He looked at me one more time before finally deciding to slam his mouth onto mine. In a heated passion, he pulled me closer. Enticing me to stay where I am, be here at this moment. I braced my hands on his thighs to have some more stability. I thought about just straddling him right there in the middle of the restaurant.

I simply melted into his kiss. He had slipped his tongue to mine, claiming it. He wanted more and I could feel him getting hard, as my hand glided across his zipper.

It was me that broke the kiss, knowing that if we continued that it wouldn't matter where we were, we'd continue and have a spot of exhibitism.

"If we don't get back to the flat, they'll think we've killed each other." I stood up about to head out to the door. "Or worse, use the facilities in under five minutes." I winked at him.

He stood up behind me, threw his arms around my shoulders to bring my body into his, "You little minx, knowing how to get under my skin. I won't need five minutes with you." He whispered in my ears.

"Is that a challenge?"

He chuckled. He kissed the nape of my neck. "That is a promise baby."

Chapter 22

Elijah

One down, six to go.

Honestly, it was six too many. The adrenaline from the museum was enough of a spark for some people to keep going.

The next few we knew where to go, just had to uncover the plan to make it happen. The next one on our list was Martine's husband's tomb.

Love has taken a soul and fed revenge,
She sits waiting for the gates to open.
To seek fury and Hell to Tomb Earth.

From Gwen's research and translation, we understood that Martine was a doting, loyal wife to a general in the French army. She was the one that started it all, wanting to make an impact in history that would go undetected, unwritten from the books. The mastermind behind the idea of the library and separating out the keys.

Her wartime mind and power explained a lot about her, unleashing the wrath unto those in her way. She sought out to make her mark and influence those around her and then her sisters followed suit.

It's easy to think of Martine as a French version of Athena and Ares, war strategies and wisdom were her strength. What a compatible match to be with a man of stature and rank.

Who knows what secret lies in that library, what influences she had in certain battles or strategies.

Gwen and I worked, research was tough trying to narrow down his burial site to certain cemeteries not being opened until after supposedly Martine's husband had been killed. We narrowed it down to Montmartre Cemetery.

The one cemetery that we knew would be a challenge. Not only is it well known, but it is in a place that might have a lot of eyes around us.

The cemetery is partially under a bridge and sprawled out across the area. It is the most atmospheric of the cemeteries in the city.

From there we had to figure out where General Toussaint laid to rest. He wasn't in a ground like a standard grave, this was a man of power but the poem said, "open the gates" and "tomb", therefore the man was in a mausoleum. Only problem is when someone searches his name, nothing pops up in the directory or archives.

As if he was nowhere to be buried, to be laid to rest in peace. Martine's own grave would be nowhere near his own.

"We must be missing something," Gwen mumbled as she flipped through the journal and her notes.

When we all got back to the flat, Winston and Gwen strolled in and vanished for a little bit, and then back, looking all disheveled.

We were back at the board figuring out the next location specifically. Gwen had gotten frustrated because we were on a good trail with the first key, Gwen became easily frustrated after the first one, which is beyond her character. Was she holding back?

"Gwen, slow down. We have time," I realized I said the wrong words when the room got quiet.

"If you haven't noticed, we don't have much of it, it's rather unpredictable, Eli. We have more obstacles than we intended." She snarled, but almost in a calm voice.

Truth be told, it was a little frightening.

"Are we missing something within the journal? A detail about Martine's marriage or life that we haven't factored in?" I suggested.

Gwen started to breathe heavily, and before Winston or Dom could come to the rescue, it was Xara that did.

Xara came around the corner where she was sitting and ended up sitting on the table where Gwen was. "Gwen, look at me. Don't be getting worked up. It's not like the time of your original project when the committee started to press you for more answers and you were fighting back." She grabbed her hands into hers and squeezed hard. "We'll figure the shit out."

Only those who are worthy.

That's why Gwen kept telling us. I had a thought, but if I continued to say something to Gwen, I might be the next one buried. But it was an idea, worthy of a shot. It may have been a shot in the dark. I chuckled at the thought.

Grave digging at night, how adventurous of us.

"Any ideas would be helpful here." Gwen mumbled.

No one else wanted to say anything or didn't know what to say. I fiddled around with the thought. But never underestimate those who sit back and listen.

"What if it's a puzzle?" I suggested.

"Care to explain?" Quinton furthered the inquiry.

"What if the name of a grave or mausoleum is an anagram or a disguised name. These women like puzzles, little tests to prove someone's worth to create puzzles and riddles to hide things they didn't want out there." I continued to explain.

"We hadn't thought of that yet. Worth a shot, maybe look at versions of his name?" Hartley shrugged, he flipped open his laptop and continued to search.

"If it's an anagram, what does that mean? That Martine continued to hide something from her sisters? Talk about a level of trust." Zacharias said.

"Sometimes families can be vicious," I eyed him, knowing that we had a long history with that.

Gwen popped up, I could see the wheels turning in her head. "Could be onto something." She looked back at Xara and Xara shrugged. "Yankee what do you think?"

Yankee, who was already a glass and a half of vodka. I think he has been on edge since we lost communication with him in the archives. He tapped the glass, "It's possible, but what would Martine have to hide? What is enough for her to hide something even her sisters may not have known."

Martine, the sister of wrath, full of fury and vengeance. I could only imagine what else she was hiding, but Quinton spoke up.

"Someone who might have a plan of their own has something in their ideal world to protect. Martine was a person of rage. She married into the military, her influence had over him, and then you factor in the trauma and emotional toll of losing her husband. Sometimes in those moments, you suppress everything and protect your own items." He rambled more about it.

The one thing you could tell from Quinton was that he was intelligent. A bit of a show off if you ask me.

"So, she protected own secrets by hiding her husband's mausoleum. Damn, I wouldn't have wanted to be at his funeral," Winston jokes.

I stood up and wrote his name on the board. Laurent Toussaint. "How many names can one form from the original?"

Everyone started to talk amongst themselves, as I went to grab the layout of the cemetery, plotting different entries and exits and contingencies plans. Looking for any possible dangers, foundation plots, or even dead ends.

"You stare at that map any longer my friend and you'll go blind." Dominic slapped my back, stirring me from concentration.

I nodded, sometimes being too quiet can be a curse. Most people would take it that I'm reserved, but you can see a lot of things when there is silence.

"We got it," Hartley said, banging on the table, making a few of us jump. "There is one name that when you cross it with the archive of names in that cemetery that pops up. Antonius Lustrate."

He gets up and marks an X on the location of the mausoleum. And if the name wasn't the hard part, the harder part was going to be this, the mausoleum laid in the middle of the land, hidden in the midst of trails of pathways.

"And we also have a slight problem." I said, disappointedly.

"Yep." Gwen said. She saw the same problem with the location as soon as Hartley marked the plot.

"Agreed." Yankee confirmed, sucking in his lips to hide a laugh.

"Got to fucking kidding me." Xara blurted out.

"In the middle," Zacharias whined a bit.

I nodded my head.

"Couldn't have been buried in a dead end where no one would go." Winston said sarcastically.

"That's what happens when you are buried in sins." I joked but it's true. What secrets and sins were buried with him?

Dominic turned back to the group, shaking his head. I had my doubts originally with Quinton, he had been struggling with leading the group, knowing how to wrangle a few of us more than some. Since Dominic stepped up it had been better. Honestly, I missed Gwen, she could see three steps ahead of the plan and others.

Dominic took one last look at the schematic and said, "We divide and conquer."

Simple instructions, knowing that most of us were not going to be going to the grave. Just myself, Gwen, and someone else.

"Divide and conquer?" Xara questioned. "You think that's wise for who's on our trail?"

"Correct. Divide as in the majority of us will be placed along the surrendering entry points." Dominic instructed. "Win, you and I are up on machinery and armory." Winston beamed a little bit, he liked when he could use his skills in any quests.

"Any particulars?" He leaned back in the chair.

"Smoke screens, a few semi automatics, give Zacharias the revolver, Xara the baton, and Gwen or Quinton, any preferences." Dominic was the real weapons master and armor master, but Winston likes to contribute. Quinton on the other hand was much of an automatic weapon, rather a crossbow or a hunting knife.

Gwen followed in his footsteps, but only had one weapon that she would carry and only that in regard to weaponry, the desert eagle. I never understood it. She didn't want a rifle, semi, or anything else, but give this woman a desert eagle, and she was a happy camper, like a kid with a danger lollipop.

"Surprise me," Quinton said.

Easy enough.

"Okay, Xara, Gwen, and Elijah will be at the tomb. Everyone else picks a vantage point. The best time is going to be at night, with less visibility. But we still have to act fast." Dominic continues to command.

"Heigh ho, we're off to rob a tomb we go." Yankee sings. He continued to hum his little tune.

"Could be worse." I said, quietly.

Xara curled her lips into a wicked smirk. "Yeah, one of us could wake up in an empty grave in his underwear after partying at Carnival."

We all burst into laughter, bringing us back into a memory of finding Zacharias and Winston in an empty grave in nothing but their underwear and we all couldn't find them until luckily Xara spoke with the locals after every other attempt of Hartley finding them. Through stories and gossip amongst everyone, we were able to find them and get the pictures to prove it.

The laughter died down and we planned to do it tomorrow, giving everyone the rest we needed from this day. We couldn't go out that night. Yankee was still coming down from a brief adrenaline high, Gwen was recovering from whatever made her bolt from the museum, and everyone else needed time to prepare for the next day.

It seemed like the more the years passed the less we wanted to jump straight into the next item on the agenda, but there was no direct urgency to get into the next key. I silently hoped that we would get to that point.

I could see everyone getting to the conclusion of continuing on after this like it was riding a bike and we just needed a push. I looked at my cousin, Zacharias felt the need to take charge over the past years, and I had let him.

He needed it more than me. He needed the sense to protect Hartley and me from being hurt anymore, considering us his main family. He saw Gwen and Quinton as an obstacle, especially when Gwen came back and asked for us to come for one more time, describing it as closure. Zach wasn't stupid, he knew that she needed everyone to come do it with her.

But now I saw my cousin wanting adventure, travel, and even the family. He was easing up more. I could see that the cold exterior that he put up for protection was melting away.

CHAPTER 23

GWENDOLYN

The second key, I knew it was close.

I could taste it, like it was the sweetest fruit to a starving man. The legend was becoming a reality and the little girl that imagined what it would be like to find it and prove to the world that women had more influence than they believed, was going to be ecstatic.

I was fulfilling a lifelong promise to myself. Fulfilling a dream that Uncle had.

This wasn't our first rodeo with a cemetery, perhaps a first in a French cemetery. We all staggered towards the cemetery. In the dark cover of the night, Dominic had cut open the chains on the side gate, a lesser known entrance to the Cemetery with the bolt cutters that we had brought along.

Everyone was dressed to the nines and their black clothing each one of us prepared with a weapon of her choice supplied by Winston and Dominic.

The bustle of city life noises faded in the background, only the night time creatures came out of their beds and awakened for their day.

Elijah had studied each crevice and turn of the cemetery, noting the correct pathways for easy entrance and exits. The cemetery was surrounded with history and came with the responsibility of leaving little to no damage upon leaving it. Each grace having a story that if you were willing to listen will unravel even the slightest unknown facts.

Each one of us had our comms in our ears. Some were concerned with the potential of armed guards for security on the grounds. Hartley had reassured us that there would be less guards or security people on the grounds but something in me screams that he was wrong.

We hadn't seen or heard from August and I didn't know what frightened me more, the fact that he was still here within the city limits or that he hadn't shown his face or made a move yet, but was still awaiting our next moves. Something in my gut told me that soon I would find out or that the crew would be in danger somehow some way.

I could feel someone behind me as we walked towards our entrance at the gates. It was a warm body pressing up against me.

"I could get used to seeing you in this gear," a low rumbly voice said to me.

I was dressed in our usual gear, black clothing and body bullet resistant gear, nothing glamorous. To Winston, it was the sexiest lingerie.

His hands grazed across my side, his warm breath against my neck. I couldn't help but have the softest smile knowing his inner dirty thoughts were turning into impulsive, intrusive thoughts. I guess the night before had assured him that we were stuck with each other now, Winston wasn't afraid to take the opportunities to make me blush or smile.

What I loved most is that he knew the signs when I needed him, when I needed a moment for peace and calm.

With all the happiness I had been feeling, my thoughts were a little lost. And unfortunately, this man could be a distraction like an Adonis, etching his way to my heart.

"Yes but if you keep being a distraction, we'll never be done with the quest and we'll never get back home. And sweetheart, if you cause a distraction during this, I will use your body as target practice. And I quite like this body and maybe the lower extremities as well." I grabbed his hand that was still teasing my side and squeezed it tight, throwing it off my side.

Before I could think he pulled me from the back of my neck and whipped me around to see him. His massive hands caressed there for a moment.

"Yes you do love my cock. Especially when it stretches you from the inside and you can feel me deep as if I'm touching your soul, buried there. You coming around my cock, squeezing it tight. Your pussy wanting to take hold. I can make that happen again and again." His words shiver down my spine and soon I would be a puddle among his feet.

The heat of my cheeks flushed.

"You know how to say the right words, Win. Maybe if you're a good boy we can have an adventure of our own. If you don't mind waking the dead." I said softly.

I wasn't much of an exhibitionist or anything, but for Winston, it was a possibility.

"You do fucking realize that we can hear you all right?" Zacharias yelled in the comms, blaring in my ear.

I could imagine what my brother's face was looking like. He was probably shaking his head and disappointed, wanting to burn the images and words from his mind.

But just like I didn't want to know what he does in his own time, either. Winston released my neck, but not before he kissed my forehead.

"Gwendolyn Griffin, get your fucking act together. May I remind you that you were the one that schemed all of us into doing this in the first place," Quinton's voice, although calm, came with brotherly, familial command. My brother was getting annoyed with adolescent behavior, or that was what he would say.

"Focus everyone! Jesus it's like working with teenagers again. I did my time handling young bucks," Dominic heads through the gates.

We split up into teams, each person would be escorted to the tomb site staggering each person that would be excavating. Dominic and Winston were with me, Xara was going to be with Quinton, and Yankee and Zacharias would walk with Elijah.

Dominic, Winston, and I kept walking through the maze of headstones and sculpted angels. The eeriness of it all would put someone in a tailspin and be filled with anxiety. But through my eyes, we were walking through history having eyes of those who have come before us watching over us. There was something mystical and yet chilling about walking through the cemetery. It was nothing like the catacombs, though Zacharias would never go in there.

Death too was a trickle thing you never knew when it would come and take everything you have. Though when it did you would never be prepared. It brought back memories of Maximus how I wasn't ready to let him go nor prepared. Just like my parents.

Unfortunately, it was something that tied us, the outcasts, to each other. We all lost somebody that was close to us that rearranged our life after their death and changed us as the years went on. We were the final puzzle piece in each other's puzzle. Some of us with jagged edges, some smoother than others, and ones that we didn't understand how they fit until they showed us.

"You're doing a lot of thinking there kiddo." Dominic said, tossing a look over his shoulder as we continued walking. The gravel under our feet, crunching under our heels.

"You know how my mind wonders." I offered him a smile. "Let me ask you something, do you believe in ghosts or spirits?" I remembered that he visited his wife and child's graves back in Chicago.

I tried to change the conversation and get my mind off of people that I had lost and focus on the mission ahead. Dominic entertained the idea for a moment, "I believe that the ones we love are never truly gone but are always watching over us though. I believe that in the end there is something out there hopefully with peace."

Dominic had a way with words both humbling and honest. He quickly changed the subject as we were nearing the supposed mausoleum. "Xara, Quinton are you nearby?"

My brother answered in mere seconds. "We're all good on the east side, Xara will be there *momentarily.*" he had said momentarily a bit slower as if he was trying to find the words correctly.

I didn't understand why I was still like this. Frightened, nervous, shaking. Any other quest or hunt would be fine. I would have eagerly wanted to move on to the next one but this one I was still trying to prove to everyone that we belonged with each other and that the adventures were not over.

Sure, I had schemed and somewhat persuaded my way to get everyone back here. But I was scared more that any movement that I made or any wrongdoing that I did would cause everybody to leave once more and them and the adventures which really stop. All lost things would never be found. and perhaps myself I would be lost again.

"Do you think there's something going on there?" I said trying to change the subject from my anxiety ridden brain, again.

Dominic looked behind him as we approached the mausoleum, "Do you really want to know the answer or do you want to keep pretending?" He chuckled, he wasn't stupid.

"Honestly, I don't want to believe it but I would also be surprised. I can only imagine that my best friend has my brother wrapped around her little finger." I joked.

Winston snickered behind me, "Baby girl, what if it's the other way around?"

Then I stilled, white as a ghost that roamed this sacred ground. I jolted back, "I really don't want to think about it now. Especially my brother"

"That's a little hypocritical don't you think?" Hartley had come through my ear. "I mean we all know now what goes through that little pretty head of yours. Especially when Winston wants to push those buttons." Hartley echoed in my ear.

"Bugger off Hartley, I don't need your dark, twistiness right now." I sneered at him.

He just chuckled.

Dominic growled through the comms, "Are we done here? If I hear one more instant of sexual tension or anybody screwing around and not focusing here we're leaving."

"Yes daddy," Yankee said, holding back his laughter.

"Yankee, I'm not afraid to bury you in the ground. Just pick a plot." Dominic sounded annoyed.

In Yankee fashion, he responded with, "Don't tempt me with a good time."

I could feel Winston smiling his little sinister smile. Dominic was yards away, clearing the way for Winston to bend down over me and placing a soft kiss on my cheek. He took out my comm and his.

"Are you going to be good this time?", he asked me.

"Me? I'm always good. I have no idea what you're talking about." I mean I made no promises with that.

He leaned forward towards my ear, "I'm just saying if you're good, a reward might be in play." Talk about making up for lost time. This man was insatiable. Like a big sexual deviant that has finally been awakened.

He tilted my head to meet his lips in a sweet, yet possessive kiss. We placed our comms back in our ears waiting for Elijah and Xara to finally arrive. Dominic and Winston went in opposite directions, heading to their specific spots.

A moment later, Xara approached the mausoleum and we waited for Elijah. I watched how my brother watched her every movement, studying every stride, every foot strike. When I acknowledged Xara, he turned and left in the same direction I had come from. We had yet to see any danger or speculation of what would come if we were caught.

Xara looked at me, we barely had conversations in the past few weeks, so when she turned towards me and grabbed my attention, I wasn't ready for it.

"Are we really going to dig up a grave this time?" she questioned.

"I mean it was on your bucket list wasn't it?" I laughed joking with her reminiscing about a drunk conversation we had one night in Japan.

Xara had been the wild one in college, disobeying her parents, setting her own path. She kept an on-going bucket list adding new ones every time we turned around.

I knew there was a slight question on her face. "I'm not going to pretend that I don't see a hint of the old Gwendolyn back. Truth be told Gwen, you're holding back and not just because you're not the leader."

I tilted my face, questioning her back, "Don't know what you mean." I said kicking the dirt around.

"Sure, you don't. We can pretend that you're not holding back because you're still scared. The crew is done punishing you, well I should say at least I am. We have all come to terms of forgiveness," She slapped my shoulders, embracing me, "But to be honest you are not yourself and I think this is your time to get back into that." my old friend tries to comfort me, try to bring me back to the land of the living.

"What happened to the woman that showed up at my doorstep with a gleam in her eyes, looking like she was ready to take on the world?" She asked me.

I snapped at her, "I'm right here."

"No, you're not. If anything, you are just the body of the old you, not the soul."

"Maybe I learned not to be impulsive?"

Lies.

"Lies." she knew it.

I didn't need to have an argument with her, but she pushed me back when I lost Maxx, and I said I wasn't going to continue my program. "Look, not the place nor the time. We have a key to find."

A couple moments later, Elijah came through with the bolt cutters. Now we were ready to rob a grave or at least find what needs to be found. With the slightest snip from the cutters the chains of the mausoleum fell to the ground planking as it did. We shine our lights as darkness fell on the ground. The only illumination was from the Moon shining full and bright.

Every creaking noise the area made you wonder if ghosts were amongst us. The mausoleum once opened released a whoosh of air as if something was trapped inside and we had just released demons on Earth. Maybe it was the vengeance that was released, the spirit of vengeance.

"I could have done without the spider webs." Elijah cringed as we started to rummage around the mausoleum. He doesn't do well with spiders or snakes. I don't blame him on snakes.

Xara looked back at me, "So I shouldn't tell you that there is a huge ass spider on your shoulder?" Elijah jumped ten out of his skin and released a deep shout. There was a little rumble in his voice.

"What was that?" Dominic asked.

"Did Elijah get attacked by a spider?" Zacharias came through.

"Awe, does Eli need a hug from Yankee." Yankee teased. I bursted into laughter.

"You all fucking suck!" Elijah growled.

"Oh, come on Eli, you know that was funny." Xara laughed.

He shined his flashlight in our direction. "Funny until someone gets hurt."

That was a low blow. I got quiet. "Way to go numb nuts," Xara walked over and punched him.

We continued to look around the place trying to find any clue or indication where the key may be. We thought that it would be too obvious for the key to be in Laurent's grave. The walls were adorned with different urns and pottery. The room smelt like death, a chill ran down my spine. It was going to be an experience to get through this without your mind taking through the possible situation.

"Hey, take a look at this," Elijah had called over to Xara and me.

His attention was on the casket that was laid in stone. It was no ordinary stone casket, there were etchings of medieval scenes, there were rectangles with Roman numerals all over the box. I wondered what the scenes entailed. Each one played out a scene, whether from history or the stories from the tales that were once told. Symbols including a flower, I could feel the etching of it, the smooth curves of the engraving.

"These women have some strange ass taste in burials." Xara pointed out that I couldn't blame her because these madames were a little ostentatious. They each had a flair.

"Did you find any leads into the key? I would imagine that it looks like the one that we found at the Louvre," I kept looking around sickly hoping that we didn't have to desecrate a grave.

But it would be obvious in the casket. Wouldn't it?

They both shook their heads but something in me knew that Elijah was thinking otherwise. "Wouldn't it be obvious to place it in the tomb but also the right answer where it could be?" Xara was starting to agree or be on the same page as Elijah.

I shook my head. "That's what these women want you to think."

"Hear me out, we know that Martine was very loyal to her husband so what if she actually laid the secret to the library aka the key and his actual grave." Elijah had started that train of thought.

They weren't completely wrong, but I wanted to believe that it wouldn't be that easy. Xara and him kept arguing, the noise echoing in the room. It made my head throb, I couldn't focus, nothing was coming to me.

"EVERYONE JUST SHUT UP FOR A MOMENT!" I yelled.

I rarely yelled at them, but I was on edge, starting to second guess myself.

I kept shaking my head. I knew my history inside and out and I knew Narcisse's journal like the back of my hand; every translation, every interpretation that there was. I was certain that her sister would not have left the key in the casket, easy enough to find or for all to know about.

After Martine's husband died she visited the library quite a few times, therefore why would she bury the one thing that granted her access. She was the mastermind behind the library. My brain was starting to rattle through all the facts and all of the historical points.

I started to get frustrated and buried my head into my hands, closing my eyes trying to look at what I was missing. I tried to see all the pieces in my head, and how they fit.

Then I heard a little voice in my comms, "Breathe, Winnie. Don't overthink." Winston tried to calm me down but I was getting frustrated with myself.

I was usually the one to point out everything and I am off my game. I had let the quest, August, the appearance of my dead uncle rattle me this bad and to top it off the pressure of not overstepping and wanting to take over myself as we got closer and closer.

I felt like I needed a slap back into reality or something because I was losing my touch. I had lost sight of all the pieces on the board and even worse, second guessing myself.

It was then that I felt the hands of my old friend grabbing me and just shaking me, "Bitch, please don't make me three stooge this. I will Larry, Curly and Moe you in a heartbeat."

She read my mind about a slap back into reality.

I nodded my head in agreement, though cautious of a slap coming my way. I took a deep breath. I started to think about what Maxx would do.

Look at everything you have in front of you.

Don't take ten steps forward when you haven't even marked your path.

What do you see, what do you know.

Those were the words that Max would tell me and Quentin whenever we were in the field with him.

What do I have in front of me? I have the casket that's etched in different patterns and different numbers *wait a second.*

Numbers. Patterns. Puzzles. Eli and Xara were right, the key was going to be in the casket but the casket is a puzzle itself just like the damn poem. I saw everything like a rush of wind waking me up.

"Elijah and Xara are right, the key in the casket," I blurted out as I started a circle around and shining my light around the casket. "But the casket is a puzzle. Just like his name on the mausoleum, it's a puzzle, it's a clue. So, the casket is some kind of lock, some kind of vault." I froze.

Jesus Christ.

There were so many connections that were running through my head.

Each sister had their key into some kind of vault. Frastine had it in a vault that unfortunately was raided during the revolution.

Esmerie, we assumed as well that it was in the family plot of their childhood home, outside the main city of Paris.

Each sister has their key in some kind of vault or tomb, as if the dead or metal would protect their secrets. The sisters, these madames, are full of patterns but they're all the same, the same thought of how to protect their key. They tried to be different but they all had the same indication of where they were going to put their key.

Question was now, how do you get into the places that are meant to be buried.

"So how do we get this key then? If it is a vault then there's got to be a passcode," Zacharias also peace in the things together. I cringed at the usage of "passcode", he could have used the word combination.

"What's going to unlock it?" Yankee asked.

"No, I do not unfortunately but we can certainly try." I reassured everyone. There had to be something in the roman numerals. Something in a pattern or a combination. My hands grazed over a block with a number on it. Trying to see if a block would move, whether pushed or twisted.

Just then there was a commotion through one of the comms.

A bit of static, which was never a good sign especially if we were split up. I didn't know which one it was until somebody spoke up. But the three of us froze there in the mausoleum, hands at our waist ready to disarm someone if it came to that. Watching the door intently, ready to strike. I silently prayed that this wasn't the beginning of another accident.

CHAPTER 24

GWENDOLYN

"Can someone tell me what is going on?" Dominic commanded. We had the respected rule that only one voice during uncertainties.

There was silence.

I could hear the thudding of my heartbeat throbbing in my ears. The only thing that we did hear was a bit of static, the crinkling of noise. I wanted to scream, I could see the confusion of Xara and Elijah's eyes.

The light from our flashlights illuminated the area. Elijah's chest started to heave, his heartbeat pounding in his chest, the worriedness in his eyes, unsure of what was going on with his cousin.

Dominic came back on the comms, agitated, "Roll call. Now."

"Gwendolyn," I blurted out without hesitation. Slowly unraveling one of my hands to count out.

One.

"Xara. I'm good." Xara came through.

Two,

"Eli," he said weakly.

Three.

"Quinton." He came through and my heart slowed down a bit, waiting for the other person that my heart was racing to call out.

Four.

"Winston. Everything is fine on my end." Thank you to whatever deity is up there.

Five.

Dominic made six in my count. Three more. I silently begged for three more voices to come through, frightening my own fear away.

We were waiting for Yankee, and Hartley and Zach. As much as Zach annoyed me and I annoyed him, I didn't want anything to happen to him. I didn't want anyone to get hurt, not this time.

We waited in silence. My eyes looked at Elijah, he was still uneasy. Seconds went by, a couple of minutes started ticking away, crunching our time from safety.

Dominic would need to come up with a plan B, because plan A was starting to catch on fire in a desert with no water.

Our prayers were starting to be granted when there was a crumpling sound as if somebody was coming back on to the feed. "Apologies. Yankee and I thought we heard something. We rushed over, we thought it was a squirrel or something." Zacharias reassured us.

Seven.

"And they made me stay behind." Hartley rang out.

Eight.

"Yankee is dandy, perhaps on the verge of a heart attack, but we're fine." Yankee came back on the comms. There was a light laughter in his voice.

And nine.

We were all on the edge, I nodded my head. "We can get back to it. Alright, so Elijah pointed out that there are blocks on the casket, in numbers. So, there is a combination. But what? Hartley, any ideas?"

Hartley usually had brilliant ideas on how to unlock something. "Okay, so I would imagine that it would have to be simply like three or four digits. This was relatively new, so maybe it's a year. Most likely an anniversary or even death. Try his death. Try the year then the date." I nodded.

The year 1786, a couple years before the actual revolution started, that year was ringing loud in my head.

Xara and Elijah surrounded the tomb alongside me. I started at the one, I tried to push it, but it wasn't like a button. But the roman numeral stuck out further. The thought of pulling it down like a slider, I wondered. I wiggled it, after centuries of not using it, I was afraid that it wouldn't budge.

Fortunately, it did.

I couldn't help but show my giddiness when a sound of *thunk* echoed.

"Holy shit," Xara exclaimed. "Those wicked women."

"Pull down the number. Don't push the block," I ordered.

Xara pulled on the seven and eight and then Elijah pulled the six. Nothing, each number pulled back down. We were incorrect.

"Try the date." Hartley reminded me.

December 29th. We tried this one. It wasn't correct. We were so close!

"What other significance?" Winston asked, trying to ponder the thought.

"Ages, maybe the ages of when they first met. We've understood she was loyal, maybe she's a romantic under that cold heart." Yankee echoes in our ears.

Maybe. Loyalty and dedication, they truly loved each other in that aspect.

Martine was 17 when she met Laurent at the age of 25. He was promoted young in the military, or have.

"17 and 25" I nodded at Xara and Elijah. Third time was going to be a charm.

1, there was another *thunk.*

7, and another one, *thunk*

2, the sound was getting there, *thunk*

5, the slab moved. It cracked open. The stench of the air hung thick from the trapped air that was in the tomb.

The three of us hurried to the side and threw off the slab.

"Stop," Winston quietly yelled through the comms. We all froze. "We have security coming through the main entrance. I'm counting three right now."

I looked at my crew and ran countless scenarios in my head. We were either going to fight, hide, or escape, but which paths. We continued to graze our waist, myself with a desert eagle to the side, Xara with her side knives, and Elijah with his Smith and Wessons.

"I don't think security is the least of our worries. I think I know what triggered it." Zacharias beamed through the comms.

I already knew the answer before Dominic and Quinton had answered and sneered. "August."

"We have a winner," Yankee said.

My heart raced, I wasn't going to have enough time to properly search for the key. We had to hurry.

"What's his location?" Dominic asked, "We'll have to create a diversion for the guards but August is going to be a different story."

"He is a few yards from our location, I say Gwen and the crew have about five minutes before he may approach the mausoleum." Zacharias took charge, you could hear the military tone peeping through, all the tactical training coming into use. "There are at least three men with him. And armed."

"It's not looking too hot, the man got smarter and acquired more muscle!" Hartley stated.

"Winston move to Zacharias, Quinton and Yankee with me. Zach take him out if you need to, Winston, injure don't kill anyone. Hartley stay with them." Dominic's gravel voice gave out orders.

I get into the casket, "We don't have much time, we have to look now!" I yelled at Xara and Elijah to move. I needed that key before August takes over or worse we'll have to choose between something and the key. I rushed through moving aside any cloth or bones. I was officially ransacking a grave.

"There!" Elijah pointed at the skeleton's heart. Hidden between the chest plate was the skeleton key adorned with a garnet gem at the top, just like Frastine's key.

"We got it!" I held the key up to the lights, "No time, we gotta go. Dominic, an escape route would be nice right now!" I yelled into the comms. I packed the key into my pack. We tried to close up the casket as much as we could.

Gunshots started to echo like an empty cave. We didn't know where nor who it was coming from.

"Everyone to the exit points, find your people. Move out. Move out." Dominic yelled out. Which meant we had to execute our plan. We'd get our group of people, and get out the nearest exit. It was going to be harder for us mausoleum area crew as we were centered around the cemetery.

We had to know, "Who's firing bullets?"

"Hold on," A few more gunshots rang out, they were close by and something told me it was from Yankee and Zach on their end of the cemetery because August was coming. "August is coming your way Gwen, you all need to run. Now!" The comms went out.

"Hartley, someone!"

"I'm still here, Gwen. Zach's comms went out. He went after one of the guys from August's crew." Hartley reassured us. Which wasn't good if his comms went out, he could be injured.

I could hear heavy footsteps, from there, we had to split up, if they couldn't get all three, then I would distract them and allow my team to escape, I could handle myself.. "Elijah, take Xara and get out of here!"

"The fuck we are!" Xara yelled at me.

"Viper you can yell at me later, I need you to take your asses to the exit points and I will be there." I started to shove them off.

Dominic started to come through the comms. "Don't do this kiddo."

"Dom, get Quinton and Yankee out of here. Hartley, I don't care what you do but get the guys and head out. I'm not losing anyone else, not again." It was a brash decision but I couldn't live with myself if we lost someone. They were going to be after me, not them. I had to run.

I saw Xara being tugged by Elijah, he muffled something but I was more concerned of going the opposite direction. Elijah grew frustrated and tossed her over his shoulder. Xara kicked and punched his back as they disappeared into the night with only the moonlight guiding them.

I didn't have time, but if we had split up I could out run and find my way out, keeping the key safe from being lost. Again.

In my head, Dominic was grabbing my brother and Yankee to their exit point, avoiding the security guards, hoping that they weren't being fired out. I imagine that Xara is hoisted over Elijah's shoulders because she is too stubborn and wanted to go back, but silently Elijah agreed with me and trusted me.

I could hear the heavy footsteps striking against the ground, my heart starting to race faster as the adrenaline was pumping through my body. If this was any other time, I'd stop and give them a taste of power, and let the bullets fly.

But too much was going to be at stake and I wasn't willing to take a chance just yet. I wanted to fight, but I had to run first. "She's up ahead." I heard one of the goons yell out.

It was like they were made of human speed because they were getting closer and closer. There were a couple of shots that flew past me, mini sparks from the ricochet off the tombstones.

More gunshots being fired off in the distance. I couldn't hear the comms or anyone else. I went to reach for my ear where my comms was and it was gone. I was in total silence.

Dominic and Winston weren't going to like the fact that I bolted again, or that I was not in the distance of being in communication. I don't retrace my steps, I plan accordingly. I'd find a spot to duck until they were out of sight and then head in the other direction to the original exit point.

I weaved in and out of the graves and tried to make sporadic moves into different pathways. But I think Hartley was right, August got smarter with the years he had disappeared and that frightened me more.

I saw my chance and I took it, there was a split way ahead of me and I took the left path and ran down there in more of a sprint and then down a hill. I kept running past sculpted angels and gargoyles, the silent protectors and hopefully mine.

The darkness fell even more, as the moon was the only illumination. I broke left again and crouched down by a smaller mausoleum. I hid in the darkness like a shadow waiting in the corner.

The approaching footsteps came closer and closer. Their ragged breathing was coming closer. The only hope was that my breathing would slow down to keep quiet. The previous gunshots were gone by now and I had hoped that meant my crew, my family were safe. They had stopped past me, and waited for a second.

"She's gone. She's quite the runner," one of them had complimented me, little did they know I was feet away.

I looked up to see who was there, peaking over the stone, but staying low to stay hidden. My eyes saw August, the lean, tall man. His lighter complexion in the moonlight made him even lighter like a ghost, but no one could mistake those light brown hazel eyes. Those eyes that could stare into your soul and keep you locked away.

Memories I knew all too well. "Yes, but she's not completely gone. She's still here," His voice woke up the nerves in my body and I couldn't stop shaking. It wasn't the weather or the current situation.

I would be lying if I said that this man doesn't still scare me.

"How do you know?" the other goon had asked.

August turned back his attention to the goon and shot him in the shoulder. The shot ringing in my ears, closing my eyes for a brief moment from the quickness of the movement.

His anger was rising, an anger that once was turned to me time and time again. "You dare question me and ask how I know the woman that got away from me is still around?" The man groaned in pain but got back up after being knocked on the ground. "I know because I know her like the back of my hand. I know every corner of her mind and that little crew of hers." His sinister voice echoed.

I started to crouch back down and back up, I did the only thing that I could do. I searched for a rock enough for me to toss it and make a noise. I patted the ground until I could feel something. Something bigger than my palm.

Please let this work.

I found a stone, turned my body behind me and threw it behind me. I bared myself to the ground and didn't move. I could hear the three of them turn around on their heels.

"I told you, little princess, you can't hide forever." He sneered before taking off.

I tried to hold back the tears and the vomit that was rising in my throat, I covered my mouth in my attempt. I let a few moments pass by and I knew I had to dust myself off and continue to my exit point.

He had power over me, again. I hate myself for it.

I slowly stood up, tugging my pack and my eagle on my side. It wasn't long before I felt a presence behind me. The cracking of a branch behind me, then a body forced behind me, their hand wrapped over my mouth. I swallowed a scream because I knew those hands, very intimately. The warmth of his body and a light vanilla scent filled me with ease.

Winston.

His hot breath over my ear, "It's okay baby girl. I'm here. Right here." He comforted me, feeling his lips softly kissing my sweaty heated hair.

Slowly I nodded my head as he let me go. I twisted my body and punched him in the gut. "You're fucking kidding me, I told you to get your ass out of here!" I shouted at him.

He wasn't supposed to be here. He was supposed to be in one of three cars and back to the flat, away from all this, so I knew that he was in one piece.

Instead, he was here with me with possible danger still lurking. I smacked his body in frustration, repeating the same hit. Thankfully he was built and muscular enough to take the hits. But my hand was starting to get sticky.

I lifted it up to the light, and saw a dark pigment.

No! No no. please.

I silently screamed in my mind. He called me stubborn, how dare he. I stopped and my hands roamed over his body. His hands cupped my face and made me look up. Such majestic in his strength and features.

"Win. You're bleeding."

"What a smart genius you are," He said. "We said no more running. We forgot one thing."

"That you are a dumbass for disobeying me."

"You're not in charge, baby, and if one of us runs, the other is going to follow," He kissed me lightly, taking every negative and horrid thought in my head and melting it away.

I whimpered in his kiss, helpless at his touch.

"You didn't listen," I said against his lips.

"You really think I would leave you? Not again." he reminded me. I loved this promise.

There was a click, a small click that broke the tender moment away. I turned and covered my body over Winston's.

August.

Pointing his gun back in my direction. "How sweet." His light English accent rang out. "Looks like someone got what he wished for. Winston, my friend, your hands are somewhere they don't belong. My woman." He snarled.

I hissed out, showing my teeth, like a lioness protecting her own, "I was never yours."

He chuckled, my stomach in knots. "Princess, you are. In every way, behind me, on your knees, and even my bed."

"I'd rather be dead than have you touch me," I said.

Winston had his arm wrapped around me, holding me tight. My one hand bracing on his arm, and the other reaching for my holster. I don't know how fast he could reach behind him and reach the automatic. I was ready to go down with a fight.

"Oh, it won't be your death, but it might be the brute, who has his paws over you." August declared and then nodded to something in front of him.

Two of his goons, including the injured one, came around the corner with their guns in our direction. Both in close proximity. I was trapped in my own nightmare where myself, feeling powerless, and the fear of losing someone else lived.

I turned back to August. More of my own mistakes illuminated painful memories.

Back then he had been a light in my life, a light that slowly suffocated me. He was handsome and dashing, now I see a devil incarnate, haunting me. "What do you want, Augustus?"

He swayed dramatically, "I want a lot of things." His lips curled in a disgusting smile. "I want the key."

"I Iuh, there are a lot of keys. Key to the city, key to a car, a key to the jail cell you rightfully belong in. You're going to have to be more specific." I sassed him.

He stepped closer, I clung onto Winston tighter. I wasn't going to lose him, but he braced himself in front of me with his arm behind him around my waist.

August took a couple more steps, his figure starting to loom over me, not like Winston. "I want that key that is hiding in your pack. One of seven."

My eyes grew wider. Maybe he didn't know that we had gotten the other one.

He laughed again, "Did you really think I wouldn't be after this as well. Ask yourself, darling." He stepped closer and held the gun to my chin, his eyes luring down at me, "Who do you think told that professor about the journal? Let alone place it in his hands?"

I shook my head in disbelief.

My eyes couldn't tear away from his look, but inside I was dying. He had beat me to the punch. He had taken the one thing that I yearned for from me again. He was ten steps ahead of me and made me think that I was the first one, that I was making headway.

The gun dug into my skin even more, jarring pain radiating, "There's that look I was waiting for. Defeat. Lost." He sneered into those words like they were the truth, his truth.

"There is no way. You couldn't have possibly made progress that fast. It has taken me years." I spat back.

I could feel Winston's tight grasp on me, trying to become one body. He knew if he made any sudden movements either August or his squad of goons that would end us. We may be quick but not matched for them, at this present time.

"I had some help. Someone else is seeking out the same thing. Call it mutual hatred. And we have you to thank for it," He was rubbing it in our face.

"Sounds like you didn't have all the brains, you had to puppet someone else." Winston retaliated. I squeezed him, telling him to shut up, his smart remarks could end us.

August cocked his head, "Winston, you don't scare me and it's only a matter of time that you'll be bored of her."

He was trying to get under his skin and it was working. Winston flinched at August, resulting in August laughing maniacally and a rifle in the back side of Winston. He had collapsed a bit over me.

I shook my head, "Enough of the pretend territory fight. What the fuck do you want?" I asked, holding up Winston from falling fully on the ground.

August extended his hand, "Martine's key. It's a nice addition to Esmerie's key. So elegant with a jade stone on it."

He found the key at the family tombs. He had one already, and we didn't see it coming, at all.

He had uncovered the ground and searched for it. He had possibly destroyed the land around it, trying to wreak vengeance on me. Taking apart the history.

"I can hear your thoughts, Gwendolyn. They are loud and delicious." The gun disappeared from my chin, as his free hand caressed my cheek, "This is one quest that won't be yours. I suggest you hand over the key, and I'll let you and your little plaything go. And you can return to that god forsaken crew." I tried to bite his hand. "That feistiness, some things do not change."

"You can't break me. Not again. If you think that I am going to give up something so easily, you are wrong, Auggie." I chuckled, knowing that he hates that nickname. I used to do it just to spite him.

I was rewarded with his backhand, twisting my head in the same direction. Winston tried to find the strength to move or strike, but the blow to his back knocks him out more than he realized.

August started to breathe heavily, his anger raging through him. I struck a nerve with him and he deserved it. But the pain in cheeks was radiating, he must have had some rings on, typically I can take a hit. I felt something warm dripping down. The bastard spilled my blood.

"Funny thing is, I already am."

"Not this time, we beat you once, we'll do it again," Winston straightened up, bringing his back behind me. Straightening up my body.

"The key if you please. Or I'll just keep spilling blood until there is none left in your lifeless bodies. I'll deliver you to the doorstep of that precious manor in the states and take everyone you love down with you." It wasn't a threat anymore, to August it was a promise. A promise that he would fulfill.

I had to give in, for once I wasn't going to let history repeat itself over and over again. I wasn't going to risk anyone else's lives other than mine. Everything was killing me inside. I was about to hand over something that I had dreamed of for so long. But history is not going to repeat itself.

I reached over into my pack, rummaging through it to find the key. I continued to think of other plans. I could have turned it into a trick and stuffed it down my shirt or slip it to Winston. But the possible consequences were too great. The key's cool metal was icy in my hands. The feeling of hope was slipping away as the key came into the light. Gripping it in my hand, I didn't want to let go.

This was for Winston and the safety of the others.

My body slumped.

I handed the key into August's outstretched hand and the weight of the key lifted out of my hand but my chest felt like it had something else on it.

"Such a compliant little princess. You say I haven't broken you, but the Gwendolyn I knew would have chosen history over others would have fought more." He made a tsking noise as the key and August started to walk away. "I expected more from the great Gwendolyn Griffin. Disappointing. Until next time my darling."

And just like that he vanished into the dark of the night.

I collapsed on the ground, and let out a blood curdling cry in frustration. I was a fool! I became too damn scared of losing that I lost again. In the corner of my mind, there was a shadow that lingered after the group had left. It was covered by fog, I couldn't see. The person walked away, fading into the background.

There was a hand on my shoulder, "We have to leave now." Those hands picked me up. My body is lifeless. I stayed silent as we made our exit and speedy getaway. Winston wasn't taking any chances, and for me, I had to change everything about my next moves.

I had enough wrath and spite in me to know, I let myself get bogged down with this. I had been too cautious and too damn scared.

Chapter 25

Winston

She was too damn quiet and at glance she was somber, depressed, barely moving. But I know her. She was like a hurricane, a storm was brewing and it was a matter of time before she released her own fury.

Through the streets of Paris, I drove us back to the flat. What she did was tough and I know that it wasn't easy for her. I could see the damage it had done. Both of us were bleeding and injured but emotionally and mentally it was taking a toll on her.

When we arrived at the flat, she didn't give me a chance to walk to her and escort her back, she rushed out of the car like it was on fire, she had to get away. "Gwen.." I started to say, she turned on her heel and held up her hand to stop me, "Don't, because the next words out of my mouth are going to be hard to take back if I let them out. So please, don't say anything else."

She walked away, not because she was done but because she was going to say something she couldn't take back.

Her footsteps echoed loudly as she went up the flight of stairs. She needed to get looked at by Zach and so did I. I abandoned the original plan to go find her and I was going to be ripped a new one by everyone.

"Fall back, everyone to their routes." Dominic had yelled through the comms. Dominic, Yankee, and Quinton were taking fire and protecting themselves from the guards that August ever so nicely acquired as a distraction. While the other end of the crew;

myself, Zach, and Hartley were taking bullets from August and his muscle.

I could hear Gwen talking through the comms, she was telling Elijah to take Xara and she was going to take the key, while the others escaped. She was going to bait. But August was too smart, he knew she would have it. Why didn't she give it to Xara?

Bullets were flying and ricocheting off stone. One had grazed me and I knew that it was going to hurt like a bitch. "Winston, Hartley, we gotta get out of here. Move." Zach was trying to give out orders as if he was back in the army. By the time we were making headway to our exits and had given us enough cover, I bolted. "What the fuck are you doing?"

"I'm not leaving her."

"She wanted us to leave." Hartley yelled at me, catching me from behind and yanking me backwards. "You go after her and you risk more than just a grazed bullet. You can end up dead."

"I'm. Not. Leaving. Her. Again." I growled out.

Zach pulled Hartley, "Let the dumbass find the she-devil, she'll tear him a new one."

"Winston, bud, I'm going to need you to re-think this. We all have been out of the field and danger for far too long, I don't think we are equipped with pieces on the board." Dominic tried to reason with me.

I didn't care, I wasn't going to leave her. She was running into the fire of August. Damn the consequences. I jerked away and weaved in and out of the paths, taking caution of the whereabouts of Augustus, the guards, or his men. My feet picked up speed, my mind and my body only knew one thing.

It wasn't until I saw from the distances a figure hiding behind a small mausoleum. Her lean, toned body hugging the stone as August and his men followed a sound in the opposite direction. She was trying to escape and be smart about it.

As soon as the coast was cleared, she started to stand up and I edged my way towards her, wrapping my hand over her mouth *to prevent any screaming. Her body tensed and between the rush of adrenaline and her body pressed against me, a thousand wrong thoughts entered my head.*

"It's okay baby girl. I'm here. Right here."

Fuck it.

I followed up the stairs as she slammed opened the door. And marched herself into her room before anyone could say a word to her. Everyone else was gathered in the main room, some stripped of their bloodied or torn clothing, some slumped on the couch with ice packs on their heads. Dominic was the first person that stood up.

He clasped my shoulders, "Thank God, you two are alright." I flinched a bit from the pain all over. As the adrenaline eased out, my pain started to blare through my skin.

"I wouldn't go that far, boss," I mumbled.

He shook his head, "I was going to chew your asses, but I have a strange feeling that it was already done" He said. He was hinting towards Gwen as she had disappeared.

Zach was in the middle of patching up Hartley, a chill ran through me, remembering when Hartley was unconscious after the last time. I thought a bullet must have grazed him as well, like me, and we were just lucky.

Quinton was on the far end with Xara's head in his lap. She passed out, which I didn't blame her for. It was getting to be dawn at any moment and none of us had slept well the previous night.

Yankee was taking a swig of something strong. Elijah was pacing the floors, didn't know if the man was nervous or still shaken. I think he was scared shitless.

"What happened back there?" Dom asked, crossing his arms.

Was I going to tell my version of the story or rely on Gwen to tell it? But she wasn't there, she was stewing in her room. I had half a mind to drag her back out and not hide from us, but what use would that be?

The fire from the fireplace across the way crackled. Small sparks of ember spitting out. The temperatures were dropping from the seasonal change. The sound of it filled the silence.

"Obviously I went back to find her and I did," I couldn't look at Dominic and risk feeling his disappointment. "And we ran into some trouble." I chewed the inside on my cheek, barely looking at anyone. "We got caught by August" the last words drawn out slowly.

We all were cautious of August and we're trying to not have an encounter with him but obviously it didn't happen like that. You could hear a pin drop.

Dominic dropped his arms in shock, "What do you mean you got "caught by"?"

I could sense that his anger was starting to bubble. Everyone stopped what they were doing and looked at me. Zacharias looked at me with the needle in his hand as he was trying to finish patching up Hartley.

Hartley had a blank stare. Xara had woken up from her deep sleep possibly from the movement of Quinton as he jolted in his position.

"He found you?" Dominic continually asked.

Before I could answer, Gwendolyn came into view. I started to answer. She had an annoyed look on her face.

"He found me." She began, "Not Winston. I had every plan to escape after I distracted him. But someone didn't listen to me nor to the team." Her anger was fuming at this point. She was ready to blow and I didn't know where she was going to aim it at. "I had every intention of running the opposite direction once the coast was clear but somebody decided to do something otherwise." Her attitude blasted louder than any other words.

"Gwendolyn, I think this would be the time for you to take a moment and," Quinton started to therapize his wording towards his sister.

Her eyes darted in his direction, stepping closer into the room. "Respectfully big brother, I'd shut up before telling me to think before I speak talk. Try again. Or respectfully shove it."

His eyes narrowed, seeing two Griffin siblings about to start a fight, "I'm just merely offering a suggestive idea that you take a step back before you explode on us. I can see it in your eyes that you are ready to explode,"

He offered but she wasn't having it. She was ready and willing to lunge across the room, she was that frustrated.

Zacharias and Hartley looked at each other as if to say they didn't know what their next move was going to be but they needed to be out of the way before objects started to fly. Whether to duck in cover or make some popcorn watch the show.

Dominic started to creep slowly towards her making sure that she wouldn't lunge at somebody. Yankee and Elijah took a step back even further as if to step away from the path of wrath. As if Martine herself was reincarnated.

"I'm assuming you didn't tell him what happened in the end?" she asked, crossing her arms in front of her, throwing her hip to the side. I shook my head no.

"August caught us, and Winston's back is the result of what happened and how bad it was." Dominic and Zach reacted, turning their attention back at me.

"What does she mean "your back"?" Zacharias asked.

I sighed, hoping that it wouldn't have come up.

"Nothing." I muttered, darting my attention back to her.

Don't start something you can't finish babygirl.

She was losing her internal battle.

"Bullshit." Zach said, slamming the needle on the table, thankfully he was done with suturing Hartley.

He yanked my shirt over my back. Flinching for a moment would cause the pain to start radiating again. There he would find the beginning stages of my bruised back from the butt of the rifle that landed there. "Fucking hell man. How are you standing?" He guided me to one of the empty seats, so he could get a better look at me. I was barely standing but had the strength to move on.

"You should take a look at Gwen's face." I said throwing it back to her, someone had to take care of her. Zach grunted and marched towards Gwen, her eyes narrowed.

"Fucking touch me Zach, and you'll lose your hand." she said, throwing her hands up to stop him.

Her face was bruised from the smack in the face, a small imprint left on her cheek. I could see the dried up blood that had been cleaned yet. Zach backed off and returned his attention to me.

Everyone stilled, waiting for the next explosion to happen. We didn't know if it was going to end up being like before when we all had to split or if she had learned from the last time.

"Why don't you take over then. You have their attention," I suggested.

She rolled her eyes and that made my blood boil for a second. It shouldn't have but it did and with our new dynamic that we have found, I could not wait to punish her for that.

One day at a time.

"Fucking someone explained what happened and why you all look like that death rolled over." Hartley yelled out, which I didn't blame him because we were all getting frustrated.

Gwen stared at Hartley, challenging him, waiting for him to take bait, anything she could do to prove that she was the strong one.

Gwen slumped to the side leaning against the door frame, trying to recount her words before she would explain. "They were following me down the path after I had told Elijah and Xara to leave. I had the key with me that way one of us had it, I was more concerned with getting them to safety that I didn't think about the damn key. I would have an easier escape especially if it was just me and not a part of the crew," she started to move around, pacing around like she was still settling in.

She took a deep breath, "I got to a point where I found a spot to hide and distracted them by throwing a rock in the opposite direction. They had gone in that direction and I was ready to bolt until *somebody* crept up on me and scared me." she nudged in my direction. I remained silent.

"Crazy bitch, why didn't you just stick with the original plan, couldn't just stick with the group." Xara shot up. Yankee and Eli watched from side to side waiting for the rest of the fight.

"Why? Because I wasn't going to lose..." she started. But she didn't finish that statement, as if the battle to figure out what she really would lose held its power. "Unfortunately, he found us. And.." she tried to continue, but either anger or frustration mixed with sadness was about to come out.

"Sweet girl, you're holding back something," Yankee tried to ask but the more that we pressed about the wise and about her the more that she grew frustrated and angrier. I think she was getting frustrated because we were asking more about her then we had in the past few months or even in the past few years. She shook her head, avoiding that.

But it was Zacharias that asked the harder question, "Where's the key Gwen?"

She looked down, fiddling with her feet, twirling it around the flooring. She didn't want to admit defeat. She didn't want to admit that she had to make a choice that was harder than anything else.

I tried to twist around even more as Zach tried to stop me. I wanted more than anything to just tell them what happened so that she didn't have a weighted feeling of disappointment or she'd let everyone down.

Again.

But I knew where her anger was going and it's understandable and I was prepared for the fight that we were about to have or we're going to have.

"It's currently in the hands of August right now." I spurted out. The amount of gasp and outcalls were outrageous, it was expected.

"What do you mean it's with August?"

"You fucking kidding me."

"How did that happen?"

"Gwen you let that happen how?"

They continued to bombard her and me with questions and Gwen stood there almost like her soul had left her body.

"We didn't have much of a choice." I sneered out as Zach kept examining my back and pressing an ice pack onto it but not gently.

"There was no *we*. It was *me*. I didn't have much of a choice." She corrected me, "I gave it to him," Gwen quietly said. At first it was missed but it was her brother that heard it the loudest.

"Gwendolyn. You gave it to him." her brother sounded like he was about to reprimand her.

"She just told you that she didn't have a choice." I growled out partially in pain but more and more in her defense. He and I were going to fight if he continued to degrade her like a two-year old.

"I'm surprised at you, little one," Hartley started to say, it was then that the bomb was about to drop.

"Everyone can now kindly fuck off." She growled out. Her hands clenched in a fist, ready to swing with fury.

Everyone was surprised for more than one reason. "We're just saying that it was more unlike you to make that kind of move." Elijah softly said.

She started to bare her teeth, like a ravenous animal showing off dominance, "Do I have to be a broken record to say again that I didn't have a choice? It was either I give him the key or I risk losing somebody else. What would you have me do? Are you glad that I actually broke down? I understand that this is unlike me," she started to pace around the floor. I was surprised at her restraint of not tossing a punch or knocking over furniture or items in the house.

"Imagine if you would if you were in my shoes? Elijah if someone made you choose between your cousin and something you have wanted your whole life and it was in your hands. You all told me years ago that I didn't think of anyone else when I risked your lives in that cave and let myself get carried away when I was so close to finding something. Now, you say that it's such a surprise when I made a decision to give it up and think of someone else other than me?" She scuffed.

"You're right. You made a better decision than before but, didn't seem like there was much of a fight." Xara spoke up, digging under Gwen's skin.

"What would you have me do?" She screamed at this point, covering the frustration in her voice.

"His two men were pointing guns at Winston and August so happily put a gun under my own chin. You know what the best part of all this was?" she started to laugh adding a dash of psychoticness. "August knew all along. He has been ten steps ahead of us. Because he had the fucking journal before me. And apparently there's somebody else in the mix as well. Someone else's life we apparently fucked up and is now seeking vengeance."

"Winnie, you don't have to continue." I tried to stand up, but was instructed not to do so.

The crew fell silent. They all turned hypocritical, underestimating that for once, Gwen had changed. They didn't know what to make of the information she had just shared.

Between having to choose between those that she loves and the history she was trying to protect. Or that she had made a choice and something blew up in her face again.

"So yeah, I lost the key to an egotistical maniac, who has not let go of me. Oh, and the other biggest part of this, on this day of shocking news, he has the next key from the family home.

Technically he has two keys where we just have the one." she continued to laugh.

That laughter was the scariest thing about her. There were no tears, there was no anger that was pouring out; it was just her.

Dominic walked slowly to her, turning her around, "Kiddo, I'm sorry that we are putting it all on you. I think we are all overwhelmed by what happened and this news. But most importantly, you are okay and you are both safe." He looked back at me.

He wrapped her in a big hug, surrounding her in warmth and comfort. She didn't return the hug. She started to muffle something, shaking her head as she pushed back from the embrace.

"What is it?" Dominic asked again.

"I need to get out of here." She started to shut down. "I can't be here."

"What do you mean?" Elijah spoke up.

"I'm not going to sit here with a bunch of hypocrites and so-called family when no one trusts me, when I know for once I made the right decision. If I sit here and stew any longer, then I will regret what I did." A spark of truth.

I stood up and pushed Zach aside, "You regret your choice."

She started to walk away.

"Gwendolyn!" I yelled at her. The first time in a while I raised my voice at her, and not the way she expected it. She turned on her heel, her fists clenched beside her.

"You. Should. Have. Listened. I had it under control." She responded. The room didn't fight her, they couldn't. "You get to do whatever you want and risk it all, but when I do what I need to, I get this. You left me to do it! Winston, damn it."

She was putting it on me. "The old me would not have hesitated on whether I would do it. I would have fought tooth and nail, I would have died going down and my soul would be okay with it. Honestly, the old me would have said to protect the lost things. I know that sounds fucking wrong, but Winston, I didn't hesitate to choose you. But I lost something. I lost the fight inside me. I felt weak. I *feel* weak," she turned back around heading out.

Weak? That she felt weak for choosing us? Choosing me? Choosing to step back? "That wasn't a weakness."

"It sure felt like it, especially after losing something we all worked hard for. We lost something more than we gained. Next time," She continued to walk away, "Just fucking listen." She hid her face. She waved her hands in defeat and left. The front door slammed shut, for her to do what she needed to do.

I fucked up. Well, we all fucked up.

The front door slammed shut, it could have woken up the neighbors. I turned back to the room, "Now y'all choose to stay quiet. A little help would have been nice. You all had something degrading to say to her, then when she chewed my ass out and left, you said nothing else."

Xara looked at Quinton, she stood up, stalked towards me.

She punched my shoulders. What was with these women and easily punching men? "Are you listening?" She asked me. I raised my eyebrow to her. She twisted around, "Are you all listening?" She scanned the room. The guys silently nodded. "She's trying to say you didn't trust her. Asshole." she looked at me and then back to everyone, "We all didn't trust her."

Hartley chimed in, "When all she did was try to earn our trust back, show us that she cared more about us, then glory."

"Can you blame us?" Zach commented, "We risked our lives last time." He sat back leaning on the table.

"Yes, I blame us. Fucking christ. She's not wrong when she calls us hypocrites. She faced the same decision as the last time and she made the choice we asked her to make years ago. Now we're telling her that she should have done it the other way around." Xara made her point.

"We're the assholes." Zach said.

"Give this man a prize. He actually said something smart." Xara snickered.

"I fucked up." I said sheepishly. Blinded by love and lust, lacking trust.

"No, my friend, we all fucked up." Quinton said.

"Alright, who's going to get Hurricane Gwen?" Elijah asked. Everyone looked around, she wasn't ready for me to come get her. This is one of those times where when she is ready for me, I'll be ready.

"I'll go," Her brother said. We all silently prayed that it would be the right choice. "I'm overdue for my own brotherly duties."

CHAPTER 26

QUINTON

Of all the times that I have screwed up, this was one of the biggest ones. When she needed me the most, I wasn't there for her again. And the guilt that riddled me was too heavy. I was the one that failed her, not her.

I gave her thirty minutes before I would go find her. But my sister is a creature of habit, and her preferences for a bar and sweets were too strong for her to hide. A few blocks down from the flat rested a pâtisserie shop that opened early in the morning. As I walked in with the doorbell rang as I opened the door, my eyes quickly found her. My sister's mouth was full of a chausson aux pommes, what we in the states would call an apple turnover.

I walked closer to her, bypassing any other patrons. She saw my movement, released an annoyed sigh and went back to looking at her food.

"I'm not fucking apologizing." She said.

I pulled the chair from the table and sat down, "Wasn't going to convince you otherwise."

She fiddled with her fork and the pastry. "They send you? Or did you volunteer?"

I started to strum my fingers along the table, "I volunteered."

We sat a few moments in silence. I kept looking at her, waiting for her to tell me what was going on in that head. Between losing a key, injuries, her former abusive partner's obsession over her, and being berated by us, her family and seeming like we were disappointed in her.

"You can stop staring at me." She said without looking up.

I arched my brow, "Why?"

"Because it's creepy when you do."

"Why?" I asked again, grinning. She was about to hate what I do.

"Because a brother wouldn't look at his sister as if she was one of his own clients," she started to play around with her pastry again.

"Why?"

She started to get furious, "Seriously, are we going to play this game again? You always do this."

"Why?"

"Because you are a cruel, evil big brother that doesn't need to know every waking thought in my head."

"Why?"

She pointed her fork at me as if she was holding a knife, "Because you don't understand everything."

"Why?" I took her coffee and took a sip of it. She was still holding the fork to me.

Her brows furrowed, "You did this to me as a kid when I didn't want to talk to anyone and you insisted on playing this 'why' question game. As an adult it's annoying and childish even still."

I start to open my mouth to repeat myself, but she cuts me off, "If you say it again, Quinton Griffin, I will return you to Xara with a fork in the hand." She slammed the fork onto the table. The rattling of the dishes startled the workers behind me.

I was just starting to tip the iceberg. She was starting to open up again. Maybe I was going to show her some trust and honesty of my own and hoped she would do the same.

"So you know about your college best friend and me." I commented. She grabbed her coffee back, and nodded her head.

"The whole manor could hear you two, in her room, the shower." She curled the corner of her mouth. Nosy sister. "But do I need to ask?"

"Ask?"

"Is this just a fling or are you two taking a shot?" A true question of the decade.

I shrugged my shoulders, I didn't know the whole answer to that. "Depends on her. I have professed what I wanted, and I believe the phrase is 'the ball is in her court'. Is that what you and Winston had decided?" I turned the tables back to her. Winston was a good man, smart, protective, and knew how to fluster my sister. He was like family.

Her mood went sour again, "Not going to talk about him."

"You can't be like that dear sister." I patted her hand that was on the table, she had yanked it back. Scrunched her face at me, as I said I was about to get to the tip of the iceberg. "You want me to admit that I am livid about how we acted, and even more so him."

"I think you touched on that subject, but I think it was Xara, the wise one, that extended the hidden message." she peered up at me, those Griffin blue eyes staring back at me. "He didn't trust you."

She took a deep breath, straining herself. It would have appeared that Xara was right, Winston nor the crew had trusted her, trusted that she could get out of the situation she was in just fine.

"He thought I would be weak." That part was not going to be something to address with Winston himself, not me.

"I think it would be wise if you discuss that with him, not me."

"Who else am I going to share this with?" She asked.

"The person you love." I didn't know if she had said those words to him yet, but I don't think she would have made the tough decision between him or the key if she didn't.

"Sister, I love you. If you didn't know it before, know it now. I am extremely proud of you." I said, reaching over towards her and grabbing her hands.

It wasn't that we were deprived of hearing people say that to us, but we were alike in the fact that we were successful in every aspect, and that it lost its meaning sometimes. "You are proud that I lost the key that the crew worked hard to get and I gave up so easily."

"I am proud that you put your love for your family, Winston, that you sacrificed a piece of you. That key wasn't a prize, it was a part of you that you had found and you had to sacrifice again. Does it seem off that you 'easily' let it go? Yes and no." That was the truth, and just like I promised our parents, our uncle, I was going to be the brother she needed me to be.

"Gwen, you have been wrapped up in the anxious thoughts of losing your family, finding the keys to the library, and the reappearance of August. Unfortunately, you had that overpower you. I believe that is why everyone is saying that you are not yourself." I searched for her eyes, seeing if there was a spark.

"What am I to do then?" She scuffed. "I can't be who I was years ago, and now I can't be who I am expected to be. Honestly, brother, it makes no sense to me." She was starting to backtrack.

"Let me ask this, who do you want to be?" I asked what could be a simple question, but to my sister it was the primary question of her life.

She took another bit of her pastry. "You can't silence yourself with food." I reminded her. She glared at me.

"I want to be the person that leads again, to find the history that is lost, to not have to lose anyone else. I want the version of myself where people hear my name and us and are terrified." She wants to be a better person without changing everything about her. That's commendable.

"Then be that person and be vocal about it. Since when did you have any troubles vocalizing what you wanted and how you want it." I reminded her that she is a Griffin, an outcast, a strong woman that can overcome anything. "Don't let a ghost or a shadow stop you from being who you are. You're smarter than that."

She paused for a moment. Letting the words echo through her mind.

"You know it sucks that you have to be right about things like this." She pointed out, "I'm not going back there right now." She gently laughed. "I don't think Zach or Hartley want to screw around with me."

I pushed the chair back and stood up, walking towards her, bending down and placing a gentle kiss on her head, "Yes, we wouldn't need anyone missing appendages. I'm sorry that I wasn't there for you again. You know I love you."

She looked at me, the soft beaming smile, "Always, brother."

I left her to sit in peace before she made her return to the flat. The sun had fully risen in the sky and before I had left we agreed that everyone needed a full day of rest before we returned with a game plan. Everyone had disbursed before I returned.

I could hear the heavy snores of Zacharias and Dominic, possibly from their time in active duty. Winston had been on the couch, possibly waiting for Gwendolyn to come back to the flat. His arms crossed in front of him, his body turned towards the door. The rest of them, Yankee and Elijah were probably knocked out from exhaustion. But there was one little demon that was wide awake and waiting.

"You survived the hurricane." she chuckled. With my sister knowing a bit more detail about whatever relationship Xara and I have was a load off of me. I had felt guilty going behind her back and not being honest with her.

"You should be asleep." I said to her.

She flashed a coy smile, "Well doc, someone told me once that I don't listen very well." She stayed leaning against the doorframe of my bedroom that I was sharing with Winston.

"I wonder who's brilliant observation was that." I glided towards her, meeting her at the door frame.

"The same person who also tends not to listen." She answered me back. I put a strand of her hair back behind her ear, caressing her cheek. She liked the tender moments of innocence. But her eyes darkened looking at me, "And you can be such a good boy when you do."

Her words flustered me, "Someone wants to play."

"Look at you blushing. It's so cute. Tell me what you want, and it's yours" She walked forward making me walk backyards into the door, closing the door behind us.

"You do understand that we still need to talk about something that we have been pushing aside." I tried to get her to start a conversation, but something told me that it would have to wait, we were both craving desire, lust.

There were a lot of things that I wanted. I wanted her to be mine and never hide that fact. I wanted her to command me like her darker fantasies. That's the best thing about her and I, it's never a power struggle. There are days that she wants me in control and there are times I want her in control. This was one of those moments.

She backed me up further to bed, where my knees hit the bed causing me to sit on the bed. She edged herself in between my legs. Both of her hands are on the sides of my face, tilting it towards her. "Tell me what you want."

My hands started to explore the curves of her muscles, her body, "Show me how I can better listen." She gripped my chin, bending down, placing a kiss, soft, but demanding.

She pulled back, with a wicked smile curling on her lips, "You'll have to remain quiet, or you're gonna wake up the entire flat." I nodded. "Let's see how well you follow instructions." her hand moves towards the top of my head, grabbing the curls in her hand. "If you don't stay quiet, you won't get to come, it will be my pleasure that I will take." I nod in agreement. The power was in her hands.

"Good boy." She loosened her grip. "Strip the shirt."

Without hesitation, I stripped the shirt I was in, giving her the view she wanted. I waited for her to tell me what she wanted next or her pleasure.

She sank down to her knees, still fully dressed. Part of me wanted to see her, touch her, feel her skin prickle under my touch. I was starting to just get hard thinking about it.

She unbuttoned the pants, "Slide them off. And keep your hands on the sides of the bed." I slid the pants and the briefs off. My erection springing free waiting for her touch. I rested my hands on the bed as instructed.

Her hands slid up my thighs, testing my resistance. The closer she got to my cock, the more my mind begged for her hands to wrap around it, asking her for the teasing to end. "Let's see how well you do listen. You don't get to touch me until I say so."

"Yes. Understood." I quietly said.

Her fingers lightly trail around every inch of me. I was already starting to ache. She was the image of power and a seductress and one day she would realize I was hers and she was mine. She stuck her tongue out, licking from the base to the top within a stroke. She trailed back up before she slowly put me in her mouth, taking every inch, knowing exactly what I liked. Starting suck me, tantalizing every tease, every move she made.

She hummed in hunger, as if she was craving every taste. This was everything. My control had faltered with the urge to thread my fingers through her own hair and take me deeper in her mouth.

Her head started to pick up pace creating a sensual rhythm, so powerful. She knew how to give pleasure but also take it away in a punishing act. Just when I felt close, she would slow down.

"Fucking hell." I could see her start to wiggle, she was enjoying this, the teasing, the pleasure of seeing me struggle and in the palm of her hand, literally and figuratively.

She laughed, and it made it harder to not touch, not move. The vibrations would send me over the edge. I didn't know what to do with my hands, my control was slipping. She had closed her legs, giving her friction against her own please. She was enjoying herself and all I wanted to do was taste her.

She released me with a pop, "You're doing good, but I can tell that you are so close."

She wasn't wrong. Another minute and I would exploding right there in her mouth and fuck the consequences. She lifted my cock up, dragging her tongue again starting from my balls to the top, taking her time before she picked up a ravenous pace.

"Xara, please." I wasn't going to last much longer.

She stopped and slowly stood up, wiping her mouth, taking all the wetness from her mouth and my cock, giving herself one last taste before her next command.

"Please what, sweet boy?" She asked me in a tantalizing voice. "You have to tell me what you want."

Testing me, that's what she was doing. Seeing what strength I had in me. "I want to touch you." She took a step back, "You may."

As quickly as I could, I sprang from the bed. I took her lips onto mine, never wanting to let go. Her passion mixing with my desire. I crave this woman everyday. I stripped her of her shirt, one she didn't have a bra on with, I devoured her, sucking on her nipples, teasing her in my own way. Her body bucked up against me, her little moans soft and quiet. With one hand taunting and teasing her breasts, the other wrapping the back and rubbing and grabbing her ass. The small little gasp she released made me want to keep continuing until one of us caves in.

"Lay down sweet boy, I have an idea. You want to touch me, make me come in two minutes and I'll reward you." Her chest started to heave, her twisted little mind had an idea, and I was putty in her hands.

I laid out on the bed. She started to stalk around it, wiggling herself out of her pants. The little demon had nothing underneath. She didn't want to waste time.

The bed dipped as she crawled over to me, "Scoot your head to the headboard." I did what I was told. "Good boy. You have two minutes, and then maybe I'll reward you."

I silently begged for nothing more than that. To please her, to relieve the ache that her and I were both feeling. She straddled my body and scooched up where her glistening pussy met my mouth. My cock got even harder if that was even possible. Two minutes would be a challenge, but I know what my woman loves and sends her over the edge. She didn't give me restrictions, it was fair game.

My hands palmed her ass closer as I feasted on her. She was sweet and wet just for me. I ate that sweet cunt like it was my last meal, switching between sucking on her clit and tongue fucking her. Her breathing staggered, but she was getting closer, she rode my face, like I was her own personal toy for use. In that moment I was happy to be that for her, knowing one day soon the tables would turn again.

"Fuck, right there Quin, you're doing so good." I grinned at her continuing my feast, I know one way for her to come immediately.

My hand gradually moved across her ass, sliding through the crack until my finger finds that tight hole that was wet from her glistening cunt, my finger started to fuck the little hole. Her thighs began to tremble, closing around me, suffocating me. She was getting there, I kept up the pace as she continued her way. Then a wave of pleasure soared over her. "Shit." she let out breathlessly. It took her a few moments to come down from her ride. I let my hands roam over her body, bracing myself in case she was going to be crashing on me.

A smiled at her winning at her challenge. She was a needy little demon.

"Such a good boy. You want your reward don't you?" She cooed.

"Yes, please."

"So polite." She glanced at my hungry cock, her hand grazed between my legs, giving a gentle stroke. I flinched at the barely even there touch. She slithered down my body, easing herself onto my cock. I bent my knees to give her some room to brace herself. She took every inch of me, the o-shape that her mouth formed. I could cum just at the sight of it.

"You and I are going to come together." She said, wickedly. My eyes grew wider, something that I enjoy immensely. I frantically nodded my head.

"Yes please," I said hoarsely.

Her hips rocked, having sunk down onto me. It was intoxicating, invigorating. She set the pace, I placed my hands on her hips, gripping her so she couldn't wiggle away. I could see the sweat dripping down her forehead.

I knew she was getting closer and so was I. I moved my hands from her hips to her face and brought her down to my face, possessively kissing her. Her hips lifted slightly, giving me the advantage to drive into her. Between our silent moans and groans, she was clenching around my cock, almost suffocating it and I would thank her for it.

"Come for me." That was all she said before her and I took off like a rocket filled with ecstasy. It had been a long while since we had last felt this way. I think we both had the same idea as both of us clasped each other's mouth from releasing a louder noise that could result in consequences. She took me out of her and just laid on top of me.

I knew in a moment or two I would need to get up and clean her up, though I know the little demon likes to be a little sticky once in a while, but I had other things in mind.

Our hearts settled down, our bodies collapsed onto each other. I kissed the top of her head, and a soft smile landed on her face.

"Xara, I think this is the time we need to have a conversation." She turned and folded her hands over her chin.

"Maybe you're right." She said softly. I inched away from her, finding my bottoms and one of my shirts for her.

I went into the bathroom, grabbed a warm cloth and came back to the bed. She had moved to the top of the bed mixed in with pillows, my shirt gracing her body. I crawled on the bed between her legs, and wiped the cum that was leaking out of her. She looked glowing as the sun painted her face with warm colors.

She let out a soft moan as I cleaned her, kissing her inner thigh. After I was done, I laid there between her and my head resting on her chest.

"You wanted to talk?" She said, her voice still in a haze. I didn't know how well this was going to go.

"I wanted to know what you wanted out of this. Us." I bluntly said. I wasn't going to sugar coat. We have a history and a history that is full of memories and stolen moments. She took a deep breath.

I looked at her chocolate eyes, I knew she was deep in thought. "Wow, that was blunt. I.. don't know." That was her honesty. To say that I was disappointed it would be understatement. "I never had to really think about this." She chewed on her bottom lip.

"I know it's hard to talk about this, especially relationships." I tried to reassure her, covering up my own emotions. I didn't need to feel like I was guilt tripping her. We all have our demons.

"What's hard is that someone is expecting an answer that won't hurt their own feelings." She said, I guess masking my own emotions was impossible for me. "Quinton, I care about you. I do. But having the expectation that we need to be in a relationship scares me."

"Because of your parents?" It wasn't a horrid observation.

"Why do you think I rebel? I break the rules they set because I learned that I don't need to fit into their expectations for my own life."

"Maybe my question should be, do you want me in your life?" I asked the question differently.

She nodded, "I want you in my life."

I started to think of ways that would make her more comfortable with the direction that we are going in. There wasn't anyone else in my life that I wanted than her. "Then instead of placing labels or expectations of what people call it, we are two people in this lifetime that care about each other enough that we don't want anyone else or looking for anything else."

"Saying it in pretty words means the same thing." She raised an eyebrow. "Putting a label on this is hard."

"Xara, I'm not looking for anyone else. How about this, we are each other's person. Someone we care about, maybe eventually grow to love and have a deeper connection. We are not calling each other a girlfriend or boyfriend. But I want to be the person you run to for the good and the bad. We don't need to hide from the crew. It would be you and me, we say what happens between us, not even my sister can dictate what we are supposed to look like." In any partnership, relationship, even marriage, it is between two people and only them.

"People will have their input." She's testing me.

"They can have their own input, the only input that matters is yours and mine."

"So, you're saying that I'm yours? Bit possessive isn't it?" She trailed her fingers down my spine.

"You were mine the moment I laid eyes on you, when you first met my sister. We just didn't know what paths would lead us here."

"You know I come with my own history, my own hurt." She tried to tell me, I lifted off of her and slithered up her body.

"I will take all of you, but you'll never have to experience any hurt with me. To see you hurt, hurts me." I hovered over here, inches away from her mouth. "But I'm not going to push you on this. This is your own decision."

She waited for a second, "Alright Doc, I want to try, but I make no promises."

I placed a kiss on her lips, her hands around my back. I pulled back, "That's all I could ask for. It's you and me, little demon."

She was mine and she knew that.

She grabbed my face pulling back to her into a tantalizing kiss. Her legs wrapped my hips. I wasn't going to ever get enough of this woman and I would be content with that.

Chapter 27

WINSTON

I waited for her as long as I could. She needed space. I couldn't wait any longer to the point where I passed out on the couch, facing the door in case she returned.

This time it was me that screwed up, and played a part in the incident while everyone turned their attention to her, placing her to blame.

I didn't want her to run from me. We just got back into a good place and we hit a tough place in the road.

I wasn't in a deep sleep yet, the sun kept me somewhat awake, I knew I wasn't going to get a full sleep until I knew she would be back. Even if she was still raging mad at me.

I heard footsteps creeping up the stairs and the turning of the doorknob. I sprung awake, wiping my eyes from any heaviness or sands in them. I hunched over, my hands folding in front of me. I waited.

She didn't see me at first, but once she closed the door, she looked back at me, her hair now up in a bun, she looked defeated still. I had hoped that the conversation with her brother gave her a boost or something. "Winston, I'm not in the mood to fight or argue." She held her hand up as she walked. The snores of the others welcomed her.

"Didn't think we needed to fight. We fought enough over the past few months." More like years even as kids.

"You can back down. Quinton has already done enough speaking to me and I have a couple of things to work out." She almost made it to the main hallway.

"Like what?" I called to her, still in a quieter voice.

She stopped, seeing her shoulders move up and down deeply. She turned, "Find a common ground between the person I was and the person people are expecting me to be."

"I liked the person you had become." I said.

She walked slowly, "Really, you liked the person that didn't put up much of a fight, second guessing herself? That's the person you liked?"

I shook my head, "I liked that I was seeing someone that was putting the needs and comfort of others before her own. But I am beginning to think that it's selfish of myself to think that." Not that I was second guessing myself, but I was blind to see that she was caring more about others and making a change to not see that the change was too much and she was lost in herself.

"Ya think? Win, this is not me," she gestured as to showcase her present self. "You can't tell me that you are falling for this person." She walked closer to me. Anger was still raging in her, she was frustrated with everything between her, the crew, the missing key, and even me. But I noticed that she winced after she said "falling for", it wasn't a discussion that has come up, at least not with the right timing.

"No, I fell for the woman that has a curve of her smile when she is ten steps ahead of someone, when she sees all the pieces on the board. I fell for the woman that fights even if she can be wrong, she is headstrong. But it wasn't until you walked back in my shop and had the look on your face like you knew what you wanted and you went for it," I leaned back onto the couch, opening myself up. "But I know that a certain woman has fallen for the man that can be a dumbass and possessive at the same time. The same one that doesn't give her enough credit for standing her ground." She scoffed at that one.

"He can be dumb, but his handsome face makes up for stupidity sometimes," She smirked. I chuckled, she was walking closer to me, enough for me to grab her by the wrist.

"I am sorry that I didn't trust you. I didn't want to lose you and that overpowered me." I gave her the apology that she didn't ask for but I know she needed. I continued, getting it out everything I could while she was listening, "I also know you are not a woman that can stay mad at me for very long. Not when he can apologize for not trusting you." I pulled her into my lap, as she cradled onto my body.

"Winston."

"That's my name."

"You're not getting off too easy." She reminded me.

"I understand. But you're not going to hide from me either." I tilted her chin to look at me. "I'll help you find your way back. Question is, who do you want to be?"

"I want to be the name people fear, especially when they come after me and our family. I want to be the hero of my damn story." There was a bite in her words, like venom ready to strike at any moment. No wonder Xara and her got along.

"Then be the little hellion that Zach is calling you. Be you. That's all I want. That's all we wanted from you." I couldn't speak for the group, and I could be stubborn but I just wanted her happy.

"Yes sir," she said sinisterly.

Well, there went my dick. "And there she is. Already starting trouble." I lifted her up as I stood up, her legs wrapped around me. I started to carry us through the hallway, also thankful that this didn't end up in a screaming match.

She kept looking at me with those sea blue eyes. "I'm still very upset with you." She pouted, whining at the same time, playfully of course, the little side of brattiness was showing. She was starting to get back at it.

I copied her whinness, "I know. You can be mad at me for as long as you want. I'll even let you take it out on me. But first, I'll make it up to you." I reached for that little pout and suffocated with a kiss before she threw her arms around my neck.

I kicked open the door, looked around to see if Xara was in here and thankfully was not. Hopefully she didn't wander off. Dominic would be pissed.

For the rest of the morning, we buried ourselves in each other, allowing for any and all frustrations to be released. Then sleep overcame us, it was the second to best sleep I had gotten in years and I had my little minx with me.

None of us resurfaced from the bedrooms until later that night, the sun had set. Each of us stumbled into the main room for food and even coffee. The cousins came out looking like roadkill, possibly from sleeping hard. I knew that Zach was snoring up a storm, but Dominic was no better.

Yankee resurfaced but looking fresh as ever. Like he stepped into a fountain of youth. Just looking like a sunshine person in a night ridden world. Dominic had walked into the room looking rough.

We knew his general rule, never speak with him until thirty minutes has passed and he has an ounce of coffee in him. Hartley was on his computer, possibly running all his systems on high. That man could work and never sleep and he would be okay with that.

The shocker of them all was Xara and Quinton himself. Walking hand in hand, and if I wasn't mistaken, she was in one of his shirts. Gwen was in my lap, giggling. "You knew," she nodded her head. Two people I would never put together. I wondered when they were going to make an announcement or say anything or even keep it to themselves.

"Look at all the bright, eyed and bushy tails." Yankee sang, followed by a few groans.

"Anyone else think that Yankee is too loud?" Elijah said.

"Oh, Eli, you like me loud." He winked. I spit out my coffee, he was ready to get under everyone's skin.

"Zach do you have any of that duct tape or sutures in your bag? I could use that to shut him up." Eli groaned, his bright golden sunshine mood hadn't woken up yet.

"Don't tempt me with a good time."

"Enough you three," Dominic growled out, and the three of them shut up quickly. "Why do I feel like I have been hit with a truck of bricks?"

"Not sure if that is the correct phrase, boss man." I said to him, smirking at Gwen, knowing full and well that Grouchy Bear was not taking to jokes.

"Because our bodies after the impact of last night are now catching up, also I need to get everyone checked out before we head into whatever direction we are going in." Zach ordered, which is precaution saying if we bleed or rip out any stitches he is going to be pissed.

Dominic sat at the main table, gulping down his entire cup of coffee. Even I wouldn't have done that. "Alright, debrief time."

The debrief time wasn't just a time to reflect on what happened and how we can make it better moving forward, but a time to air out any unwavering feelings or words that if not said now, were not to be brought up in the future or used against us.

It wasn't a Dominic rule, it was a Quinton rule.

"Kiddo, I'm going to let you take the floor." Dominic said, hinting at Gwen. She shook her head, "I have done enough talking in my defense. But someone told me that I needed to remind myself who I am and stop being dramatic."

"I never said you were dramatic." Quinton said defensively.

As a group we all responded, "Yes you are." It was what we loved about her as a person.

"You're right I had my own flair."

"Is Gwen hour done now?" Zacharias groaned.

"You got something to say?" Dominic turned around peering at him.

"Yeah, we are a hot mess express. One turned into a possessive asshole that could have made things worse, we have one prima donna that was willing to risk her life, again. Then you have us that just follow along. We are a hot mess." Zacharias relayed, crossing his arms.

"Agreed, we are a mess, but we have not fallen apart," Dominic reassured us. "Anyone have any gripes or items they want to get off their chest?" A moment went by and everyone was waiting for someone to speak.

Hartley finally looked up from his computer, he had been quiet for the most part. "Time to stop dicking around and actually get to work," Bold words from the man that remained quiet. Gwen wiggled around in my lap, if she kept doing that we would have had a repeat of this morning.

"Elijah, anything?" Dominic went through the roll.

"All good," He responded.

"Yankee?"

"Anyone else see the hand holding and the t-shirt wearing Xara?" He pointed out. Xara smacked the back of Yankee's head.

Dominic glared at Yankee, "Bud, shut up. Not your place. Zacharias, anything else?"

"Nope, other than I would like to not stitch up anymore people, please." He muttered while taking a sip from his coffee.

"Noted, Hartley, anything else?"

He shook his head, headed back onto his computer.

"Anything from the couples?" Dominic bluntly said.

Xara and Quinton jolted back, trying to not make it obvious. "If you are going to be in each other's clothing and don't want to make it obvious then, be careful what you come out wearing." Dominic grumbles in his coffee.

"Told you they would figure it out." Xara smacks Quinton in the stomach.

"Only you and me." He kissed the side of her head.

Dominic continued "Anything else from the other couple?" Pointing in our direction.

"No, I think I'm good. Babygirl?" I said, letting her answer for herself.

"All good."

"You know the rules, once this ends, nothing else can come up that should have been said in this conversation. If you didn't say anything, bury it now, write it down and throw it away, whatever you need to do to get it out of your system. I'm giving everyone thirty minutes to get themselves together and in their own clothing. We have a key to find." Dominic instructed.

Everyone separated on their own accord, I followed Gwen through the hallway, "You heard the man everyone needs to be in their own clothing," I growled in her ear.

"You're not getting the sweatshirt back, it's mine now."

"Okay," I smiled at her and smacked her ass as she went into her room.

Moments flew by and we were gathered once again with the crew and immersed back into the world of unknown history and lost things. Hartley seemed to have been hard at work.

"Hey brother, what's going on with you?" I slapped him on his back. He flinched, he was lost in cyberspace. He had even darker circles under his eyes. "Seriously, you were supposed to get sleep, not look like a death hangover." He shook his head. He had mumbled something, I couldn't make it out.

"Sorry what?"

"I don't understand," He said again. "There is no way that Augustus should have been to be steps ahead of us. Every firewall, every search within the dark web. How could he just reappear and move without a trace?"

"How were we to know? We were much in the dark and taken by surprise." I reassured him.

"That is where we need to start." Dominic echoed through the hallway, being the final piece to start the plan of how we get through the next half of this quest.

CHAPTER 28

DOMINIC

As Hartley bluntly put it, we needed to stop dicking around and pull ourselves back together. We hadn't been a unit in that two year span split. Or at least, the unit that we used to be like.

We came back thinking we could pick up where we last left off or suffer through a last quest together and leave once and for all. We had forgotten our flow. We missed listening to each other, respecting one another, and even knowing ahead of the next move.

My hope was that we have cut the shit and are ready to move on. We played the blame game and the pointing fingers. We have done the trial and error of acting as individuals rather than a team.

I opened up my own notes and files, thanks to Hartley and Xara, "We need to understand things from the beginning."

Gwendolyn sauntered over, sitting on the table next to me. We had our makeshift board from the manor in front of us. "Starting with the journal, he was the one responsible for getting it into my hands." She said, "His words were similar to 'how do you think you got the journal in the first place'. He boasted about it. As if this was his credit in everything."

"He had a hand in the dealing, especially with your professor associate." Yankee said.

"Fucker made me barter too. I had to promise I would guest lecture anytime he needed a guest lecturer. Or really when he didn't want to teach."

"Ew. Undergrads." Yankee shivered with sarcasm.

"Point being that he had the journal before us." Gwen said, pausing as Xara stepped in, "Which means he had time to go through it. I even second guessed myself that he put in false evidence to throw me off."

"Any conclusion?" I raised the question.

She shook her head in relief, "No, none of this is new. Even Yankee had it in his possession back in the manor and never said anything about fake paper or entries." Smart deduction.

He nodded in agreement, "You can't get around the paper quality. In this journal, it's extremely hard and years in the making to make a perfect replica of this paper." Yankee added.

"So, we don't even know how long he's had it." Zacharias pointed out.

"Are we concluding something then?" Elijah asked.

"The son of a bitch knew exactly where to look." Winston growled out.

Gwen was a little solemn, "And he has two keys in his possession."

The room fell silent, "Come again?" Xara exclaimed. It was a little piece of information that was left out.

Winston spoke up from the corner, "Augustus gloated to us that he had Esmerie's key, it was a jade stone key. Presumably like the others."

Augustus came back like a hydra, multiplying how many heads were going to surface. My head started to pound. We needed to be careful with the keys, safe guard as much as possible.

"Talk about being prepared." Yankee chimed. "And now he's ahead in this game."

"He waited this long? To do what? Snake his way back in?" Zach commented.

We took some of his dignity and his image after what he did to Gwendolyn and us. He fought back after we regained her in the crew and away from him. He shot his ammunition at us and we fought back. Fortunately, we won the battle but apparently not the war.

"He pulled a Hartley," Elijah joked. But it was different. Hartley grunted, not appreciating the fact that Elijah was comparing him to August. Pulling a Hartley just meant that someone popped in when you least expected it.

He was different.

Gwen walked over to Hartley, stood behind him rubbing his shoulders, "Hartley is not like him. Hartley is playful with his way of getting into the minds of others, he just likes to fluster, make you blush, innocent. Augustus is a cruel evil man that waits to take something and use it against you. His mind tricks are more than cruel, they are more like hell's punishment in flesh." She gave him a peck on the cheek.

"Wasn't my intention to do so." Elijah said somberly.

"I know. But we have to remember who we are dealing with." Gwen reminded everyone, returning to her spot near me.

"Fucking crown prince of hell." Yankee sneered.

"And one mystery person." Quinton noted.

We had another piece of the board that we didn't know anything about, only a personal vendetta against the Griffins.

Xara walked towards the board, "So we have to assume that he has figured it out on his own."

"Shithead didn't know the difference between ruling monarchs of his own country, what makes you think he did this on his own." Gwen fired back.

"Easy kiddo, aim that fire at someone else." I calmed her down.

"In layman's terms, he knows the majority of where the keys lie, if he had help, there may be a couple things he can't figure out." Quinton pointed out.

"We might have an advantage." I said. "There are locations that we can pull together."

"We'll have much more than an advantage, we have more than he'll have in a lifetime." Gwen beamed.

"But the next one on our list was the prison, Chateau d'If." Elijah had said.

"That is a long travel! We takin' a helicopter or something?" Zacharias spurted out.

There were a few chuckles. "Slow down, we'll get to that point. After the prison what locations do we have?"

"We have a church for Ameline which we are still looking into possible locations. Desiree's lover, whoever that may be, and then Narcisse's mirror in her home, which we are still inquiring about." Gwen ran through the list.

"The last three are ones that we still have to research in." Winston asked.

"Correct, and if we know our enemy's mind set, we have some time." Quinton continued.

Gwen started to chew on her bottom lip, a sign that she was lost in thought. She started to fumble through the journal, going through each page looking into every word.

"We still have to think of a way of getting back the keys that we are missing." Yankee pointed out.

We had a few items and we kept jumping around. I had to make notes of where they were in conversations.

"Let's put a pin on the notion about the locations, we need to plan ahead for Chateau d'if." I demanded their attention and focus. Little steps at a time.

Hartley got up from the other table bringing his laptop, placing it on the table, projecting the screen on the wall next to the board. He gathered Elijah, "Lucky for us there is a day where it is not for the public, which is in the next two days. We have to be diligent."

"But, unfortunately," Elijah continued.

Yankee piped up from the back "I don't like the sound of that."

"I second that," Gwen chimed in.

"There is not enough evidence to believe that there is a safe or something similar to a safe within the prison." Elijah pointed out the only entrance to the fortress part of the prison.

The prison is surrounded by water and I would say a ten minute or twenty minute boat ride. The city has grown over the centuries and it is not as discrete or hidden as the island once was off the coast of France. The only way a prisoner would be able to escape is by death or within the Count of Monte Cristo, pretending that you are deceased.

"Which means, it can be somewhere on the island," Hartley said.

"Then where?" I asked.

No one had an answer, we had anticipated that it would be in a safe. But in this case, it may not have been the case. Hartley and Elijah looked through the possibilities, taking in every crevice of the structure. The layout of the historical prison.

This was not my domain, not my speciality, I couldn't say much. I was getting frustrated more and more by the moment. "I guess we are all going to be gluttonous for punishment, especially some punk getting ahead of us," I uttered. Thinking that I was saying it in mind. Obviously not.

All eyes were set on me, "What?"

"Say it again." Yankee said.

"Say what again?" I asked.

"You big oaf, the beginning part." Xara said.

"Guess we're going to be a glutton for punishment?" I said again, "I'm just saying nonsense right now."

"You might be onto something." Gwen followed the lead of Xara and Yankee.

"I think we were off by saying every sister had a safe. What if the keys are places that the places where the sisters thought it was hidden like a safe? Shit, we are overthinking this." Xara pointed out.

"Even twins have differences, but sometimes their differences have a similarity, like what is considered safe or hidden. Perhaps away from unlikely eyes." Quinton put his own spin.

It could be possible that's why we were stuck. Another perspective.

"Punishment, Nanette didn't have to hide it in a safe..." Gwen jumped off the table, pacing the floors, something sparked in her eyes, and there she was, the fearful had turned back into the fearless, her spirit had come back.

I'm trying Maximus, I'm trying to keep that promise.

Winston came up behind her, "Talk it out," he said. Her eyes searched for something in her mind, like her brain was working over time. I swear you could see the sparks flying out of this kid. Little mad genius.

She stopped, and the biggest smile came across her face, "She hid it in the one place that no one dared to go, even back in the eighteenth century." There was a small hint of a menace, something that she lost and perhaps had found again.

"That smart bitch," Xara figured out what she was trying to say.

"Someone want to enlighten us Neanderthals?" Zacharias groaned.

Gwen popped a chair out and plopped into it like she queen sitting on her throne, she clasped her hands towards her chest, still with that smile on her face, "The dungeon, the one place where continental torture, brutal, and cruel punishments were given."

Elijah turned back to the board, pointing out the lower level where the dungeon was still intact.

"What about the well?" Hartley asked, noticing the center of it all, a place that not too many think about.

"It's an idea, the well symbolizing hope, taken from the prisoners. It's a stretch." Xara noted.

The whole island is a damn punishment, secluded away from others and only death to escape the constant torture, to be honest, history still repeated itself no matter what country or time period you were in.

"What, we are all going to go together? I mean I vote we leave Gwen in there." Zach laughed, then dodged as Gwen threw an apple at his head. "Missed me."

"You want to go there Langley?" Gwen snickered, "Remember what happened last time you did that?"

"Actually, no because that was Winston and you missed his ear by inches." Zach taunted again, referring back to one of the quests we were on.

"Children please," I growled. "Answer to your question, no we are not all going to the dungeon and at least I will not be leaving Zacharias and Gwen in the same group."

We continued to plan transportation, figuring one phone call to Massey and we'll have two helicopters and a boat waiting for us. We were all very anxious to get back into the game. Each of us finding the true groove. Breaking the group up for security purposes was essential.

"Three groups. One to stay with the boat, Zacharias, you will be driving, Yankee, and Elijah will be with him on the docking station."

Yankee snickered.

"Did I miss something?" Elijah asked, I was confused alongside. But apparently the women also chuckled with Yankee.

"Nothing you poor shelter big man," Yankee sat back, with a gleam in his eyes. He beamed at the ladies who suppressed a laugh as well.

"Xara, Winston, and myself will go down to the dungeon, the lower level. Gwen, Quinton, and Hartley will check in the center and possibly any of the cells." I continued. I had to separate the couples, I wasn't going to risk another incident like the graveyard.

Everyone nodded in agreement. I was going to allow Quinton to do his diligence with Massey, being Massey was more of a family friend than a benefactor.

We all knew that if we couldn't move forward with the other locations just yet. We had to research. Quinton left the room to make the call with Massey, ensuring transportation was covered and at least giving an update.

Zacharias started to examine everyone, especially Gwen, as she had stormed off before he had the chance to examine her. There was bruising around her forehead.

Night was falling and we only had two days to rest up before we moved on to the next destination. Being here for nearly a week or so has taken a toll on us and we don't know how much longer or even we'll be here for Christmas.

Xara started to walk towards the board, looking at the pages and strings attached to theories and points of interest. She started to mutter something, Winston leaned forward. Gwen arched her eyebrows.

"Viper, whatcha doing there?" Gwen asked.

"*No dedication to Almighty power and heavens, Little effort, no movement, no Bells to ring. She can expect the unexpected, no one else.*" She read aloud.

"Yeah, that's the sister of Sloth." Zach looked as he broke his concentration from Gwen.

I leaned back in my chair, she was thinking. "Xara?"

"No Bells to ring" She repeated, she was lost in a trance. She kept repeating it as if it was some sort of mantra. She touched the strings following it to a picture we had placed of a church. Just a visualization, a symbol of what we are looking for.

"I think she's broken, quick, someone go get Quinton," Elijah jokes. Gwen suddenly groaned at the image of them two and also from the pain.

"Watch it," she continued to hiss.

I turned and saw Zach yank Gwen's head back, "Then stop moving. You keep moving and the more you move the more I keep reapplying the disinfect."

"No one told you to be fucking rough. I thought doctors were supposed to have a healing touch."

"Well, devil woman, I will leave that roughness to Winston." I swear they are like true brother and sister hating each other.

Winston slapped him on the back of the head.

"Fucker," he said.

"Spawn of Satan lover," Zach retorted.

"Hey at least they had a game to go for it. What's your track record like?" I said back to him.

"No one asked you to side with them," Zach threw his hands up in the air.

"No Bells to ring," Xara continued to repeat, followed by mumblings in another language, I wasn't sure if it was French or Latin, or hell even Farsi.

"There should be a broken record over there that you should be worried about." Zach pointed To Xara and returned to work on Gwen.

Yankee joined her, trying to see what she was seeing. Elijah and Hartley spoked what they were doing. "Do I need to go get Quinton?" Hartley kindly asked. I shook my head. Moments passed by, I saw the same trance like Gwen does when she's on to something. Then the lightbulb went off.

"The Bells." Xara screamed. Most of us were surprised, but not like we weren't watching her like hawks.

Quinton's timing was perfect, "What about bells?" He snapped his head up from his phone, "I take it from the group's attention span that someone either acted out or made a theory."

He wasn't wrong.

"I think the board broke Xara." Elijah joked again.

He walked over to her, looking at her, "Xara, babe, I think you need to talk it out with the group before they make me tranquilize you." He grabbed her shoulders looking at her at eye level.

The curl of her smile gave it away. "The Bells. A bell tower."

"Okay, most churches have bells, I don't think that is a dead give away." Zach said.

"Obviously, but what bells of a church are famous and notable? Oh and I don't know, a whole ass book and that is set there." Xara dragged the answer out, but it was Zach that stood up, "Notre Dame!"

There was a small clap from Gwen, sarcastically as usual.

"Small problem though, does no one remember the fire that broke out?" Winston noted.

"It's in the middle of a restoration," Gwen commented.

"I smell a ploy coming on," Hartley said, "Are we going to pull another Canada?"

"I mean, the bells, or the tower would be interesting," I said.

"Can we focus on one location at a time?" Quinton spoke up. "We need to focus on the key we know for a fact is there."

Another good point.

I nodded my head, "Two days folks, we have two days until we are secluded on an island."

"But without the beach umbrella drinks and the hot cabana boys," Yankee snickered.

CHAPTER 29

AUGUSTUS

Come and get me, little princess. I'll take everything from you, just like you did to me.

CHAPTER 30

GWENDOLYN

A warm body pulling me closer woke me up. It was the day of travel to the island. I was ready to get on the road, I wanted to wipe the smug look on August's face. I wanted to prove to him that I was more than a pawn, or a pretty face. I was someone to fear, that we were a crew to fear.

I knew who was behind me, the same spirited man that has consumed me over the past few months. His warm vanilla smell lingers, the scruff of the beard nuzzling my neck. It was obvious that Xara went with Quinton and Winston snuck into my bed.

"I know you're awake, little minx." His voice grumbles in my ear. I smiled, for the first time in a long time I felt nothing but love and happiness. Something I could have had a long time ago.

He trailed kisses down my neck, brushing off the sweat stuck hair off my neck, his arm grasping me tighter, keeping my ass glued to his pelvis. I could feel his morning wood, I joked with him, "Someone is in a mood."

"Always with you." He said, as his hands traveled up my shirt, caressing my breasts. I leaned my head back into him, "You are trouble this morning, Win."

"True, but I'm not the one that is releasing those little moans. And you know what happens when you start going." He nipped at my ear. His fingers pinched my nipples, the pain and the pleasure rushed through me. "I think someone wants my fingers somewhere else." my mind silently wishes, no begs for it to happen. "What do you want, Gwen?" He taunts me.

Two could play at that game, I yanked his hand out of my shirt, and twisted myself around pinning his arms above his head. I started to grind against him, he wanted to be a tease, and karma is a bitch. "I will never understand how you can just pull a stunt like that." Winston groaned.

"You can thank Uncle Maxx for that, he was the one who wanted me to protect myself and know how to fight. Little did he know that it would come in handy for this."

"Brat."

"Would you have it any other way?"

He shook his head, "That's what I thought" I said.

I slammed my mouth on his, taking control and possessiveness of it. Our tongues collided, taking a taste of each other. Normally I would have him and I brush our teeth, we had a thing about morning breath, but that went out the window this morning.

I nipped at his bottom lip. I pulled back, letting go of his hands, placing my own on his bare chest. The little dark hairs sprinkled on his chest.

"Admiring the view there baby girl." he asked, I nodded my head, dragging my nails across his chest, he released a small growl, warning me to behave.

"What do you want?" I turned his question back on him. His eyes darkened, and I silently thanked in my mind I had turned into brat mode.

His fingers snaked to the hem of my shirt, "I want this off and that cloth you call underwear off." Hinting at the barely there thong I was wearing, "Then I want you to take me out and ride my cock. Then you're dripping from me playing with your swollen clit, I want you bent over to where I will drive into you without mercy. And you know what?" I stilled, my pussy already throbbing from his words. I tilted my head, waiting for his response.

"You're going to take it like a good girl," His words echoed in my ears.

I nodded my head quickly, I wanted that. I'd wake up every morning with this man and want to sink myself into him.

Right when his hands started to fumble around with my shirt, there was a sharp knock on the door and a killjoy voice through it.

"We leave in an hour. Stop fucking around," Zacharias yelled.

"Fuck off Zach." I responded back, still grinding against Winston. He started to chuckle.

"Griffin you make us late because you and Winston want a morning booty call, I will personally lock you in a cell!" His annoyance was lingering.

His footsteps echoed knowing that he walked away, "You get five minutes." I said.

"I only need one," Winston challenged.

Within one minute, I was floating on cloud 9. And apparently Winston was mentally giving himself a pat on the back.

After a round two in the shower, Winston and I packed the gear we needed for the trip. Winston and I made our way to the main room.

Zacharias checking the case of medical supplies. Hartley and Elijah crowding around the screen with the schematic of the island. Xara and Yankee talking to each other as they examined their own gear. Quinton and Dominic are waiting for Win and I to come together.

"Winston, help me with the artillery." Winston nodded and placed a kiss on my cheek and walked out with Dom with the boxes of weapons and gadgets.

My brother loomed over me, "You look well rested, sister." He bumped shoulders with me and turned in the same direction, looking over the rest of the group.

"Well, that is what happens when you thorough fucked," I knew it would get under his skin.

He scrunched up his nose, "I really wish that you don't use that language around me. Nor tell me of your sexual history."

I laughed and looked at him, "You got some nerve, considering what you and my best friend are doing. I promise you that you use worse language than me."

The difference between my brother and I varies from time to time. We are both stubborn, though I am too outwardly showing it. Quinton was more influenced by Uncle Maximus and his mannerisms and speech and then there's me who had more influence over my sense of adventures.

We were too young when we lost our parents but they instilled the way we look at the world, with wonder and the love of family.

"How are you doing now?" Quinton asked me.

Honestly, I was trying to figure out the best path but was feeling more confident about myself and where I was. Even if I never lead again, it was the true motivation and inspiration that I contributed.

I was at the point in my journey where I still itched for control, but knowing Dominic was taking over and taking the lead, the itch wasn't pressing.

"I'm doing okay."

"Is that the truth?" He could always sense when I wasn't completely honest. It's the body language, human lie detector.

"Fine, I'm still fighting with my internal fear. We get into a grove and either I fuck it up or something happens to where we all get in a haze."

"And that is different from any other time we have been on a quest? Gwendolyn, push those anxious thoughts away. You have us." He threw his arm around me. "And plus dear sister, it's time for a win."

He was right. Time to get back what was lost.

"Alright everyone, roll out." Dominic boomed through the stairwell. We started to head out, I was the last one in the loft, before he stopped me, "Gwen, I would leave the journal here."

"Can I ask why?" as I grabbed my messenger pack, reaching for the book.

"We don't know what to expect, and if we are outnumbered.." He tried to explain.

He didn't want what happened in the graveyard to happen again.

"Don't give me the look." He said, almost fatherly. "Kid, it's not what you think."

"I understand." I said, extending out my hand.

"I don't think you do. If anything happens to you or the crew is outnumbered because August has prepared for this, then the last thing we need is to lose you, anyone else, and then the journal." I wasn't denying that he had a point, it just hurts to think it would be that would screw it up.

"You are a capable, amazing woman. You have grown over the last few months." He grabbed the journal from my hands, and pulled me into an embrace. "I don't think the group would survive if we lost you."

His words reminded me of sentiments from Maxx, and it felt like home.

"You are important to us, and yes, even Zacharias." He joked. "Come on, we need to get to the airfield."

Through the traffic of downtown Paris, we weaved our way to the airfield, where Massey had come through with the transportation. The nerves were setting in, each one of us had an altered goal, or a personal vendetta. I didn't blame them.

I started to shake my knee in the midst of the helicopter ride, it took Yankee placing a hand on knee to stop me.

Was I anxious to know if my ex-partner would show up, yes. I was going to be well prepared for that even if I needed to go down with a fight.

An hour or so later we had landed in the city of Mariselle. There was a big difference between 18th century Mariselle and the city we saw before us.

One of the oldest cities in France, and bordering the southern region. It was the biggest port in the country and still was. There were churches that were still standing with their romanesque-Byzantine influences.

The stories and histories that lived in those buildings, one day I would have ventured into. I wanted to walk down the busy streets, make memories with the locals and have a moment where I could hear history recalling their stories.

Every detail, every curve of stone and etchings, a story to be told, I knew Elijah would have been entranced with the details. The city had continued to build throughout the years, essences of history ingrained in the streets.

Down the winding hills and streets, you could see the shoreline and soon the secluded island in the distance. The fortress beckoned to those who wondered about the tales of the people of long ago.

We arrived at the docks, seeing the many docked boats lined up.

"Which one did Massey obtain?" Hartley asked, as he and Elijah carried the container of the comms and tech he would need.

After loading the items out of the vans, I went searching for, hopefully, a boat. Winston and Dominic were searching behind us, carefully looking elsewhere.

"That was Quinton's department." I yelled from the back. Quinton pulled out his phone, Massey had sent over the tags and picture of the transportation. Quinton pushed forward the group, looking at each docking station, trying not to overlook the boat. He ended up a few yards from us.

Xara popped next to my side, I started to joke with her, "Look at your man like a bloodhound, still I don't see what the attraction is about."

There was a hint of color on her cheeks, "I'm surprised that you are okay with this."

"What were you expecting me to deny someone from being happy and throwing a tantrum, hold on." We kept walking, "Oh. my. Gosh you're fucking my brother. How. dare you." I say in the most dramatic valley girl voice.

Xara laughed, breaking any tension or nervousness that she created, "No, Xara, not upset. Is it weird that my friend is dating my brother? Yeah, but does he make you happy is the real question."

She nodded her head, "Yeah, he makes me happy."

"And as long as you don't break his fragile, weirdly attached heart, we'll be fine. I won't have to smother you in your sleep." I joked with her. I am the protective little sister, but my brother knew how to take care of himself.

"As if you'd get the chance to smother me." She laughed.

"Yeah, you'd already have a knife to my throat." I said.

"Found it." yelled my brother from the end of the dock.

We quickly approached the vessel. It wasn't a normal boat, no Massey acquired as a fucking yacht. Well, a smaller one. I looked back at Zach, "You do know how to drive this."

"It's been a long while, but yeah my license and certifications are still intact. Winston can help with the ropes, and Elijah can help."

"As long as you don't whip it like you did on the lake." Elijah said, cocking an eyebrow to him.

"I wasn't the one that wasn't sitting down and drunk off my ass." Zacharias threw back at him. Oh, I could see it now, Elijah not listening and Zach giving him a lesson. "That was one time."

"Try more than ten." Apparently the lesson was never learned.

"Alright, let's load it up. After we get pushed off the dock, let's convene on the main deck." Dominic gave us a command.

Everyone splits up, either taking in the equipment or gathering up the ropes. The wind and weather seemed fair and although it was a twenty minute boat ride. The engines started to roar and we were off.

The guys finished up below deck cleaning up all the ropes and stored them away. We all met up on the main deck awaiting the next bit. Zacharias was at the helm as he navigated the smooth seas to the secluded island where the next key was waiting for us to find it.

Dominic had laid across the table all the rest of the gear that wasn't already attached to us and our comms. "Does everybody know their groups? Do we need to go over any additional details."

He had split us up into three different groups, splitting up the ones that were coupled up which was smart of him. He then looked at me and asked "Are you sure that there aren't any other details that were missing? It seems like it's a wild goose chase with this one with as much land and fortress covering this place."

It was a valid question with as much uncertainty from the start even when we started with the journal, for all we know it could have been this island or it could have been Bastille. But here with as much history I was fairly confident with the help of the crew that we were heading in the right direction.

But, of course, history always has a way of repeating itself, a lesson that we continue to ignore.

CHAPTER 31

DOMINIC

As we headed to the island I felt the crew was anxious about what awaited us. As each one of us had placed our comms in their ears and attached different weapons of choice to their holsters, I couldn't help but wonder what it was going to be like once we finished all this.

Once we had gone back to the states and fully debriefed, I wondered which ones wanted to stay or go. And the past few weeks I've seen people treat this as the one last time and I've seen others treated it as a second chance or a second start.

"Once we get to the docks, we'll go through the main entrance and then the team with me will go through the stairwells. And then the team with Gwen will search around the center of it all." I reviewed the plan even though we had all heard it two to three times already. but the team nodded and no one responded back with any additional questions.

"You all ready for this?" I asked, trying to fill the silence without hearing the clicking of gun chambers and knives being placed and holders.

"Heads up everyone ten minutes out. Winston, Elijah I'm going to need you on deck in 5 minutes." Zacharias had said through the comms.

Yankee was the first one to respond to my question, "I'm ready to find this key so we can get the others so find this damn library. Going through all this trouble, it better be incredible." Always the inner con man.

"Should we make it better? Who finds the key first, a little friendly wager?" Xara asked as she settled with her knives.

"I'll take the bet," Hartley had said.

"All right my man, fifty bucks on my team being the one to find it" Xara extends out her hand ready to take the bet. Hartley thanks for a minute.

He gripped his chin to think. "I'm going to say Gwen is going to find it because she's Gwendolyn and I'm going to do a hundred."

Xara chuckles, "You're on."

It seems like the spirit of the team was rising between the banter and the friendly bets and even the occasional threats and memories that have been brought up. It was starting to feel like family again. Even Zacharias was starting to turn around. He had been one that I was concerned that would turn his back at the very end and it was still my thought but there was hope.

We could see the island approaching closer and closer. Quinton and Xara getting closer, his hands on her shoulders rubbing them. I still couldn't get over the fact that they were an item but then again no one thought that my wife would go for me.

Winston and Elijah went to go and help. Zacharias had done his job of getting the boat to where needed to be. I had looked over the railing trying to see if there was any indication of Augustus. the little punk wasn't going to mess anything up anymore than he already has.

"You know I never did get to thank you for taking over." Gwen's voice came from behind me. "Thank me, why would you have to thank me kiddo?"

She started to bounce on her toes as I turned to see her. "You didn't have to take over for Quinton. I had full hope that he would rise to the occasion should we say."

"Kid, if anything he was following your lead and just reinforcing that. But you don't have to thank me. Soon you'll be back in your shoes."

The engine started to cut off. It was about time to get off this boat and start searching for the next piece of the puzzle.

"Yeah about that after this I'm not sure if the crew is fully ready for me to come back." she admits to me. I folded my arms across my chest leaning back on the railing looking at her home confusion.

"What do you mean if they're ready for you to come back. Hell, I'm surprised you haven't tried to talk over me as much as you haven't."

She stuffed her hands in her pockets, "Oh, trust me the itch is still there but trust still has to be formed and earned and I still have a way to go to gain the full trust of everyone."

"I trust you."

"I know you do but Zacharias, my brother, Xara and hell even Winston. You know as well as I do dumb that it's not given overnight. I'm not going to harp on the fact anymore because I feel like we've been around in circles with what I've done. But it's nice to know that you trust me and the crew trust you."

"Don't give up, you'll end up back where I'm at. It might take time yeah but it will happen," I was sure that it would happen.

We weren't blind, it was a constant fight for her not to step up and over speak to everyone and she was handling it with more grace than anybody was giving her credit for. If that wasn't a real leader trying to earn their place back I don't know what was.

We had pulled into the dock and the boys had finished up down below. Hartley had moved forward and asked if everyone had their comms and they were working. "And please remember I do not want to hear any sexual talk over the lines. I hope everyone got it out of their system either this morning or last night." I wasn't dumb nor was I deaf. Part of me couldn't wait to get back to the manor to hopefully never hear those sounds again but one could only hope.

"Aye Aye Captain," Yankee mocked.

I gave him a look just to shut him up. "All right Zacharias, Yankee, and Elijah you're staying here. Needless to say Zach if there are any signs of trouble or unexpected visitors you know what to do." Zach nodded at his head as he prepared his weapon of choice. Yankee and Elijah were going to be on the docks in preparation.

"All right the rest of us let's go. Move on out."

The stone fortress laid ahead of us. There was no one in sight for a change, no security measures to worry about. I wasn't sure if that was a good thing or a bad thing. I was surprised that there was no security for this historical monument.

"Could you imagine if there were ghost tours?" Xara had commented.

"Who would want to come on a ghost tour here?" Winston had responded as we had walked down the deck and to the main entrance up to the main grounds.

"I sure as hell wouldn't want to be on that ghost tour." Zach had come through the comms.

The sun was shining bright allowing good light for hopefully finding the key. If we were lucky it would go a lot faster when we have a drive.

We were there for one thing and one thing only and we were all determined to find it no matter what was to come our way. As we approach the main grounds it's like you could hear the whispers of the tortured Souls. The sisters had a funny sense of humor. it seems like they found the place where secrets were hidden from the lives that once were.

"Can you imagine the revenue that those goes towards would have made," Yankee had commented.

"Hey buddy, I think I found your new con. If the crew doesn't continue to work out you could always do ghost tours." Gwen had playfully said giving him the idea to do something like that.

The stone setting was getting closer and closer as we continued to walk. I felt comfortable and secured enough not hearing any other sounds other than the waves crashing against the rocks below us. I was still on edge but had some hope that no one would show up.

With the Chateau there was only one entrance and exit. You go in one way and you come out the same. It wasn't known if there were any hidden roots or dug out tunnels.

"How do we look and Zach any updates? Elijah anything on your end?" I double checked with the guys down below.

"All good boss," Elijah had responded.

"Copy. We are about to split up. Hopefully Hartley's updates or modifications won't allow for any disconnections," I was trying to poke fun at the fact that the comms gave us a scare back at the Louvre.

Harley gave me a look in his defense, "Look Xara and I were very confident that this wouldn't happen. But never underestimate the French."

"All right, crew, let's split up. Xara, Winston you're with me. And y'all three within this main area hopefully it doesn't take us long to find where this key is." I instructed everyone to start to split up. I had more confidence in the daylight because at least we could see. The sooner we find it the sooner we can leave, and move on.

"Also, I need to win the bet I could use a hundred bucks." Xara taunted as she walked alongside me and we started to walk away from the group.

"Says the millionaire hacktivist," Hartley teased her back.

"Hey that's Ms. Millionaire hacktivists to you," She teased back.

"Somebody was trying to turn you into a sugar mama." Winston bumped into her shoulders as we found the stairwell down to the dungeon.

In my old age my knees aren't as good as they used to be but I still went on. I could hear the chatter of the other group as Gwendolyn was starting to think of where she could find the key.

We weren't quite sure which location was going to be the best but if I was a betting man I would say the dungeon was a better place.

Through the winding stairs we came across different cells that were darkened with no light to seep into. It wasn't the physical torture that made this place a living hell but it was the loss of hope and the mental strength that it took to continue on that broke these people.

The ironclads surrounded us with the different cells but there was one room that as we let the torches it showed us the way.

"What are we supposed to be finding exactly? All we're seeing is a wall." Xara had called through the columns.

"I don't know exactly. I don't know if I am supposed to be looking for a certain person or a symbol or maybe just a hole in a wall." she had responded.

As we entered the big room of the dungeon you could tell between possible scratch marks on the walls the stones etched into it. There was a static sound. "Everything okay? Zacharias? Hartley? Gwen?"

The signal was getting jammed, I didn't know what was happening. But I was losing confidence, we needed to fall back and regroup.

"Y'all come look at this," Winston shone a light at part of the wall. It was an unusual sight, possibly not something from one of the prisoners but something man made. Xara started to rub her fingers over it. On one of the brinks was carved a flower Xara faced as her fingers grazed across the stone, but she had seen something before.

"Hartley is going to owe me money." there was a Cheshire cat-like smile on her face. She grabbed her knife from her side and started to dig into the wall. The dust was settling from pulling the brick out.

Low and behold, something was wrapped in cloth, as Winston had started to unravel it, we heard the creaking of a gate closed.

A commotion goes on upstairs, sounds of yelling and a gun fired echoed in the caves.

We started to book it!

Fuck!

CHAPTER 32

GWENDOLYN

The group split away from us as they walked down the winding stairs towards the dungeon. It was just Quinton, Hartley, and I exploring the center of the big tower. It was truly amazing the history that was left behind. The ground beneath our feet, taking in the steps of those who suffered more than we will ever know.

We started looking around the main area. The Well had sat in the middle for all to wander over. The idea of those who wanted to end the life they had, the slightest of hopes.

The prison had become some sort of Museum piece. Each of the empty cells echoed their stories of misery, pain, and the screams of the deceased. Hartley had taken one part of the quadrant. My brother went up to the second level of the cells. We all were searching for an indication of a pathway or answers.

I heard Xara's voice coming through the comms, "What are we supposed to be finding exactly? All we're seeing is a wall."

I responded, "I don't know exactly. I don't know if I am supposed to be looking for a certain person or a symbol or maybe just a hole in a wall."

We didn't know what we were looking for. We didn't have a map. There were no clues within the journal, we were coming in blind. The secrets were hidden well within the journal, their history and even the unknown.

Quinton didn't find anything just yet, neither did Hartley. I had walked through the bottom cells, reading off the information the curators had gathered. The light from the sun illuminated the hollow cells, no stone unturned. Something wasn't sitting right in my mind, we were missing something. The Well wasn't something that had easy access.

But none of us had looked at the well. It appears that the well was rarely used or the top never opened. I had to go to the lock to see what I could find.

When I did I shined my light down there hoping to see something grab my attention. Suddenly there was a little static within the comms and I got nervous. because the last time that happened we lost all communication with Yankee.

I looked at Hartley looking for an answer. He tried to take out the tablet that he had in his pack to see if there was any indication of problems.

I continued for a moment to look into the well. Reminding myself this was not a wishing well for even the wishes of those prisoners from long ago had never come true.

"Hey Quinton, come look at this real quick," I called my brother down from the second floor. Something did catch my eye. I don't know if it was a hoax or even the real thing but I was going to find out.

My brother quickly came to my side holding the flashlight as I was bending over the well studying myself. The last thing we needed was for someone to either fish me out of the water or I get stuck down the well. And there would be no Lassie to go tell everyone that I had fallen nor would I have lived it down especially from Zacharias.

"What do you see, sister?" He asked me, I could feel his hand cuffing around my ankle, airing on the side of caution.

I couldn't give him a straight answer, at least not just yet. Hartley had gathered towards the well also.

I had traced my fingers over a symbol. It looks like an upside down flower. Etched on one of the stones of the Well from the inside.

My fingers traced it as if it was familiar, as if it was something that I had felt or seen before. And suddenly it hit me that the emblem resembled the one that we had found in the mausoleum. The one that had the casket of Martine's husband on it. I wondered if this symbol is a common symbol with the sisters indicating to someone that they were in the right direction.

"Someone hit me with a fucking knife," I stretched my hand back out towards the guys hoping that somebody would fill my hand with a knife to cut this brick out. Hoping that it was old enough that I wouldn't harm the blade nor be a struggle for me to get it out.

I could feel one of the guys hands me the knife and I reached back down into the well and started to carve the outline of the brick.

With enough grit and strength I had finally carved into it deeply enough to utilize my second hand that was studying myself and grab the loose brick.

"Okay now would be the right time for someone to grab the hips and hoist me up please," My voice echoed traveling down down into the well.

The hands of Quinton and Hartley had yanked me from over the edge before I could lose balance and who knows what would have happened next.

"What did you find, sweetheart?" Harley questioned.

"Don't know, hopefully it's the key. Did you get anywhere with the static of the comms?" I had asked him as I was still examining the torn out brick.

"I was just about to go down to the dungeon with the guys and Xara and see what was going on. I don't know why it's been this difficult." He had said tapping on his ear hoping that it was just a miss error of human usage.

"The last thing we need is for Dominic to have a hernia because of technological error," my brother had noted. Hartley went back to rapidly tapping on his tablet and then he stilled. "Partly you're right." I called after him.

"I don't think we are alone," he said.

My brother and I turned towards him and hoped that he would further explain what he meant. Then the light quickly turned into darkness. A rush of cool air came through the center. The tiny hair on the back of my neck started to stand up.

"What do you mean we are not alone," I started to press for answers but suddenly something had already answered it.

I could smell smoke from a familiar smell that I thought I had buried from a long time ago. "He means dear princess, the snake has become a hydra." Before we could respond with guns blazing we were surrounded by his men pointing heavy artillery in our direction.

"I knew I should have killed you when I had the chance," I had snared, turning on my heels to see the devil incarnate alive again.

This time he wasn't going to take anything away from me.

"Did you really think that I wouldn't come to play? Obviously you don't remember." Augustus said as he took another drag of a cigarette before stomping it out on the ground. "Do you remember what I told you in the graveyard?"

I started to reach down for the desert eagle that was hidden in my back, but one of his men charged at me. Already knowing my next move. We were surrounded even more so than at the graveyard and with more men. It didn't seem like Augustus was going to go down without a fight.

"I try not to remember the words of a pitiful excuse of a man." I sneered at him. He wasn't going to get under my skin like he did in the graveyard not again.

"Oh Gwendolyn, I'm hurt." He placed a hand on his chest and clutched it. His teeth bared in a grimace smile, "You would do well to listen this time around dear one" He commented.

I tried not to look in his direction but his men started to knock around Hartley and Quinton. Every blow and hit to the chest and sides. He hadn't touched me yet he was waiting.

Every kick and punch was a twist in my stomach, I wanted to stop it. I needed it to stop.

I could hear my brother groan in pain as he had braced himself for impact and Hartley had gone to his side.

We hadn't fully recovered from the graveyard and Lord only knows what other injuries were about to happen. I go to defend them but the man behind shoves me with his gun. I looked back at August. I started to run towards him, ready to whip out everything I had. Knives, guns, anything to bury him once and for all. His men stopped me in my tracks, grasping my arms with force and holding me back.

"You're not getting the key. Not this time. I beat you fair and square, Auggie," I smiled devilishly at him, not breaking for him.

"And since when did that ever matter? I take what I want," he started to walk closer to me like he was trying to intimidate me as his prey.

I had hoped that the guys in the dungeon would soon rejoin us or with our calms being down there was no way of knowing what was going on. I started to look around and hoped for some glint of hope.

Then I heard the clinging of a metal door. I didn't have to guess, I knew. He would get rid of any obstacle that he had.

Shit.

He had closed the door. He had them close the door and keep them locked up. Where was Yankee?

Where was Zacharias?

Where was Elijah? I can't lose them again, I just couldn't.

"By that nervous look in your eye princess it looks like your hope is running out." he taunted me. His men started to drop kick more into the guys and I had grown frustrated and yelled "stop,"

Before I knew it I had split second to yank the gun out of my back and aim in the direction of August's head. "You should have stayed buried. A snake should have been hidden under his rock."

"You know I had hoped that your little group would stay broken. You did a bang up job tearing it apart," I jerked back at his comment holding my arm steady thought. "Oh yes, I know about your little split. Why do you think I set it up with the journal."

This was the part of any movie or book where the villain would suddenly spell out his plan. and that was my hope that August would still be stupid enough to reveal all his secrets.

"Because you're a low life leech, limp dick for brains that couldn't handle that he was bested by your group that no one would challenge or give a second glance. So, what did you do? You ran and cowered," I spit back at him.

"I call it re-evaluating the situation. I'll have to admit, the split caused a lot more consequences. You are rusty, second guessing yourself, and even out of moves." he started to lean forward at the front of my gun.

He raised his eyebrows, "I mean it took one swipe of my tech genius to defeat your security and hacker." His cruel smile spread from ear to ear. Hinting at Hartley who was still on the ground with a guy's foot to his chest. His body was partially lifeless.

Anyone would fall for his charm or the way that he would look at you. But all I could see were the flashbacks of pain.

My eyes grew in defeat, here I thought that we were going to best him once again. That we were going to win this one. But unlike me, he was already three more steps ahead. "You all have lost your touch. You underestimated me. I'll tell you what princess." he started to walk around me again like a vulture. My gun followed his every movement.

I glanced over at my boys and there was pain in their eyes. I can see a gush of blood in the corner of my brother's head.

It was the graveyard all over again. I had a feeling I was about to make another choice. I had to go down fighting. The brick was still in my hand and I had glanced at it. There was nothing in there. No key but old paper wrapping. Which only means one thing, I didn't have it and hoped that the team found it somewhere else.

I could play this off. I could trust that my team was down below and had found something. I could save more people than risk them all again.

I could keep everyone safe.

"What's your deal Augustus? What do you want?" I raised an eyebrow at him.

All of a sudden a thunderous roar of screaming and yelling of Winston and Xara. I could hear their echoes of them shouting.

"First that brick that is in your hand." He pointed to the brick, he had no idea that there wasn't anything in there, I used that to my advantage.

"Over my dead body," Poor choice of words, but the only thing I could think of.

"That could be arranged."

He would do it too, without hesitation. "But if you won't hand it over, you can come with us."

I jolted back, I lowered my eagle, "What makes you think I would come with you?" playing this the way I needed to. I relied on trust, trust from the team to know I could do this.

"Because you wouldn't want the three bodies down below on the docks to be submerged in the waters, but that could change." He wickedly said. He nodded towards the men at the entrance, ready to take his orders. One slight movement and the game could be over.

My gut twisted. More blood had been spilled than we wanted. He had gotten to the guys below, my stomach tightened. Augustus found my weakness, my family.

"You don't have to do this Gwendolyn," my brother weakly said.

The blood was still dripping from his head. I couldn't leave him there. I couldn't bear to think that in all this, revenge and vendetta drove the decisions of others. August's men surrounded both Quinton and Hartley ready to strike brutally. I lowered my weapon.

"How do I know that you won't leave anyone with more than a bullet hole," playing the innocent part, the submissive role he saw me in.

He was behind me now, he lowered himself to my ear, "Because the true prize is watching everyone you love see you walk away from them. That they lost you. Again," He softly kissed the top of my head. I flinched, a cold chill running through my body.

"But the choice is yours. Come with me with the key, and let your rag tag rats live another day, or the gates of Hell will welcome nine of you and be buried here."

He stepped back letting his men circle us. I looked back at Hartley and Quinton. Their eyes pleading with me to not give up. But it was too late, I was. But not entirely.

"Okay," I muttered. Throwing my hands up in surrender. Dropping the eagle, clanking on the ground beneath me.

"Perfect. Now do yourself a favor," he reached for two pairs of handcuffs, "Handcuff these two to the gate over there the one that is trapping the rest of your measly crew." He threw the handcuffs my way.

He allowed me to help my brother and Hartley up by being careful of any other internal injuries. Praying that Zacharias was okay, and Yankee and Elijah. "Everything is going to be okay." I whispered to my brother. He looked at me pleading that I turn back and rethink my position, I could see the anger but the heartbreak in his eyes. The disbelief that this was happening. I offered a weak smile.

"Better get a move on, you remember that I am not a patient man." Augustus taunted. I was ready to end him. I'll get my chance, but the timing wasn't there yet.

His men followed me with the guys in tow. As we made our way to the gate, I could see Dom, Xara, and Winston with anger and confusion in their eyes seeing the guards surrounding them. Winston and Dom had their guns out ready to fire. Until they saw me, confused about what I was going to do. Their bodies slumped, shaking their heads, trying to make sense of what was happening.

I moved one of the guys to a part of the gate, clasping the cuffs on their wrist, weaving it through the bars. The clicking of the cuffs burned in my mind. That sound echoed continuously. I handled the other pair and quickly clasped.

"Kid, what are you doing?" Dominic asked me, the shakiness in his voice.

I forced a smile at him. "Saving you all. Like you saved me."

"I don't understand." Xara said, her eyes searching mine.

My sweet friend.

"Take care of my brother please." I looked between her and Quinton. Xara shook her head. "It's going to be okay." I offered her a smile without trying to break.

"Babygirl, don't do this," Winston begged me.

My sweet man. I held back tears knowing that I was breaking his heart once again, but this time with better intentions. I knew I would be okay, but if anything had happened with anyone else, I don't think I would survive.

I leaned forward, trying to get to him, trying to steal one last kiss, the tears welling up in my eyes, the heaviness in my chest. "Winston, I.." I started to say.

"Don't you dare say it." he choked out. He tried to grab the scrap of clothing on me, anchoring me to the gate. It wasn't the right time, but it was needed. If I was going to leave this Earth, I wanted the words said rather than to be left in wonder.

"I love you," I pressed a kiss on his lips, before being yanked away, "Come find me."

The words ached with sorrow, a deep agonizing pain hit my chest.

His yells and screams ingrained in my mind. I needed him, but I wasn't going to lose him. I wasn't going to lose anyone. We all needed each other, but I would rather give them a fighting chance to find strength than to make another mistake that could cost us more than just losing keys.

We got back to the middle and there was Augustus with a sick smile, like he won the war. "Let's go princess, your chariot awaits."

My hands then tied behind me and forcefully pushed to walk. He walked like he was the damn king that saved the maiden, and was about to imprison her in a tower. Unfortunately, it doesn't look like this maiden would get a happy ending.

His men filed in behind me, allowing me no room to escape or plot. Down the stairs to the docks, I could see Elijah and Yankee slumped over the rocks. My heart sunk further in my chest, I didn't see Zacharias though and I grew worried.

"Don't worry they are just sleeping it off, maybe," August had called from behind him.

The fucker had tranqed them or tased them. That's how they were able to get by, with no way of warning us. He was the reason why the comms were jammed, why signals were weak.

We continued walking, the wood from the docks thunked with our steps, the only other sound mixing with the waves from the water, crashing against the wood of the dock. Something caught my eye, and suddenly my heart started racing, my whole body tingling from nerves and shock.

Zacharias.

He was limping and huffing with weak breath, pointing a rifle in Augustus's direction.

"Don't you make another move." He said. He was trying. "You are not going anywhere with her." Through all the banter, and the hate, he did love me like family.

I had to stop him before he made a stupid error that would cost us everything. I shook my head hoping that he would get the point and back down.

"Zach. Stand down," I yelled. Trying to push past the men. Urging him to stop to allow me to do what I need to do for everyone.

"Dumb bastard, you think you have leverage." Augustus chuckled out. "One lowly man trying to play soldier again." He tsked.

"You think that having one of your men tase me is going to stop me. Kind of low, don't you think." He sneered. I prayed that he would stop.

"What I think is that the special Army man should understand to cover his six." August said, before I could say anything, there was a man that crept up behind Zach and stabbed him in the shoulder. He cried out in pain, agony. A blood curdling scream came out of me. I threw myself in front of August.

"Stop, please. Augustus. No more, I told you I was going with you. You said you wouldn't hurt anyone." I ran in front of him, almost begging him.

"I said something along the lines of no more than a bullet hole, I never said knife or anything else." He spat out, almost turning his words into a cruel laughter. "You should get down on your knees and beg me." A low feeling in my gut.

I wasn't going to end up on my knees for this man. I had to bargain for it.

I turned to see the man raise the knife again. "Wait, if you stop this, I'll tell you where the next location might be."

That got his attention, his eyes widened. He held up his hand. "You're not lying to me are you?" Possibly.

I shook my head, "You know my weakness, you know what I would do to protect everyone. Why would I lie now?"

He hooked his finger under my chin, "You'll be on your knees for me." My eyes started to water. "Very well. But if you do lie to me, there will be consequences if you lie to me or play your little games, princess. And it will start with a certain mechanic." He nudged his chin, signaling everyone to get on his boat.

I staggered towards Zacharias who had been laid out on the ground. The brick in my hands, holding tight to something. I bent over, trying to do more to get him on his feet. I looked for any injuries, anything that was hidden.

"Gwen, come on. Not the hero act," he whispered. All I could do was offer him a fake smile.

I looked at him, "Take care of them, find me, my friend, please," was all I could say before I was shoved onto the boat. He grunted, trying to stand up. He winced with every movement, and at that moment I was back feeling weak and helpless, wondering what the hell I just did.

We just left him there. I just left him there. Weak, bleeding, perplexed.

Augustus ushered us further into the boat. I was slowly giving into the fact that I needed to be more cautious.

As the engines started to turn on, I was escorted to the main level where I was placed on a couch. Of course, his money would buy him a big ass yacht. He didn't know how to survive with less. He sat down in the single chair with a glass in his hand, crossing his legs. "Get comfortable my dear, we have a long journey ahead of us."

I was shoved onto the couch, waiting for something to come my way.

Before I could retort and spit out my own venom, I felt the pinch of a needle in my neck. My eyes got heavier and my vision started to get blurry.

There was a fuzzy white blur that stepped next to Augustus and clasped his shoulder. He was almost like a familiar ghost. The last thing on my mind and on my lips was the thought of Winston.

Then it was dark. I was swimming in a black of hole of emptiness. No dreams to lull me, no memories to revisit. It was a nightmare caressing a lost soul. All I could think about was Winston.

Come find me.

CHAPTER 33

WINSTON

She was gone.

She was physically gone. I had kept yelling for her, the guys struggled against the bars. My voice was becoming more and more hoarse.

She surrendered herself again to that man, the one that broke her once. My mind raced with those thoughts, she walked away.

She had the audacity to say those words as a goodbye. I refused to accept them. She was taken from me. I was going to get her back. I kept banging against the bars, hoping the age of metal would allow easy breakage. But the metal wouldn't budge.

I had been held by Dominic at one point, from doing any more harm to myself. "Son, you have to take a step back. We're going to get her back!".

Hartley and Quinton looked defeated, failure written across their faces. They underestimate the fucker again, underestimated the fact that he had years on us, we only had only weeks, not even months.

He had the time, and we didn't.

"Guys, hold still." Xara had instructed. She had whipped out a lock pick, trying to undo the cuffs from them.

"How long have you been holding that?" I growled out, furious that we were waiting until they had left the coast.

"You stole that from Yankee." Hartley noted.

She shook her head, "No, he taught me and thankfully he did." With that, under seconds she had released the guys from the cuffs. "These are my own."

She continued to work the locks, trying to take one step at a time.

Once they were free, Dominic instructed them to check on Zacharias and the rest of the crew. "I'll get us out of here. Give me a moment." Xara looked between us, heading to undo the ironclad gate. She had climbed the bars to get a better angle of the lock.

I couldn't focus, I could hear my heartbeat through my ears. The blood rushed through my head. Everything had gone under fire and we were still wondering where the smoke was coming from.

My chest heaved with anticipation, I couldn't focus on the goal ahead. She flooded my thoughts.

If there was conversation, I couldn't hear anything. Nor did I want to.

"Got it." Xara said, but bluntly. Little emotion in her voice. Needless to say, we were all flooded with emotions, and were walking on eggshells with each other.

I had one objective and that was to get the hell off this island and get her back.

Damn the keys.

And for a moment, damn the crew.

She offered herself like a sacrificial lamb. It wasn't a damn hero complex, it was a chance she was willing to take to fight for us. Fight for survival. And I was furious at her.

We rushed through the fortress, down the winding stairs to the port.

Hartley had dragged Yankee and Elijah on the board dock.

Elijah and Yankee were slowly coming back to reality. Luckily there wasn't any blood shed.

We froze, our eyes widened in surprise. "Are they?" Dominic started questioning.

"Alive? Yes. Either stunned or tranqed." Hartley said. "If I had to guess, something weak, but enough to subdue them for a length of time."

Quinton was at the end of the dock, hunching over Zacharias. Xara and I rushed over to him. He was bleeding from his back. Waves were crashing around us.

"He's suffering from a knife wound. One of the men came up from behind." Quinton had said. Anger was rising in me. Stabbed in the back, no fairness, that was what Augustus was, a monster.

"I'm alright, we just need to stop this bleeding." He staggered out. He wasn't okay.

"So, half the crew is down, and we need to get off this fucking island. We can't afford to risk anyone else right now." Xara winced at the thought.

"Risk anyone right now?" I said, bluntly." Xara, the one person that knows this quest like the back of her hand and is stubborn enough to risk her own damn life so that we didn't lose ours, is gone." I started to raise my voice.

"I tried to stop them." Zach said, his voice frail. Quinton had taken off his jacket putting pressure on the wound, risking the icy winds of the seas, the winter weather was coming.

Zach slumped, his shoulders sagged, a bit of swallowed breath, his look of disappointment had spread across his face. The internal thought of failing surrounded him.

We all failed, and were scrambling to comprehend it.

"I can see that. But no success." Quinton remarked.

"They tried to protect her, give her leverage, but she stopped them." He hoarsely said. "Bastards tased me first, and then knifed me." He clenched his teeth as Quinton moved the rag over his back. "I don't think the man," he started to let out again, "knew where to plunge it, it's not as deep." He said.

"Yeah, but you're going to have some limited movements." Dominic said walking up. "We're not going to like the road we're on, but we can get through it."

Zach sighed, "There's more I'm afraid, they tore the engines, I don't know the damage, but it's not to know the engines won't start up."

Fuckers messed with the engines, preventing us from tailing them. Smart and cruel.

I looked at Dominic, "What are we going to do? You're still the leader." He nodded, but I didn't think he had a strong answer that would work.

"First thing is getting off this island before we capture the eyes of anyone else." Get off the island and then find Gwen.

"Then we'll find her." I said, hinting for him to acknowledge it. He nods his head, "And find the other keys."

"Fuck," Xara exclaimed, like she remembered something. She reached into her pack and unzipped the pocket where she put the thing we found in it. "They didn't get the key though." She unraveled the cloth that was found in another brick in the wall, "We do."

Zach cocked his head, "Wait, so does August think she has, if we have it." It took him a moment, "Fucking hell. She played it off as she did. And he doesn't know." He started to think further and the gloom on his face told us that we were missing something. "You're not going to like the next part."

"Man, if you don't spit it out, we are on borrowed time here." Xara snarled out.

He sucked his lips between his teeth, "She bargained, telling him that she would tell him where the next location was at. She bargained for me."

It was a dangerous game and August was not one to just take lying lightly. But Gwen just granted her own death wish.

I took a deep breath.

"We're going to get her back." Quinton looked at me.

"In what state?" I threw out angrily.

He and Xara shook their heads. They couldn't give an answer to something they didn't know or promised to know. Yankee and Elijah were starting to regain consciousness, you could see the small movements. This wasn't a battle anymore, it was war.

I love you. That is what she said to me. Like it was her final goodbye. *Come find me.* A whisper of a wish.

"We need to get the boat up and running, Winston, you think you can take a look. We'll have to call Massey, hopefully with some additional help." Xara asked.

Dominic nodded his head. "Zach, you still have any contacts with old army medics?"

"I think so. As long as the jackass didn't jam our communications." Zach started to move slowly, walking towards the boat.

"How are you all so calm, not shaken?" I angrily said, "You all are acting like this is a regular Tuesday."

Out of the corner of my eye, Elijah started to sit up, his eyes blinking from the sun beaming in his eyes, Yankee didn't move as fast.

Quinton stood up and jerked my shoulders to his attention.

"You don't think I am furious at the situation? That I am not fuming that my sister, endangering her own life? I am seething here! But right now is not the time to show emotions. Once we are off this god forsaken island, then we can have some type of release. But I'm holding out hope that she is smart and allows us to do what we do best." Quinton looked at me sternly in the eyes. "Find the lost things."

My whole body was shaking, finding no peace.

"If I can promise you something it's this, my sister is a damn fighter, she has gained back that strength. We will get her back, safe with us. Then we'll put an end to all this."

He promised that we would get her back.

But I didn't promise that there would be blood on my hands after.

CHAPTER 34

GWENDOLYN

I wished that there were dreams, I wish I could have hung on to his face one more time. I didn't know the path that laid ahead of me. Maybe he'll forgive me and in time love me even more. His beautiful brown eyes, his hard muscles, the way he makes me smile.

I tried to hang on to a piece of everyone. Something to ground me and weaken that empty and alone feeling I was having.

My brother's ramblings.

Dominic's chuckle when he's ready to strangle one of us.

Xara's fun-loving attitude.

Yankee's jokes as he jokes with Elijah.

Elijah's sunny perspective and pranks.

Hartley's little flustering games.

Zach's grumpy grumbles.

My head hung heavy, like a rock. Like all the weight had been shifted to my head.

Maybe it was the drugs.

Maybe it was my mind giving up already. No one should have to suffer through a dark abyss.

Silence.

Darkness.

Hopelessness.

You are a damn Griffin.

I give myself a mental slap.

"Come find me, baby." I said softly. My vision was coming back. Gone was the day, night had fallen. I was knocked out the rest of the day.

My nerves were walking up slowly, the feeling of my body taking over coming to the surface. This was worse than a hangover.

"There's the little princess. Trying to call out for that pathetic lover?" That taunting tone woke me up faster than I could believe. I see a living room, donned with the expensive taste. Glistening in gold and black decor. There was a roaring fire that lit half of the room. Night had fallen, time escaped me.

I tried to move, but my hands were still tied behind my back. No longer was I on a cozy couch but I was in a chair. I could easily break this and escape. But the cuffs were too tight and I was in a very uncomfortable position, not enough for me to get out of them.

There was a click of a gun, "What did I say about lying to me?"

My voice gravelly saying, "That would require me to have said a lie. Thus, I have not."

There was a bang, the clattering of glass.

I blinked my eyes, adjusting to the sight, August had gotten up and strode across the way and gripped a chunk of hair, I released a yelp.

"Give me your eyes." He said. I held them closed. He pointed the gun under my chin, "Let me see those Griffin blues. Genetics are strong." He gripped harder. I held back tears.

I blinked, slowly opening them. He held up the empty brick, "You didn't have the key." He slammed the brick in my lap, then cold metal slapped across my face.

"Easy, Augustus. We wouldn't want her to bleed too much, after all, her treasured outcasts." I knew that voice all too well, the slight proper English accent.

"Come on, let me have some fun. It's been a long time." He sneered. I couldn't see where the voice was coming from. There was clicking of the heels.

"We have done enough for today, old friend. I have a feeling she's going to be shocked enough." The echo of the voice was behind me, I started to crane my neck. I started to tremble with fear that ghosts were amongst us.

I looked back in the haunted eyes of a ghost of the past but in the form of a spirit, an evil spirit. The delish grin flashed me.

Those ocean blue eyes. The cruel handsome face that haunted me still. The embodiment of someone I knew. He was one we thought was dead, never to be resurrected.

It wasn't my uncle that I had seen everywhere. But rather the man that broke his heart years ago.

"Charles."

His deep rumble answered under a cruel, vicious smile. "Cousin."

Thank You

This first damn book of the series is done! It has been a journey for sure. I didn't know what this was going to look like or even if it was going to be good. Honestly, I didn't think this book was going to be finished but it is. I went through a huge writing slump for this and then ended up coming up with other ideas for other books.

To my parents, who continue to support me through all this. I may not be a big time author, but in your eyes I am. Thank you.

Thank you to my friends, those in my life that have inspired these characters and providing me memories that will last me a lifetime.

Thank you Bee for bringing my vision to life in this cover!

To my Fritz Clan. You have been stuck with me and taking on everything. Thank you for loving me and supporting me, honestly, best clan in the world.

To Caelyn, June, C.E, Mariah, Erin, Misty, the ones that checked in with me and gave me the support to continue on whenever I started to doubt myself. Also who aren't afraid to give me a swift kick in the pants.

To anyone who says that they are not able to do this, just start doing it and let your mind roam free.

More Books and What's To Come

Grim Wolves MC
Wild Cub
Savage Angel
Shiloh and Rawlings (Coming Soon)

The Treasured Outcasts
Buried in Sins
Unearthed Sins (Coming Soon)

Autumn Press Publications Series
Writing at Bat (Coming Soon)

Saint's Outlaws MC: Memphis Chapter
Hound Dog's Howl
B.B's Queen (2026)

About the Author

Jamie Fritz is a full time social worker with her masters in Social Work, that works in various populations such as family services, veterans, homelessness domestic violence, and pediatric health care. She lives in Eastern Virginia, where the weather never is correct.

Author of the Grim Wolves MC, Saint's Outlaws MC: Memphis Chapter series, and the Treasured Outcasts series. She is known to be the author of stories that takes genres by the horns. Stories that don't fit into one category. She hopes that some of her writing will shed light into the vulnerable communities that have a special place in her heart.

She's still waiting for prince charming but he might have gotten lost or the dragon burned him to a crisp. When she is not immersed in the community and writing, she is attempting to go through her TBR list with her dogs, and surrounded by family. She enjoys a good whiskey and coke, while doing whatever her ADHD tells her to do.